From Paris to Zion

Louise Ashworth

Contents

Dedication

I dedicate this book to the memory of my soul mate who now resides
in heaven. May you find everlasting peace and love with God.

Thank you for the beautiful poem you wrote for me, set deep in
my heart for evermore.

In the corner of lagoons, I travel constantly with enthusiasm inspiring
puffs of perfume, your body operating in the streams
of your larmes.

Escaping punishment and return to the thousand delights
feverish peau.

I have travelled time on this earth;
I have thought of you often encountering this illusion
that masks the life.

I've crossed the faces of a hundred eyes,
but only one rocking the rhythm of my nights.

I'm standing on the rose, I just understood it was you.

Chapter 1

Young Mother

⸻◆⸻

It's 1964. Delmare is a eighteen-year-old French Jewish girl. She is three months pregnant and living in Rabieh, a beautiful and expensive part of Lebanon.

Splendid white villas are scattered across the hills in amongst luscious green tropical plants and trees. Her boyfriend Claude's family are Lebanese Christians and have invited her to live with them in their magnificent house. Claude is three years older than Delmare and is half Lebanese, half Italian.

Delmare receives a phone call from Paris. It's her mother, Mirabelle.

"You're going to have to come back to Paris. You can't stay in Lebanon. It's not safe for the baby. Your father and I are worried that when you have the baby, the family might take it to ensure you both stay there in Lebanon. You must return home, Delmare. We'll buy you a ticket."

"But they're nice to me Maman. Don't worry. I'm fine."

"You don't understand," her mother insists. "You must return, Delmare."

"Maman, what will I tell them?"

"Nothing. Tell them nothing. Just pack some of your things, and in one week you will fly back. It's safer this way, dear. You must return. Your father and I will raise the baby here in Paris. Don't say anything to the family there."

"But Maman—"

"Goodbye, Delmare."

As the week passes, Delmare begins to pack her things, careful not to arouse suspicion. Soon, her last day in Lebanon arrives. As night falls, Delmare is ready to catch her flight back to France.

It's 10:30 p.m. After ordering a taxi and then checking from room to room to ensure the family members are all in bed, Delmare creeps across the vast white stone floor lugging her bulging suitcase. She knows any sudden noise would be disastrous. Panting and puffing, she takes one last look over her shoulder, then she goes outside, closing the mosaic peach-coloured door behind her.

Though sighing with relief once she's safely outside, her heart feels heavy. She sheds a tear, still unsure if she's doing the right thing.

As she makes her way down the street, where the taxi has been instructed to wait, she gasps when she spots Claude's young cousin, Malak, who is only a year older than her. They have become good friends since her arrival in Lebanon. Delmare panics, knowing that her secret is out.

"Don't tell the family, Malak," she pleads, her voice anxious.

"Don't worry, Delmare," she says. "I heard you on the phone. Uncle will miss you." She places her hand on top of Delmare's, her eyes filled with tears. After kissing her on the cheek, they embrace.

"Goodbye, Delmare. And good luck."

"Goodbye, Malak. Thank you."

The taxi arrives, and the driver opens the rear door. As Delmare steps inside, she looks back at Malak. Malak blows her a kiss, and in that moment, both girls realise they will never meet again.

CHAPTER 2

Goodbye, Papa

Five years old and standing in front of the tall, elegant black iron gates of his school, Francois gazes upwards as the gates appear to go on forever, deep into the hot summer sky.

"Francois," a voice says, trying to get his attention.

Francois looks up at the face of a big, scary man standing next to him. His weathered skin has seen many battles. The menacing snorting of his broken nose is like that of an angry bull waiting for the matador. The man is a mixture of Italian and Lebanese descent. Stretched across his broad, powerful shoulders a perfectly tailored grey suit, the trousers clinging to his bulging thigh muscles. His eyes are pale blue, his light brown hair thick and wavy and immaculately styled.

The man crouches down before Francois, and their eyes lock. Francois's lower lip starts to tremble. He is afraid of this man, his father.

As Francois blinks nervously, his father grabs the kippah from Francois's head and throws it to the ground. There is a short silence between them as Francois's eyes search for answers in his father's face.

"Are you going to follow me and become a Christian, or are you going to become a Jew?" he bellows. Francois looks at him with a shocked expression on his face. He's scared, but he's also dead certain of what he wants to be.

"P-Papa," he replies, his voice small and trembling. "I ... I want to be Jewish, like grand-mamie."

His father leans forward until they are almost touching nose to nose, taking a few snorting breaths as they stare at each other.

"Then you won't see me again."

Standing up, he then turns on his heel and walks away, leaving Francois at the school gates, his mouth wide open and alone.

"Papa," Francois whispers, too afraid to shout. Tears roll down his face as he watches his father walk away.

Just as he is about to turn down another street, his father stops and looks back at Francois. His pale blue eyes are glazed over, and he's breathing heavily, his fists clenched. He raises his left hand as if to signal to Francois that he has changed his mind. Francois takes a few steps forward in anticipation of his father's return

"Papa!" he screams, waiting for his father's next move. But Francois's desperate expression soon turns to terror as he sees his father change his mind. Turning away, he heads down a side street and disappears behind a building.

"Papa!" Francois's screams again, his voice echoing down the street. Then his screams turn to wails. It's too late; his father is gone.

Francois stands alone for several minutes, unsure of what to do. Then he feels a gentle hand on his shoulder, followed by a warm, reassuring voice.

"Come with me, dear."

Francois turns around to find a tall woman in her forties with green eyes and auburn hair tied up in a neat bun standing next to him. She's dressed in dark green trousers and a peach blouse. It's Madame Buzyn, the deputy head teacher. Noticing Francois looking upset on her way into the school, she has been observing Francois and his father from afar.

"I'll walk with you into school. Come with me, Francois."

As they walk together, his hand in hers, Francois forgets that his kippah is still on the ground. Several children trample on it as it goes unnoticed in their rush to get to school on time.

"Don't worry, dear," Madame Buzyn says. "I'll call your grandparents to come pick you up. Come and sit with me in my office."

Sitting on a chair in Madame Buzyn's office, looking around at the old oak panelling on the walls and the shelves filled with books and files, Francois is still shocked and saddened at his father's disappearance. Upon a wooden desk sits a vase full of pink flowers, along with piles of neatly stacked papers and a gold pen pot in the shape of a swan, housing a variety of coloured pens. Francois looks on as Madame Buzyn telephones his grandparents.

"Your Grand-papa is coming to collect you, dear. Are you alright, Francois?"

"I don't know. Papa's gone … gone." His voice now desperate and afraid, he begins to sob.

"I know, my dear Francois, I know," she replies, her voice soft and reassuring. Opening a drawer at her desk, Madame Buzyn takes out a jar of sweets. Reaching deep inside, she takes one out, then offers it to Francois.

"Take it, Francois."

Francois looks up at her, not very interested, but he decides to take it anyway, sniffing as he pops the sweet into his mouth. Reaching into her pocket, she takes out a floral-patterned handkerchief and hands it to him.

"Take it, Francois. It's clean"

His eyes red, he gazes at her, then takes the handkerchief and dabs his nose. The desire to confide about his family life is overwhelming.

"Madame Buzyn, my family fights, and my uncles are mean to me sometimes. Maman and Grand-mamie love me though, and so does my Grand-papa, but my maman is ill."

Madame Buzyn looks at Francois with a confused expression. "What do you mean she's ill?"

Before Francois can answer, there's a knock at the door.

"Come in," Madame Buzyn says. The school secretary enters. She's wearing a light grey suit, and she has thick black glasses and frizzy black hair.

"I've come for Francois. His grandfather is here."

"Thank you, Beatrice."

"Madame Buzyn," Francois says, wanting to continue his confession about his family, but she cuts him short.

"Now come on, dear. Everything is going to be okay."

Hugely disappointed, he crosses his arms around his body. Francois stands up and walks slowly towards the door, sighing deeply that Madame Buzyn has lost interest. Glancing back at her with his tear-stained face, looking for reassurance, he is met by a sad, sympathetic smile. Then Beatrice ushers Francois out, closing the door behind them.

CHAPTER 3

The Ninja Warrior

Francois is now six years old and is living in a thirty-bedroom hotel run by his grandparents and mother in Neuilly-sur-Seine. This opulent part of Paris, full of elegant buildings, splendid shops and expensive restaurants, is the place to be. The residents are fashionable in their designer attire. Well-groomed men and immaculately made-up women are followed by trails of expensive perfumes and colognes as they shop.

Francois is pacing up and down one of the beautifully decorated halls in the hotel. The carpets are thick and pale green, with delicate gold leaves running along the edges. Gold-framed mirrors hang upon the walls, each with its own elegant table beneath lining the halls, along with beautiful porcelain vases placed precisely in the middle of each table. Francois is eavesdropping upon a conversation inside room twenty-seven, where a strange voice and unfamiliar language can be heard.

"Who's in there?" he whispers creeping forward. As he presses his ear up against the door, the voice inside stops, and there is silence. Without warning the door swings open, causing Francois to stumble forward and almost fall into the room. To his astonishment, in front of him stands a tall Japanese man dressed in a long black robe, his long hair tied back. He is middle aged, and in his hand is a long, sharp samurai sword, Francois looks at the sword and gulps as it glistens in the sunshine beaming through the window. Frozen in fear, Francois stares at the man, open mouthed. The man stares back at him for a moment. Then he smiles.

"Hello child," he says in a Japanese accent.

"Hello," Francois squeaks. "How did you know I was there?"

The man smiles again. "I felt it."

Francois is mesmerised by the sword. Encircling its black onyx hilt are gold Japanese symbols and the shape of a small dragon with emerald-green eyes. He is just about to ask the man a barrage of questions when he is brought back down to earth by the voice of an old lady who is coming up the stairs and into the hall.

"Francois, Francois!"

The voice grows louder. It's Francois's Grand-mamie Mirabelle.

"Where are you, dear?"

Francois looks up at the man's face as they listen together, both of them smiling.

"I hope you're not in the guests' area again. Come down this minute and eat your lunch!"

"You must go," the man says.

"Will I see you again?" Francois asks, backing out of the room.

"What is your name, child?"

"Francois. My name is Francois."

The man nods, still smiling as he closes the door.

It's Saturday morning, and whilst most of the guests are out exploring the sights of Paris, in the main kitchen of the hotel is Eugène, Francois's grandfather. A handsome, elegant man, his strong chiselled jaw is complemented by well-defined cheekbones and deep blue eyes, his hair wavy and grey. Wearing an expensive lilac shirt ironed to perfection decorated with a purple silk tie, his black shoes shine like freshly cleaned mirrors, and the fragrance of his expensive cologne lingers throughout the hotel apartment.

He is sitting at the breakfast table in the kitchen drinking orange juice, having just finished his croissant and eggs, as he listens to traditional French music playing on the radio.

The tranquility of the moment comes to a grinding halt as the door flies open, and Francois comes hurtling into the kitchen, sliding across the crème-coloured marble floor, coming to an abrupt stop just short of the breakfast table.

"Grand-papa, Grand-papa, where have you been?"

"I went to see my cousin yesterday. What's the problem?"

"I've been waiting to tell you. I met a warrior yesterday, like the one in my book."

"You met a what?"

"A warrior, Grand-papa, a warrior."

"Oh, I see. Very good, Francois. Now eat your breakfast."

"But, Grand-papa—"

"Eat!"

Francois sits at the table and begins nibbling on some toast. Francois's mother, Delmare, enters. A perfectly formed lady with a head full of large dark brown curls and oval eyes hazel, she looks much like a younger and more petite Sophia Loren.

"Morning," she says. "Where's Mother?"

"She's at the salon having her hair done. She'll be back at noon."

"Maman."

"Yes, Francois."

"Why did my Papa leave me?"

"Francois, now not this now," Delmare replies as she pours herself a coffee, taken back by the unexpected question. "I told you not to talk about your father, Francois."

"But, Maman, why?"

"He's not a good man, Francois." Delmare glares at Eugène, indicating she needs his input.

"Francois, sometimes people are no good, my darling," Eugène explains. "It's the way life is. People are good or people are not, and I'm afraid your papa is not. Now, don't waste your time speaking about him. Finish your breakfast, and let's go get your bicycle. It's repaired now."

After breakfast Francois waits near the reception desk, watching the guests come and go, bored and eager to go out.

"Bye, Fran," Mollie, the hotel receptionist, says as she walks by, having just finished her shift. "See you tomorrow."

"Bye, Mollie."

Francois's eyes follow her reflection in the large mirror in the lobby as she makes her way to the entrance. Then, as if by magic, another face appears, startling him. It's the Japanese man. He smiles before disappearing again. Francois looks toward where he came from, then runs towards the hall. It's empty, so he rushes into the opposite hall, darting back and forth between the two, but the man is nowhere to be seen.

Deciding to make his way towards the restaurant at the rear of the hotel, overlooking the garden, Francois pushes open the glass doors and steps outside. In the garden is a large pond centred around a renaissance sculpture of a woman wearing a robe. The gentle patter of a fountain raining water down on her head. In the pond delicate pink lilies rest on the water's surface.

Several white iron benches with curling handles sit throughout the garden. The walls are a wash of pink and red, and the air is filled with the sweet fragrance of roses. Making his way towards an old white locked gate leading to the woods behind the hotel, Francois scrambles up it, teetering at the top, before jumping down and landing in a heap in the long grass on the other side. Leaping to his feet, he runs towards the woods. After wandering through the foliage for a few minutes, he hears a strange but familiar voice coming from his left. He cautiously makes his way towards it.

Standing in a clearing in the woods, with the sun beaming down upon him, is the Japanese man. His back to Francois, he's wearing his black robe and making some sort of chanting noise, practicing ninjutsu with ritualistic precision.

Looking through a gap in the foliage, Francois is transfixed, watching with fascination as the man stamps forward, followed by lighting kicks and rapid punches, his forearms stretched out fully. After a minute or two he stops, then turns and looks Francois in the eye.

"Hello, deshi," he says.

Francois gasps in surprise. Unsure what to say, he says the first thing that comes into his head. "You remember me?"

"Yes. I've been waiting for you."

Francois comes out of the foliage with a big smile on his face.

Over the next few hours, the Japanese man shows him the techniques of ninjutsu. The time passes quickly as the two of them practice in unison, with Francois trying to mimic the man's movements, having completely forgotten that he is supposed to be going with his grandfather to collect his repaired bicycle.

"Enough now," the Japanese man says, stopping. "Time for you to go."

"But I want to stay," Francois protests.

"There will be time again."

"What is your name?"

"Kiyoshi, you must go, Francois, but before you do, I want to tell you something. You have the gift, and you must continue to learn ninjutsu. It's very important because in the future it will save your life."

"What do you mean?" Francois asks, frowning in confusion.

"Just remember what I said, Francois. Remember."

"Why, are you leaving the hotel soon?" Francois asks, looking sad.

"Goodbye, Francois."

As he trudges back through the woods, only then does Francois remember that he is supposed to meet his grandfather. He stops, his mouth open, then he breaks into a run.

"Grand-papa!"

Back at the hotel, Francois makes his way towards his grandparents' apartment in search of Eugène, but he is nowhere to be seen. Deciding to seek out the chef instead, a source of much information about the comings and goings at the hotel, Francois follows the divine aroma coming from the hotel kitchen, finding the chef conjuring up another delight.

"Maurice, have you seen Grand-papa?"

A mountain of a man with frizzy blonde hair, with his large face large and small features, much like a caricature of the Michelin Man, Maurice's huge stomach hangs over his belt. He's a nosey but friendly man who loves to sing whilst he cooks for the guests.

"Yes, I've seen Eugène. He's in the office. He asked me if I'd seen you. He said if you didn't return soon, he'd call the police, so I suggest you go quickly to the office, Fran."

"Thanks, Maurice."

"You're welcome."

Francois opens the door to the office to find Eugène sitting at his desk with a large pile of paperwork in front of him. Eugène leans forward, placing his hands on the desk, a stern look upon his face.

"Where have you been? Your grandmother and I have been very worried. I got your bicycle repaired for you, and you disappear!"

"Sorry, Grand-papa."

"Have you been in those woods again? I've told you not to go off on your own like that."

Francois blushes. "But, Grand-papa—"

"Come then, Fran. Let's go get your bicycle."

When they arrive at the repair shop, Eugène pushes open the door, causing an old rusty bell to ring. The stale smell of bicycle oil mixed with cigarette smoke fills the air. Various bicycles, both old and new, and some in a state of half repair fill the shop. In the corner a grubby ginger cat sleeps on a rug. At the rear is Cedric, a skinny old man with a crinkly face wearing a brown French beret upon his head. His white shirt is dirty, its frayed cuffs hanging over brown checked trousers. His bare feet are clad in old beige moccasins as he sits at a desk fixing a chain. He mutters something to himself, annoyed at being disturbed.

"I'm coming," he announces, his voice that of a heavy smoker, gravelly and deep. Frowning to himself, he shuffles through the doorway of the office and into the shop.

"Oh, it's you Eugène. You're late. Remi repaired the bicycle this morning."

"Yes, I know, Cedric. We were held up. Now, where's the bicycle?"

"Over there." Cedric points to a blue bicycle in the corner of the shop. Francois goes over to it, then wheels it back to where Eugène and Cedric are standing. He looks down at the bicycle with a puzzled expression upon his face.

"How much do I owe you, Cedric?"

"Well," Cedric begins, "it was a lot of work, umm ... I would say around three hundred francs, Eugène."

"Three hundred francs? Are you crazy? That's what the bicycle costs new. Who are you trying to fool?"

"But Eugène, the parts are the best steel in Paris, and they will last a lifetime. I had a new seat put on—the old one needed replacing—and it's the best bicycle leather on the market."

"Grand-papa—"

"Not now," Eugène snaps.

"But, Grand-papa—"

"I said not now!"

"But, Grand-papa—"

"What is it?" Eugène asks, exasperated.

"The bicycle is old, Grand-papa. It's not mine."

"Are you sure, Francois"?

"Yes. Mine had my name on the frame. I scratched it on the frame with a knife. It's gone, Grand-papa."

Eugène's expression changes from irritation to anger. "Get me my grandson's bicycle now, or I'll wring your neck!"

Grabbing Cedric by the collar, he shakes him like a ragdoll.

"But Eugène, let me explain. There must have been a mistake!"

"The only mistake here, Cedric, is me trusting you. You haven't changed. You're still a little snake. Where is Francois's bicycle? I won't ask you again."

"It's in the backyard," Cedric squeaks, starting to panic.

"Francois, get the bicycle," Eugène says.

Francois runs to the yard at the rear of the shop, finding his bicycle leaning against a wall. He wheels it back into the shop to where Eugène is still holding onto Cedric's collar.

"Francois, we're going. Take your bicycle outside."

Francois does as he's told, Eugène releases Cedric's collar, causing Cedric to crumple to the floor, gasping with relief. Eugène turns and walks towards the door.

"But Eugène," Cedric pleads, his voice trembling. "You haven't paid me. Remi repaired Francois's bicycle too."

"Good," Eugène replies. "You're lucky I didn't break your thieving little neck."

As Eugène opens the door to the shop, he looks back at Cedric, shaking his head. Then, with a sigh, he goes out.

Arriving back at the hotel, Francois searches for his mother. He runs up and down the halls between the kitchen and the restaurant, but she is nowhere to be seen. Finally giving up, he heads to their adjoining apartment.

"Maman!" he calls, flinging open the front door. "Guess what happened with Cedric? Maman, where are you?"

Excited to tell her of the events in the bicycle shop, Francois searches all the rooms, eventually finding her sitting on the end of her bed.

"Maman, why are you sitting in here?"

"Stop! Go away, Francois!" Delmare shouts, getting into the bed and pulling up the cover. "I want to be alone. I'm feeling blue."

Francois stops still, his mouth open, feeling confused. "But, Maman, what do you mean by 'blue'?"

"Sad, depressed. I need to be alone, Francois. Go!"

"But, Maman—"

"Go!"

Francois turns and runs towards the door, his eyes filled with tears. Hurt and confused, in his hurry to leave the room, he trips on the corner of a thick lemon-coloured rug, landing in a heap on the wooden floor. Scrambling to his feet, he races out of the bedroom. After running to the end of the hall, he heads for the living room, where he finds Mirabelle sitting in an armchair looking over some papers.

"Grand-mamie," he wails, tears rolling down his cheeks. "Maman told me to get out because she's blue. What does she mean?"

Mirabelle pulls Francois close to her as he climbs onto her lap. "It's okay, Fran. Your mother is ill."

He looks up at her. "What do you mean?"

"I will explain to you when you're older, Francois. Now tell me, if you open my heart, whose name do you see?"

"Mine," Francois replies, sniffing as he cuddles into her bosom.

"That's right. Don't cry, Fran. Go and fetch your grandfather."

Francois walks slowly out of the room, passing by one of the many mirrors aligning the walls. He stops, looking straight ahead staring at his reflection as his mother's words echo in his mind.

I want to be alone. I'm feeling blue.

As the sunbeams dance through an open window, they creep up his shoulder and into his face, their warmth offering comfort. He wipes his tears away, then heads back to the door leading to the adjoining hotel.

The next morning, Francois wakes early. He stumbles out of bed, yawning, his ruffled hair sticking out in every direction. Looking out the window of his large bedroom, his eyes move slowly from left to right as he watches a small boy walk along the pavement holding his father's hand. Francois continues to watch as they enter a building. Then, climbing back onto his bed, he lies down, folding his arms behind his head and staring at the ceiling.

He begins to daydream, his thoughts turning to his father, Claude. Then, sitting upright looking at his chest of drawers, he remembers something he placed inside. Leaping off the bed, he pulls open a drawer and feels around inside under a heap of socks until he finds what he's looking for: a small blue book. Opening it, he reveals a little photograph. He studies the facial features in detail, the only photograph of his father that he managed to save after finding them in the trash. He wonders what it would be like to have a papa at home, a papa who wanted him, who loved him, he closes his eyes and imagines them embracing. Then, letting out a big sigh, he returns the photograph to the book, placing it back into the drawer.

Hungry and ready for breakfast, Francois makes his way to the kitchen, still wearing his pyjamas, humming as he skips along the carpet. Hearing raised voices, he stops and listens, then tiptoes towards the voices until he realises Delmare and Mirabelle are having an argument. Francois listens at the door.

"He's my son!" Delmare screams.

"No, he's mine!" Mirabelle retorts. "You're not capable of looking after him!"

Francois nudges the door open and peers through a small gap as the fight becomes physical. Mirabelle and Delmare are wrestling next to the table. Delmare finally strikes her mother in frustration and then storms off. Francois races into the kitchen and flings his arms around Mirabelle.

"Are you okay, Grand-mamie?"

"Yes, my dear, I'm fine," Mirabelle replies, tidying her hair.

"Why are you and Mama fighting?"

"Your mama is ill, dear. Remember how she goes into the hospital sometimes?"

"Yes, the psychiatric one, Grand-mamie."

"Yes, dear. She was very young when you were born. I know it's hard for you to understand. Come, let's make some eggs."

After breakfast Francois decides to go to the living room to look for Eugène. To his surprise he finds his Uncle Gustave, Delmare's brother, sitting in one of the armchairs drinking coffee. He's the eldest of Eugène and Mirabelle's three grown children. Immaculately dressed in a light blue tailored suit, lined with silk, he's also wearing a white shirt and sand-coloured Italian shoes. His shoulders are broad, his hair light brown and wavy and swept back, and he has a strong, masculine jaw and green eyes. He trained as a doctor, later becoming a plastic surgeon.

"Here it comes." He laughs, trying to tease Francois, but Francois scowls at him as an uncomfortable mixture of emotions fills his body. Glaring at Gustave, his hurt and distrust apparent for all to see, Francois tries to ignore his comment.

"Where is Grand-papa?"

"I don't know, Francois. Are you behaving yourself?"

Francois starts to walk away.

"Francois," Gustave says with a sarcastic undertone, "where are you going?" He grins at Francois, taking pleasure in belittling him. Francois doesn't answer. As he nears the door, he turns around to look at his uncle, his expression weary and defeated as he leaves the room.

At dinner time, the family tucks into chicken in cream sauce along with a delicious side portion of steamed vegetables. Francois is chatting with Mirabelle and Eugène. Eventually, Delmare appears.

"Come and have some dinner, Delmare," Eugène says. "The chicken is good."

Delmare pulls out a chair and sits. They eat together in silence until Francois decides to confide about his earlier encounter with Uncle Gustave.

"Grand-papa, Uncle Gustave is mean to me sometimes. He doesn't like me, does he?" he asks whilst pushing a large piece of chicken into his mouth with his fork.

"He's just jealous, Francois. Don't take any notice of him."

"Why is he jealous?" Francois asks, his eyes wide and full of confusion.

"Just know this," Mirabelle says. "Grandpapa and I love you, Francois."

"I'm Jewish, aren't I?" Francois asks.

"Of course!" Eugène replies. "Your father is half Italian and half Lebanese Christian, as I have told you, but you are a Jew, Fran, like everyone else in our family. Why do you ask?"

"Uncle Gustave makes me feel like I'm not part of this family."

"You are Fran. We told you; Uncle Gustave is just jealous, darling."

"You both spoil Francois, though," Delmare says.

"He needs a mother and a father!" Mirabelle snaps.

"I'm his mother!" Delmare retorts.

"Now, stop," Mirabelle orders. "Let's eat!"

CHAPTER 4

Meeting with a Monster

It's early summer, and the sky is blue as a warm breeze criss-crosses the rooftops of Paris.

Now eight years old, Francois is riding his bicycle with two of his school friends. As they weave in and out of the streets near the hotel, each one lining up one behind the other, they take turns as leader. Now it's Francois's turn, and he's way out front.

"Hey!" Patrick shouts from the back. "Fran!" Francois doesn't answer, so Patrick calls out to the boy riding ahead of him. "Phillipe, tell Fran to get to the back. It's my turn to lead."

"Fran, get to the back!" Phillipe shouts, but Francois ignores him and giggles as he picks up his pace, pedalling faster and faster. Grinning, he lowers his head, his curly hair bouncing in the wind. His face flushes red as beads of sweat form upon his forehead, caught up in his moment of glory.

Eventually, he forgets about his friends, whom he leaves far behind, and begins to tire, his legs feeling like lead. He squeezes the brakes, bringing the bike to a screeching stop.

Putting one foot on the ground with the other on the pedal, he looks behind him, ready to gloat to the others about how fast he can ride. Much to his surprise, they are nowhere to be seen. Realising they must have gotten separated, Francois's looks worried as he surveys the area around him.

The shops and buildings are unfamiliar to him, and he's not sure if he should go forward or backward, conscious he will be in trouble for straying outside the restrictions set upon him by Eugene, having been told numerous times to stay near the hotel. He looks down the street in front of him, then to his left, trying to decide what to do.

On the street corner is a tall plum-coloured building with a sign that reads "Argent Architects." He doesn't recognise it either, but he decides to make his way down there anyway, hoping it will lead back to the hotel.

When he is two thirds of the way down the street, he puts his foot down and stops, noticing the street is becoming narrower. Puzzled, he sees that the street leads to a dead end. Realising there is no quick route back to the hotel this way, a worried expression creeps across his face.

"Am I lost?" he whispers, unsure what to do. Feeling tired, he notices a bench up ahead and decides to head towards it and rest there for a while.

As he pedals, he notices a young man in his early twenties leaning against a building and smoking a cigarette. He is tall with dark straight hair. His long fringe is parted on the side and swept over one ear. One of his dark brown eyes is noticeably smaller than the other, displaying a slight squint. His eyes are encircled by dark rings upon his sallow skin. Above his upper lip, the light feathering of a moustache underlines his rather wide nose. Dressed in a slightly stained blue shirt rolled up at the sleeves, his dark brown trousers are frayed at the knees. Without warning he moves forward, blocking Francois's way and forcing him to stop.

"Hey, kid, what are you doing down here?" he asks, his voice uptight. Appearing nervous, he looks behind Francois toward the direction from which he came. Then, looking up, he casts his eyes across each of the nine windows on the side of the building, as if to be sure that nobody is peering out.

"I think I'm lost," Francois replies.

"Lost? Really?" Throwing his cigarette to the ground, a grin creeps across the man's face. "Where are your parents?" he asks, looking back down the road behind Francois again.

"Papa's gone. I live with Maman and my grandparents at our hotel."

The man chuckles, not believing Francois. "A hotel, eh? Listen, do you want to come into my apartment? You can use my phone to call them. Do you know the number?"

"I'm not sure. I know the hotel name if you can ring it. "

"No problem."

"They walk along the side of the building leading to the dead end. Then Francois stops, feeling uneasy.

"I don't think I should come in with you."

"Why not?" the man asks, trying to hide his sudden frustration.

"You're a stranger, and Grand-papa says I must not talk to people I don't know."

"Listen, kid, your grandfather is right, but I'm going to let you in on a little secret. You see, I'm a secret agent, so you can trust me. I just bought a new dog. He's really lovely. Come on, you're safe with me. Let's make that phone call. You can see my new dog and then we can get you home."

Francois looks up at him, not sure what to think, anxiously blinking his eyes. They stare at each other for a few seconds. Then the man pats Francois on the head. Beckoning for Francois to follow, he starts walking. Francois wheels his bicycle behind him.

They arrive at a door. Francois parks his bicycle against the side of the building. Then the man leads him through the door and down a short hall to the elevator. The man presses a button, and a cranking noise can be heard as the elevator starts to descend. As they wait, the man impatiently presses the button a few more times.

"Damn thing. Come on, come on."

Eventually, the elevator doors open. As they step inside, the man looks down at Francois's angelic face and smiles, causing Francois to smile back.

As the elevator passes each floor, there is silence between them, each level displaying a red lit-up number on a panel: one, two, three, four … Just before the lift comes to a stop at the fifth floor, Francois looks up at the man, noticing beads of sweat have started to form upon his face. Francois's eyes move down to the man's shirt, and he sees that his underarms are wet with patches of sweat. Looking intensely at Francois again, the man wipes his brow on his shirt sleeve. Just then a strange expression seeps across the man's face, and he begins to make a strange grunting sound, appearing to go rigid. This unnerves Francois.

At last the elevator comes to a stop. As the doors open, they walk out together.

"What's the dog's name?" Francois asks.

"Wait, wait, boy." The man's voice deepens as he becomes agitated. Then, putting his hand on the small of Francois's back, he hurries him forward. Francois smiles up at him, totally oblivious of the danger ahead.

Glancing behind him to make sure no one is around, the man turns to look at Francois again, and his grin reappears.

"What's the dog's name?" Francois asks again. The man still doesn't answer as he leads Francois a few yards down the hall to his apartment door. Pulling out a bunch of keys from his trouser pocket, his hand trembling, the man groans and huffs, becoming exasperated as he is seemingly unable to find the key quickly enough. After finally selecting the correct one, he slides the key into the lock and turns it. The door opens, and he pushes Francois forward, making sure he enters the apartment first. Then he quickly closes the door behind them. At that moment Francois senses something is very wrong. He looks up at the man, full of fear.

"Where's the dog?" Francois asks. The man's eyes seem to glaze over, like a wolf having just captured a lamb.

"There is no fucking dog!" he bellows, grabbing Francois by the arm. Francois screams as the man drags him towards the kitchen.

"My arm, my arm! You're hurting my arm!" Francois begins to cry.

"Stand there, and don't fucking move." The man bends down, his face opposite Francois's, glaring and snarling. "Or I will kill you," he hisses, emphasising each word. Terrified, Francois realises he has become the man's newest victim.

Taking a huge gulp of air, his mouth dropping open in shock, Francois starts to tremble, tears rolling down his face. He is frozen in fear. As the man leaves the room, Francois looks around the drab, dirty kitchen. A cheap plastic clock with a caricature of an infant upon the clock's face hangs on the wall. In the brief moment of silence, Francois stares at it as it ticks. The chequered black-and-white lino flooring is split and broken. The countertops are piled high with an array of dirty dishes.

The man returns and yanks open one of the kitchen drawers so hard that it falls out, crashing to the floor and sending its contents flying everywhere. Forks, spoons, knives and then ... a big, heavy black gun slides across the floor, coming to a stop in front of the stove.

Their eyes lock. Francois is transfixed with terror as they stare at each other. A sinister grin creeps back across the man's face. Sweating profusely, droplets of perspiration slide down from his forehead and drip from his chin. The man picks up the gun, then lunges towards Francois, digging the gun's muzzle into Francois's temple. Then, to Francois's horror, the man shoves his hand down Francois's shorts.

Sobbing silently throughout the horrendous experience, Francois's eyes are wide with fear. Then it's finally over, and the man stops, his evil perversion satisfied.

Grabbing Francois's arm and marching him to the front door, he slams Francois against the door, leering at him. Francois sobs uncontrollably. In a state of panic, he begins hyperventilating as he tries to draw breath, terrified and confused.

"Listen, kid, I want you to forget you ever saw me," the man says, his voice softer, calmer. "Never tell anybody what happened here today, because if you do ..." The tone of his voice changes into that of a hissing monster, spitting venom into Francois's face as he grabs Francois by the throat. "I will not only kill you, but I will also kill your family too. Do you understand me?"

Francois is unable to speak, glued to the spot and trembling.

Losing his temper, the man begins to yell. "I said, do you understand me?"

"Y-yes," Francois squeaks, his voice tiny and meek.

With that the man then opens the door. Kicking Francois's bottom, he sends him hurtling to the floor in the hallway, where he lands in a heap. After the deafening slam of the door, all is silent.

Francois looks up nervously to be sure the man is inside. Then, scrambling to his feet, he runs.

Passing the elevator, he sees the stairwell. He pushes the swinging doors open with such force that he leaves them banging and clapping to a stop. Leaping down several steps at a time as fast as his legs can carry him, he struggles to catch his breath. His heavy panting is filled with fear as he descends floor by floor. The sound of his steps echoes up and down the stairwell bouncing off the walls, until finally he reaches the ground floor. Yanking open the big wooden door leading outside, he grabs his bicycle, and in a second he is gone.

CHAPTER 5

Bar Mitzvah

Now thirteen, Francois's bar mitzvah is in three weeks' time, booked at the Synagogue de Neuilly Paris. Feeling excited, Francois spends hour upon hour in front of the mirror reciting a poem he has written, and with help from Eugène, he practices reading from the Torah. Having arranged to meet the rabbi at 2:00, they make their way to the synagogue to discuss the upcoming day.

Francois rushes out of the car and up the path.

"Grand-papa come on!"

"Hold on, Francois, not so fast."

Inside, Rabbi Halevy is waiting to greet them.

"Hello Francois, how are you?" he asks, placing his hand upon Francois's head.

"I'm okay."

"Are you looking forward to your bar mitzvah?"

"Yes, I am. I've been practicing my reading."

"Good boy. Do you know what you're going to say in your speech afterwards?"

"Yes, I'm going to read my poem."

"A poem, really?"

"Yes."

The morning of the bar mitzvah arrives, and everyone is excited. Delmare and Mirabelle watch proudly as Francois walks to the car wearing his smart white shirt and immaculately pressed trousers.

Driving to the synagogue, Eugène looks into the rear-view mirror at Francois and smiles. Francois's voice is hushed as he recites his poem over and over, occasionally glancing out the window at the ice-covered buildings glistening in the crisp January sun.

Entering the synagogue, family and friends sit as Francois walks to the rear accompanied by Eugène. They make their way towards the Rabbi, who is standing in front of a plinth. Upon the plinth is a large scroll, open in the middle, Francois puts his beautifully embroidered white tallit over his shoulders, then wraps the leather tefillin around his left bicep three times, wrapping the remainder around his forearm seven more times before doing two final wraps, one around his palm.

Then, placing the other leather box upon his forehead, he looks up at Eugène, who smiles and gives him a nod of approval. Holding his silver-and-white yad pointer to the Hebrew scripture, Francois begins to chant the words as family and friends look on.

There are gasps of wonder and whispers, everyone in awe as Francois reads his deep, meaningful poem, glancing up occasionally at the congregation, the people stunned into silence and impressed at his maturity and deep wisdom despite his tender years. Soon, it's time for everyone to celebrate. Francois's journey from boy to man is complete. They all make their way to the party.

The following January, having turned fourteen, Francois is becoming increasingly worried about his mother and her repeated low moods, often followed by patterns of highly stressed behaviours. She has lost her appetite, hardly wanting to eat at all.

One afternoon, Francois decides to take matters into his own hands. After making some soup, he takes it on a tray to her bedroom, hoping to entice her to eat. Wanting so badly to help, he knocks on her door.

"Maman, hello. It's Francois. I'm coming in."

"No, don't come in. I want to be alone," his mother replies in a sad, despondent voice.

"I'm coming in," he insists. "I have some soup for you."

"I don't want it, Francois."

Ignoring her, Francois enters her bedroom. He finds his mother sitting on the bed staring out the window. Placing the tray on her bed he ignores her disinterest and scoops up some soup gently raising the spoon to her lips.

"Maman, please eat," he pleads, his voice hopeful.

"No, Francois, I don't want it."

"Please, Maman. Eat it for me."

Delmare turns her head away, rejecting the spoon. They both sit in silence for a while. Francois searches her face, hopeful she will change her mind, but she does not. Eventually, he gives up, removing the tray from the bed.

"I'm going now. See you later."

Carrying the tray out of the room and feeling profoundly sad, he goes in search of Mirabelle, eventually finding her with Eugène in the hotel garden, planning their new seating arrangements.

"She didn't want my soup," he says.

"Fran, she's ill," his grandmother replies. "I told you."

"But I don't understand what you mean."

"Not now, Fran. Come back in a little while. We have a meeting with the garden planner in a few minutes."

Francois wanders around the hotel for a while, feeling miserable, until eventually he goes to his room and decides to read his Torah.

Several months pass. It's now June, and a major change has happened in the lives of Delmare and Francois. After a lot of persuasion, Delmare has managed to convince Francois to relocate abroad with her to Tel Aviv, Israel.

Having settled in the exclusive neighbourhood of Herzliya Pituah, things begin well for both of them, Francois enrolls in school, and Delmare meets a wonderful gentleman who is kind and polite. They spend their spare time exploring the country. After several months Delmare is hopeful that the move will become permanent.

But ten months on, Francois is starting to miss France, triggering arguments that occur more and more frequently, both of them frustrated with the other. Francois has started to rebel.

In his continued confusion, with Delmare and Mirabelle still fighting over who is to play mother, even though they are on opposite sides of the world, he feels torn between them.

With his natural father long gone, the internal turmoil Francois feels becomes increasingly profound. A storm is brewing, with Francois refusing to take any direction from Delmare. Slamming doors and yelling, Francois is having none of it.

"Come back here now, Francois!"

"No, I'm going out."

"It's late. You come back right now. You have school tomorrow."

"No, you're not my mother."

"Yes, I am!"

One night Francois runs off, spending the night walking from street to street. Feeling lost, he watches others pass him by having fun in the bars and restaurants. Finally returning to his house, he finds his mother asleep in an armchair.

After two more months, with things getting progressively worse between them and Francois growing increasingly homesick, Delmare reluctantly agrees to move back to Paris.

CHAPTER 6

Papa's Revenge

Having turned fifteen, much to his surprise, Francois's father, Claude, comes back into his life. Having returned to Paris, Claude and Delmare have decided to give their relationship another go. They move into an apartment with Francois near the hotel.

It's early morning, and all three are having breakfast, the topic of conversation about how Paris has changed, leading into recent news of an armed robbery at a high-class jeweller. Francois is fascinated, his head turning from left to right as he listens intently to his parents' conversation. This new and curious sight captivates him. He's not used to seeing them together, let alone talking. This state of temporary equilibrium is a rarity for him.

"It wouldn't happen in Lebanon, you know," his father says. "They would shoot him with a gun in two seconds. In Italy, well, maybe."

As they move on to another subject, Francois's thoughts are still on the robbery. The conversation has awakened something deep inside him. He sits and stares straight ahead, thinking about the guns used in the robbery.

Just then a dark memory stirs within, gradually seeping to the surface. After years of having to keep it secret, he remembers the threats that the paedophile made if he ever told what happened. He also remembers the gun, buried deep in the depths of his mind, too traumatic to re-visit. At that moment, however, the need to disclose what happens becomes overwhelming. After six years, he is finally ready to tell.

"I can't breathe," he says. Francois begins to tremble, panicking as his heart pounds against the walls of his chest and starting to hyperventilate.

Delmare and Claude stop talking and look at each other, then at Francois, both of them confused.

"Francois, what's wrong?" Delmare asks.

"Papa, Maman, I have something to tell you." Tears run down Francois's face.

"What is it?" Claude asks.

Francois swallows hard, realising he is about to disclose his dark, heavy secret. Francois wrings his hands, recalling that terrible day that he'd spent so long shutting out of his mind. All the fear comes bubbling back to the surface, his forbidden memory box now wide open.

Although scared of his short-tempered father's probable reaction, Francois decides he must disclose his secret regardless of the consequences.

"What is it?" Claude demands, becoming impatient.

"It's about a pervert, Papa. A pervert hurt me. He said he would kill my family if I told. He hurt my privates."

Francois bursts into tears. Finally, his secret is out, having weighed upon his subconscious mind for so long. Delmare pats him on the back, too shocked to know what to say. Claude's mouth drops open, not quite believing what he has just heard.

"Who did this, Francois? What, who, where did this happen?"

Francois explains how he was kidnaped and sexually assaulted with the gun held to his head, Claude listens intently, his face full of horror and then anger.

"He said he would kill me and my family if I told."

Claude's fists thump down on the table. Then, exploding with rage, he hurls his breakfast plate across the kitchen, sending it smashing into the wall. Delmare and Francois jump in fear and shock.

"Who is this man?" Claude yells.

"I don't know, Papa."

"Where does he live? Can you remember?"

"Maybe. I'm not sure."

"I'm going to kill him!"

Francois and Delmare look at each other, not knowing what to think.

Leaping to his feet, Claude orders everyone outside to the car. Then they set out to find the man's apartment.

Claude begins by searching the neighbouring streets, driving erratically, his fury spilling over as he swerves in and out the traffic, causing Delmare and Francois to sway from side to side. In his determination to teach this man a lesson he fails to notice that they have driven down the same streets several times. Francois is becoming increasingly anxious, finding his father's impatience draining as he asks repeatedly if Francois recognises each building they pass. They have now been in the car for over an hour, making Claude increasingly exasperated.

"Where is it, Francois? Surely you can remember something!"

"I don't know, Papa. I really don't."

Francois puts his hands over his ears as it all becomes too much for him. Then flashes of memory resurface, and he remembers the street, cycling down it, the man leaning against the building, and in his mind's eye, he finally remembers that the street has a dead end.

"Papa, the street was blocked! It was a dead end. I remember that, and there was a big wooden door near the end of the street of the apartment block."

"But where? Where, Francois? How far? How far were you from the hotel?!"

"It's near here. I'm sure," Francois replies, desperate to pacify his father.

As they pass by a tall red building, Francois notices a sign on the front that says, "Argent Architects." It looks familiar, and suddenly, it all comes back to him, eight years old, alone and afraid.

"It's back there! Back there!" Francois yells. "Turn the car around, Papa. Turn!"

Claude spins the car around, causing the tyres to screech. Gripping the steering wheel, his rage is becoming more and more apparent. He is ready to kill.

As they near the dead end of the street, he slams on the brakes, causing Francois and Delmare to lurch forward.

"Let's go," he instructs, and they all get out of the car.

As Claude strides towards the door at the end of the building, Francois and Delmare follow. Francois has a flashback as he remembers how he naively followed the man, relieved that however this time the danger is from Claude, seeking revenge on Francois's behalf. As stressful as the situation is, Francois feels a strong sense of love for Claude, pleased to experience his father's protection.

"Is this the place, Francois?"

Francois nods. Claude pauses for a moment as if to compose himself. Then, with a look of determination on his face, he nods for them to follow him into the building.

His expression menacing, though now strangely calm, he smiles. He is going to enjoy this, oh yes, his sweet revenge.

In the elevator, they're all silent.

"Which floor?" Claude asks, but Francois doesn't hear him. Gripped with fear, he is reliving that horrific day again. The sensation of being dragged backwards through a tunnel overwhelms him as his traumatic memory unfolds further. Looking at his father's face, he notices he's sweating, and his mind plays tricks on him. Suddenly, he sees the paedophile's face and then his father's face again. Francois's eyes move down to the wet patches of sweat that have formed upon Claude's shirt, but instead he sees the paedophile's shirt again, and starts to tremble.

"Francois, which floor?"

Francois still doesn't answer, too busy watching the numbers, one, two, three, four ...

"Which floor!" Claude bellows, causing Francois to snap back into the present.

"Five, Papa, five."

"Are you sure?"

"Yes, five," he repeats, his voice breaking as he sees the red number in his mind's eye.

They exit the elevator, and Francois points to the right. Now he remembers everything. He leads his parents straight to the man's apartment. Standing outside the door, Claude waits for a moment, his expression determined.

"Shhh," he whispers, putting his finger to his lips. The music of "Comme IIs Disent" by Charles Aznavour can be heard coming from inside the apartment. Claude looks at Francois and Delmare, then knocks on the door. Nothing. He knocks again, harder this time, and movement can be heard inside. It's followed by the sound of a lock turning. As the door opens, the music floods the hallway like an orchestra riding a giant wave.

Standing there with a puzzled expression on his face is the paedophile, now in his early thirties with that distinctive smaller eye. First, he looks at Claude, then at Delmare. Finally, he looks at Francois. Then, like a flicker of light igniting a dark secret, he remembers. That unmistakably beautiful and angelic face, that head with its abundance of curly hair, and those aquamarine eyes. Now fifteen years old, Francois is taller, but his face is practically the same.

The man's mouth falls open, and in a panic, he rushes to close the door, but Claude wedges his foot in the gap to stop him.

"It's him?" Claude asks, looking at Francois and then back at the man, already knowing the answer.

"Yes," Francois replies.

Claude lunges forward, swinging his fist at full force and punching the man in the face, sending him flying backwards into a cabinet. Blood trickles from the man's broken nose. Lying in a crumpled mess on the floor, he groans in pain. Claude grabs Delmare and Francois's hands and pulls them into the apartment. Kicking the door shut behind them, he turns the lock. Francois and Delmare clutch each other in terror as

Claude grabs the paedophile by his shirt and drags him into the bathroom as the music plays on.

"You dirty bastard! You're going to pay for what you did to my son!" Claude yells.

The man begins to whimper. "Please, please no."

"Shut up, you nasty pervert! Like children, do you? Let's see how you like drowning."

Holding onto the scruff of the man's neck, he turns on the cold tap and puts the plug in the bathtub, Francois and Delmare peer into the bathroom, still holding onto each other.

"Claude, stop!" Delmare screams.

"Stop? Stop, you say? Remember what he did to Francois?"

"But this isn't the way, Claude. Let the police deal with him. You'll only get into trouble."

"Not yet!" Claude says, smiling. "Suffer, you nasty bastard, suffer."

When the tub is half full, Claude pushes the man's face under the cold water. Francois stares in disbelief, his eyes wide open in shock as the man struggles, large bubbles erupting from his mouth as he gasps desperately under the water, held tight by Claude. He thrashes about like a trapped alligator, rolling left and then right, struggling to break free, but he is no match as Claude's iron grip. His powerful arms hold the man down with ease. Finally, the man gives up and stops thrashing as he begins to drown. Just then Delmare races up to Claude, hitting him on the back.

"This is not the way. Stop, Claude, stop! Let the police deal with him. You'll go to jail. We'll all go to jail. Stop, Claude, please!"

Suddenly, Claude lets go. The man lifts his head out of the water, choking and spluttering and totally exhausted.

"Rot in hell!" Claude hisses.

Still standing in the doorway of the bathroom, Francois is transfixed, his mouth wide open, frozen to the spot. Then there's a loud bang as the apartment door crashes open, and three police officers' barge into the apartment. With all the commotion going on, a frightened old man living next door rang them.

"What's going on here?" one of the officers asks as the other two officers push into the bathroom behind him. They look at the paedophile and then at Claude, then back to the paedophile again.

"Let's just say I've taught this child molester a lesson. You hurt my son, didn't you? Didn't you?" he yells, grabbing the paedophile's hair.

"Yes!" the man cries in defeat.

"Okay, okay," the first officer says. "We'll deal with it now. Leave your details with my colleague in the living room. It's time to stop, sir.

Your son will need to come to the station with you to make a statement."

"Okay, officer, he will," Delmare says, putting her arm around Francois's shoulder. The officer looks at Francois, who appears depleted and shell-shocked.

"It's okay young man," the officer says. "Time to leave."

CHAPTER 7

Caging of the Innocent

Francois, now seventeen, is quite the stunner. It's almost 10:00 p.m., and a particularly mild October evening is welcomed by all of Paris.

The fine dining restaurants are full, groups of people in high spirits making their way to the glamorous eighth arrondissement. Francois is sitting in the lounge area of an upmarket nightclub, laughing and joking with friends, enjoying a few drinks and an occasional dance.

"Get another drink in, Christophe," Francois says as Christophe stands up. He's a tall, slim handsome man, his brown gelled hair sweeping the top of his shoulders. His face is chiselled and tanned. Dressed in a long black leather jacket, dark blue fitted trousers, a silver patterned black T-shirt and leather ankle boots, one could mistake him for a rock star.

"I only want juice."

"Is that all?"

"Yes. I'm not drinking, not with the ninjutsu."

It's the 1980s, and the speakers are pumping out a song by the pop band OMD. As Christophe strides toward the bar, a group of girls gathers near to where Francois is sitting. Fluttering their eyelashes, they whisper to each other while looking at him in fits of flirtatious giggles, each girl hoping to get noticed.

As the other girls stand, one girl sits, not wanting to participate in their game of fighting for Francois's attention. Disinterested in competing, she is tall and slim with pale green eyes and is very pretty, her long dark hair reaching down her back.

Francois notices her pretty face and is intrigued by her quiet, confident demeanour. He smiles at her, ignoring the others, and she smiles back. Then he nods his head, motioning for her to come over.

She stands up. Dressed in a silky lilac-coloured dress and purple heels, she makes her way over to him, glancing back at her friends in gloating motion. Some scowl with jealousy, and others giggle, curious to see what might happen next as she approaches Francois.

"Hi, sit down," he says. "What's your name?"

"Sabine."

"How old are you, Sabine?"

Francois's friends' smirk and whistle, poking fun as yet another girl is enchanted by their friend.

"Seventeen," she replies.

"Me too. I haven't seen you here before."

"Oh, well, I've just moved here from Lyon."

"Lyon, eh?"

"Yes. My father opened a dental practice near here."

"Really. Oh, you have very good teeth."

She breaks into a fit of laughter.

"Want to get out of here?" he asks. "I've got a motorbike. I could take you home. I always keep a spare helmet."

"Okay then."

Francois grins. "Good."

They stand up to leave.

"Hey," Christophe says, arriving with the drinks. "Where are you going?"

"See you Monday, Christophe," Francois replies with a wink.

"Again," Christophe mutters to himself. Then he approaches the group of girls to try his luck.

Weaving in and out the traffic with Sabine on the back of the motorbike, they eventually arrive at the hotel. Pulling up outside, they park in a small gap between the steps and an enormous stone flower pot. The lights from the hotel shine down upon them as they dismount. Francois takes off his helmet, and Sabine does the same.

"Why are we here?" she asked, a confused tone to her voice.

"It's my hotel," Francois gloats, trying to impress.

"Yours? But you're only seventeen."

"Well, my family owns it. Come on."

Hanging their helmets on the motorbike's handlebars, they climb the curved limestone steps leading to the entrance.

Inside the hotel lobby, two huge, elegant chandeliers reflect the gold flecks of the cream-coloured marble floor. The walls are a pale peach colour with swirls of flowering orchards. Several grand mint-coloured embroidered seats with high, curved backs line the walls. Tiny rainbow specs reflect from a large oval glass table in the middle of the lobby, with a gold vase centred on top, displaying a freshly cut bouquet of pink roses. The reception desk is empty. The decorative white porcelain clock on the wall behind it shows midnight.

"Sophia's finished work. She's our receptionist," Francois remarks. He flips up the countertop, then grabs some keys and shakes them, smiling. Hanging from the keys is a tag with the number twenty-nine on it. It's a room he knows well, a place he uses often to take friends and to store some of his things.

"Come on." He takes her hand. "Best to take the stairs, just in case the staff or my family are still awake. They always use the elevator."

Making their way up, they pass each level until they reach the top floor.

"Here we are."

Francois leads her down a long hall. Several gold-framed mirrors are positioned in between each door. Tulip-shaped glass lamps illuminate the luxurious olive-patterned wallpaper.

Sabine notes the numbers on the doors, looking left and then right, counting down. Each of the hotel's three floors has ten bedrooms, a total of thirty.

As they reach room twenty-nine, Francois puts his finger over her lips. "Shh," he whispers with a smile. Taking the key out of his pocket, he unlocks the door. They step inside, closing the door behind them. Then Francois switches on the light.

Inside the room is an array of belongings and musical equipment. The black and gold scabbard of a samurai sword hangs on the wall, and various pieces of clothing are draped over the backs of chairs. On a table opposite the bed, a television is surrounded by piles of books about philosophy, French law, ninjutsu, and elite army special forces, to name but a few subjects. Bottles of expensive cologne sit on the bedside tables, and study papers litter the floor in varying piles of untidiness. On one of the pillows lies a white leather Torah with a pale blue embroidered kippah on top.

"Welcome to my room," Francois says, placing his hands on her cheeks as he moves in for a kiss. She kisses him back.

"Come with me," he says, leading her to the bed. Picking up the Torah and kippah, he places them on the television and then smiles at her, but she hesitates.

"You don't have to do anything," he assures her. "You're beautiful, Sabine. You just want to talk?"

"I bet you have lots of girls come here, Francois."

"Actually, no. I'm fussy."

"Yes, me too."

Leaning forward for another kiss, they flop onto the bed together as things begin to heat up. Their kissing becomes more passionate, and they caress and explore each other's bodies. She stands up, taking off her dress and revealing a toned, athletic physique. He takes off his trousers and shirt and switches on the bedside lamp. Then, getting up, Francois goes to switch off the main light, and she follows.

Taking her hand, he leads her back to bed. They giggle as they slide off their underwear under the covers, both tossing them onto the floor. Then, pulling the covers up over their heads, Francois reaches out to switch off the bedside lamp. In the darkness, they make love.

Two weeks pass. It's late morning, and Francois is sitting opposite Delmare in the hotel office watching as she works on some documents. Somewhat proud of the attention he is getting, but fed up with the constant calls, Francois designates Delmare as his filter to fend off yet another girl he met ringing the hotel, wanting to speak to him.

"Hello, who is this now?" Delmare snaps, impatient and exasperated. "He's not here. He's out. Will you stop ringing here?"

"But I love him," the desperate voice sobs on the other end of the phone.

"Love him?" Delmare quips. "You've only met him twice. Now stop calling here, and leave him alone."

"Thank you, Maman," Francois says, feeling relieved.

"You sort it out yourself," she replies. "Don't give them this number."

"I don't. They find out about the hotel from other girls."

"Well, then I'll tell Sophia that if any other girl phones reception for you from now on not to put the calls through and be done with it."

"Have I had a phone call from a girl called Sabine?"

"Who's Sabine?"

"The only girl I want to speak to."

"No, Francois, no Sabine. By the way, Cyrille and I are going to have dinner tonight at the hotel."

After allowing Francois's father, Claude, back into her life a couple of years back— following countless arguments about his suitability from family members—Claude left again six months later, breaking all contact with Delmare and Francois. Having been alone ever since, Delmare has recently taken a new partner.

"Not that idiot again."

"Stop, Francois, he's good for me."

"He's good for your money, no more."

"Francois, stop."

"He's an asshole."

"Stop using that language!"

"He hates me."

That's because you keep fighting with him."

"He fights with me, Maman."

"Stop it, Francois."

Francois stands up, unable to stop his frustration boiling over. He sweeps his hand across the desk, sending a pile of papers flying. He glares at Delmare as she scowls at him. The papers flutter in slow motion like a flock of low-flying doves littering the floor behind him. Francois shakes his head and then leaves, slamming the office door behind him.

It's lunchtime, and Francois is sitting at the kitchen table with Eugène.

"What time's lunch?"

"I don't know, Francois. Whenever your Grand-mamie gets back from the hair salon, I expect."

"Cyrille is stupid, Grand-papa. Why is Maman with him?"

"I don't know, Francois, but don't get involved in it."

"I'm going to see where Grand-mamie is. She's taking ages."

Francois leaves the kitchen and makes his way back to the hotel. He spots Cyrille, standing next to the reception desk. He is tall and slim and in his early forties. Expensive designer glasses sit on top of his layered dark blonde hair. He's wearing a beige pullover draped over his shoulders on top a lemon-coloured Ralph Laurent polo shirt. His mustard-coloured slacks hang loose over his dark brown leather shoes.

The lobby is busy with guests checking in and out. An old gentleman sits in one of the mint-coloured chairs reading a newspaper as a pair of newlyweds near the entrance hold a guide of central Paris, excitedly discussing where to explore.

Cyrille is trying to get Sophia's attention in between her helping a succession of guests. Francois sits on one of the chairs, partly hidden by a group of high-spirited American tourists who have just arrived at the hotel.

"Sophia, my darling, come on," Cyrille says. "When are you going to let me take you out?"

Sophia is in her late thirties. She is short, slim, and attractive, with large oval brown eyes and curly dark hair that tumbles down her back. Wearing a blue polka dot dress, she holds a pen to her lips as she smiles flirtatiously at Cyrille, her long red nails matching her lipstick. Furious, Francois jumps up to his feet and strides over to Cyrille.

"Cyrille!" he snaps.

Cyrille turns around slowly to face him, a sarcastic expression on his face. "What?"

"I heard you trying to take out Sophia. You're Maman's partner."

"Not at all," Cyrille replied. "I was simply explaining where I'm from."

"You liar!" Francois shouts, causing the group of Americans to look over.

"Now, Francois, you don't want to upset the guests, do you? Your mother will be angry."

Francois glares at him. Looking over at the guests, he decides to leave it for now and makes his way back to the apartment.

Mirabelle has returned, and lunch is waiting on the table.

"Eat up, Francois," she says. "Grand-papa and I are having an early lunch. We have some new breakfast staff to meet."

"Okay," Francois replies, still upset at Cyrille's betrayal of his mother. Deciding not to share it with them, he begins to eat.

After lunch he makes his way to his bedroom. Still angry with Cyrille, he wants to be alone. As he passes by the living room, he sees Delmare and Cyrille in an embrace. Cyrille spots Francois out the corner of his eye and grins. "There goes the troublemaker."

Francois stops. Not quite sure of what to do, he walks into the living room. Furious and unable to take anymore, after months of lies, deceit and manipulation from Cyrille, Francois has reached his breaking point. After being inspired by the Japanese man back in early childhood and training in ninjutsu incessantly, he is well on his way to tenth dan. Exploding into a fit of rage, he rushes forward and punches Cyrille in the jaw, causing him to stagger back and cry out in pain.

"My jaw! My jaw … the little bastard almost broke my jaw."

Having never believed Francois's ninjutsu skills were real, Cyrille is shocked to discover that before long Francois has him pinned to the floor in a foetal position.

"Get off me, you idiot! Delmare, he's crazy. He needs locking up. Get off me, you crazy boy!"

"Get off him Francois!" Delmare yells.

"But Mama, do you know what he did with Sophia? He tried to take her out."

"I did nothing with Sophia!"

"You are a liar!" Francois shouts as he continues to hold him down.

"That's it!" Delmare snaps and then storms out of the room. Francois finally lets go of Cyrille.

"I know you don't care about Maman. She doesn't see it, but you're just using her."

Cyrille grabs his broken glasses from the floor and stumbles to his feet. Brushing himself down, he stares at Francois, wincing in pain as he tidies his hair. "You really are crazy," he says.

Francois glares at him with hatred in his eyes, then decides to leave it for now. He goes in search of Mirabelle, his only sanctuary.

Unable to find her, he decides to seek refuge in one of the bathrooms instead. Looking into the mirror at his hot, sweaty face, he turns on the tap and splashes his face with cold water. Gripping the edge of the sink, feeling hurt and confused, the disappointment of his mother not taking his side plays heavily on his mind. Mumbling under his breath, he closes his eyes and sighs deeply as he tries to calm himself down.

Sitting on the bathroom floor enjoying the silence, more than an hour has passed when he hears raised voices. Unlocking the door, he races down the hall towards where the voices are coming from and finds Delmare and Mirabelle fighting in the kitchen. Delmare lashes out with her hands as they yell and scream at each other, Delmare's denial of Cyrille's true character having brought them to blows.

"It's your fault Maman. Cyrille is horrible!" Francois shouts. "I'm going to the police. Stop hurting Grand-mamie!"

Francois runs out of the apartment and through the hotel. Making his way up the street, he turns down a side street, then onto another and another until he stops in confusion.

"Where is it?" he says, frustrated that he can't find the nearest police station. Stopping by a small pharmacy to ask for directions, an old man dressed in a white dispensing robe steps outside the store and shows him the way. After thanking the man, Francois follows his directions and eventually finds the station. Once inside he strides up to the front desk.

"I have a terrible problem," he tells the duty officer.

"What is it, young man?"

"My mother is hitting my grandmother. I want to register a complaint."

The officer gives Francois a sceptical look. "How old are you?"

"Seventeen. Why do you want to know my age? I want you to stop this problem and help my Grand-mamie."

"Well, young man, what is your name?"

"Francois. My name is Francois."

"Francois, eh? Well, Francois, we can't just march into your home. Where is your evidence?"

"My words are your evidence. Aren't you going to take notes?"

"Where did this happen?"

"At our hotel. We run a hotel."

"And what is the name of this hotel?" the officer asks, raising his eyebrows.

"Hotel Charmarine. My mother's name is Delmare Ronen."

"Okay, sit here." The officer points to a wooden chair. As Francois sits, the officer disappears through a door at the rear of the reception desk, closing it behind him. Wanting to find out which one is telling the truth, the officer decides to find out what Delmare has to say. Once out of sight, he telephones the hotel.

"Good afternoon, Hotel Charmarine," Sophia says.

"Hello. I'm Officer Durand. Can I speak with Madame Delmare Ronen, please?"

"What's it about?" Sophia asks, hoping to find out some gossip to share with the other staff.

"That is for Madame Ronen and Madame Ronen only, I'm afraid. Is she in today?"

Sophia blushes, feeling a little annoyed, and transfers the call through to the apartment.

The telephone rings in the lounge, and Delmare picks it up.

"Hello?"

"Hello, is this Madame Delmare Ronen?"

"Yes, who is this?"

"It's Officer Durand. I have your son here at the police station. He says there's been some violence in the home. Is that correct?"

"Violence?" Delmare replies, her heart almost missing a beat. "What are you talking about? That's nonsense. Of course not!"

Cyrille overhears the conversation and creeps up behind her. "Your son is crazy," he whispers into her ear, causing her to jump.

"Madame Ronen, are you still there?" Durand asks.

"Yes, yes. We'll call a psychiatrist. He's ill, very ill indeed. He needs an assessment. He has psychiatric problems. It's him who's violent, not me!"

Delmare hangs up, looking very stressed.

"It's for the best," Cyrille says, smirking. "I'm off to the hotel bar," he informs Delmare as he walks away, a big grin on his face, knowing full well that between them they have just managed to obtain an emergency psychiatry order against Francois.

Officer Durand returns to the counter and gives Francois a sympathetic look. "Hold on, Francois. I need to make another call," he says. Then he returns to the office and calls for a duty psychiatrist to come to assess Francois. Once he's done, he comes out once again.

"Francois, would you like a drink?"

"No. Have you called the hotel? Are you going to see my mother and Grand-mamie? you need to tell my mother to stop. Are you going to help me?"

"Francois, everything is going to be okay. Just wait there."

With a suspicious expression on his face, Francois sits and waits. Eventually, two smart-looking men arrive, followed by another police officer. They look at Francois, speaking in hushed voices to Officer Durand. Then they walk over to where he's sitting.

"Hello, Francois, is it?"

"Yes."

Francois's eyes dart from one face to the other as an uneasy feeling creeps up his spine, sensing something is wrong.

"Come with us. Let's talk," the officer says.

"What about?"

"We're here to help you, Francois," one of the smartly dressed men replies. Oblivious to the situation he has found himself in, Francois stands up and follows them into an interview room. One by one they sit around a large desk. The first of the two men is thin, his face almost concave, dark circles around his small piercing brown eyes. He's dressed in very creased grey jacket and black slacks.

"Francois, I am Doctor Legrand," he says, gesturing towards the other man. "And this is Doctor Morel."

Doctor Morel is the polar opposite of Legrand, overweight with large bulging blue eyes. He's wearing a smart but very tight pale blue linen suit.

"Hello, Francois. It's good to meet you. We're here to help."

"Help? Help who? Me? Help me with what? Are you going to speak to my mother? She's the one who needs a psychiatrist, not me."

"We're going to ask you some questions, Francois," Doctor Legrand continues. He opens a book, his pen poised and ready to write. "First, we would like to ask what is going on for you. Have you ever been aggressive? Do you ever hear voices?"

Francois looks at him in astonishment. "What do you mean? Voices in my head? I'm not crazy. No, I don't!"

"Francois, you have walked into a police station and told the officer that your mother is violent. Now, it's you who's violent, isn't it, Francois?"

"No, no, it's my mother. Sometimes she fights with my Grand-mamie, and her boyfriend makes trouble. It's them, not me."

"They tell me it's you, Francois and that you're getting worse and worse."

"No, that's not true!" Francois screams, his voice full of fear as he jumps up, kicking over his chair. "Touch me and I will put you on the floor. You're trying to trick me. It's not me, I tell you. Listen to what I say."

Francois's hands begin to tremble. Then the door swings open, and three officers rush in. Grabbing hold of him, they pin him to the floor. He starts to struggle, knowing he could use his ninjutsu skills, but thinking better of it, he gives in, hoping the situation will change. He allows them to cuff his hands behind his back.

This misjudgement only makes matters worse for him. Now he's powerless to act and to state his case. The three officers drag him outside to a waiting van.

"Wait, wait, where are you taking me? You're wrong. You'll see! You'll see!" Francois cries as they bundle him into the rear of the van. Two of the officers get into the van with him. The third shuts the back doors and then gets into the driver's seat. Their destination is Flanc de Coteau, a private psychiatric hospital.

Arriving at the hospital grounds, the van passes by two buildings and then comes to a stop outside a third, the male wing. At that point, Francois decides he's had enough of being complicit in this perceived game.

"Where are we? I want to go home now," he demands, but the two officers remain silent, avoiding eye contact. Francois starts to panic.

"Where are we?" he yells, but they remain silent.

"I said, where are we?"

The sound of keys being shaken can be heard. A moment later, the rear doors swing open to reveal three men standing outside. Two are dressed in white cotton nursing uniforms, name tags pinned to their chests and beepers attached to their belts. The other is dressed in jacket and slacks.

"Time to go," one of the officers next to Francois says. Eager to escape the stifling heat and the claustrophobically small space, Francois steps out, taking a deep breath of fresh air. However, his relief is short lived as he stands looking bewildered, not understanding the gravity of the situation.

"Hello, Francois," one of the men in white says. "My name is Marc. I'm a nurse here. I'm going to take you in. This is Franc," he says, pointing to the other nurse, "and this is the ward manager, Pierre," he adds, pointing to the man in the jacket and slacks.

"What do you mean you're a nurse here?" Francois asks, his hands beginning to tremble. "Where am I? Why am I here?"

"It's a psychiatric hospital, Francois," Franc says.

"A psychiatric hospital? That's where Maman goes sometimes when she gets ill. I'm not ill, so why am I here!"

"Come on, Francois, we'll explain more inside," Marc replies. "Please come with us."

Still believing he will be sent home once they realise their mistake, Francois follows them inside.

As he enters the building, a nurse on either side of him, he is met by plush modern furniture and a half-moon lime-green reception desk, all of which gives him a false sense of security.

"This doesn't look like a hospital," he says, looking around.

"It's a private hospital, Francois, very expensive, one of the best in France," Marc replies.

"I don't care how expensive it is," Francois snaps as they walk towards the desk.

"Hello, Belinda," Marc says to a woman typing at a computer. She looks up and smiles at Marc and then at Francois, then carries on typing.

"When are you going to take off these cuffs?" Francois asks. "I'm not a criminal!"

"Soon, Francois, soon," Franc replies.

The two nurses lead Francois to the rear of the lobby.

Marc presses a buzzer, and a female nurse appears, looking through a glass square in the door. The door clicks, and Franc places his hand on the small of Francois's back to guide him through. For a split-second remembering the paedophile doing the same thing, Francois shudders at the memory, not realizing that, yet again, he has just walked into the eye of the storm.

At the hotel, a call comes through to Mirabelle in the apartment.

"There's a girl on the phone for Francois," Sophia says.

"So, what's new? Tell her he's out."

"I did, but she won't listen."

Mirabelle sighs. "I'll deal with her. By the way have you seen him, Sophia? He said he'd be back for dinner, but I haven't seen him yet."

"Oh, really?" Sophia replies. "Well, this girl says that Francois would like to speak to her. Her name is Sabine."

"Well, put her through. I'll get rid of her."

She waits for a moment until Sabine comes on the line. "Hello, dear, what do you want? Francois isn't here."

"Hello. My name is Sabine. I would really like to speak to Francois. Is he there?"

"I already told you he's not. You are one of many girls who would like to speak to my Francois. Please don't waste your time calling here again."

"But I haven't heard from him. Is he okay?"

"Yes, dear, now I'm very busy, so please don't call here again. If he wants to, he'll ring you."

"Excuse me, Madame Ronen, but would you tell him I rang when you see him?"

"Goodbye, dear." Mirabelle hangs up the phone.

Back at the hospital as the door shuts behind Francois, making a loud clunk. That sound is followed by an electronic buzzing sound, securing the lock.

"What's going on?" Francois asks.

"Come on, Francois," Marc relies. "Time to meet the doctor."

"What doctor? I'm not ill. Why are you taking me to see a doctor? What do you mean, a psychiatrist?"

"Come on, Francois." Marc extends his hand, gesturing for Francois to move.

"Take these cuffs off me now!" Francois shouts.

"Do you promise you'll be calm?"

"Yes, yes."

Retrieving a key from a pouch on his belt, Marc unlocks the handcuffs. Francois rubs his red, pinched wrists.

"Okay, Francois come on."

"No, I will not!" Francois shouts, his broken voice echoing down the corridor. In a panic, he begins hammering his fists on the door.

"Open this door! Open it! Let me out! I'll get you put in jail! My family will sue you!"

As Francois kicks the door, two more male nurses arrive. Marc and Franc grab Francois's arms and wrestle with him. The other two grab his feet. With his arms held behind his back, they carry him, still struggling, down the corridor and into a small pale grey room.

As they lay him on a plastic mattress on the floor, a female appears with a needle on a tray. Before Francois can say another word, Marc pulls Francois's trousers down a little, and the nurse injects a drug into Francois's buttock. They continue to hold him down, and before long he loses his ability to struggle, letting out a final terrified scream like that of a child having just injured their limb. His eyes roll back into his head, and he becomes weaker. Still, he desperately tries to fight them off, huffing and panting with all his might, but little by little the powerful drug takes hold, and he finally succumbs. Franc turns Francois's head sideways, so he can breathe. His eyes closed and his face full of sweat, saliva trickles from his half-open mouth. One by one the others leave, locking the door behind them.

The next morning Francois wakes early. He coughs, his mouth dry and sore. Trying to raise his thumping head, he looks around the room. Suddenly he jolts into a sitting position, a panicked expression on his face.

"Oh, my head."

Rubbing his forehead, he recalls the previous day's events. Then he scrambles to his feet, his legs weak and heavy, and staggers across the room.

"Let me out of here! Let me out!"

He shouts and pounds on the steel door with his fists. Nobody comes. He continues until a face appears at the thick window. It's Marc.

"Stop, Francois. If you're calm for an hour, we can let you out."

"Let me out now, you idiot!" Francois screams, continuing to pound on the door, but Marc goes away, and after a while Francois gives up. Returning to the mattress, he lies down, feeling furious and frustrated. Tears well up in his eyes and stream down his face.

"Evil bastards," he mutters. Then he eventually falls to sleep.

A few hours pass, and Francois finally wakes up. As he tries to open his tired, puffy eyes, he jumps with fright as he sees two blurry figures staring down at him. As he rubs his eyes, his vision becomes a little clearer. He recognises Franc. Still feeling drowsy, he stares at the other.

"Hello again, Francois," the other figure says. "It's Doctor Legrand."

Francois scowls, ignoring him.

"How are you feeling, Francois?"

"How do you think I'm feeling, stupid? You pump me full of poison, you keep me in this prison, and I haven't done anything wrong!"

"Francois, we're not keeping you here because you've done something wrong, I promise you. You're here because your mother said you're ill and there's been some violence at home. You're here for treatment."

"Violence? Ill? Treatment? You're crazy, Doctor. She's the one who's ill, and her boyfriend is a troublemaker. He's not honest. He's only interested in money. She doesn't understand that I was trying to protect her. She fights with my Grand-mamie, and I complained to the police."

"Well, Francois, let's concentrate on your treatment."

"When are you letting me out? That's all I want to know."

"When you're well, Francois, when you're well."

"Well? With this poison in my blood, you're making me ill."

"Francois, Franc is going to take you to your room. Come on, it's breakfast time."

"I don't want a room!"

Francois gets up, clenching his fists, but then somehow, he manages to stop himself from getting any angrier, realising any outburst will only make matters worse. Instead, he decides to play along.

Arriving at the breakfast room, he sees that the tables are laid with plastic cups and plates and that several other patients, male and female, are already eating. Spotting an empty table and keen to sit alone, he rushes over to it, scowling at any passing patients who attempt to sit with him. Picking up a cup filled with chilled orange juice, he gulps it down. The welcome taste soothes his sore throat somewhat. Then he scoffs down some toast, satisfying his hunger. Unfortunately, his small moment of peace is rudely interrupted.

"Hey," a voice behind him says. Irritated, Francois turns around to see who is disturbing him. He is met by the smile of a tall, thin, handsome black man. His jaw is strong and his cheeks are dimpled. He's wearing glasses, his hair short in ringlets tied back with a large blue band.

"Listen, friend," he begins. "Don't sit there. You'll get in trouble with Lucian."

"I'm not your friend," Francois snaps. "Leave me alone."

"I'm just warning you, my brother. My name is Joel." He extends his hand to shake Francois's hand, but Francois refuses.

"Listen, I said, leave me alone!" Francois jumps to his feet and raises his hands in ninja mode, ready to fight, causing two male nurses to rush over.

"Okay, okay, calm down, Francois, calm down," one of them says. "You don't want to end up back in the isolation room."

"Try it," Francois snarls, glaring at him. Then he sits down to finish his toast.

After being shown his room, Francois is keen to take a shower. Picking up the small bag provided by the hospital on top of his bed, he looks inside, finding shampoo, soap and a toothbrush along with some toothpaste. Stripping down to his boxer shorts, he walks barefoot down the long pale green hall toward the shower room, passing Franc along the way.

"Hi, Francois. How are you settling in? I hear you had had some breakfast. Your medicine is at four o'clock, okay? I'll see you then."

"Why don't you get lost?" Francois retorts, then continues walking, causing Franc to roll his eyes and walk away.

Entering the shower room, Francois notices there are three shower cubicles. Deciding to use the one in the middle, he slings his towel over the door. Taking off his boxer shorts and hanging them on a peg, he turns on the tap, moaning with delight as hot water rids him of the itchy sweat and dirt of the previous day. Pouring shampoo onto his hand, he lathers his hair. As the bubbles creep down his face, he closes his eyes and inhales the fragrance of the shampoo.

"Yuck, shit shampoo," he mutters to himself.

After drying himself, Francois goes to retrieve his boxer shorts from the peg, only to stop and stare at the peg in astonishment. His boxers appear to have vanished. Wrapping the towel around his waist, he looks down at the floor, not seeing them there either, he opens the cubicle door and checks the cubicle to his right and left. They're both empty. Being the only person in the shower room, or so he believes, he becomes irritated, unable to understand where they could possibly be.

"Where are they?" he shouts in frustration.

"Looking for these?" a sneering nasal voice asks.

Francois turns round to see a thin tanned man in his thirties with snake-like blue eyes. His leathery skin is full of acne scars, complete with a large scar running from his nose to his cheek. His blonde is styled in a buzz cut. Emerging from one of the toilet cubicles, in his hand are Francois's boxer shorts. The man grins from ear to ear, exposing jagged teeth as he sniggers.

"Give me my shorts back!" Francois demands, feeling vulnerable with only a towel to hide his modesty.

"Feisty little thing, are you?" the man replies with a wink as he runs his eyes over Francois's strong, muscular body. "Come and get them, darling."

Francois tightens his towel around his waist, then starts forward, maintaining eye contact. As he nears, the man's expression becomes serious, and he reaches for something in his pocket. Still holding onto the boxer shorts, he pulls out a small sharp piece of metal and lifts it up to his mouth. Staring at Francois, he grins as he runs his tongue along the edge of the metal. After breaking into sinister laughter, his mood switches like lighting to a look of aggression. Francois stops, keeping his eyes locked upon the man's face, realizing the threat has become real. At that moment he remembers the Japanese man all those years ago at the hotel, telling him that ninjutsu would save his life, and he raises his hands to defend himself.

Standing with one foot behind the other, his heart pounding, he rushes at the man, taking him by surprise. With one hard swipe of his hand, Francois immediately disarms him, sending the blade clanking down upon the tiled floor. Just then the door to the shower room crashes open, and in runs Joel.

"Leave it, Lucien. The nurses are coming!" he shouts, putting himself between Francois and the man. "Move back, Francois."

The man looks at Joel and then at Francois, grinning as he rubs his arm.

"Next time, pretty lad," the man warns, blowing a kiss at Francois. He slings his boxer shorts across the floor he leaves.

"Are you okay?" Joel asks.

"Yes, yes I am," Francois replies, a little shaken up. "You know, I could have taken him out."

"He's not worth it, Francois. You'd get trouble from the staff. Just leave it,"

"He is crazy. What's he in here for?"

"He's a danger to men, a sexual predator. He's been in jail too, but they keep putting him here."

"Why isn't he in jail if he's a danger?"

"Rich parents. Remember, this is a private hospital. I've heard they pay an enormous amount to let him stay here."

"That's crazy."

"Yes, some of the doctors are as crazy as some of the patients."

They both laugh.

"Why are you in here, Joel?"

"I killed my mother's boyfriend."

Francois stares at him in shock.

"Don't worry about me," Joel assures him. "You're completely safe. The bastard beat me and my mother for years. He was a violent drunk. One day he was choking her, so I tried to knock him out, but he died".

"How did you knock him out?"

"I smashed her hair drier over his head."

"Oh, well, maybe he deserved it."

"Yes, I've been in and out of psychiatry ever since. It's my memories from childhood that get me into trouble."

"I am sorry about what happened to you. I've had family troubles too. Well, maybe you are my friend after all."

Francois reaches out his hand, and they both shake, smiling.

"Why did you come to help me?"

"I was your age once, and I know what it's like to be in this shithole for the first time. Stick with me. There are some weirdos in here, Francois."

Francois picks up his boxers, after he slips them on under his towel, they leave the shower room together.

Back at the hotel, there's a panic, Eugène is pacing back and forth across the living room. Mirabelle is sitting in an armchair, her brow furrowed with worry, as Delmare sits on the sofa, looking on.

"I'm going to call the police," Mirabelle says. "Maybe they can help us find him."

"Look, you don't need to call anyone, I know where he is," Delmare says.

"Where?" Mirabelle asks.

"He's in Flanc de Coteau, a private psychiatric hospital."

"What on earth is he doing there?" Eugène asks, astonished.

"Look, he's getting more and more aggressive, and he needs treatment. Anyway, it was the judge's decision. It's out of my hands now. I paid for him to stay there for six months. He needs help."

"He needs love, that's all. What have you done?" Mirabelle screams, then begins to cry.

"This isn't right," Eugène snaps. "It could destroy him."

They sit in silence for several minutes as Mirabelle weeps. Then the phone rings, Eugène answers it.

"Hello, Eugène. It's Sophia. There are some friends who keep calling for Francois. Have you found him yet?"

Eugène doesn't answer, unsure what to say and sensing that Sophia is fishing for information. He glances over at Delmare and then Mirabelle. Delmare waves her arms, indicating not to tell her anything whilst Mirabelle puts her finger to her lips.

Eugène frowns.

"Yes, we have, thank you very much, Sophia."

He hangs up.

Sophia purses her lips, scowling, and crosses her arms in annoyance. Another opportunity lost to spread gossip around the hotel.

Two months pass, and Francois is reaching his limit. Desperate to leave the hospital, he marches up to Franc, who is on the medicine round.

"I want to see Doctor Legrand."

"Not now, Francois. Come see me after the medicine has all been disbursed."

"I want to see him now!" Francois insists. "I don't need to be here any longer. I'm fine. This medicine you're giving me is toxic. It makes me ill. Look at my tongue."

"Francois, we stopped your injection, and you're on tablets now. But you've been spitting them in the toilet, haven't you? Doctor Legrand won't let you go yet."

"You call this medicine? It's poison. My mouth is dry, and I'm sweating and shaking. You're trying to kill me."

"Don't be silly, Francois."

"But I'm not sick!" Francois shouts. "Look at my tongue again. It's white. What are you doing to me?" Francois sticks his tongue out a few inches from Franc's face.

"Calm down, Francois, calm down."

"Oh, fuck off. I've had enough, let me out of this hell."

Becoming increasingly annoyed at having nowhere to go, coupled with the staff's lack of understanding, Francois snaps. Racing into the empty breakfast room, he begins to throw the chairs around sending them crashing into the walls.

"I've had enough. Let me out!" he yells.

Franc runs to the nurses' office and presses a buzzer. The sound of a pulsating alarm fills the wards as four nurses rush out to assist Franc. They run to the breakfast room, where they find Francois with his back against the wall. He is wild eyed, his forehead covered in sweat as he stands ready to use his fighting skills.

"Don't touch me. Leave me alone," he warns as they approach. His voice is desperate, and he's close to tears. Three nurses grab his arms, pulling them behind his back. Franc and the other nurse grab his legs, and together they put him to the floor to restrain him.

"Inject me and I'll kill you!" Francois screams, but before he can say another word, he lets out a huge gasp as he is injected into his buttock. Instantly, he feels weaker. As the drug takes hold, his heart begins to beat faster, and a hot rush travels through his veins. Unable to fight any longer, he gives in.

The nurses carry Francois to the isolation room and place him onto the mattress. A female nurse enters, carrying a small white pot containing some pills and a plastic cup of water. They sit him up, still holding his arms.

"Here, Francois, take this," she says. "It will calm you."

"You want to give me more? You take that shit!" Francois snaps.

"The injection was to calm you. This is your actual medicine, Francois."

"Bastards, poison you mean."

Unable to find any way out of this situation, Francois gives in, and they release his arms. He grabs the pills and swallows them.

"Don't you want to take a drink of water to help wash them down?" the nurse asks.

"No, now get out," he snarls, crossing his trembling arms. One by one they leave, locking the door behind them.

Lying on the mattress, Francois looks up at the window in the door. Franc stares back at him.

"Where am I, in a zoo?" Francois shouts, sticking his tongue out at Franc. Franc merely smiles, then walks away.

Returning to the nurses' office, Franc makes a coffee for himself and Marc.

"He's strong, that Francois, isn't he?" Franc says.

Marc nods. "Yes, I know. His notes say he can do ninjutsu. We'll have to watch him."

"What's his diagnosis?" Franc asks. "Remind me."

"We're not sure at the moment. Apparently, Doctor Legrand is still working that out."

Franc looks at Marc with a slightly alarmed expression. "Oh, okay," he replies, then begins to drink his coffee.

Francois's legs are like lead weights as he stumbles over to the window. His head still thumping from the injection, he rubs his eyes before looking through the window in the door. Seeing that no one is outside, he spits the tablet into the stainless-steel toilet and then flushes it, flushing once more to be certain it's gone.

Muttering and swearing to himself, he begins to pace back and forth across the tiny room like a caged animal. After coming to the realisation that there's nothing more he can do, he lies down on the mattress and goes to sleep.

Later on, that day, Franc arrives at the door with Marc, who peers through the window at Francois, who is still sleeping, then unlocks the door.

"Francois," Franc says. "Coming for dinner?"

Francois opens his eyes, then closes them, ignoring him.

"Francois, you can come out now," Marc says.

With hunger getting the better of him, Francois gets up and, without saying a word, walks out, making his way to the breakfast room.

Sitting at the fourth table again, ignoring Joel's advice, it doesn't take long for Lucian to appear. Standing in front of Francois, grinning, he sits down opposite him. Francois doesn't move.

"Hey, pretty boy, you don't learn, do you? Move this is my table."

Francois doesn't budge and continues to eat.

"I said move," Lucian hisses. Then, grabbing hold of the table, he flips it over, sending Francois's food flying. Armed with another sharp object, Lucian's expression turns cold and menacing, but this time Francois is ready. Putting his arms in front of him, he stands ready to fight. As Lucian lunges forward, several nurses run into the room. Before they can intervene, Francois disarms Lucian with one swift kick. He sends the piece of metal flying into the air, landing a safe distance away from them both. Then, leaping on top of Lucian, Francois grabs Lucian's head and locks it under his arm. Pinned to the floor and unable to move, Lucian groans and whimpers. Joel watches in astonishment, the group of nurses alongside him.

"Whoop, whoop!" Joel claps his hands in delight. "Well done, Francois!"

Marc picks up the piece of metal. "Thank you, Francois," he says. "We'll take over now."

Lucian is marched out of the room, and Francois never sees him again, finding out later he has been sent back to prison.

"Is there anyone you'd like to ring, Francois?" Franc asks.

"Yes," Francois replies. "I have an uncle, Olivier, on my father's side. He can prove that I shouldn't be here."

Franc takes Francois down the corridor, stopping at a locked green door. Selecting a key from the bunch hanging from his belt, he unlocks the door and pushes it open. Inside the room is a wooden chair and a black telephone on a small table.

Francois follows the instructions displayed on a little placard on the wall to get an outside line. Then he dials, waiting in hope for someone to answer.

"Hello?" a voice says.

Francois smiles with delight, it's Uncle Olivier.

He spends the next fifteen minutes explaining what has happened to him, leaving his uncle shocked and bewildered.

"Uncle Olivier, can you help me?" he asks.

Back at the hotel, Delmare receives a call from Olivier.

She pulls a face, surprised to hear from him.

"I'm at Hospital Flanc de Coteau."

"Why?" Delmare asks, her mouth open with shock.

"Listen, you better come down here now and sign the release papers for Francois. If you don't, I'll create hell."

"It's not all my fault he was fighting with my partner."

"I don't want to hear it. You sign the papers to release him, or there'll be trouble."

Before long, Francois is free.

Chapter 8

Death of the Saviour

Summer arrives in Francois's nineteenth year. After studying law at university in Israel, Francois returns to France, having decided to complete his degree at the University of Paris.

Having discovered a passion for music, after getting to know the owner of a small record label in the city, in addition to helping at the family hotel, he also works as a talent scout for the record label.

Taking his new position very seriously, he spends his nights at various music venues, hoping to spot the next big thing.

It's lunchtime, and Francois, Mirabelle, Delmare and Eugène are sitting at the dinner table in the kitchen. An argument has broken out.

"Francois, are you keeping on top of your studies?" Delmare asks.

"Yes, yes."

"But you're out nearly every night. How can you get any studying done?"

"Not every night."

"Most nights."

"Oh, leave him alone," Mirabelle says. "He's okay. Let him eat."

"Don't interfere, Mother. If he's to become a lawyer, he needs to study."

"He can work at the hotel, Delmare."

"The hotel? He can do more in law!"

"Yes, and running the hotel is easy?" Mirabelle retorts.

"No, I'm not saying that, but he must study!"

"We'll see."

Before the war of words can erupt further, Eugène intervenes to calm the situation, banging his fork on the table. "Stop!" he shouts, and silence falls for a few moments.

"I have some work at a record label," Francois informs them.

"Doing what?"

"Looking for talent."

"Looking for talent? Francois, that's not a career!"

"I don't want to be a lawyer."

"You see? He doesn't want to, Delmare," Mirabelle says, a hint of a smile on her face.

"He's not your son," Delmare replies. "I make the decisions, and this is a good career for him. I told you to stop interfering."

"He is my Son. You know nothing, Delmare. Now be quiet!"

Before Delmare can say another word, Mirabelle gets up and leaves the room.

"I will finish my degree here, Maman," Francois assures his mother. "I have already applied to transfer to the University of Paris."

"Well, the university in Israel was excellent. Why the change, Francois?" Delmare asks.

"I want to finish here, to be near my family and friends."

"Francois, don't forget your studies with this music thing, please." With that Delmare leaves the room.

"I'm off for a lie down, Francois," Eugène says, sighing as he leaves the table.

Now sitting alone with his elbows on the table, Francois rests his head in the palms of his hands as he stares at the wall in front of him. Loneliness engulfs him, and he feels confused. For a moment he wonders if he should have stayed in Israel after all. Getting up he heads to the living room in search of Mirabelle, finding her sitting upon the sofa watching television. He sits down next to her.

"Is Grand-papa okay? He looks pale."

"Of course, he's fine, Francois. You want to be back in Paris, my darling?"

"Yes, I miss you."

"If you open my heart, whose name does it say?"

"Francois."

"That's right, my darling, and don't forget it."

"I won't."

The following day after breakfast, Francois makes his way to the hotel office in search of the hotel book of enquiries. In the book are all the contact details from interested parties he's collated for weddings and business group stays. After working his way through the list for a few hours, making endless phone calls and securing bookings, he decides to head out.

Deciding to visit his old friend Nylah, a thirty-two-year-old Arabic princess living in Paris, he rings her private number and is then connected via her security.

"Hello, Nylah."

"Hello, Francois, how are you?"

"I'm okay."

"Still having problems with your uncle?"

"Yes, Maman and Grand-mamie are still fighting too. I don't know who to trust. My uncle says don't trust your Maman, and she says don't trust him."

"I keep telling you we'll adopt you, Francois."

He chuckles.

"I'm free for an hour or so," she says. "Do you want to visit for a cup of tea?"

"Yes, why not."

"See you soon, Nylah."

Francois arrives outside a magnificent white building situated in one of the most expensive parts of Paris. Following the instructions for entry, as he has done many times before, he waits for security to escort him up to the huge penthouse apartment, which covers the entire length of the top floor. Upon exiting the elevator, he is met with floor-to-ceiling gold and white marble, exquisite furniture, glorious chandeliers and luxurious rugs lining the floors.

"Hello, Francois. Come sit," Nylah says as he enters the living room.

They sit on matching plush red couches decorated with precisely positioned gold and crème cushions. An employee arrives carrying two small teacups and a beautiful bone China teapot on a fancy tray.

"You look upset, Francois. Family problems again?"

"Yes. How are you, Nylah?"

"Things are okay now. I had some trouble again from my ex-husband, but it's sorted out now. My cousin is coming to visit next week. Maybe you'd like to meet her. She's very nice."

"Maybe."

Their conversation soon progresses onto other subjects, including their mutual interest in philosophy. Soon, it's time for Francois to leave.

"Take care, Francois dear."

"I will."

Deciding to call in at the record label a little early, Francois finds a group of three men in discussion with the label owner, Erwan.

"Hi, Francois. You're early today," Erwan remarks. "I'll be with you soon."

Erwan is a tall, attractive and slightly flamboyant middle-aged man. He wears blue patterned designer glasses on the edge of his nose, and his hair is shoulder length, light brown and sleek with flecks of grey. His light green designer polo shirt hangs over orange jeans. He's a successful music producer, having built up a wealth of hit songs after investing in a carefully selected collection of groups and artists.

Francois goes to the kitchen area to sample the delights in the refrigerator, often a source of delicious cakes. He makes himself a coffee and then returns to the studio, munching on an apricot pastry. Erwan is there alone.

"Who were they?" Francois asks.

"Investors. They're interested in Barr."

Barr is Erwan's new dance act, a trio of talented musicians, two male and one female. They write synthesizer-based pop songs, and they are Francois's pride and joy, having spotted them in a club on the outskirts of Paris and then recommending that Erwan meet them.

"Excellent. You think they might invest?"

"Sure, why not? We'll both be winners, Francois. Listen, I want you to check out this new club tonight. It's called Ambiance. There are a lot of great acts there. Find me someone. I know you're the one to do it."

"I will for sure."

"Have a listen to this track, Francois. You'll love it."

They listen together, chatting excitedly about its potential. Francois hangs around the studio for another couple of hours, then makes his way to the new club in search of the next big thing.

It's almost 8:30, time for the first act to begin. Having bought himself a drink, Francois manoeuvres through the crowd to the front left of stage, standing upon a slightly raised platform to get a good view. After the compere is finished, the first act arrives on stage, a four-piece band playing songs similar to Big Country but not as well. Francois is utterly bored. Having noted their copycat attempt, he spends his time crowd watching, the other people looking as disinterested as he is.

A few more acts follow. Then a trio of guys struts onto the stage, oozing charisma. Instantly, they have the attention of the room, and the chatter of the crowd dies down. One of them sits behind a piano. The bass player slings his guitar across his chest, and the third member, dressed in silver and black, positions himself behind the drums. A few seconds later, on walks a fourth guy. He looks striking. In his twenties, his hair is pulled back into a bun with just a few carefully placed ringlets of hair flopping over his handsome, chiselled face. Wearing a blue leather jacket over white T-shirt and blue-and-white vertically striped trousers, he introduces the band and their first song.

Within three minutes the room is captivated, including Francois, who instantly sees their potential. The melodic beauty of the first song enchants the room, accompanied by the singer's emotional and distinctive vocals. Having heard enough, Francois takes the band's details from the club owner and rushes back to share the news with Erwan.

When Francois arrives at the studio, Erwan is hard at work recording an artist. He raises his hand to Francois to indicate that he needs to wait before opening the inner soundproof door. Once the singer finishes the track, Erwan beckons to Francois to enter.

"Hey, Erwan, I just saw a great band at that club." Francois pulls out the band's details and hands them to Erwan.

"Great, Francois, but forget that for a moment. Your mother just rang the studio, and she wants you back at the hotel right away."

"My maman?"

"Yes."

"What's she ringing here for? It's probably nothing."

"She said it was urgent. She said you need to return to the hotel."

"What's so urgent?"

"She wouldn't say. Best to go, Francois. I'll see you next week. You can tell me about the band then."

"Okay, okay. See you next Friday."

Francois reluctantly leaves the studio. "What's so important that it couldn't wait until tomorrow?" he mutters to himself.

When he arrives back at the hotel, he makes his way to the living room of the family apartment. He's surprised to find his entire family waiting for him there: Delmare, Mirabelle, Uncle Gustave, even his other Uncle Jacques, everyone except Eugène.

"I had to leave the studio. What's so important?" Francois asks, looking at the faces of the other family members one by one. Delmare looks flushed, and her eyes red. She doesn't answer; she just looks at Mirabelle. Then Francois notices that Mirabelle is crying. Gustave looking stone faced.

"Francois, come, my dear," Mirabelle says at last, opening her arms to him.

"Where's Grand-papa?" Francois asks, hugging her.

Delmare gets up off the sofa and puts her hand on Francois's shoulder as he kneels on the floor facing Mirabelle. His grandmother places her hands on either side of Francois's face. "Francois, my darling, I'm sorry. It's Grand-papa"

"What? What is it?" Francois whispers, his eyes filling with tears and his body rigid with fear, not daring to believe what he already knows he is about to hear.

"Sorry, my darling, but Grand-papa has died. He's in heaven now."

Francois hears her words, but they don't register. He stares into her face, unable to move, then he removes her hands from his face, lays his head on her lap, and sobs.

CHAPTER 9

Rejection from a Stranger

Now twenty-one, Francois has become more and more interested in finding his father. Sitting on a train, having just pulled out of Gare du Nord Station Paris, he thinks of the journey ahead. His destination: Belgium.

Having neither seen nor spoken to Claude for seven years, he yearns for his father to want him. He decides to track him down in a last-ditch attempt at a successful reunion. Having been given some details regarding Claude's whereabouts by his Uncle Olivier, the only family member who knows where Claude could possibly be, Francois is determined to find him.

Dressed in a light grey pullover, jeans and boots, he takes off his scarf, placing it on the table top in front of him, his rucksack and jacket on the seat next to him. Sitting back watching the raindrops moving diagonally along the window, he looks up at the grey sky of November as the scenery rushes by.

As his thoughts turn to Mirabelle, he smiles, remembering her words spoken so many times before: *"If you open my heart, it says Francois."* he feels warm inside, her love and influence a comfort from what lies ahead. Remembering his grandfather, his mood becomes sad. He still misses him dreadfully, wishing he was accompanying him on this journey.

The train reaches full speed. As the landscape flickers outside the window, pictures of a hundred past events enter his head from years gone by.

An hour passes. Starting to tire, Francois's heavy blinking eyes soon close. He tries to stop his head from falling forward, but overcome with tiredness, he finally nods off.

Suddenly, he is abruptly awoken by a deep voice.

"We arrive in Gare du Midi in fifteen minutes."

Francois looks around him. The people who were sitting near him before are all gone, replaced by others. He realises he has slept through almost the entire journey.

Standing up, he puts on his jacket, then wraps his scarf around his neck. He sits back down and waits for the final fifteen minutes to pass, sighing deeply as the reality of the situation sinks in. Feeling anxious about his father's reaction to him turning up unexpectedly, for a split second he considers returning to Paris. Then, steadying his thoughts, he decides to carry on.

"After all, I'm almost in Belgium," he mutters to himself.

The train pulls up at the station, and Francois gets off. Standing on the platform, he pulls out a piece of paper and reads it.

"Uccle."

Checking the name of the probable area where the nightclub his father owns is located, he looks at the name of the club, Rose Bleue, but there is no address. Armed with this bit of information, he decides to head there, feeling sure he can find the club.

After catching a small connecting train, he makes his way through Uccle. Feeling hungry, he goes to a café for a late lunch. After ordering a chicken salad and coffee, he sits and gazes out of the window, watching the people going about their business. He sighs, feeling unsure about reconnecting with his father.

A pretty young woman brings his meal and coffee, placing it on the table in front of him.

"Merci," he says, forgetting he's not in France, but the young woman smiles, looking slightly flustered. She blushes as she notices his handsome face.

"Vous etes les bienvenus," she responds in a strong French accent, telling him he is welcome. He smiles, realising she too is French.

"One moment," he says as she turns to walk away. He pulls out the piece of paper. "Do you know where this club is?"

"Rose Bleue?" Her demeanour instantly changes. Looking shocked, she points out the window, giving quick directions, then walks away. Francois is puzzled. He glances over at her a few times, trying to catch her attention, but she ignores him. Confused, he shakes his head and eats his meal.

After finishing his coffee, he gets up to leave. He looks over at the young woman and sees her whispering into the ear of a female colleague. They giggle, then frown as they watch him leave.

Outside, Francois is bewildered, not understanding their strange behaviour. He follows the directions she gave him.

After walking down several streets, he stops. "Where is it?" he says, standing in front of an up-market restaurant. A small blue van pulls up in front of him, and a man gets out and unlocks the rear doors. He begins unloading boxes of fruit onto the pavement.

"Excuse me, do you know where the Rose Bleue nightclub is?" Francois asks. "I've been told it's around here somewhere."

The man laughs and winks. Francois looks confused at yet another strange reaction to his father's club. Then the man points diagonally across the street. Feeling slightly annoyed, Francois doesn't thank him. He merely walks away, crossing the street in the direction the man has given.

As he reaches the other side, he recognises some of the buildings and realises he has already walked down that street. He looks left and then right, not knowing which direction to take. Feeling utterly fed up and thinking that the man gave him the wrong directions, he decides to give up and try again the following day. He is just about to walk away when he happens to glance down an alley in front of him. He sees a blue carpet along a white stone floor. At the end of the alley he notices large glass doors, and above them a large gold sign that says, "Rose Bleue." He's found it.

Standing there staring at the sign, his heart beats faster. Feeling a mixture of excitement and anxiety, he walks down the alley, not quite believing he's finally found his father after six long years.

Standing at the doors, he looks at his reflection in the glass. Holding onto the handle to steady himself, his heart beating faster now, he puts his other hand to his chest and waits for a moment to compose himself. Looking through the glass doors, he is unable to see much, as the club is dark. After pulling the door handle and finding it locked, he looks through the glass once more before deciding to return in the evening.

He recalls passing by several hotels a few streets away. He looks forward to resting in the warmth of a room. Francois heads back towards them, checking into the first one he sees.

Closing the door to his room, he kicks off his boots, takes off his jacket and pullover, loosens his belt, then sits on the large soft bed. Flopping backward, he lies down, feeling relieved to be able to rest. He tucks his arms behind his head, closes his eyes, and sighs deeply, letting out all the emotional ups and downs of the day. Before long he drifts off to sleep.

A couple of hours pass. Waking up and stretching, Francois gets up to look out the window at the dark street below. He looks at his watch and sees it's 7:00. The cold November evening has arrived early. Feeling less enthusiastic about going out for dinner, he decides to order room service.

Sitting at a small table by the window waiting for his meal to arrive, he suddenly feels very alone and begins to worry about what his father's reaction will be like upon seeing him. After eating dinner, he opens his rucksack and takes out his Torah. He reads it quietly to himself, trying to gain some comfort. Then he begins to pray.

"God help me find the way tonight. Protect all my family: Grandmamie, Granddaddy in heaven and Maman."

Following that with a short prayer in Hebrew, he gets up and looks into a mirror on the wall opposite his bed. Images of his father flicker in his mind. Immediately, he is transported back in time as he recalls the events of his past, being abandoned outside the school when he was five, when they searched for and found the paedophile, who was subsequently imprisoned and eating dinner with his father. The memories are few, but they are strangely comforting to him.

Closing his eyes for a few seconds, he sits on the bed, wringing his hands in anguish. Feeling afraid as he thinks about the evening ahead, he decides to take a bath. Taking out a neatly rolled up dark blue shirt from his rucksack, he places it on the bed. Then he pulls out a small bottle of expensive cologne and takes it into the bathroom, placing it on the sink. Then, returning to his bag, he begins to rummage through it.

"Shit," he says, realising he forgot to pack shampoo.

As the bath begins to fill, he switches on the television. Having stripped down to his boxer shorts, he flicks through the channels. Deciding there is nothing of interest, he turns the TV off and returns to the bathroom. After getting into the bath, he opens the hotel shampoo bottle and smells it.

"Ooh la la, horrible," he says, sighing as he pours the shampoo onto his large soft curls. After working up a lather, he lies back, submerging his head underwater and blowing bubbles, which pop on the surface. Sitting up again, he rests his head on the back of the tub. With the steam surrounding him, he begins to relax. After soaking in the bath for a while, he exhales a deep breath of calmness. Feeling refreshed, he gets out.

Having wrapped a fluffy white towel around his waist, he touches the gold star of David that hangs around his neck as he walks into the bedroom. The light from the two bedside lamps shows off his toned and defined physique. Catching his reflection in the mirror, he smiles. Then he reaches into his rucksack for one of his most important possessions: his hair brush. He sits at the desk and begins to dry his hair, taking great time to arrange each and every one of his beautiful curls perfectly.

After getting dressed and dabbing some cologne on his neck, Francois retrieves a small umbrella from his rucksack. Then he leaves the hotel and makes his way to the club.

It's Friday evening, and despite the cold and rain, people are out enjoying the end of the working week. As he walks past several bars and cafés, Francois glances through the windows and sees people having fun. Feeling very alone now, he continues down the street.

The rain becomes heavier, and a gust of wind makes walking more difficult. It blows his umbrella inside out, causing two of the spokes to snap. Quickly getting soaked, Francois takes off his jacket and holds it over his head, tossing his umbrella into a bin. Soon, he reaches the end of the street where the club is located. As he makes his way towards it, he stops. Losing heart, he begins to question himself.

What am I doing here? Why bother?

He steps into a shop doorway to shelter from the rain, feeling utterly miserable as thoughts race through his head.

Did I make the wrong decision to come here? Why do I have to force a relationship with my own father? What if he rejects me?

He begins to feel angry, angry at Claude, angry at those who have normal fathers, angry at the people out enjoying themselves, angry at the world.

As a middle-aged couple walks past, chatting and smiling under an umbrella with a young man, Francois notices the similarities between their faces, assuming they are father and son. As they pass, he notes how happy they look. Feeling emotional now, he is in turmoil.

"Should I just give up?" he whispers. He gives himself another ten minutes to decide. During that time, the rain eases off a little, so he decides to go to the club.

Stepping out of the doorway, he makes his way down the alley towards the club's entrance. The lights are on inside, and people are gathered in the foyer. Feeling anxious, he pushes open one of the glass doors and enters.

The walls of the foyer are sky blue. In the middle of the glittery pale stone floor is a sculptured silhouette of a naked woman painted in gold, the edge of her body displaying tiny white lights. Francois stares at the sculpture in surprise. Behind the large reception desk is a large sign that says, "Rose Bleue." He looks over at the counter, noticing the edging of blue neon lights. A group of men is forming a queue, their clothes expensive, with shoes to match. Behind the counter are two women dressed in tiny matching red dresses, displaying lace-edged breasts exposed to the maximum. Their faces are heavily made up, along with false eyelashes and long painted nails. They talk and flirt with the wealthy-looking clients as they arrive. Only then does it dawn on Francois that what his father owns is an exclusive up-market gentlemen's club.

As he makes his way over to the reception counter, one of the women notices him.

"Hello, beautiful," she says, looking surprised at seeing such a young, handsome man arrive. "Looking for fun tonight? I haven't seen you here before. Are you sure you're a member?"

"No, I'm not a member."

"Oh, so how can we help you, darling? Would you like a glass of champagne?"

"No thank you," Francois replies, watching the man next to him hand over a huge amount of cash to the other woman.

"What do you want then, honey? Aren't you a little young to be in here?" the woman asks, her voice sarcastic.

"I'm here to see my father."

"Your father?"

Francois nods. "Yes, Claude."

The woman stares at Francois for a few seconds, blinking her false eyelashes in surprise.

"Wait here," she instructs, then disappears through a side door. A few minutes later, a tall, muscular looking man appears at the counter.

"I hear you're looking for Claude." His voice is gravelly and a little aggressive. He looks Francois up and down, not believing he's Claude's son. "What do you want with him?"

Starting to feel annoyed Francois finds his footing. "That's between me and him."

"Come with me," the man says, stepping out from behind the counter.

Francois follows him down a long hall that leads between the foyer and the entrance to the bars. The oval ceiling is lit up with hundreds of tiny twinkling bulbs. In amongst them more blue neon lights. Lining the walls are paintings of beautiful semi-naked women.

At the end of the hall, the man pushes one of the curved gold handles in the dark blue double doors. Suddenly, Francois is transported into another world, as a wall of slow, seductive jazz surrounds him.

"Stay there for a moment," the man instructs. Francois looks around him. More wealthy looking men are sitting at circular tables covered with glasses of fancy cocktails and whiskeys and gins laced with ice. As the club starts to fill, young women walk seductively in between the tables, flirting and giggling while offering themselves on display in their tight bras and matching skimpy shorts. They serve drinks and keep the clientele happy.

At the rear of the club is a large bar. On the wall behind it is a blue rose with tiny gold lights etched into it.

Francois notices the tall man talking to another man who is sitting on one of the barstools. White and blue lights dance over their heads as they speak, reflecting from one of the stages, as a woman begins to dance topless, wearing tiny sequined panties. Her nearly naked body is covered in shimmering sparkles.

Francois gasps when he realises that the man sat on the barstool is his father. Francois's heart sinks. He feels embarrassed and disappointed in his father for not setting his standards higher.

Claude turns to look at Francois, but he doesn't move. A mixture of emotions cascades throughout Francois's body, dominated by sadness and confusion.

Still standing there waiting, he becomes inpatient, wondering why his father is still staying put. Francois feels angry with himself, standing there like a fool when his father is sitting at the bar.

Who does he think he is? he wonders. Then, ignoring what he's been told, he strides up to the bar and stands right next to his father. Signalling the man to leave, Claude turns to look at Francois. Francois sees a flicker of shock and then happiness in Claude's eyes. Francois smiles, feeling both relieved and happy.

"Hello, Papa. I came to find you. Are you happy to see your son?"

Claude's expression changes as he surveys the club as if to confirm they can't be overheard. Then, looking Francois square in the eye, his expression turns serious, causing Francois to step back a little. Francois doesn't know what to say. Finally, Claude speaks.

"You're not my son."

Francois stands rigid in shock, his mouth open. Did he hear his father right? This is not what he was expecting. Wanting his father to want him, his stomach is knotted in anguish.

"But Papa, I am, I am," Francois pleads, not understanding his father's behaviour.

"You're not my son," Claude repeats, his ice-cold stare piercing Francois's heart. "Go."

"But Papa, it's me."

"I said go!"

Feeling crushed, Francois's hands begin to tremble. The sudden disappointment overwhelms him. Feeling exposed and alone, the vulnerable, lonely little boy inside comes back to haunt him. He can't believe it, his own father rejecting him.

He stares into Claude's face for a few more seconds, hoping that a mistake has been made and longing for him to say something, but instead Claude turns away and picks up his drink. Unable to bear the pain of rejection any longer, Francois turns and runs out of the club, his eyes filled with tears.

Back out on the street, it's still raining. Francois continues to run, unable to feel the rain as his hair and clothes become wetter and wetter. He's too full of pain to notice. Eventually, totally exhausted and unable to run any longer, he steps into a dark doorway and sobs.

Utterly heartbroken, all the pent-up emotions and disappointment overcome him. He stays there for another hour, staring blankly into the cold wet night. Then he finally starts back toward his hotel.

Once in his room, Francois takes off his wet clothes and throws them into a heap on the floor. Reaching into his rucksack, he pulls out the little blue book from his childhood that contains the small photograph of Claude. In a rage, he rips it up, throwing the pieces onto the floor.

"I hate you!" he yells. Then he switches off the bedside lamp, the room dark except for the light from the street. He watches the raindrops run down the window for a while in silence. The faint sound of laughter can be heard people enjoy themselves out in the street. He sighs, then gets into bed. Once under the covers, he prays quietly, then drifts off to sleep.

CHAPTER 10

A Very Important Guest

It's late September 1993. Now twenty-three, Francois has reached his ultimate dream in martial arts. After five years of dedication, he has achieved the top rank of eighth dan.

Neatly folding his ninjutsu uniform upon his bed, he places it inside his sports bag. Having moved out of the hotel, he is now living in an apartment in the same area of Neuilly-Sur-Seine Paris.

Music blasts from the hi-fi system, playing "Enjoy the Silence" by British pop band Depeche Mode. Singing along while wearing a dark blue fitted jogging suit along with red tennis shoes, Francois is pleased to have made a new friend, Elijah, the older brother of his friend, Fabrice. Excited about meeting them later, he checks his hair in the mirror smiling at his reflection. Then he slings the sports bag over his shoulder and heads out.

When he arrives at the street that leads to the small and exclusive training club, he feels free, away from some of his family troubles. As he passes a group of girls, they smile at him, impressed by his handsome face. He looks back at them and grins, then continues on. After a few minutes he arrives at an old black wooden door set back from the pavement. He presses a button and waits to be recognised by the tiny spy camera.

"Hello, Francois," a deep voice says. A buzzing sound can be heard, and the door clicks. Pushing it open, Francois walks up some steep black stone steps. When he arrives at the top, he pulls open a second door, closing it behind him.

Francois enters a small room to his left situated at the beginning of a short hall. He places his bag on a wooden bench, then changes into his black uniform, taking time to carefully wrap his black belt around his waist. Then he makes his way down the hall and into a large room.

Reflected in the mirrors upon the far wall is a wooden floor along with a number of green mats placed horizontally across it.

"Francois!" a man in his forties says as two younger men stop their training to look over as Francois enters the room. This talented young man has captured their respect and admiration. Smiling, they resume their practice.

"Hello, Astor," Francois replies. Astor is tall, tanned and powerfully built. His hair is shaved short, and he has brown eyes. His powerful square jaw displays a prominent mole on one side. Having spent his life as an elite military service professional, he is super fit and skilled in combat.

"Ready?" he asks Francois.

"Sure."

They begin to spar. Just as skilled as his older counterpart, Francois has no fear of the taller and much stronger man. They attack and defend over and over using every move possible, each outwitting the other in turn.

After around thirty minutes they stop, and take a break

"So how are you Francois? Family still giving you stress?"

"Same old thing Astor yes."

"Are you still training the new elite recruits?"

"Yes, but less now I am a volunteer at the military hospital now."

"You are everywhere Astor."

"Well, I try to be."

They both laugh

"I have got to know a few people in the elite police forces RAID and the GIGn."

"Why are you interested in joining them Francois?"

"Maybe."

"Come on let's get back to it."

Astor takes out two wooden practice samurai swords from a long black box on a bench. He hands one to Francois. They bow and begin an array of complex moves, demonstrating the skill and full power of their knowledge. They manoeuvre their swords with grace and precision, both offering an impressive and deadly display. After a while they stop, and Astor returns both swords to the box.

"Wonderful, my friend. See you in next week, Francois."

"Goodbye, Astor."

When Francois arrives back at his apartment, the phone is ringing. It's Mirabelle.

"Would you like to come to dinner tonight?" she asks. "I haven't seen you for a while."

"Sure, okay. I love you."

"I love you too, dear. See you at six. Kisses."

After taking a shower, Francois blow dries his hair and dabs on some delightful citrus-fragranced cologne. He takes a look in his elegant walnut chest of drawers at his vast collection of polo shirts, settling upon a peach and white one. Grabbing his black designer jeans hanging over the back of a chair, he dances around as he pulls them up, finishing with a pair of black suede ankle boots.

It's almost 5:00 when Francois arrives at the hotel. He's early, keen to see Mirabelle and his mother. Making his way to the kitchen, he glances into the living room as he passes. Then he stops, seeing an unfamiliar but important-looking man sitting on the sofa. His wavy, glossy black hair is swept back off his face. He's immaculately dressed, wearing an expensive tailored dark grey suit. His crisp white shirt is aligned with a blue silk tie. Upon his feet, shiny black brogues reflected the lights of the room. Sitting in an armchair, Delmare is deep in conversation with him as they both drink coffee. Upon the table is a selection of beautifully decorated cakes upon china plates. They both then look over at Francois and smile.

"This is my son, Francois," Delmare says.

"Hello," Francois says, wondering who the man could be.

"This is Nicolas Sarkozy, Francois, the Mayor of Neuilly-sur-Seine—the future President!"

Nicolas chuckles. "You are so kind, Madame Ronen."

"Mr Sarkozy is visiting all the hotel owners Francois," she explains.

"It's good to meet you," Francois says. Nicolas nods, then resumes his conversation with Delmare.

Continuing to the kitchen, Francois is met by his Uncle Gustave and his Uncle Jacques. The table is set for dinner. Francois walks around to the other side to avoid sitting next to, or opposite, Uncle Gustave.

"Francois," Uncle Gustave says, his greeting cold and half-hearted. Francois looks at him and then looks away, not wanting to answer after hearing his lack of warmth.

"So, how are you?" Uncle Jacques asks. He is slim with dark green eyes hidden by black thick-rimmed glasses. His face is small and sports a moustache. He is a gynaecologist with his own private practice.

"I'm fine, Jacques," Francois replies. He decides to say very little after learning long ago that the more he says, the more sarcastic criticism comes his way from both of his uncles, especially Gustave. Just then the door opens, and in walks Mirabelle and Delmare.

"Hello, darling," Mirabelle says.

"Hello, Francois," Delmare adds, sensing the uncomfortable atmosphere as she sits.

"Anyone for wine?" Mirabelle goes to the fridge, taking out a bottle of rosé.

"Yes," Uncle Gustave replies.

"Not for me," Jacques says.

"Now," Mirabelle begins, placing the wine bottle on the table, "I expect manners and kindness tonight. Otherwise, I will be furious."

Mirabelle takes a roast beef from the oven. After laying out a variety of vegetable dishes and trimmings, they begin to eat.

"Has Sarkozy gone?" Jacques asks.

"Yes, of course. He's not hiding in the lounge, is he?" Delmare replies.

"I don't know why he met you anyway. I'm surprised you didn't scare him off," Uncle Gustave sneers.

"Oh, shut up, Gustave," Delmare snaps. "You're just jealous. He visited the hotel before last year, and Maman and I met him. It was our turn again. You don't know what you're talking about."

"Stop, eat!" Mirabelle says, and silence falls. Francois shovels his food down, eager to meet up with his friends.

"You have finished already, Francois?" Delmare asks. "We have a beautiful dessert."

"No, it's okay. I have to go."

"Already?" Mirabelle asks, sounding disappointed. Francois gets up and kisses her on both cheeks.

"Bye, Maman," he says, blowing Delmare a kiss. Ignoring his two uncles, he leaves.

Riding his motorcycle through the streets of central Paris, passing between the tall, elegant buildings, Francois weaves in and out of traffic, eventually arriving at his destination, L'oranger, a large up-market lounge on the corner of a long street. As he enters, the sound of "Voyage" by Desireless can be heard.

The bar is a favourite haunt of the young and wealthy of Neuilly Sur Seine. It is the place to be seen. Chattering in their finest clothes, a large crowd is already gathered, men in designer jeans and beautiful shirts, wearing expensive watches and smart leather shoes without a sock to be seen, women in slinky dresses draped in beautiful jewellery, immaculately made-up faces and high-heel shoes. The air is intertwined with the sweet smell of expensive perfumes and colognes as the patrons laugh and drink fine wines and cocktails. Small bowls of fresh green olives and flickering white candles in small glass domes sit on each table. The walls are a mass of colours, depicting a repeating pattern of the Eiffel Tower surrounded by orange trees. The seats are covered in pale blue leather, and the dark blue marble floor with its silver flecks reflects the lights. It's a regular venue for Francois and his friends to have fun, meet girls and hang out.

"Elijah!" Francois calls, waving to him. Spotting him and Fabrice sitting at a table in a corner of the huge room, Francois makes his way through the crowd. Several girls glance at Francois as he passes, admiring his beauty.

"Hello, Francois," Elijah says as they embrace and kiss each other on both cheeks.

"Francois," Fabrice says, patting the empty chair next to him. "Come and sit."

The brothers look very different from each other. Elijah's hair is dark and full of small curls. His big blue eyes have long lashes that compliment his oval face and dimpled cheeks. Fabrice's layered hair is light brown. His face is longer with a strong square jaw. Both of them are wearing polo shirts and smart designer jeans.

"What do you want to do later, Francois?" Elijah asks after they've caught up with each other. "I have a new moped. It's better than Fabrice's."

"No, it's not. You're joking," Fabrice replies. They all laugh.

"Want to go for a spin?" Elijah asks.

"Sounds fun," Francois says.

"It's a good thing we don't drink alcohol. Do you need a helmet?" Elijah asks.

"No, I have mine."

After finishing their drinks, they get up to leave the bar.

"Hello, Francois," a pretty blonde woman says.

"Hello," Francois replies, trying to remember who she is.

"I rang the hotel, you know. Remember when you took me to a restaurant late last year? I wondered what happened to you," she says, hoping for another date.

"Oh yes." Francois suddenly remembers her. "Sorry, but I have to go. My friend is ill."

All three friends rush out of the bar, giggling as they push each other through the crowd.

"That was a close one, Francois," Elijah quips.

"Yes, I remember her face but not her name. I also remember her mentioning marriage after one date. After she discovered we had the hotel, she kept on harassing me, calling me a millionaire. Money hungry, that one. Never again. Let's go."

Parked outside the bar are two shiny new mopeds, one pale blue with a tan leather seat and chrome trim and the other red and black. Fabrice puts on his helmet, then gets onto the red one and starts it up. Elijah does the same, sitting upon the blue one. After putting on his helmet, Francois jumps on behind Elijah. Elijah revs the engine, making the moped roar. Then they make their way up the street, Fabrice following closely behind.

Turning up a side street, Elijah cranks the throttle. The engine's high-pitched whine causes pedestrians to turn and look. An old man jumps in fright, furious at the noise, and shouts whilst waving his fist.

"Whoo!" Elijah shouts, looking back in his wing mirror as Francois punches the air in delight. Wearing a faceless helmet, Fabrice grins as he overtakes them. Turning the throttle further, Elijah races ahead, Francois holding him tight. Now neck and neck, each brother edges forward a little, trying to outdo the other as the beams of their headlights shine down the street. Just then Elijah notices a car heading towards them. He quickly drops back, raising his hand in the air to warn Fabrice. As they near the end of the street, Fabrice slows down, and they pull over and park. Francois takes off his helmet as he gets off the moped, feeling exhilarated.

"That was great!" he says, laughing.

"Excellent moped, eh, Francois?"

"Yes, Elijah, I love it!"

"That was fun," Fabrice says, "but I need to get back now. I have another date later with my sexy Florentine."

"Lucky you," Francois replies. He and Elijah watch as Fabrice drives off into the darkness.

"How are you, Francois?" Elijah asks, turning back to him.

"I'm okay. I'm still fed up though. Maman's boyfriend is using her just like the one before."

"Is Gustave still being a horrible asshole?"

"Yes, both him and Jacques, but Gustave is worse."

"Sounds like he's just jealous. Try to ignore him, Francois."

"I try, but it's not easy, I love him but I want to punch him sometimes. He's always horrible to me. It confuses me. He's a manipulator, clever too. I don't know who to trust, him or Maman."

"You have your Grand-mamie, Francois. That's all you need, my friend."

"I know."

"Come on. I'll take you back to your motorbike."

When they arrive back at the bar, Francois gets off the moped and takes off his helmet. Elijah does the same. They embrace, and Elijah kisses Francois on both cheeks.

"See you soon, my friend."

"See you," Francois replies as Elijah drives away.

Looking through the window at the people in L'orange having fun, Francois sighs, feeling a little lonely. He looks up at the moon and the stars, muttering a few short words to God in French and then in Hebrew. Finally, he decides to leave.

As he nears his apartment, Francois feels hungry. He decides to take a shortcut down an alley, knowing there's a Japanese takeaway nearby. He cranks the throttle, hoping to reach it before it closes. So determined is he to get there that he ignores the dim lighting. Faster and faster, he goes. Just a few more buildings. He's almost there when ... bang!

Someone opens their car door, and Francois crashes straight into it. The impact sends him flying, and he lands in a heap on the road. The mangled front wheel of his motorbike is lying a few feet away from him. The bike's engine is still running, and the back wheel is spinning. Then the engine cuts out, and the street goes silent.

"Oh my god! oh no!" a man yells. He's a Canadian tourist who has just arrived in Paris. After opening his car door, intending to visit the same takeaway as Francois, he gets the shock of his life. He shines his cell phone in Francois's face, noticing his helmet is split, exposing the left side of Francois's blood-covered jaw. He groans in pain.

"Are you okay?" the man asks, in a panic. "I'm so sorry. Are you okay?"

Having heard the impact of the accident, customers and staff at the takeaway come running outside. One person quickly returns back inside to call an ambulance. Eventually, Francois is taken to the nearest hospital, in a state of semi-consciousness.

The following day, Francois is awakened by the sound of voices. Thinking he's dreaming, he tries to open his eyes. Then, crying out at the pain coming from his jaw, he slowly moves his head from left to right. As his vision clears, he sees Delmare in a chair, with Mirabelle beside her.

"Francois!" Delmare cries. "My son, are you okay?"

"My son," Mirabelle says as they put their hands on top of Francois's hands, both of them fighting for his attention.

"Francois, can you hear me?" Delmare asks, her voice frantic. "You're in the hospital. Can you hear us?"

Francois tries to move, but his head feels like lead, and his jaw is aching so badly it makes him want to vomit. Nodding slightly is all he can manage for now as a tear runs down his grazed and bruised face, which is bandaged from his jaw to his head.

A doctor enters the room and smiles at Delmare. "Good afternoon. I'm Doctor Arnaud. I was the surgeon who operated on Francois's jaw.

He's awake, good. Don't worry; he'll recover. Lucky for him it was a jaw injury, not a brain injury. We mended his jaw, but it was not easy, as part of it was shattered. We inserted a small piece of metal, which we will take out in six months once the bone regrows. The only problem for you, young man, will be going through metal detectors at airports for the time being."

"Thank you, Doctor Arnaud. We were so worried," Mirabelle replies.

"I will leave young Francois to rest now. I'm here tomorrow afternoon if you wish to speak to me. Goodbye for now."

The doctor leaves the room.

"I told you not to buy him a motorbike," Delmare snaps. "This has made me ill with worry."

"Francois wanted it. He wanted one for a long time."

"Yes, and look what's happened."

"Stop, Delmare. Francois, are you okay, my darling? It's Grand-mamie."

Francois's eyes start to close. The powerful painkillers are making him drowsy, and he has to fight to keep his eyes open.

"Stop arguing, both of you," he mumbles.

"Let him get some rest," Mirabelle says. "Go home. I'll stay with him."

"No, I'll stay," Delmare replies, her frustration growing.

"No, you go," Mirabelle orders. "Let him rest. Let my son rest."

Furious, Delmare gets up and leaves.

A little later a nurse enters the room, informing Mirabelle that Francois needs to rest, and it would be best if she returns tomorrow. Mirabelle kisses Francois on the head and then leaves.

Later that evening, Francois wakes up. He tries to focus his eyes on the objects around the room, but things still look blurry due to the medication.

"Grand-papa," he whispers. In his confusion from all the trauma of the past twenty-four hours, he thinks he can see his grandfather, only to remember he is no longer alive. A feeling of utter sadness fills his body.

Chapter 11

The Curse

Francois, now twenty-five, has arranged to meet Elijah for lunch at a popular Italian restaurant and bar. After they finish their meal, they chat and laugh together, sipping coffee.

Francois gets up to use the bathroom. As he makes his way through the crowded bar area at the rear of the restaurant, he feels an abrupt push from behind, causing him to stumble forward. Feeling annoyed, he turns around to see a man standing right behind him.

"Hey, don't push!"

"Do excuse me, sir," the man says. "Someone pushed into me too, which made me bump into you. I'm new in Paris. Can I get you a drink as an apology?"

The man looks down at Francois's chest, making Francois uncomfortable. Pulling up the zip on his top and hiding his star of David, he looks the man up and down, feeling suspicious. He finds it odd that a stranger would offer to buy him a drink.

The man looks to be in his mid-thirties. His thick jet-black hair sweeps the top of his collar. His eyes are dark brown, and he has a small goatee. Draped around his neck is a black-and-white chequered shawl. His thin wide lips are smiling.

"No thanks," Francois replies, sensing something is off with the man. He turns to walk away.

"Listen," the man says. "I'm just looking to make a friend. Does it matter that you don't know me?"

He extends his hand for a handshake, taking Francois by surprise. Francois hesitates, looking him in the eyes for a few seconds. Then he smiles, lowering his guard as he shakes the man's hand.

Elijah looks across at them, trying to eavesdrop on their conversation, but he is unable to hear a word over the din. He feels annoyed with Francois's sudden trust of a stranger.

"My name is Tariq, and yours?"

"Francois. Buy me a drink, and I'll tell you the best places in Paris to explore."

"Great," Tariq replies. "What are you drinking?"

"I don't drink alcohol."

"I don't either, Francois."

They both smile.

"Just get me a fruit cocktail. They'll know at the bar. I'm sitting over there with my friend, Elijah."

Francois points at Elijah, who is talking to Nadia, a woman he has just started dating,

"Oh, I see," Tariq replies, looking over at Elijah. Francois looks at Tariq again, feeling uneasy but not knowing why. He dismisses his instinct again and decides to be kind to his newfound friend.

As Tariq makes his way back from the bar with his drink, Francois beckons him to follow back over to Elijah.

"Hey, Elijah, this is my friend, Tariq," Francois says, patting Tariq on the shoulder. Elijah looks up at Francois and then Tariq.

"Hi," he says, his tone unenthusiastic as he notes Tariq's tasselled black-and-white cotton scarf.

Angry at Francois's naivete, he has an instant distrust toward this new "friend."

"How do you know Francois?" Elijah asks, knowing full well that Francois has never seen him before.

"We just met!" Francois laughs, then sips his cocktail through a straw. Just before Francois sits down, Elijah grabs his arm.

"Francois come outside for a minute. I've lost something."

"What?" Francois replies, wanting to sit. As Tariq sits down, looking around the busy restaurant, Elijah glares at Francois, then tilts his head, indicating Francois should follow. Reluctantly, Francois sets down his drink and follows him outside. Tariq watches them as they make their way towards the doors.

"Who is this guy?" Elijah asks.

"I don't know. What's the problem? He's new to Paris. I'm just being friendly."

"Friendly? You don't even know him. How can we trust this guy?"

"Don't be so dramatic, Elijah. He's okay. Not all Arabs hate Jews, you know."

"I know that! It's not his scarf; it's him. There's something odd about him. He's weird, and sneaky."

Francois chuckles. "No weirder than anyone else."

"Well, it's up to you," Elijah replies. "I just offered to drive Nadia home."

Elijah returns to the restaurant to collect Nadia whilst Francois waits. When he comes back outside, Elijah kisses Francois on both cheeks. Francois reciprocates and then Elijah leaves.

"See you soon, Elijah."

"See you, Francois."

As he watches Elijah walk away, Francois feels sad. Glancing through the restaurant window, he sees Tariq standing near the door, smiling at him. Once again, an uneasy feeling forms a pit in his stomach, but he brushes it off yet again, his compassion and empathy getting the better of him.

Returning inside, Francois sits with Tariq, and they begin to talk. Before long they are laughing and joking fills another couple of hours. Francois enjoys telling him the best places to go in Paris. He also finds Tariq's accent intriguing.

"What country are you from?" Francois asks.

"Syria. I have an uncle in Paris. He encouraged me to come look for work. He has a small food business but no space for me, I'm afraid, so I'm finding my own way."

"Oh, I see, well, good luck." Francois looks at his watch. "It's almost four o'clock, I have to be off. It was good to meet you, Tariq, but I really must go."

"Oh, okay, Francois," Tariq replies, looking a little glum.

"I will have to try and find a hotel for the night then."

"Goodbye, Tariq."

"Goodbye, Francois. Good to meet you."

Francois leaves the restaurant, but after walking for a few minutes, he looks back behind him, thinking of his new friend. Then he turns round and heads back into the restaurant to find Tariq is still sitting there.

"Tariq."

"Oh, hello, Francois, you're back."

"Yes. Come on. I have a large apartment. You can stay in one of the spare bedrooms. You're not a thief, are you?" It's a joke, but it also contains a hint of warning.

"No, my friend, certainly not. Don't worry. Thank you, Francois."

"Sorry to say such a thing, but I don't know you, so I'm just being careful."

"Of course, no problem, Francois."

Tariq stands and slings a large brown bag over his shoulder. Then they leave the restaurant together.

As they walk, Francois notices Tariq's expensive-looking tennis shoes. He finds them strangely reassuring, convincing him that Tariq can be trusted.

The offer of one night turns into three weeks and then two months.

The new friends get along well. Francois enjoys having a new companion at his apartment. Then one night Tariq makes a suggestion.

"Shall we have a little party tonight, Francois?"

"A party? What for?"

"I have some people I'd really like you to meet, five friends of mine, in fact. They have arrived in Paris unexpectedly. They are wonderful people. It would be really nice, if you don't mind, Francois. They don't drink alcohol, just like you."

Francois pulls a face, unsure about the suggestion. "Well, Tariq, maybe, but I thought you were moving out soon. I thought your uncle had a job lined up for you now. I have many things I must do. I must help in the hotel with my family."

"Sorry, Francois. I will be moving on very soon, maybe next week. This could be my farewell party. How about it?"

"Well, okay," Francois replies reluctantly. You organise it, the food and everything else. Are these people, okay?"

"Absolutely, my friend. They know my family."

"I see. Right. I'm off now, Tariq."

"Okay. Come back at nine o'clock for the party, Francois."

"Nine? That's a little late, isn't it? Well, alright. See you later."

Francois leaves his apartment, closing the door behind him. He has a bad feeling, sensing something isn't right. He stops and looks back at his door, unable to understand why. Then he dismisses it and makes his way to the hotel.

The phone in the kitchen rings.

"It's for you, Francois," Mirabelle says. "It's Elijah."

After exchanging greetings, Elijah gets down to business. "You haven't still got that guy living off you, have you? He's using you, Francois. When are you going to throw him out?"

"He says he's leaving next week. His uncle has work for him now."

"He said that a few weeks ago, Francois. Get rid of him!"

"But he can be good fun."

"Yes, Francois, because he's living off your back. He's having fun, alright."

"Okay, okay, don't keep telling me what to do."

"You're stupid, Francois. Keep him there then!"

"Don't call me stupid! You're just jealous, Elijah."

"Jealous? Are you joking?"

Francois slams the phone down. Then he grabs a nectarine from the fruit bowl on the kitchen table and hurls it across the room. It bursts against the wall, leaving a giant snowflake pattern. Realising what a mess he has made, Francois gets a tea cloth from the kitchen drawer and makes a vigorous attempt to clean the stain from the wall, grumbling to himself in annoyance at having made the mess in the first place.

After calming down, Francois feels sad, full of regret at having fallen out with Elijah. He sits at the kitchen table, staring into space. Finally, he gets up and wanders off to see where the rest of the family members are.

In the living room he finds Delmare and Mirabelle engaged in another argument.

"Francois, Francois, come in, I have a new idea for you," Delmare says.

"No, Delmare, he can work in the hotel," Mirabelle retorts.

"No, Maman, stop. He's clever. He can do something else."

"He works here, and that's final." Mirabelle stands up. So does Delmare.

"It's not final."

Suddenly, the argument becomes physical, and Delmare and Mirabelle start to push each other.

"Stop, stop!" Francois yells. Feeling even more upset, he leaves the room.

Delmare runs after him. "But Francois, I'm trying to ensure you have a good future. I don't want you to waste your life."

"I won't, Maman. Stop."

Delmare bursts into tears and walks off.

Feeling anxious, Francois returns to the kitchen and sits at the table. He is lost in thought, still unable to understand his place in the family. He closes his eyes, trying to steady his mind. After a few minutes he calms down. Getting up, he goes to the refrigerator and takes out a packet of his favourite fruit, apricots. After washing two of them, he sits back down to eat.

"Francois," a voice says. Francois turns around to see his mother's tear-stained face as she enters the kitchen. "Listen, don't be too angry with me. I'm fragile today, and there's something I want to tell you, Francois, something good."

"What, Maman?"

I want to take you to New York. You can bring a friend. Will you come?"

"New York? Why?"

"Because you're my son, Francois."

"I don't know, Maman."

"Well, think about it. It'll be fun."

A disapproving expression creeps across Francois's face. Delmare pulls out a chair and sits down opposite him, extending her hand across the table and gesturing for Francois to do the same. Unsure of herself, when he hesitates, she retracts her hand, triggering more disappointment in Francois. They sit in silence, looking at each other periodically for a minute or two. Francois waits in anticipation that she has something important to say, but nothing comes. He glares at her in anger, causing her to lean back in her chair.

"Just think about it, that's all, going to New York with me. It's been really difficult for me since Grand-papa died and with my two brothers on my back. They're jealous that he left me a bigger share of the hotel, and I get very depressed."

Delmare places her hand on her chest as if to express herself better.

"I know that, Maman."

"I'm your mother, Francois, not Grand-mamie."

"Yes, but you get ill."

"I had a brain aneurysm, and I had you when I was very young, Francois."

"Grand-mamie helps me."

"So do I."

"You're erratic."

"She's neurotic."

"She loves me."

"So do I."

"I don't want to talk about it anymore."

"I don't either!"

As Delmare leaves the room, Francois shakes his head, feeling confused. His hands trembling, he rubs his face. Letting out a big sigh, he leaves the kitchen and makes his way to the hotel office. Sitting at the desk, he begins working his way through the enquiries book, ringing a list of potential customers and group bookings, his newly designated role in the family business.

At 7:00, Francois smiles as he suddenly remembers the party that Tariq has arranged for later that evening. This little ray of sunshine warms his heart after what has proved to be a stressful day. Feeling happier and a little hungry, he decides to leave the hotel and go home.

When he arrives back at the apartment, Francois turns the key in the lock, but before opening the door, he stands still for a moment, listening. Hearing nothing, he's confused. Expecting to hear excited voices and music, he feels disappointed that perhaps a party hasn't been arranged after all. When he enters the apartment, however, Francois is met with a peculiar sight: a group of six young men are sitting in a circle in his lounge, all of them dressed similar to Tariq, wearing long black cotton kaftans.

"Hello, Tariq," Francois says. "What's going on? Where's the party?"

"Ah, Francois, welcome. I'm afraid we don't drink, and we're a little fussy about what we eat. Come, join us."

Tariq gestures for Francois to sit in the middle of the group. Francois notices that dark veils have been draped over the shades of his table lamps, dimming the light, and a circular deep red rug has been placed in the middle of the group. The men are sitting cross-legged in a circle around it.

Francois feels uncomfortable, wanting to speak out but feeling overwhelmed by the weirdness of the situation. After convincing himself that he is in the midst of a traditional Syrian party, he remains silent and sits down. Choosing to ignore all that he has been taught in ninjutsu, as his solar plexus contracts, he foolishly ignores this signal of danger.

"Francois, we're going to chant now, a very beautiful chant. It's part of the party. Relax and enjoy, my friend," Tariq says, noticing Francois's discomfort.

At that moment Francois recalls a week he spent in Japan to meet a ninjutsu master, during which he visited a temple of chanting monks. Against his better judgment, he allows himself to relax. Sitting as instructed upon the mat in the middle, he decides to try and embrace this unusual and unexpected situation.

"To all people here, close your eyes," Tariq says.

Francois looks at the others. Each man's eyes are closed. Tariq begins muttering, and they all start to chant.

Sitting in the middle of the rug, Francois notices a small dark wooden box near his feet. It has a red symbol on top. As he looks up at the faces of the group again, their eyes still closed as they chant, he assumes something spiritual is happening, and he decides to go along with it.

The chanting continues for another few minutes, still led by Tariq. Then the tone of the chanting becomes deeper, darker and more intense. The sounds the men make resonate together, encircling the air around them much like the eye of an incoming storm. The atmosphere begins to change, becoming increasingly sinister, causing Francois to open his eyes. He looks at Tariq, who has started to rock from left to right and blink rapidly. Tariq's eyes roll back as he begins talking in foreign tongues. The rest of the group continues to chant, their voices intense and aggressive as their words spill out faster and faster.

Francois feels unnerved as he looks at the faces around him. Just then he feels a slight tug on the back of his head. Turning around, he sees Tariq holding a small blade in one hand and in the other, a piece of Francois's hair.

Tariq begins to laugh, his tone menacing. Then he stands up as the others fall silent. Crouching in front of Francois, Tariq opens the box. To Francois's horror, inside is a dead crow's head covered with blood. Tariq places Francois's hair in the box and then snaps it shut. He turns to Francois and smiles. His smile is cold, evil and unfamiliar, and the whites of his eyes are darker. All eyes are on Francois, and at that moment he realises he has been the victim of a black magic ritual.

Before Francois can say anything, Tariq looks him in the eyes. "I have always dreamed of cursing a Jew, and now I have. May you be cursed forever."

Francois jumps up and grabs Tariq by the neck. "Get out of here, you evil bastard. Get out!"

The men clamber to their feet and scramble out of the living room. In the chaos they knock over one of the lamps, sending it smashing onto the marble floor. They squeeze out the apartment door like rats escaping a flooding drain. Francois is still holding Tariq by the neck as he watches them leave. Then he slams Tariq up against the wall. He glares at him face to face. Tariq doesn't fight back; he continues to smile; happy his dream is complete. Francois drags him out of the living room to the front door.

"I trusted you," he says. Then he opens the door and, with all his might, kicks Tariq from behind, sending him crashing into the opposite wall, smashing his face. Unfazed, Tariq turns around to look at him, licking blood from his split lip, still smiling.

"If you ever return here, Tariq, I'll kill you, do you hear me? I will kill you!"

Tariq hobbles down the hall, stopping just short of the exit to the stairwell. He looks back at Francois before pushing the door open. Francois stands outside his apartment watching him, wanting to be sure he leaves. Then he returns inside his apartment, slamming the front door behind him. He races to the window and sees Tariq hobbling away from the building.

With the realisation of what has just happened beginning to dawn upon him, Francois grabs a packet of plastic bags from under the kitchen sink and, in a state of panic, stuffs Tariq's belongings inside several bags. Then he rolls up the red circular rug.

He remembers the box. Hoping to burn it, he searches the living room for it, swearing and whimpering when he is unable to find it. Finally, he realises that Tariq took it with him. Taking his keys from his jacket pocket, he picks up the bags of Tariq's belongings, tucks the rug under his arm, and leaves the apartment.

Too anxious to wait for the elevator, Francois runs down the four flights of stairs to the ground floor. Then he exits the building and runs off into the darkness.

Francois heads for the river, struggling with the bags and the rug. Sweating and panting, he finally reaches the water's edge. He tosses the rug into the water, followed by the bags. He watches as the bags float away, illuminated by a nearby streetlight. Completely exhausted, he trudges back to his apartment.

Once he arrives back home, he strips off his clothes and turns on the shower. His hands trembling, he frantically scrubs himself, hoping the hot soapy water will free him from the curse.

Not sure whether to believe it or not, he's locked into a state of trauma. As the hot water runs down his body, flashbacks of the evening's events flicker through his mind. The chanting, the piece of his hair that Tariq cut and Tariq's words. Sinking to the shower floor as the steam builds up around him, Francois lets out a desperate cry, praying to God for protection.

Chapter 12

Blood Shoes

Francois is now thirty-two. It's 1996, and he has recently moved to a new area in Paris. He's excited to find out what his new life will bring.

It's Saturday morning, and warm spring sunshine fills the streets of Paris. After accepting an invitation from some new neighbours to meet up, Francois is happy and looking forward to the evening ahead. Lying down and relaxing on the sofa, he decides to ring Christophe.

"Hey, my friend, do you want to come out tonight? I've been invited out by some new neighbours."

"Sorry, Francois, but I'm meeting a girl tonight."

"What? Another one?"

"Yes, I'm almost as popular as you, Francois."

"Are you sure? I'm taking a break from girls for a while. Problems and more problems. They won't leave me alone."

Christophe laughs. "Let's meet up on Friday. I'm on my way out. Speak soon."

"Okay, ciao."

Francois decides to ring another old friend, Herve, who has recently returned to Paris from down south.

"Francois, it's so great to hear from you," Herve says. "How's the new apartment?"

"It's great. I am meeting my new neighbours tonight."

"Nice. It would be good to catch up. Are you free after lunch for a coffee?"

"Sure. Why don't you come around and see my new apartment?" Francois gives him his address, and they agree to meet at 2:00.

Feeling tired, Francois decides to go back to bed and sleep a little longer.

Once he wakes, he checks the time, then turns on the radio. "Love's been good to me" by Frank Sinatra is playing. Putting his hands behind his head, he begins to daydream. His thoughts turn to his father, then his grandfather, and he begins to pray.

"Dear God, you're my father now. Keep my Grand-mamie and my

mother safe. Oh, and also help me find my future love. Amen."

As the song ends, he switches off the radio. Pulling the covers up to his chin, he turns on his side and sleeps a while longer.

After an hour he is rudely awoken by several loud voices coming from outside the apartment. Leaping out of bed, he goes to look through the spy hole in the door. Three men and a woman are standing outside the apartment across the hall, laughing loudly. Francois frowns as he presses his ear against the door, listening to their conversation. After discovering it's a birthday celebration, he looks back through the spy hole. The apartment door opens, revealing a large red-and-white flag on a wall inside. He watches until the last of the three enters and the door closes, cutting off his view.

Returning to his bed, he lies down for a few minutes, thinking about the flag and feeling a little uneasy, though he doesn't know why. Soon he begins to rationalise that it's all in his head, remembering that they were friendly. Dismissing it as nothing, he decides to let it go.

It's lunchtime. Francois is standing in front of the long mirror on his living room wall doing some stretching exercises. Then he starts to practice ninjutsu. After going through every technique several times, his thoughts turn to the flag again. He decides to stop, returning to the bedroom to check the time again.

"Ooh la la," he says. It's 1:30, and Herve will be arriving soon. Rushing into the bathroom, he steps into the shower. He dances beneath the water, trying to wash quickly, rubbing his favourite citrus fragrance shower gel all over his body.

Stepping out, he wraps a towel around his waist, shaves, cleans his teeth, puts on some cologne, and then returns to the bedroom. Balancing on one leg to put on his boxer shorts, he grabs his blue designer jeans from the back of a chair, then takes out a long-sleeve light blue polo shirt from his wardrobe. After blow drying his hair, he styles his curls in the mirror. Finally, he is ready.

In the kitchen, having just finished making coffee, he hears a buzz from his intercom.

"Hello, you ordered pizza?" a silly high-pitched voice asks.

"Hello, Herve," Francois replies, smiling. "Come on up."

Francois presses the door-release button, and soon there's a knock at the door. Looking through the spy hole, he sees Herve. He's tall and dark, and he looks strong. He has thick eyebrows and broad shoulders.

"How are you?" Francois asks as he opens the door. They kiss each other on both cheeks. "Come in, have a look at the apartment."

Herve takes in the living room as Francois closes the door. "Nice Francois, nice."

Herve takes a look out of the window at the street below.

"Do you want a coffee?" Francois asks.

"Yes, that would be great."

Sitting on the pale blue sofa, Herve relaxes as he watches Francois returning from the kitchen.

"Here." Francois hands Herve a cup, then sits in a matching chair.

"So, how are you, Francois? What's happening? Are you still working at the hotel?

Are your uncles still interfering in your life?"

"Yes, especially Uncle Gustave. He will never forgive Grand-papa for giving the majority share of the hotel to Maman. He hates me. He's jealous of the love Grand-mamie has for me. I don't think I'll ever escape this problem."

"Me neither, Francois. Your Grand-mamie adores you, and that's their problem."

"I know. I don't know who to trust sometimes, Gustave or my mother. They both say the other is crazy. Maman had an aneurysm in her brain, you know, when I was very young. It affected her mental health."

"You look drained, Francois. What else has happened?"

"You don't want to know."

"Try me."

"It's a long story."

"What happened?"

"You know that lodger I told you about?"

"Yes, that Syrian guy."

"I had some trouble with him. I threw him out a few years back."

"Why?"

"He was crazy. Evil too."

"Evil?"

"Yes. He cursed me in a ritual, although I didn't realise what was happening until it was too late."

"How horrible. That's disgusting. I hope it can't bring people bad luck."

"I hope so too."

"Want to come out with me tonight to the bar, Francois? Maybe it will cheer you up."

"I can't. I'm meeting some new neighbours tonight. They invited me out. You can come along if you like."

"No, you enjoy it, Francois. Maybe I'll try to meet up with a girl I met last week instead. She might be about tonight. It's a shame you don't have your father about," Herve said, changing topics.

"He doesn't want a relationship with me. I tried."

"Really? Are you sure?"

"Yes, I'm sure."

"Oh well, that's his problem. You think this area is okay, Francois? I haven't been around this part of Paris before."

"I think so. I hope so. You mean because of me being Jewish?"

"Well, yes."

"It seems okay."

"Have you eaten at the Chinese restaurant below this apartment block?"

"Not yet, but I've spoken to the owner, and he seems friendly."

As the afternoon comes and goes, the friends continue to catch up on each other's lives until.

"Well, I have to go," Herve announces.

"Okay, Herve, no problem. Great to catch up. See you soon."

After saying goodbye to Herve, Francois gets ready for the night ahead. Having arranged to meet his neighbours at 7:00, it leaves him just enough time to try out the Chinese restaurant.

As Francois enters the restaurant, the short middle-aged owner looks up from behind the counter.

"Mr Ling."

"Ello, Mr Francois. You come to eat tonight? What you want?"

Francois looks at the menu on the counter.

"Chicken and noodles. Is it good?"

"Of course, Mr Francois, of course."

Francois sits in one of the booths, awaiting his meal. Hearing shouting coming from outside the restaurant, he looks out the window as a group of men pump their fists in the air. Two have shaved heads, and the other three do not. Francois continues to watch them as they pass.

"Enjoy," a voice says. Francois looks down to see a plate of food in front of him and a waiter walk away.

After finishing his meal and paying his bill, he goes to say goodbye to Mr Ling, who is still behind the counter.

"Mr Ling, I'm going now. I have a question for you. Do you like living here? Is it a good area?"

Mr Ling looks a little unnerved and then looks down. "Yes, yes, it okay, it okay."

Sensing his discomfort, Francois decides not to press the matter.

Upon leaving the restaurant, he looks back through the window at Mr Ling, feeling confused. Shrugging it off, he goes to meet his new neighbours.

When he arrives at the bar, the first thing Francois notices is that nearly everyone appears to be very local and male, not the usual crowd he's used to drinking with in Paris and not what he was expecting at all. Feeling disappointed, he wonders if the evening is going to be a little dull. Deciding to leave early if things become boring, he wanders through the crowd looking for his new friends. Eventually, he spots all three sitting on barstools. As Francois walks towards them, one of the three looks up and smiles.

"Hello, Francois. You're here. Good to see you," says a tall man with short blonde hair and wearing blue-rimmed glasses. His two friends turn around to look at Francois. One has dark hair with a long fringe and a small beard. The other has a buzz cut. He's wearing a bomber jacket and tight khaki-green trousers. The man wearing the bomber jacket, Guillaume, smiles. The other does not.

"Francois, this is Alix, and this is Paul," Guillaume says, introducing the other two. "Do you want a drink?"

"Yes, a fruit cocktail please. I don't drink alcohol often."

Alix, the man with the long fringe, pulls a face. He looks Francois up and down, obviously a little surprised at his choice of drink.

Guillaume smiles, pushing his glasses farther up his nose. He turns around to order. There is an uncomfortable silence as Francois stands looking at the other two.

"So, where are you from?" Paul asks.

"Here in Paris," Francois replies, not wanting to give too much away.

"Paris where?"

"Neuilly-sur-Seine," Francois says, deciding not to mention the hotel.

Paul raises his eyebrows. "Oh," he replies, unable to hide his surprise at the thought that someone from such an affluent area would now be living locally. "What do you do?"

"I work at a hotel," Francois replies, still not wanting to give too much away after sensing a slightly unwelcome undertone from Guillaume's friends. Glancing at Paul's neck, he notices part of a tattoo poking out from under his shirt. He recognises the top of the tattoo but is unable to figure out why. Then he runs his eyes over Paul's military-style clothing.

"What do you do, Paul?" Francois asks, mirroring Paul's formal questioning.

"I work with a friend printing T-shirts and gifts. We print just about anything."

"Is it your company?"

"No, it's my friend's, but I've been there for years."

"What other things do you print?" Francois asks, starting to feel bored.

"Flags of all sorts."

Alix listens to the conversation but remains silent.

'Francois your drink."

"Thank you, Guillaume," Francois replies, feeling a sense of relief that Guillaume has finally turned back around. The evening passes slowly, and 10:00 comes and goes. Feeling tired, Francois decides to go home.

"See you again, Francois!" Guillaume shouts as Francois waves goodbye. Alix smiles for the first time as he watches Francois leave.

Feeling a little lonely after he returns to his apartment, Francois decides to call an ex- girlfriend. He lies in his bed as they chat late into the night.

"You want to come around tomorrow, Ariane?"

She giggles, knowing exactly what Francois means.

"Okay, see you tomorrow," he says, laughing. "You can come and wake me up."

As he hangs up the phone. His thoughts turn to Alix. A suspicious feeling comes to mind as Francois recalls how unfriendly he was.

"Miserable idiot," he mutters as he gets out of bed and heads to the kitchen.

After gulping down half a carton of milk, he returns to the bedroom and strips off his clothes. They fall in a heap on the floor. Yawning, he tramples over them and gets back into bed. Reaching across, he switches off his bedside lamp. Soon he is sound asleep.

The next morning, Ariane arrives early. After hearing the buzzer, Francois gets up and unlocks the door. Then he gets back into bed wearing a big smile upon his face.

Ariane is slim and beautiful with long brown hair, blue-green eyes, a small, upturned nose and perfect slender legs.

"Hello, Ariane. What are you doing here?" Francois askes as she enters the bedroom. Throwing back the covers to his waist, Francois exposes his toned physique. Ariane smiles. Then she strips off her clothes and climbs on top of him, straddling him. They begin to kiss passionately and make love.

Morning soon disappears, and as they rest side by side, chatting. Then Ariane asks him a question.

"Why did you move here Francois?"

"I wanted somewhere different, not so close to the hotel. I was fed up with the drama at home and endless girls also knowing about the hotel and only wanting money."

"Francois, don't put me in that category. I don't just want your money."

"What do you mean, 'don't just want'?"

"I'm joking, Francois."

"I know, darling. That's why you're here. You're one of the few genuine people I know."

"So, why did you end things with me then, Francois?"

"I told you I'm not ready for marriage. I thought we agreed we would just be friends. Well, almost. I don't want to hurt you again. Maybe we shouldn't do this anymore, sweetie. Maybe it's wrong. What do you think?"

"But Francois, you know I love you."

"Ariane, you want more than I can give. I'm sorry."

"Okay, okay, Francois, then let's just be friends. I have to go anyway. I have to go to a family dinner tonight. Today's my father's birthday."

She gets out of bed and showers. Then she returns to the bedroom and gets dressed. Blowing a kiss at Francois, she walks toward the bedroom door. Then she stops, the expression on her face serious.

"Goodbye, Francois," she says, her tone final.

"Goodbye, Ariane."

Francois sighs, his happiness diminishing somewhat. Being nowhere near ready to marry anyone, he knows he has done the right thing. He decides it's best to let her go.

Later that afternoon, he feels hungry. Francois surveys the kitchen cupboards, finding them all but empty. So, he heads on out in search of the nearest supermarket.

Standing outside the apartment block, he looks up and down the street, unsure which direction to go. Deciding to cross the road, he eventually comes across a small bakery. After buying a pastry, he munches it as he walks, stopping to look at a window display for a martial arts shop, which features an array of uniforms and weaponry. He casts his eyes over every intricate detail of a sword sheath, noting each part of its design. After finishing his pastry, he continues to explore the area.

As he passes by a group of people sitting outside a bar, Francois notices a small supermarket on the opposite side of the road. Standing on the edge of the pavement, he waits for a gap in the traffic. Hearing laughing behind him, he turns back for a second. Then the traffic clears. Just as his foot leaves the pavement's edge, he hears a word that he didn't ever think he'd hear.

"Satan."

When he reaches the other side of the street, he looks back and notices a small group of men sitting outside the bar, glaring at him. Francois feels angry, but carries on walking, deciding not to respond.

"Idiots," he mutters, looking back at them again. Then, to his horror, two of the men give him a Nazi salute. Feeling utterly shocked and upset but not wanting to give them any satisfaction, he walks straight into the supermarket, showing them that he won't be intimidated.

He takes comfort as he strokes his star of David around his neck. Then, grabbing a basket, he begins to shop.

After paying he walks towards the exit. Feeling anxious, he looks through the sliding glass doors across the road. Seeing that the men are gone, he sighs with relief.

Back at home as Francois puts his groceries away, he notices that his hands are trembling. He decides to run a bath, feeling a strong desire to relax. Hoping to diminish the anger and hurt he felt earlier, he slides into the steaming water, which offers him some comfort. He runs his trembling hands through his hair and sighs. Then, holding his nose, he submerges for a few seconds before placing his head back upon the slope of the tub. He rubs the palms of his hands over his eyes and blinks nervously. As his eyes reflect the glare of the ceiling light, a mixture of emotions runs through his body like a train hurling down the tracks. Little by little the hurt and anger begins to disperse, his heart rate slows and he closes his eyes.

"Grand-papa," he whispers as he prays to Eugène, finishing with a few words in Hebrew to God. Then he gets out of the tub and puts on a robe.

After resting on the sofa, Francois goes to look through the spy hole in his front door. He checks the lock and then returns to the sofa, deciding to ring Elijah, who is now married with one child and another on the way.

"Are you okay, Francois?" Elijah asks after some chitchat. "You sound sad. What's wrong?"

"I had a horrible anti-Semitism encounter today. Some assholes outside a bar shouted 'Satan' at me and gave me the Nazi salute."

"What? Idiots. Careful, Francois. You didn't respond, did you? Careful that you're not attacked."

"I didn't. I could have put them on the floor and given them a shock with my ninjutsu, but I didn't. I felt really angry though. It made me feel anxious."

"I know, Francois, but it was best you got away from them, my friend. How did they know you were Jewish?"

"I was just about to cross the road in front of them. They must have seen my gold star of David as I passed."

"I had someone throw a bottle at me the other day," Elijah says. "I didn't hear what they said, but I'm sure it was 'dirty Jew' or something. They disappeared quickly, cowards."

"Cowards, yes, cowards."

"Are you sure that new area you're living in is safe Francois? It's not an extremist area, is it? Did you check it out before you moved there?"

"No, I didn't. I took the apartment quickly because it's near the train station."

"Francois, be careful. Maybe it's not safe for you there."

"I can't move now. Why should I anyway? I can live where I like. I've just settled here. I'm also trying to find a way to not work at the hotel anymore. I'm fed up with all the arguing. I don't know who to trust anymore."

"I know, my friend. I understand. Keep safe. Let's meet up soon after I finish the projects I'm working on for my Papa."

"Okay. Ciao Bisous."

"Ciao Francois Bisous."

As dawn breaks, Francois is up early and making his way to the hotel. As he nears the end of the street, he bumps into Alix, the least friendly of the three neighbours he met the night before.

"Hello, Francois, isn't it?"

Francois stumbles, caught off guard, surprised to meet anyone who might recognise him so early in the morning.

"Oh, hello."

"Are you settled in okay, Francois?"

"Yes, I'm fine, thank you. I'm off to work, actually."

"Where do you work?"

"At our family hotel in Neuilly."

"Really. I thought you said you just work there. Your family owns it?"

Instantly regretting having revealed that detail, Francois tries to change the subject.

"I have to go. I'm late."

"You are a rich guy, aren't you?" Alix replies, wanting to press further, which only makes Francois feel even more uncomfortable.

"I better hurry. It's good to see you again."

"Hey, Francois, before you go, I'm off to a meeting. In fact, all the guys are meeting today. I'm in the local 'Front' group."

Francois gives him a puzzled look, not understanding what he's talking about.

"Why don't you come along? There's another meeting tonight at Victory Hall near the bridge. Two groups are joining up. It could be interesting."

"Okay, maybe."

"Hope to see you later then. It starts at seven o'clock. Come have a drink with the guys afterward if you like."

Francois nods and then starts walking away.

"See you later!" Alix shouts. Francois waves without looking back, then disappears around the corner of a building.

The hotel is full, and the day passes quickly. Francois works with his mother now, Mirabelle now too old to want to be involved in the day to day running of the hotel only coming back to help on the occasion, has retired to Nice, happier to be in a sunnier climate. The end of the day cannot come soon enough, and finally he heads off home.

After making dinner, Francois sits down to eat in the living room. He flicks through the television channels, but nothing grabs his interest, so he switches it off. Once he finishes his meal, he feels lonely in the silence of the apartment. He goes to look out his living room window, watching the activity on the street below with a blank expression on his face. Then he remembers Alix's invitation. Looking at his watch, he sees it's 6:40, just enough time to check out this mysterious group. He grabs his jacket and heads out, making his way to the hall near the bridge.

When he arrives at the hall, Francois notices a large group of people gathered outside, most of whom are men. As he gets nearer, they make their way inside. Francois tags along behind them.

Once inside, Francois looks behind him as an old man shuts the doors. He looks around but doesn't recognize anyone in the crowd. He's not sure why he has come and with no clue as to what it's all about, he considers leaving.

Suddenly, someone shouts his name. Francois spots Guillaume making his way towards him. He's accompanied by a powerfully built man with short blonde hair.

"Welcome, Francois. Glad you could make it. Alix told me he bumped into you this morning. This is Leon," Guillaume says, gesturing to the other man. "Perhaps you'd like to join our group."

"What is this group?" Francois asks.

"The Front."

"The Front?" Francois replies.

Guillaume nods. "Yes, of course."

Only then does it dawn on Francois what this meeting is. A knot forms in his stomach, and his face flushes red as his eyes dart around the crowd. Then at the back of the hall he notices a huge red-and-white flag with a swastika in the middle. Instinctively, he lifts his hand to touch the star of David around his neck, ensuring it's hidden from view.

"So, Francois, are you going to join us?"

Francois is unable to answer as anxiety grips his body. Desperately searching his mind for an excuse to leave, he says the first thing that pops into his head.

"I'm late for something. I have to go."

"Go?" Guillaume replies, frowning in confusion. "But you only just arrived."

Francois's brow breaks out in beads of sweat, and he begins to back away, pulling the zip up higher on his jacket. Then he turns and rushes toward the rear entrance. He yanks the old wooden doors open, and in an instant, he is gone.

As Guillaume and Leon watch him leave, their puzzled expressions turn to suspicion. Then they're interrupted by the announcement of the first speaker, and they move further into the crowd to listen.

Francois hurries down the street toward his apartment. When he gets there, his fingers tremble as he struggles to put the key into the lock, dropping his key twice in the process. Swearing, he looks back over his shoulder to reassure himself, he has not been followed. He grits his teeth as he steadies one hand on top the other, finally opening the door and then slamming it behind him.

After locking it, he peeks through the spy hole. Once he confirms the hallway is clear, he lets out a huge sigh of relief. He takes off his jacket and drops it onto the floor, then making his way to the bedroom, where he collapses onto his bed in exhaustion.

It's 5:00 in the morning, and Francois is unable to sleep as disturbing thoughts swirl around in his head regarding the previous night's events. Switching on his bedside lamp, he opens a drawer in his bedside cabinet, takes out his Torah, and reads, trying to distract himself. After a few pages he grows tired. Yawning, he puts the Torah back and then switches off the lamp and falls to sleep.

The following morning on his way to the hotel, Francois stops at the first coffee shop he sees. As he waits, a man joins the queue behind him.

"Francois, isn't it?" the man says.

Francois turns around to see the man who was with Guillaume the night before.

"It's Leon. I met you yesterday, well, briefly. You had to leave."

Francois feels a sudden mixture of fear, followed by anger, at having bumped into the last type of person he wants to see at that moment.

"Oh, yes," Francois replies, trying to look disinterested. After paying for his food, Francois walks past Leon on his way out of the shop.

"What's the hurry?" Leon asks, his tone aggressive. Sensing danger, Francois rushes out of the shop, but Leon follows. They stand outside the shop facing each other, Leon blocking Francois's way.

"I'm late for work. Excuse me," Francois says, glaring into Leon's eyes. Then, as if in slow motion, Leon looks down, stopping at Francois's neck. The gold reflection of something in the sunlight flashes, and his eyes widen. At that moment, Francois realises Leon has noticed his star of David.

"Jewish, are you?" Leon asks, his expression serious. A wave of anger rises up through Francois's body. He yearns to flatten Leon, to teach him a lesson, but he manages to resist the urge.

"So, what if I am?" Francois replies, his voice defiant as he goes to leave, but Leon steps in front of him, blocking his way again.

"Why are you living here, Jew?"

"Don't push me unless you know how to defend yourself, Leon, because I do. You want to find out?"

Instinctively, Francois assumes a defensive stance, ready to use all of his ninjutsu skills to defend himself. He keeps his eyes fixed on Leon, remaining silent. Leon begins to lose his nerve, realising he may have bitten off more than he can chew.

"Out my way, Jew," Leon snarls, deciding to back off, then he rushes away.

As he reaches the halfway point in the street, he stops when he hears Francois's voice shouting one specific word, penetrating the air like an arrow coming for him.

"Coward!"

Leon turns and looks back at Francois, then disappears down a side street. Little does Francois know he has become a marked man, a target and an object of hatred, and this will not be the end of it.

After reaching the hotel, Francois decides not to tell anyone in the family what happened, not wanting to cause them to worry. He spends the entire day rushing to complete every task, too anxious to take a break, trying hard to take his mind off his negative encounter with Leon.

By late afternoon Francois is on his way home. When he reaches the corner of the street to his apartment building, he passes a small group of men sitting on some benches. As he continues to walk, a deep voice calls out a word, the most unpleasant and darkest of words, a word he thought he would never have to hear again, but he does.

"Satan!"

Francois looks back at the men, not recognising any of them. After looking around at other people strolling down the street, he hopes it wasn't directed at him, but deep down he knows it was. As he continues to walk, he hears it again.

"Satan," another voice hisses. "Yes, you. We're talking to you, Satan."

Feeling afraid, Francois quickens his pace. When he reaches the Chinese restaurant, he yanks the door open and hides behind a red curtain at the side of the window. Peering through a gap in the curtain, he sees the group of men running past the restaurant and realises they're looking for him.

"What you do?" Mr Ling asks.

"Nothing, Mr Ling. Nothing at all."

Mr Ling watches as Francois steps outside to see if the men are gone. Then he makes his way up to his apartment.

As he turns the key in his door, something catches his eye: tiny bits of paper scattered over his doormat. Kneeling down for a closer look, he picks up a piece of paper and immediately notices Hebrew writing on it. He gasps as he realises, he's holding part of his Torah. After gathering up all the pieces, he shoves them into his pocket and then stands up. Turning the key in the lock, afraid of what could be waiting for him on the other side, he slowly opens the door.

His heart is pounding as he steps inside. Immediately, it's clear somebody has been in his apartment. Deciding to leave the front door open, his only escape route, he creeps inside, his trembling hands ready to defend himself from attack for the second time that day. He checks each room, looking behind doors and inside his wardrobe. Finally, he decides that whoever had entered is now long gone. Just then he sees his Torah on the living room floor, and his heart sinks. It has been torn up.

Rushing over to it, he sinks to his knees in disbelief as the hurt cuts deep. His precious book given to him by Eugène, ripped up and broken, is almost too much for him to bear. His heart breaks as he picks up all the pieces, putting them on his coffee table.

"You're not going to drive me out!" he yells, his defiant voice echoing around the apartment.

He sits at his breakfast table and looks out the window, not sure of what to do. He's concerned that if he tells Mirabelle or his mother, they will worry, and he will have to return to the hotel.

Should he call the police or not?

As a sense of isolation creeps into his thoughts, realising he's alone in this, he begins to feel anxious. As he paces up and down the length of his apartment, at a loss for what to do, something catches his eye as he passes the entrance to his bedroom. A pair of his shoes have been pulled out from the bottom of his wardrobe and placed in the middle of the floor. Not understanding why, he eventually loses interest, deciding to leave them there.

He tries to call Elijah, but it goes to voicemail. His anxiety growing, he decides to go to the police station. Grabbing the pair of shoes from the bedroom floor, he puts them on quickly, in too much of a rush to consider wearing socks.

After locking the door, he rattles the handle, trying to satisfy himself that the door is truly locked. Panting with fear and anxiety, knowing full well his apartment has already been invaded, he rushes out of the building and heads to the police station.

Half running and half walking, he is only a few streets away from the police station when he takes a shortcut across a grassy square surrounded by trees. Just then he feels a burning sensation in his feet. Unable to walk any farther, he stops and sits on a small wall, desperate to look at his feet.

Wincing in pain, he pulls off his shoes, only to discover, to his horror, that the soles of his feet are covered in burns and blood. As he peers into one of his shoes, he gags, a strange chemical smell wafting out from it. Frowning in disbelief, he looks inside the shoe again. Then it dawns on him. Whoever broke into his apartment poured a burning chemical into his shoes.

Still in immense pain, he continues in his bare feet, deciding to keep his shoes for evidence. He carries them upside down, careful not to put his fingers inside. The pain is so unbearable that he has to stop every so often to rest his dirty, bloody feet. Finally, he reaches the police station.

CHAPTER 13

Satan's Knife

Now thirty-seven, Francois is in turmoil. Things are not going well. Despite having made numerous complaints to the police over the last year about having been harassed and followed, he continues to feel unsafe.

Still determined not to return to the hotel, unable to be around the conflict and the continuous hostility from his two jealous uncles, Francois stays put. Gustave in particular is trying to drive a wedge between Francois and his mother, still upset that she has been made majority shareholder in Eugène's will, causing even more resentment.

It's a warm morning, and as the sun creeps up the buildings, Paris awakes. After ringing Elijah to talk over the problems he's having, Francois decides to head out. Wanting to clear his head, he makes his way to the nearest park.

When he reaches the end of the street and turns right onto another, something causes him to stop dead in his tracks. The sound of a sinister voice hissing a word he was hoping he would never hear again, the word of darkness, has raised its ugly head again his bright and sunny morning, which is now turning grey.

"Satan," a voice says. Francois looks to his right to discover a group of three men are standing next to a building, staring at him. He turns away quickly, trying not to look afraid.

"Satan," they hiss again, grinning as they await his reaction. Francois tries his best to ignore them, quickening his pace as he continues on.

He arrives at the park feeling hurt and angry that the same thing has happened again. The leafy shrubs and brightly coloured flowers help to ease his mood a little, offering a distraction as he walks across the grass. Feeling a little calmer, Francois stops to look at a group of pretty birds chirping inside an aviary. Deciding not to let the men upset him, in defiance he holds his head up high, striding purposefully toward the nearest bench.

He sits quietly for well over an hour. Then he looks up at the clear blue June sky and sighs, feeling utterly alone. Pulling a packet of sweets from his trouser pocket, he pops one into his mouth and watches two children playing with their father for a while. Eventually, he heads back to his apartment to make himself some lunch.

After leaving the park and crossing a busy street, he heads for a familiar shortcut, a quaint leafy ally between two buildings. As he passes the only shop in the lane, a flower shop, he peers through the window, hoping to catch a glimpse of the pretty woman he has noticed there a few times before. He spots her arranging a huge bunch of pink roses. He smiles to himself as he continues on. Then his smile turns to horror as the three men from earlier in the morning jump out from behind a gap in the wall, causing Francois to stumble backwards in fright.

"Satan," they hiss again. Two of them are dressed in military-style clothes, the other in jeans and a pale blue polo shirt. This time Francois is ready, knowing there is unquestionable danger ahead. His heart pounding in his chest, he assumes a defensive stance.

One of the men lunges at Francois, throwing a heavy-handed punch. Francois darts to the side, and the man misses his head, though he catches his shoulder with a hard thud. Francois winces in pain. Then, using the full force of his ninjutsu, he launches an assault, pounding the man with both arms, his hands locked together. The man cries out in pain as he crashes to the ground, unable to move, his neck injured.

"You'll pay for that," the second man growls. A skilled fighter, he attempts to kick Francois's feet out from under him, catching his right knee. Francois cries out in pain. Then he rains down a series of heavy blows and kicks using his skills to confuse and overpower the man. Following a precisely aimed strike to the side of the man's neck, he collapses to the ground. He is finished.

Francois turns around, ready to face the third man. His face is covered in sweat, and his eyes are wild, but the man is nowhere to be seen. He looks behind him and then up and down the alley, thinking he must have run off.

Placing his hand on his damaged, bloody knee, the agony overwhelms him. Francois feels a lump and realises it's broken. As he limps forward, he suddenly lets out a piercing scream when he receives a sharp blow to his stomach, followed by a long tear of his flesh. He feels dampness as blood seeps from the wound. As he looks up and sees the face of the third man, who had been hiding behind the wall, holding a blood-covered knife. Looking down, Francois realises his stomach has been sliced open, his polo shirt now crimson red.

"Die, Jew," the man hisses, his expression the ice-cold look of a killer.

Summoning the last of his inner strength whilst holding onto the wound with one hand, Francois kicks with full force, sending the man crashing backwards into the wall. Francois looks down at the man, who is lying in a crumpled heap on the ground. Only then does Francois notice a swastika tattoo on the man's neck. The man looks up into Francois's eyes as blood trickles from his mouth. Then his eyes roll back as he falls into unconsciousness.

Only when he is sure that the threat is over does Francois make his way out of the alley. Still clutching his stomach with one hand, he puts his other hand on the wall, trying to maintain his balance. As his vision blurs, he begins to feel cold, the blood from his stomach trickling over his hand.

Once he makes it to the end of the alley and onto the busy street, he collapses. An old man rushes over to help him. A young woman working in a shop sees him collapse and runs out, yelling at the stunned owner who is standing nearby to call an ambulance.

The next morning, Francois opens his eyes, wincing in pain from his stomach. He sees it's wrapped tight in bandages. Then he remembers the day before. He looks around to discover he is in the hospital, but it is no ordinary hospital. It dawns on him that he is in some sort of military hospital.

As he's still getting his bearings, a doctor appears at his bedside.

"How are you feeling, Mr Ronen?"

Francois looks at him. "How do you know my name?"

"Don't worry about that."

"My stomach is painful. Where am I?"

"The hospital."

"Yes, but which hospital?"

"Never mind that. You'll be okay. You've had an operation to repair your injury."

"I was attacked."

"Yes, we know."

"We found this in your pocket." The doctor holds up a razor attached to a handle.

"I was attacked. That's not mine."

"Yes, Mr Ronen."

"I don't know where that came from, but it's not mine. I was attacked. Someone put that in my pocket."

"Okay, Mr Ronen, rest now. I'll see you later."

"Promise me, Doctor, that you do not tell my maman or grand-mamie about this. They will be so worried.

Nodding, the doctor turns to leave.

"Doctor, before you go, did you hear anything from the police about what happened?"

"Only that when they arrived your attackers had vanished."

Francois's mouth drops open in shock, knowing how badly he injured one of them.

"They must have had help," he mumbles to himself as the doctor leaves the room.

The day is long and frustratingly slow. After spending hours unable to sleep, his stomach tender and uncomfortable, Francois notices the doctor is standing just outside his room talking to another man. They both look over at him, smiling and nodding. The other man looks strangely familiar. As Francois tries to sit up to get a better look, the pain of his wound forces him back. Then Francois's mouth drops open as he recognises the other man. It's Astor, his old friend from ninjutsu. Francois realises he must have come to help.

CHAPTER 14

The Stalkers

It's been a little over a year since the knife attack, and Francois is not sleeping well. His anxiety is at its worst, and it's starting to take a toll on his mental health.

The events of that horrific day remain at the forefront of his mind, and he's unable to move forward, locked into a continuous cycle of torment, his nights filled with horrible recurring nightmares. He has decided to return to work at the hotel, the familiarity of his environment helping to keep him distracted.

Predictably, a few days in, another argument breaks out between him and his uncles. Their continued belittling and bullying have reached the boiling point. After storming out of the hotel, Francois returns to his apartment feeling emotionally drained, seeking refuge in the silence.

He's afraid to continue living where he is, but he's more afraid of the harassment he's enduring endangering his beloved grandmother if he moved back to the hotel, knowing he could never forgive himself if anything happened to her. He decides to stay put, partly out of defiance and partly due to fear as he tries to cope alone.

Taking solace in his ninjutsu, his mind is in a continuous heightened state, fight-or-flight mode ever present. Night after night, he goes through the same ritualistic pattern of techniques, preparation to meet the enemy consuming his every thought. Without any reassurance from anyone helping to dampen his fears, he begins to develop an unhealthy obsession with being attacked again.

Punching and kicking rapidly, he moves through various complex positions, ready for combat. Francois executes each move to perfection, his eyes staring straight ahead as, hour after hour, he continues until exhaustion gets the better of him. At times his fragile mind plays tricks upon him, making him think the shadows on the walls of his apartment are his attackers,

"I see you," he snarls, the intensity of his stare like a stalking mountain lion ready to pounce on its prey. Only then does he realise the shadows are, in fact, his own.

One afternoon as he stares at his reflection in the mirror on the living room wall, his red, sweaty face looking back at him, his cell phone rings, snapping him out of his compulsion.

"Kai!" he shouts, formally ending the practice.

Finally satisfied, he lies down on the sofa to take the call.

It's his friend, Christophe.

"You sound rough," Christophe says. "You want to come out tonight? I've met some girls, a lovely one for you too, a real beauty."

"No thanks."

"Come on, Francois, why not? You need some passion, some fun."

"Passion? After passion there's trouble, Christophe."

"I'm not taking 'no' for an answer," Christophe replies. "I'll meet you at L'arc. Be there at eight thirty."

Before Francois has time to respond, Christophe hangs up.

Francois sighs, preferring to be alone. However, not wanting to let Christophe down, he decides to meet up later, and his mood begins to lift somewhat.

After taking off his ninjutsu uniform and showering, he heads out to do some shopping.

After crossing several busy streets, he arrives at a supermarket. He picks up a basket and wanders aimlessly up and down the aisles, unable to decide what to buy. Having just picked up a packet of apricots, he hears a woman call his name from behind.

Turning around, he sees a pretty woman with grey-blue eyes and shoulder-length light brown hair. Francois doesn't know whether to smile or frown seeing as she's interrupted his decision making.

"It's Florence," she says. "How are you?"

Trying to remember who she is, Francois rubs his cheek, looking puzzled. Then, blushing slightly, he recognises her. They met at L'arc quite a few years back, the same club he is due to meet Christophe at later. Memories of their long week of passion come racing back to him. He smiles. After having forgotten so many things, seeing Florence offers him a flicker of sunlight, momentarily lifting the heavy grey clouds from his mind. She giggles, noticing his discomfort.

"So, how are you?" Francois asks. "I haven't seen you for a few years."

"Good, Francois, and you? How have you been?"

Her eyes study every detail of Francois's handsome face. A feeling of awkwardness arises between them, fuelled by a fresh revival of attraction.

"I'm going to L'arc tonight," he says. "You want to come along?"

"Oh, L'arc," she says, smirking. "Yes, um, why not? I'm not doing anything tonight. Okay, I'll see you there, Francois."

She smiles as she looks into his eyes, her voice sensual and flirtatious, knowing full well where this will lead.

"Good. See you there Florence, eight thirty, okay?"

Francois smiles and then walks away, continuing his shopping.

Back at his apartment, Francois cooks one of his favourites, white fish and crème fresh with tomato sauce. Feeling a little happier with the possibility of not being alone again all night, his mood begins to lift.

He turns on the radio, and classical music swirls around the apartment. After plating his meal, he sits at the kitchen table to eat.

After dinner, Francois strips off everything but his boxer shorts and sits on the sofa to telephone Delmare

"Hello, Francois."

"Grand-mamie! What are you doing there?"

"I wanted to surprise you. Are you still coming tomorrow? Your Maman said you were. I've come to stay a little while to help out."

"Yes, I am. I was going to make the bookings."

"Wonderful! I can't wait to see you"

"Me too. You know, for a moment I was expecting Grand-papa to answer."

"Oh, my darling Francois, I miss him too, but if you open my heart, whose name is written on it, darling?"

"Francois."

"That's right. Never forget it, darling. Are you okay?"

"Yes, I'm fine," Francois lies, not wanting to worry her. "I love you, Grand-mamie."

"I love you too. See you tomorrow."

"Tomorrow."

Francois hangs up. After that much-needed dose of comfort, he makes his way to the bathroom.

Following his shower, with a white towel wrapped around his waist, Francois catches his reflection in the mirror on the bedroom wall. He stares for a moment as a succession of images flash through his mind.

His mood flips back to black again as that fateful day comes rushing back like a volley of arrows, each one fired containing an image, the fight, the faces of the men and the knife attack. Soon his calmness deserts him, replaced by anguish. His hands trembling, he is frozen to the spot, his fingers following the line of the crude scar upon his stomach as he remembers it all. The trembling worsens as the images in his mind become too much to bear. He cries out, and a sad and haunting sound leaves his lips. Grabbing a glass from on top the chest of drawers, he hurls it at the wall. As the pieces of glass spray across the room, he watches the sunlight reflect upon them, as if time has stood still for a moment, like a thousand tiny rainbows scattering through the air. The impact of the smash pulls him back to a place of calm, and his mind is still again.

"Ooh la, la, no, no!" he shouts, his life now marked by flashbacks. Realising his bedroom is covered in glass, he rushes to the kitchen, returning with his vacuum cleaner. He pulls back his bed cover and folds in the four corners. Then he carries it to the bin, deciding to dispose of it completely. Then he cleans up the rest of the glass from the floor, vacuuming it up until he is sure it's all gone.

At 8:00, Francois makes his way to L'arc. As he approaches, the pumping music spills out onto the streets, mixed with the sound of laughter as people make their way inside the club. As he nears the entrance, he notices Florence standing just outside the door.

"Hello, Florence. Why are you waiting here?"

"I thought I'd catch you on the way in."

"Oh, okay," Francois replies, feeling slightly uncomfortable at her choice of words, but he decides to let it go. Wanting to enjoy the night ahead, he takes her hand.

After paying their entrance fee, he leads her down a short hall full of flashing blue lights and crisscrossing chequered mirrors. At the end of the hall, they enter a huge crowded seating area and make their way to a silver dance floor. Still holding hands as they're showered in multi-coloured, pulsating lights, they weave through the swaying arms and twisting bodies, heading to the largest of the three bars at the rear of the club. Covered in twinkling tiny lights, the bar is surrounded by a huge arch, with the word "L'arc" written on it. Francois spots Christophe standing by the bar with two women and goes over to greet him.

"Francois, this is Estelle, and this is Bella," Christophe says. Francois glances at them both, realising within seconds that neither are his type, not caring which of the two Christophe has claimed.

"Christophe, this is Florence."

One of the women glares at Christophe, obviously expecting to have been paired with Francois. An awkward silence follows.

"Anyone want a drink?" Francois asks.

After buying everybody a drink Francois takes Florence by the hand and looks for a place to sit, finding two empty seats towards the rear of the bar.

Suddenly, Christophe appears next to him. He bends down to whisper into Francois's ear.

"Francois, what's wrong? Bella was for you."

"I have Florence tonight," Francois replies.

"But Francois, I remember this girl. You said last time she wouldn't leave you alone."

"I know, but she knows I'm not looking for a relationship."

"Well, good luck. We'll be over in a minute. Bella's gone to the bathroom."

Eventually, Christophe reappears with Estelle.

"What happened to Bella?" Francois asks.

"Don't ask," Christophe replies. "I think she left."

Francois starts to relax as he sits watching people on the dance floor, his arm draped over Florence's shoulders.

As the night wears on, the four of them are having fun. They laugh and joke, followed by the occasional dance. The night passes quickly, and before long it's 1:00 a.m., and the club is beginning to clear out. Soon they decide to leave, all four of them making their way to Christophe's apartment.

When it's almost 2:30, after drinking coffee and chatting, Francois begins to tire, deciding it's time to go.

"Want to come to my apartment?" he whispers to Florence, smiling.

Florence nods knowingly, and they creep out of the apartment, leaving Christophe and Estelle, who had disappeared into one of the bedrooms.

As they make their way along the street, Francois stops, pulling Florence close to him. They kiss passionately before continuing through the darkness, eventually reaching his apartment. As Francois turns the key in the lock, Florence giggles.

"Shh," Francois says. "You'll wake the neighbours."

As soon as they enter, they begin pawing at each other, stripping off their clothes. Francois leads Florence to the bedroom, and for the rest of the night they make mad, passionate love, eventually falling asleep in each other's arms.

When Morning comes, Francois wakes up and is startled to find that Florence is already dressed and is standing by the bed, staring at him. He sits up straight.

"Are you okay?" he asks. "What are you doing?"

"I'm fine. I just wanted to have a chat with you, Francois."

Francois's heart sinks, knowing what's coming next, and begins to regret agreeing to hook up again.

"What about?"

"Us."

"Us?"

"Yes, us, Francois. I … I want to marry you. I love you. I need you to know that."

Francois jumps out of bed, naked, grabs the robe from the back of his bedroom door, then rushes to put it on.

"Florence, I seem to remember this conversation last time. I'm not looking for marriage. It's only been one night. That's too much!"

"But we were seeing each other before," she replies, her voice distressed.

"But that was only for a few weeks a few years ago!"

Suddenly, her mood changes, as her face reddens in anger. "You horrible shit! I hate you! I hope your life is hell!"

She hurls one of his shoes at him. Francois ducks, and it bounces off the wall behind him. Then, turning on her heel, Florence marches out of the apartment, slamming the door behind her.

"Christophe was right," Francois mutters to himself, relieved that she is gone. Sitting on the bed, he gazes at the floor for a few minutes, remembering everything she said and feeling a little sad about it. Finally, he gets up to make a coffee.

Francois spends the rest of the morning tidying his apartment, absorbing his sadness in music, flicking through his vast collection of CDs and changing the mood every so often with another song. Turning the volume up, he busies himself tidying each room. Then he leaves to go to the hotel.

He catches a bus a few streets away from his apartment. As Francois makes his way down the crowded aisle, he spots an open seat and hurries to claim it. At the same moment, a fat, balding man gets up to make his way off the bus, and they bump into each other.

"Hey, watch out," the man says.

"Sorry, but you bumped into me too," Francois replies. As they glare at each other, the man then notices the star of David around Francois's neck.

"Well, I might have guessed. Stupid, greedy pigs, the lot of them."

"You what?" Francois replies, furious.

"You heard me," the man says.

For a split-second Francois considers putting him on the floor, knowing full well he could easily overpower the ignorant man, but not wanting any more trouble, he thinks better of it and goes to sit down.

"Ignorant idiot," he mutters as he watches the man leave the bus.

Moments later, he feels a soft touch on his hand. Looking down, he sees a feeble old hand on his. Then he looks up into the smiling face of an old lady. Her white hair is in little ringlets, and she's wearing a purple hat with a matching coat. Her face is lined and crinkled. Francois notices a silver crucifix around her neck. She smiles at him.

"Be proud of who you are, my dear," she says, then places something in Francois's hand and closes his fingers. "There are not enough of us who know him," she remarks, pointing to the sky. Then she stands up and makes way off the bus, which has stopped outside a large church.

As the bus pulls away, Francois looks out the window and sees her still smiling as she looks back at him. She raises her hand and waves. Francois opens his hand to reveal a Christian booklet with a picture of Jesus on it and the words *God Loves Us All*.

Francois looks back out the window, but the old woman is gone. He smiles as his heart warms a little, then puts the booklet in his jacket pocket, knowing he will never forget her.

When he arrives at the hotel, Francois makes his way to the office. After spending the afternoon ringing customers and arranging group visits and booking events, he goes in search of Mirabelle. He finds her asleep in a chair in the apartment's living room. Bending down, he whispers in her ear to wake her, then places his hand on her shoulder and smiles.

"Francois," she says as she wakes. "How are you, my darling?" She studies his face, noticing dark circles around his eyes. "Are you okay, Francois?"

"Yes, I'm okay, Grand-mamie."

"Are you sure? You look troubled."

"I have a bit of a problem, but I'm okay."

"What problem, darling?"

Francois sits on the footstool opposite her. "I don't want to worry you."

"I'm a strong lady, Francois; you know that. Just tell me. It won't worry me."

"Well, I've had—am having—some problems with anti-Semitism."

"With who?"

"I don't actually know who they are, but it doesn't matter. I shouldn't have mentioned it. I don't want to worry you."

"Francois," she replies, frowning with impatience, "tell me, my love."

"Some neo-Nazis, I think, but I'm not sure who they are really."

Mirabelle looks shocked. "Oh, I see, well, where are they? Where do they live? We can get the police involved."

"I have. They didn't do anything; they just took some details from me."

"Details? What use is that? Is that all?"

"Don't worry. I'll be okay."

"My darling, maybe you should move back to the hotel."

"Why should I leave? I won't let them win."

"But darling, you'll be safe living back here with your mother"

"No, I'll be okay. Please trust me."

"Francois, I'm worried."

"If it gets too much, I'll move back home, back to the hotel. I love you."

"Promise me you will. I love you too."

"I promise."

"Come on, Francois, it's time for dinner."

Francois gets up and hugs her, and they exchange kisses on each other's cheeks.

After dinner Francois decides to visit the one bedroom in the hotel that was never let to guests, his old bedroom. He would stay there amongst the guests once he reached adulthood and wanted more independence from the rest of the family whilst working at the hotel before moving out. Having left a lot of his stuff there, when he opens the door, everything is just how he left it. Several piles of books are sitting on the chest of drawers, titles referencing the elite military training and ninjutsu among them. A collection of empty cologne bottles of varying shapes and sizes is grouped on the bedside cabinet, and a mass of old, discarded CDs sits on top of a large music system.

He sits on the bed and casts his eyes over all his old treasured possessions, each one with a memory attached, reminiscing about times gone by. His thoughts turn to his grandfather, and he begins to visualise himself talking to him. Each memory is unlocked, one by one, of conversations and the times they spent together. Hearing his grandfather's voice in his head, he smiles, then begins to pray in Hebrew.

"I love you, Grand-papa. I need you," he whispers, wiping a tear from his eye. Then he lies back on the bed, and before long he drops off to sleep.

Francois is abruptly awoken by a knock at the door. It's Mirabelle.

"Francois, I want to discuss something with you. Can I come in?"

"Of course."

Francois looks at his watch. It's almost 8:30.

"I have a document I want you to sign."

Mirabelle sits next to him on the bed.

"A document? What sort of document?" he asks.

"Listen, darling, I'm getting older This is something I have prepared for you. You need to sign it, darling. It gives you a share of the hotel upon my death."

"I don't want to. I love you, but I'm not interested in your money."

"I know that, Francois, but please sign it. It will help you. You know what your uncles are like. They won't help you when I'm gone or if your mother gets ill. Sign it, darling, for your future."

"No."

"Francois, be sensible. Please sign it."

"No, I really don't want to, Grand-mamie."

"Well, listen, I'll leave it for you, and if you change your mind, talk to me."

Standing up, they embrace.

"If you open my heart, whose name is written across it?" Mirabelle asks, smiling.

"Mine."

"Yes."

"I'm going to go back to my apartment now," he says.

"You should stay here tonight. It's safer."

"No, I'll go. I don't want to run. I'm French. They can't drive me out."

"But Francois, it's late."

"It's okay, Grand-mamie."

As they leave the bedroom together, Francois feels anxious at the thought of Mirabelle dying.

"Don't leave me, Grand-mamie."

Mirabelle places her hand on his chest. "Francois, I'm not ready for heaven just yet. Don't worry, darling."

They embrace and then Francois turns to go.

"See you in a couple of days," he calls out as Mirabelle watches him leave.

Stopping at a bistro on his way home, Francois decides to visit an old friend. After ordering a cappuccino, he sits on one of the cushioned barstools, a row of which are perched on the grey marble floor. The bistro belongs to Jean, an ex-employee of the hotel. A tall thin man in his sixties, he wears half-moon glasses perched on the end of his nose and attached to a chain. Francois is very fond of his old friend, and as they laugh and joke, reminiscing about old times, time passes quickly. As the last customer leaves, it's time for Francois to go too.

"See you again, Jean."

"See you soon, I hope! Take care, Francois."

Francois heads out into the night, then stops to look at the time on his wristwatch. It's almost 10:00. Crossing the street, he darts in and out of traffic, then makes his way to a familiar and cobbled back lane, which runs behind several restaurants.

As he passes each one, heavenly aromas of international cuisine waft out of the rear doors, each with its own mouth-watering delights.

At the end of the dimly lit lane is a major street with several bus stops, many of which are a good route back to his apartment. He begins to walk, his black suede shoes make a clipping echo upon the cobblestones, breaking the silence.

Soon another sound can be heard, the echo of other footsteps walking behind him. He listens, identifying three pairs of feet but no voices. The hairs begin to stand up on the back of his neck, and he stops, standing perfectly still, like a deer sensing a predator, as a knot forms in his stomach. The footsteps stop, and Francois knows that something is very wrong. Several thoughts rush through his head as he contemplates whether to run or fight. Then he turns to look behind him, his arms raised, his knees bent, and one leg positioned behind the other, ready for combat, but no one is there.

"Who's there?" he shouts, his voice echoing down the lane, but no one answers.

"I said who's there?"

Once again, nothing. Then, about thirty feet away, three men appear from the rear door of one of the restaurants. They stand still, looking at him. Unable to make out their faces, Francois becomes anxious. He starts walking backward, keeping his arms out in front of him and his fists clenched, ready to fight. They don't move. Then Francois hears a single word: "Jew."

He turns on his heel and runs, and they give chase.

Instead of turning left at the end of the lane to head to the bus stop, he turns right and decides to return to the hotel, his heart pounding, and his entire body gripped with fear. Faster and faster, he runs, his forehead thick with sweat. He can't believe it's happening again. Finally, he manages to lose them, but in the distance, he hears a voice cry out into the night.

"We'll get you, Jew!"

Their words linger in the darkness for a moment, floating on the night air. Francois reflects on the absurdity of it all. He is baffled at first and then angry. By chance he sees a taxi coming, and he steps into the street, anxiously flagging it down. The driver stops and lowers his window.

"What's the problem?" he asks once he sees Francois's frantic, sweating face.

"I need a ride."

The driver eyes him suspiciously. "I don't want any trouble. Besides, I already have a booking."

"No, please wait. My family owns a hotel. I can pay you. Please take me. I promise you no trouble. I really need to get there."

"Okay. Get in."

Once they reach the hotel, Francois takes one last look behind him. Satisfied that he hasn't been followed, he pays the driver and then goes inside to find Mirabelle.

After searching the apartment, unable to find her, it dawns upon him how late it is. Thinking she must be asleep, he heads for her bedroom. Francois notices a light coming from under her door. Relieved that she's still awake, he knocks anxiously.

"Who is it?"

"It's Francois."

"Francois! What are you doing back here?"

"Can I come in?"

"Yes, yes, come in."

Francois rushes in, closing the door behind him. Mirabelle's mouth drops open as she looks him up and down, noticing he is covered in sweat, and his hands are trembling. Exhausted, his adrenaline now faded, Francois stumbles over to her and switches off the bedside light, draping the two of them in darkness, the only light coming from the streetlamp outside.

"Francois what's the matter? Are you in trouble?"

"Shhhh," Francois replies, walking over to the window and peering out a small gap in the curtains.

"Francois, what happened?"

"I shouldn't have come."

"No, Francois, it's okay. I'm glad you came."

Francois sighs and then sits next to her on the bed, where she had been reading.

"No, I might have put you in danger. I could have been followed."

"Francois, it's okay. I'm not afraid of them."

She sets down her book and holds out her arms, wanting to comfort him. As they embrace, Francois so badly wants to sob and to be in the safety of her arms forever, but not wanting to worry her further, he holds back.

"They're gone. I can go now," he says, switching the bedside lamp back on.

"No, you must not, Francois. You could be in danger."

"But I shouldn't have come. I could have put you in danger."

"I insist you stay."

Reaching into the drawer of the bedside cabinet, Mirabelle pulls out a key, then gets out of bed and locks the door. She places the key in her night dress under her bosom.

"You are going nowhere, Francois, and that's final."

Mirabelle sits back down on the bed and is soon followed by Francois, who sits next to her. She takes his hand in hers, and they sit in silence.

Before long Mirabelle's eyes become heavy, and she lies down, leaving Francois sitting on the edge of the bed. Unable to fight the tiredness any longer, she drifts off to sleep.

Francois switches off the bedside lamp, then sits and watches her for a while, her face lit up by the streetlamp. Exhausted, Francois succumbs to the lead weight of his eyes, and he lies down next to her to sleep.

By 4:00 a.m., Francois is wide awake, still worried that he may have been followed. He decides to leave after all, not wanting to bring any trouble with him.

"Grand-mamie, are you awake?"

"Yes, Francois. I was unable to sleep. I'm too worried about your safety, darling."

"I need to go."

"No, Francois. Wait until morning."

"I really want to go. Please give me the key."

"No, dear. It's not safe for you."

"I'll be fine, Grand-mamie. Don't worry."

"Why don't you move back to the hotel, Francois?"

"I'm not going to be driven out of my apartment. Why should I go? It's not right."

Just then their conversation is interrupted by a loud knock at the door.

"Who's that knocking at this hour?"

"I have no idea, Francois."

"Give me the key, Grand-mamie. I'll take a look."

Mirabelle takes the key from her night dress and places it in Francois's hand, then leans over and switches on the bedside lamp.

"Be careful, Francois."

Walking slowly over to the door, Francois unlocks it. Just as the door begins to open, Uncle Gustave comes striding into the bedroom, pushing past him in a rage. Francois and Mirabelle look at each other in shock.

"What are you doing in my mother's bedroom?" Gustave bellows.

"Gustave, calm down. What is the problem?"

"What's the problem? Him, that's the problem. How dare he stay in your room."

"How did you know Francois was here, Gustave?

"Yes, how did you know, Gustave?" Francois asks.

"Get out, you squatter!" Gustave yells, his face red with fury.

"Gustave, stop! He's in danger."

"Danger? What danger? Nonsense."

"He has been followed by some neo-Nazis. They've been harassing him for some time. I told him to stay here, Gustave!"

"He's trouble. Get out!" Gustave yells.

"You're an idiot!" Francois snaps. Filled with rejection, he runs out of the bedroom, desperate to get as far away from Gustave as possible.

"Francois!" Mirabelle cries. "Francois, wait!"

Once out on the street, he looks back at the hotel, heartbroken, no longer feeling welcome. His body is like a lead weight, full of dejection, as he walks away.

Crossing one street after another, mumbling to himself, he sighs and then wipes away a tear as he makes his way back to his apartment.

As the night wears on, Francois slows his pace, in no hurry to get home, knowing he will be alone there. He decides to go to the synagogue instead.

When he reaches the gates, he tries to pull them open, but they're locked. He looks up and notices a light on in a small window. After waiting a few minutes, hoping someone will come down, the light goes out, and he gives up.

When he turns the corner of the next street, he notices a figure coming towards him in the dark. Stopping dead in his tracks, he is immediately on his guard, ready for conflict. Deciding to stand his ground, he waits as the figure gets nearer. It turns out to be a bearded old man.

"Hello," the man says. He looks like a fox creeping around the gloomy dead of night. "Do you have a light son?"

Francois looks him up and down, noticing his clothes are grubby and torn. "No, I don't smoke."

"Oh well, no point in asking you then is there?" The old man chuckles, and Francois finds himself smiling back.

"What are you doing out in the middle of the night?" the old man asks. "The bars and clubs are shut now."

"Nothing."

"Nothing always means something. What's bothering you, son?"

"Why would something be bothering me?"

"Because you're walking around the street in the middle of the night, and you tried the synagogue didn't you? It's closed, you know."

"Have you been following me?"

"A little."

"Why?"

"Something's wrong, son, isn't it? It's okay. You don't have to tell me. I'm just a dirty old tramp." The old man chuckles again.

"No, it's okay. I'll tell you. Actually, I'm glad to speak to you. I've had some trouble, that's all. People harassing me."

"Who are they? Why are they harassing you?" The old man looks Francois up and down, noticing his fine designer clothes. "Oh, I see. Harassing you, eh? I know what that feels like. I get it all the time."

Francois hesitates for a moment not sure whether to mention that he is Jewish. Then he decides that the man is no threat.

"I'm Jewish. I have some problems with neo-Nazis, thugs, I'm not sure who they are."

"Jewish, eh?" The old man scratches his chin. Then he places his hands on Francois's arms and looks him directly in the eyes. "Courage, young man, courage."

"You survive out here?" Francois asks.

"Yes, I get by, but my mind is lost sometimes. It's why I live here." The old man points to the street.

"You live on the street? You're homeless?"

"Yes."

"Maybe I can help you find somewhere to live. Here, take some money." Francois pulls out his wallet.

"No, I don't need money. Put it away, son. Others have tried to help me. I'm a little difficult, a little damaged, my friend, but my courage, they can't take that away from me. I am amongst friends here. I have many friends on the streets, and I'm too old to change. Listen, don't worry about me. This is nothing. Now that place, that place was something.

"What place?"

"The institution, of course. Terrible. But now I'm free, as free as a bird."

The old man flaps his hands like a bird. Then, looking up at the clock on the church tower, he begins to walk away. "I must go. I promised to meet a friend. He has chicken for me, you know."

Francois watches him as he walks away.

"Goodbye, Francois. I will pray for you. May God be with you!" he calls out, his voice penetrating the still night.

"Goodbye," Francois replies, sad to see him go.

After the encounter with the old man, Francois's mood begins to lift, and his footsteps feel a little lighter.

With another half mile to walk, Francois picks up his pace. He glances up at one point, noticing a light on a balcony above a shop. An old lady is sitting at a table reading a book. He smiles to himself as she temporarily feels the empty void of his lonely walk. She notices him looking up at her.

"Good evening," she calls down, her voice old and delicate, as she raises her glass of cognac.

"Good evening, madame," Francois replies, smiling. The world becomes an even brighter place for a moment.

"Just a few more streets," he tells himself. Feeling more confident now, he takes an underpass that leads to the other side of the road instead of the longer, safer route.

Once he reaches the halfway mark, he looks back over his shoulder, the deafening silence unnerving him. Something doesn't feel right, and sure enough, moments later he hears a hissing voice in the darkness.

"Satan."

"Oh my god," Francois whispers, realising they must have been looking for him.

As if he's being pulled backwards in time, he can't believe it's happening again, and he stops dead in his tracks. His heart pounding through his chest, he almost vomits with fear. Then, getting into fighting mode, he assumes a defensive stance and looks behind him again, then in front, hoping he imagined it, but he hears it again.

"Satan," the voice hisses, louder this time. Not knowing whether to race ahead or turn back, he looks around in a blind panic, then decides to run. Just as he nears the end of the underpass, three figures step out in front of him.

Francois turns, almost tripping over his own feet, and races back into the underpass, not wanting to have to fight again. As he runs, his head fills with terror when he hears their footsteps behind him. Looking around, he notices he's not far from Elijah's apartment block. He darts down a narrow alley filled with bins and hides behind a large metal crate.

In the pitch-black silence, all he can hear is his beating heart. The moonlight illuminates the beads of sweat on his face as he waits, not daring to move. Hearing their running footsteps drawing near, he tries to curl up smaller and holds his breath. Just then he hears the enemy's voices, only a few yards from where he is hidden.

"Where did he go?" asks a deep, menacing voice, standing dangerously nearby.

"Maybe he's down there," another says, pointing.

Francois puts his hand over his mouth to stifle a cry of fear as one of the men walks down the alley.

"I don't think he's down here. There's nothing but bins, and it stinks. Let's go."

As they run off, Francois sighs with relief. He waits a few minutes to be sure they have gone. Then he creeps out from behind the crate and looks up and down the street to ensure it's safe. Elijah's apartment block is only three streets away, and Francois runs there as fast as his legs can carry him.

When he finally arrives at the entrance, in a panic, he's unable to remember Elijah's apartment number. He frantically presses all eight buzzers on the panel. Before long lights go on all over the apartment block as angry residents shout down at him. The buzzer in Elijah's apartment rings over and over again, but his apartment is empty, as Elijah and his family have gone away for a few days, visiting cousins outside Paris.

"What do you want? Go away!" a voice shouts.

"Get lost, or we'll call the police!" shouts another.

"Elijah, help!" Francois yells. "Help me!"

Francois looks up, desperately hoping that Elijah's face will appear at one of the windows, but it does not, and now it's too late, as Francois hears the echo of running footsteps coming towards him.

He sprints around the corner of the building and sees some gates belonging to the concierge quarters. Grabbing hold of the gates, he begins to climb, jumping down on the other side. As he scrambles to his feet, something tugs him from behind. Turning around, he realises his trouser leg is caught in the gate. Gasping and whimpering in fear and desperation, he tugs. The running footsteps are getting nearer, but he's stuck. Then, yanking with all his might, he hears a rip and falls to the ground. Clambering to his feet, he races up the white stone steps, reaching a dimly lit door at the end of a split-level landing.

Now completely hidden, he struggles to catch his breath. He slides down the door to the floor, not daring to move. Exhausted, he stays all night, but at least he's safe.

CHAPTER 15

The Tormentors

It's 2002, and Francois is thirty-eight. Having arranged to meet a friend, he strides with purpose, wearing a crisp pale blue shirt, designer jeans and his favourite black Italian suede ankle boots. The fragrance of his rich citrus cologne fills the mild September air as he stops every so often, admiring his reflection in the windows he passes.

His destination is Le Poirier, a large, vibrant restaurant that entertains the chic and wealthy of Paris. Dressed in their expensive attire, drinking fine wines and downing cocktails, at Le Poirier they enjoy some of the best food Paris has to offer.

Waiting for Francois is Arnold, a handsome, jovial man, who runs a wedding business in Paris along with his wife. It's been eighteen months since the attack. Having spent many sleepless nights filled with anxiety and nightmares, Francois is happy to be meeting his old friend.

When he enters the restaurant, he spots Arnold sitting near a window on the left just like he said he would be. Upon the table are two glasses of white wine, one of which is waiting for Francois.

"Arnold, my friend."

Arnold stands, and they embrace, kissing each other on either cheek.

"Francois, how are you? Are you okay? I'm shocked to hear about what happened to you, really, really shocked about what you told me on the phone. Is that why you've hardly been in contact for the last eighteen months? Why didn't you tell me sooner or ask for help? I tried to call you several times, but you did not answer. I was wondering what was going on. Here, I've got you a drink. Oh, I just remembered you don't drink."

"I do now. Well, sometimes. I'm okay. Well I'm getting there. I'm still struggling with anxiety, but I'll get there."

"That's understandable, Francois. Have the police found them yet?"

"No, nothing much seems to have happened."

Francois shakes his head. "Do you have any idea who they were?"

"I'm not really sure. I thought they were from some extremist group. Maybe neo-Nazis. I just don't know."

Francois nervously sweeps back his hair as Arnold looks on, noticing Francois's hand trembling. A blank expression crosses Francois's face as he stares at the table. Then, closing his eyes, he grits his teeth as the memory of the knife closes in. Arnold puts a reassuring hand on Francois's shoulder. Immediately, Francois opens his eyes, brought back to the present.

"Whoever they are, they hate Jews, unfortunately."

"What they did to you, Francois, it's horrible, terrible."

"Yes. Look." Francois lifts his shirt to reveal a long, vulgar scar across his stomach. "It was like they were trying to destroy me, like they knew about my ninjutsu, trying to make me weak or kill me."

Francois picks up his glass, his hand still trembling as he sips his wine.

"My god, Francois."

Too shocked to say anything else, Arnold sits in silence for a minute.

"Francois, do you think they were professionals?"

"I don't know. I don't think I'll ever know who they were."

"The police will catch them. You'll be okay, Francois. It will take time, but you're strong. Don't let this destroy your life, my friend."

"They were gone by the time the police got there. I think they were helped. They must have been especially the one I knocked out. He was out cold. He was the one with the knife. It always happened when I was alone. Someone found out I was Jewish. I stuck up for myself and became a target."

Francois smiles. "I used to be friendly with the GiGN and RAID in Paris, but I've lost contact with them now. I was hoping they would protect me.

"Really how did you get to know them?"

"It doesn't matter. I shouldn't have mentioned it."

"Francois, listen, I've already ordered some food for us, so let's eat."

A waitress arrives with two oval plates of succulent beef in a red wine sauce, accompanied by a decorative arrangement of vegetables. They begin to eat, ordering another bottle of wine to share and chatting well into the evening. Eventually, Francois begins to tire, and he decides it's time to go home.

"Francois, keep in touch. Call me."

"I will."

Leaving the restaurant together, they kiss each other on the cheek, then part company, each making their way down the street in opposite directions.

The evening air is cool, and Francois walks quickly, not having brought a jacket with him. Feeling a little light headed after drinking a few glasses of wine, he decides to buy a coffee to take home.

As darkness falls, he passes by a man leaning against a wall. Not taking much notice, Francois continues walking. Then, to his disbelief, he hears a word he was not expecting to ever hear again. The shock upon hearing it causes him to drop his coffee cup, sending it rolling into the traffic. Looking across at the man, he's unsure if he imagined it. A feeling of trepidation raises its ugly head, as the last eighteen months of peace suddenly evaporates, taking him right back to where he was.

"Satan."

He hears it again, now sure he is in the midst of danger yet again. His ordeal is not over just yet.

A flurry of thoughts rushes through his mind. Should he fight? Run? Ignore it?

In spite of his ninjutsu skills, Francois decides he does not want to get into another fight, not knowing if more of them are lurking around. He watches as a car squashes his coffee cup flat. At that moment he decides to run, but then he hears another voice.

"Leave him alone."

Francois stops, not quite believing what he has just heard. He looks behind him to see a man standing in the middle of the pavement, his hood up. Unable to make out his face, they stand facing each other for a few seconds. Then the man walks away.

Not knowing if it's a trick, Francois decides not to follow to find out who he is. He looks back, but the man who was leaning against the wall is gone. Feeling relieved but confused, Francois rushes home.

When he arrives back at his apartment, Francois cautiously unlocks his door. Then he performs a safety ritual, noting that the cotton he has set diagonally across the entrance is still intact. Sighing with relief, he shakes the door handle a few times to ensure it is locked. Then he slides down the door to the floor to catch his breath.

Several minutes later, he gets up and looks out the window in the living room to ensure no one is lurking outside. Then he goes to his bedroom and climbs into bed. Fully dressed, minus his shoes, he's too tired to undress. As he pulls up the cover to his chin, his mind turns to the man who protected him earlier. Then he puts a name to the voice.

Was it Astor again? How did he know he was in danger?

Confused and overwhelmed by the night's events, his eyes grow heavy. Unable to fight his fatigue any longer, he finally surrenders to sleep.

It's 2:20 in the morning, and Francois's eyes begin to twitch as he enters a deep, dark nightmare about a faceless man coming towards him with a knife. Francois's body shudders as, in his dream, he cries out for help, but nobody comes. He moans in his sleep, his body soaked in sweat. His heart pounds, and he gasps, fighting for breath.

In his dream, he tries to cry for help, but a hand covers his mouth. The grip is almost super human as he fights to pull it off, punching and scratching at it in desperation. Just as he lets out a piercing scream, the hand disappears, and Francois wakes up.

Leaping out of bed in the darkened room, he swings his fists, fighting an invisible enemy.

"Leave me alone!" he screams, kicking and punching the air. "Leave me alone!"

In a panic, he races from room to room, checking his wardrobe, the windows, and behind the shower curtain, looking for his tormentors. Then he stops and screams. "I'm not Satan!"

Desperately thirsty, he runs into the kitchen and turns on the tap. Leaning over the sink, he gulps down water. Then he yanks a drawer open, looking for something to arm himself with. He spots the bread knife. Now at his breaking point, the sight of the knife overwhelms him, and his world comes crashing down.

In blind panic, his eyes wild, he screams and shouts. As he crashes around the kitchen, knocking over chairs, it doesn't take long for the noise to reach the neighbours. Lights go on above, below, and on either side of his apartment. Before long the police are called.

"No, no, they're coming. They're coming!" he yells, now in the midst of a full nervous breakdown.

At first he's unable to hear the knocking at his door. When it continues, louder this time, like a propeller coming to a sudden halt, his mind snaps back to reality.

Realising someone is at his door, he stumbles over to it and looks through the spy hole. He frowns in confusion when he sees three police officers.

"Open the door," one of the officers orders. Turning the lock, Francois opens the door a crack as the three officers stare him up and down, noting his messy hair, raw red eyes and sweat-soaked clothes. Francois stares back at them, bewildered.

"Sir, you're coming with us," one of the officers says.

"Why? Where?" Francois asks, his voice croaky and sore.

Without answering, the officers enter the apartment. While one of them gets his keys, the other two officers grab Francois, each of them taking one arm. Too tired to resist, Francois allows them to lead him out of his apartment, watching as the third officer locks the door behind them.

As the elevator descends, silence falls. All four men watch the numbers decrease as they approach ground level.

In the back of the police van, his hands cuffed, neither Francois nor the officers sitting opposite him say a word. As dawn breaks, his thumping head is a lead weight, rolling back and forth throughout the journey as he fights to stay awake. Eventually, they arrive at their destination, a large psychiatric hospital on the edge of Paris.

The back doors open, and a police officer beckons Francois to get out. As Francois stumbles out of the van, he is met by a psychiatric nurse who introduces himself as Bruce. He asks Francois to follow him.

"I'm not Satan," Francois whispers, confusion and exhaustion starting to set in.

"I'm sure you are not. What's your name, my friend?" Bruce asks.

"Francois."

"Hello, Francois," Bruce replies as they enter the hospital foyer.

Francois is taken to a door on the right leading to an adjacent building. Bruce informs the police officers that he will take over now and they take off the handcuffs. Then he presses a code into a keypad, activating a high-pitched sound that indicates the door is unlocked. Francois looks through the thick square window in the door at two nurses waiting on the other side. Bruce opens the door, and Francois follows. Francois looks behind him when he hears the door click shut as it locks.

Now at the mercy of psychiatry, Francois is now committed, and any refusal of medication will be forcefully administered whether he consents or not. As Francois begins to grasp where he is, realising what lies ahead of him, several images flutter in quick succession from his memories of his hospital stay at age seventeen. Then a tidal wave of fear and panic sets in, and he begins to lash out.

"Let me out of here!" he yells, his voice terrified and hoarse. Turning towards the door, he bangs the glass with his fists, "Let me out! There's nothing wrong with me!"

Three male nurses appear, Francois tries to run away from them, then he rushes at the door again. Leaping forward, his leg outstretched, he delivers a powerful ninjutsu kick at the door. It trembles, but Francois is no match for its thick steel, designed to keep people in.

Francois stumbles backwards, falling to the floor. The nurses rush in and pin him down, holding his arms behind his back. Francois gives up, too tired to resist. A female nurse appears and injects him at the top of his left buttock. Letting out a final squeal of fear, Francois succumbs to the medication's effects. Before long he is lost in a drug-induced haze, and it's game over.

Several hours pass. At 10:00 a.m., Francois begins to wake. When he opens his eyes, his vision is blurred. He looks at the ceiling and frowns. Looking down, he realises he's lying on a thin mattress only a few inches from the floor.

As his vision clears, he takes in his surroundings. The pale grey floor and green walls are unfamiliar to him. Then he notices the stainless-steel toilet and sink. His hands trembling, he sits up and rubs his wrists, which are sore from the cuffs.

"Oh," he gasps, his head hurting from the medication. "Oh no. Oh my God," he whispers, realising where he is. He tries to stand, but his thumping head causes him to stumble backwards onto the bed. Determined, he tries again, this time managing to get to his feet. He staggers to the door and bangs on it. After a few minutes, a female nurse appears at the small square window.

"What is it, Francois?"

"What is it?" Francois repeats. "Get me out of this room!"

The nurse shakes her head. "I can't."

"Why not?" .

"We're waiting for the doctor to see you."

"Why?"

"You're ill, Francois."

"No I'm not! You're the ones who are ill, you lot!" he shouts as the nurse leaves.

Feeling unsteady on his feet, he makes his way back to the mattress and lies down, realising there is nothing he can do but wait.

As evening approaches, the door opens, and in walks a tall thin man wearing a crumpled but expensive looking brown suit. He's accompanied by two male nurses. His circular, black-rimmed glasses are perched on the end of his nose.

"Hello, Francois. I'm Dr Bisset. I wanted to have a little chat. Is that okay?"

Francois looks at Dr Bisset's thick curly black beard, which partially hides his lips, and immediately distrusts him.

"Don't patronize me," he retorts, sitting up on the mattress. "We can have a little chat about letting me out of here. How about that?"

"We'll see. We need a little time to see how you are, Francois."

"I'm fine. You can't keep me in isolation forever. I know my rights."

"Well, if we let you out, will you stay calm? That would be a good start, would it not?"

"Yes, yes I will," Francois replies, realising that his only option if he wants to leave that room is to cooperate.

"Come, Francois," Dr Bisset replies. He exits the room, followed by Francois and the two nurses.

They make their way down a wide, dreary hall and into a meeting room.

"Take a seat, Francois."

All four pull out chairs and sit around a large oak table.

"I understand you have had some problems at your apartment," Dr Bisset begins. "You're here because there was a lot of concern from your neighbours. They reported you screaming and banging. The police said you weren't making sense on the way here, repeating a lot of unusual thoughts and words to them."

"Like what?" Francois asks.

"Like the word 'Satan,' for example. You've been telling people that you're not Satan, have you not?"

"That's correct, I'm not," Francois retorts, his voice sarcastic.

"Francois, we're trying to help you. What made you say such a thing?"

"I'm not crazy, if that's what you mean."

"Francois, nobody is saying you're crazy. Maybe you're just having some difficulties."

"So, if you don't think I'm crazy, let me go."

"We don't think you're crazy."

"Of course not. That's why I'm a prisoner here, eh? Listen, I've been attacked, and I've been called Satan many times. They've harassed me for almost two years, and they still are. They follow me in the street."

"Francois, can I stop you there? Who do you mean by 'they'?"

"I don't know, but they hate Jewish people."

"But who, Francois? You must have some idea. Could it be that you have developed a fear? That it could possibly be some sort of paranoia?"

"No way. It's happening. I'm not paranoid. Are you?"

"Now, Francois, there's no need for that."

"They're extremists, anti-Semites. I don't know who they are, but they always appear when I'm alone, when there are no witnesses."

"But why would they do that, Francois?"

"What a stupid question! Why do you think? Look!" Francois pulls up his pyjama top, revealing the scar across his stomach. "Look at this. Do you think I'm dreaming, that this is just paranoia?"

"No, Francois, but is there a possibility that this was self-inflicted? I don't believe you're dreaming, but I believe that maybe you're suffering from delusions. Have you ever heard of such a thing?"

"Self-inflicted? Are you crazy? This was done by a knife. You think I could self-inflict this? That's ridiculous. I'm not suffering from delusions; I am traumatised. You're stupid. You don't know what you're talking about. I want to go home."

"Not yet, Francois, I'm afraid."

"Why not?" Francois asks, his voice faltering. "I need some water."

One of the nurses leaves the room and reappears with a plastic beaker, handing it to Francois. Francois takes the beaker, his hand trembling as he gulps the water down. The room falls silent as Doctor Bisset and the nurses watch him drink, not stopping until the water is gone.

"I want to go home," Francois repeats.

"When you're well, we'll consider it."

"When I'm well? What are you talking about? I am well."

"That's enough for today, Francois." Doctor Bisset replies, bringing the meeting to a close. "I'll see you tomorrow, when I do my rounds."

"Ridiculous," Francois replies.

Following the meeting, Doctor Bisset goes to his office to ring Francois's family and inform them that Francois has been committed.

The week creeps by. When Tuesday arrives, Delmare arrives at the hospital to visit Francois, having brought toiletries and chocolate. She is taken to a small visiting room off the ward where Francois is waiting for her. When she enters the room, Francois begins to cry.

"Maman," he says, throwing his arms around her.

"It was difficult for me to come today, Francois. Uncle Gustave tried to stop me."

"I missed you. How's Grand-mamie? Get me out of here, Maman, please."

"I can't, Francois. It's up to the doctor. When you're well, maybe then."

"But Maman, you can tell him I'm well now. Help me please. They're making me take this really strong medicine, and it's making me feel ill. Look." Francois holds up his trembling hands, then pokes out his tongue. "See?"

"Okay, okay, Francois. I'll chat with the doctor. I must go soon."

"Go? But you only just arrived."

"I need to look after the hotel, Francois."

For the next hour they talk. Finally, Delmare gets up to leave.

As she closes the door behind her, Francois eats the chocolate, feeling utterly alone and frustrated. Tears run down his cheeks. After popping the last of the chocolate into his mouth, he stares out the window, feeling nothing, seeing nothing, abandoned and alone.

Several weeks pass, and Francois is sitting in the lounge, looking pale and despondent. He gets up every so often to knock on the nurse's window to ask when he's leaving the hospital. Irritated at having to answer the same question over and over again, they take longer and longer to respond. Finally giving up, Francois returns to the lounge.

Just then, Bruce arrives. He puts his hand upon Francois's shoulder and smiles.

"You have a visitor."

"Who?"

"He says his name is Elijah."

"Elijah? Thank you, God."

Bruce leads Francois to the visitors' room and unlocks the door.

"Francois, there are a lot of visits today, so you have forty minutes."

"Okay, okay," Francois replies, eager to see Elijah. He peers inside the room to find Elijah sitting and waiting for him. Elijah jumps up, and they embrace, kissing each other on both cheeks.

"I had a problem seeing you, Francois, Gustave said you're not allowed any visitors. I tried to come last week."

"What? He's always interfering. It's not his business. I hope to leave soon. The doctor said I'll only stay another twenty-eight days. They're crazy, these doctors. He has no idea that the medicine is making me ill."

"Don't worry, my friend. You'll be out soon. It happened to my grandmother. All they did was give her drugs, drugs, drugs, never therapy or a solution, always drugs. Be careful, Francois, and stay well."

"It's the memories. I can't shake them. I can't sleep. I haven't slept properly for weeks on end."

"You must try, Francois, or you'll end up in here again."

Elijah looks down at Francois's hands and realises they are trembling. He places his hand on top of Francois's and they talk about old times. Before long their time is up, and the door opens. A short male nurse enters the room. His name is Seb, and he wears thick black glasses. Francois doesn't like him.

"Yes?" Francois asks, scowling.

"It's time for your friend to go," Seb replies in his usual dismissive manner. Irritated, Francois looks up at the clock on the wall.

"We have another three minutes yet."

"Doesn't matter. There are lots of families and other visitors today, not just yours."

"Don't worry, Francois, really, I'll go," Elijah says.

"Okay, my friend."

They embrace.

"Keep strong, Francois."

"I'll try."

Elijah follows Seb out of the room. Then, looking back at Francois, Seb's lips purse into a slight smile. Francois glares at him as he shuts the door.

As one day morphs into the next, utterly bored, time and the medicine become Francois's worst enemies. Knowing that any resistance to taking the medication will be met with force, Francois discovers more inventive ways of keeping up the pretence that he has swallowed it. Fearful of the long-term damage it will have on his body, he has begun hiding tablets inside his cheeks, later spitting them into the toilet, then flushing them away, proving to himself that he has recovered without them.

Each passing day he humours the nurses. "Yes, I've swallowed it," he says, poking out his tongue. "Stick your poison up your ass," he mutters.

Day twenty-eight finally arrives, and Francois is brought into a meeting after his tribunal the previous day.

"Welcome, Francois, sit," Doctor Bisset says. Francois rolls his eyes, feeling slightly patronised, but he sits and folds his arms in annoyance at being made to feel like a child. Along with Dr Bisset in the room are two nurses and the ward manager.

"It went well for you yesterday in the tribunal, Francois," Doctor Bisset says. "We don't agree entirely—some of us think you should stay a little longer—however, we are willing to give you the benefit of doubt and let you leave, so, I'm pleased to tell you that we are discharging tomorrow. But Francois, you must take the medicine when you return home. Promise me you will."

"Yes, yes I will."

Francois smiles as he exhales deeply, relieved and delighted to have regained his freedom.

The next morning comes and goes. Francois waits anxiously near the entrance clutching onto two green plastic hospital bags full of his belongings. A taxi has been called to take him back to his apartment, but it's running late. Francois paces up and down the foyer, anxiously awaiting its arrival. When it finally comes, Bruce accompanies Francois out into the sunshine.

"Good luck, Francois," he says. "Here's your medicine."

He hands a white paper bag to Francois. Francois takes it reluctantly, pushing it into one of the green bags as they lock eyes. Bruce holds out his hand. Francois eyes him suspiciously. Then he smiles, and they shake hands.

"Thank you, Bruce."

Letting out a huge sigh of relief as the taxi pulls away, Francois looks back at the hospital.

"Goodbye," he mutters, his voice defiant.

CHAPTER 16

Invasion of the Devils

Seven months have passed. Now feeling ready to venture out a little further, Francois decides to contact an old friend. Having found out he has just returned to Paris after touring, he arranges to meet American music artist Gary Mudbone. They agree to meet at the first place they ever met, Rainure Violette, a favourite VIP music club of theirs.

Inside the club the atmosphere is relaxed and welcoming. The sweet sound of a saxophone can be heard accompanied by a funky bass rhythm. The music swirls around purple half-moon upholstered sofas, accompanied by flickering candles upon opaque glass tables. Francois feels relaxed as they laugh and joke about old times and then discuss Gary's recent tour.

"Did you play New York again, Gary?"

"Sure did. That was the last place after the west coast, like before."

"Excellent, my friend. Have you written many more songs?"

"Yeah, but I had no time for the studio. Now that the tour is finished, I'm going to get back to recording."

"The same studio in Paris?"

"Yep. I have a great friend flying over soon. We've been working on some ideas together. He's got soul, man."

They laugh together.

"You still in touch with Dave Stewart? How is he?" Francois asks, making reference to Dave Stewart of the Eurythmics.

"Sure. Dave is cool, man. Love him. Want a drink, Francois?"

"Yes, great."

Gary orders two more cocktails.

"So, how have you been, Francois? Women still chasing you?"

They both smile.

"I've been good, yes, fine, fine," Francois replies, deciding not to mention his problems. As they continue to chat into the night, one o'clock comes and goes, and soon after they decide to leave.

Standing outside the club, Gary gestures to the driver of a taxi as it arrives. Then he turns to Francois, and they embrace. "It was great to see you, Francois. Take care. Until next time."

Gary opens the taxi door, then turns around and takes Francois's hand, squeezing it to his fondness for their friendship. Still smiling, he shuts the door and waves as the taxi pulls away.

Francois goes back inside and asks for a taxi to be called for him as well, not yet feeling safe enough to walk the streets of Paris alone at night.

Feeling peckish when he arrives home, Francois opens the refrigerator and pulls out a large circular block of camembert cheese. He slices off a large section, then spreads a thick layer of it on a stick of French bread. He takes a large bite, licking the corners of his mouth in delight.

As he eats, he hears a strange thud, causing him to jump in fright. It's coming from beneath his apartment. A moment later, the kitchen light dims. He stands there motionless, waiting, still holding the French bread as the light brightens again. He looks out the window and sees that the street below is empty. As his fear starts to diminish, he decides to dismiss it and carries on eating. Leaning against the kitchen unit, he takes the last bite of the bread, then guzzles down some chilled milk. After switching off the light, he makes his way to the bedroom.

Taking off his clothes, he slings them over the back of a chair and then gets into bed. He decides to leave his bedside lamp on for a while. A million thoughts are running through his mind as he faces the ceiling, his hands behind his head. Soon, tiredness gets the better of him, and he switches off the lamp and falls asleep.

In the still of the night, something disturbs Francois, and he wakes up. His ears prick up as he lies perfectly still, sensing a presence nearby. Hearing nothing but the sound of his beating heart, he swallows deeply, knowing something is about to erupt. Then, to his horror, he hears it: the sound of the creaking floor. He knows it can only mean one thing: an intruder.

As the footsteps edge nearer, he sits up and gently rolls down the bed cover, ensuring he is ready, all his ninjutsu skills locked securely in his mind. Then Francois realises there is more than one intruder present, as the steps are out of sync. Now they are just yards away, edging towards his bedroom. Francois is ready, but he's gripped with fear as the reality that this happening again is almost too much to bear.

Wearing only his pyjama bottoms, he creeps out of bed, his arms outstretched, his legs wide apart, one foot behind the other, knowing an attack is imminent.

Suddenly, his bedroom door crashes open, and someone switches on the light in the hallway, illuminating the faces of four neo-Nazis standing facing him. Saying nothing, they encircle him. They grab Francois and try to get him back onto the bed, wrestling with him as he kicks and struggles. He kicks one, who stumbles backward in pain. He swears, then grabs Francois's leg again.

"Get Satan on the bed!" the ringleader instructs. "Keep hold of his legs."

They fling Francois onto his bed. As he thrashes about, struggling to fight them off, he finds that they are skilled fighters. To Francois's horror, one of them starts yanking down his pyjama bottoms. Francois cries out in terror with the realisation that they are attempting to rape him. As he struggles to free himself from their grip, his pyjama bottoms slip down to his knees, and they try to turn him onto his front. Then everything seems to fall silent as if being played out in slow motion around him. Digging deep, he locates his courage, and his fear is transformed into anger. Seeing red, Francois begins to fight harder.

"Get off me, or I'll kill you!" he snarls. Then, freeing his right arm, he seizes his opportunity. He thrusts his elbow deep into a Nazi's throat, causing him to gasp in shock. The neo-Nazi's face turns blue, his windpipe damaged, and he stumbles backwards, holding his throat. His eyes are wide as he stares at Francois before collapsing into a heap on the floor.

Francois grits his teeth and kicks legs harder as another neo-Nazi loses his grip, and before long they all let go. Seizing his chance, Francois pulls his pyjama bottoms up, then leaps up and stands on his bed in a defensive position, ready for the fight of his life.

Silence falls as the remaining three attackers look up at Francois with hatred in their hearts. Then the injured Nazi hobbles out of the bedroom, still gasping for air.

Francois goes on the attack. Leaping off the bed, he kicks one of the neo-Nazis full force in the chest, sending him crashing into the wardrobe. Badly injured he too decides to leave, doubled over and groaning in pain.

Now there are two, one strong and one uncertain. The weaker one looks at the ringleader for support, fear upon his face, but the ringleader doesn't flinch, even though he realises they have underestimated Francois's skill and strength.

A huge fight breaks out. They punch and kick each other, crashing into walls and furniture. Several minutes pass and then the third Nazi lets out a scream. Francois has broken his arm.

"Go, go! It's time to go!" he pleads, his arm bent backwards, but the ringleader doesn't move. "Go! Let's go!" he screams again, wincing in pain. He looks at Francois, then at the ringleader, and sees they are staring at each other, their faces dripping with sweat. Having had enough, he heads for the door. "You're on your own! Do him! Do him!" he shouts as he runs out.

Now just the two of them remain. Francois waits for his chance to strike.

"Come on, Jew, try your luck," the ringleader says, smirking as he holds out his thick, muscular arms. Francois looks him up and down, noticing his stance, which reveals he too has skill in martial arts. This is going to be a tough fight, and Francois realises there is a real possibility of one of them dying.

Finding his voice, Francois speaks. "This Jew isn't afraid," he says. "This Jew is here to stay."

The ringleader laughs. His voice is deep, dark, and ugly.

Seizing the opportunity, Francois rushes forward, taking the ringleader by surprise. He locks him in a stranglehold, and the ringleader gasps for air.

"Had enough?" Francois whispers.

His lips turning blue, the man scratches at Francois's arms, trying desperately to break free. Then Francois lets go, and the ringleader crumples to the floor, coughing and gasping.

"Get out of my home!" Francois yells, and the ringleader scrambles to his feet. As he exits the bedroom, he stops and looks back at Francois. Then he leaves the apartment.

Francois waits for a minute or two and then races out of his apartment, to be sure his attackers are gone. He yanks open the door to the stairwell and looks down. He sees the ringleader stumbling down the stairs, floor by floor.

Francois runs back into his apartment, slamming the door behind him, then rushes over to the window in the living room. It's now an hour past dawn. Soon he sees the ringleader walking away from the building, holding his neck. Then he stops and turns around, looking up at Francois. His bloody face is filled with hate and defiance. He holds up his arm, grinning, and gives a Nazi salute. Then he turns and walks away.

"Coward," Francois says as the man disappears between two buildings.

Curious as to how they gained entry, Francois is shocked to discover the lock on his door has been skilfully taken out from the outside. He goes to the living room and drags a heavy cabinet in front of the door to block it.

Then, dropping to his knees, Francois begins to sob, the horrific events of the night finally getting the better of him.

Later, he still has not moved. He sits and stares at the wall opposite him, his expression blank and his hands trembling, unable to comprehend or understand what he has just experienced.

Finally getting to his feet, he feels immense pain coming from his right leg. He hobbles to the bathroom. When he switches on the light, his mouth falls open, startled by the image of his war-torn face staring back at him. Turning on the tap, Francois splashes cold water over his face, dabbing it with a towel as blood drips on the floor.

Afterwards, he makes his way back to his bedroom, surveying the damage. He searches for his mobile phone and finds it wedged between the bedside cabinet and the wall. Returning to the living room, he sits on the sofa and calls the police.

CHAPTER 17

Death of Mirabelle

It's November 2004. Having turned forty, Francois is living a much quieter life. With help from Mirabelle, he has invested in an apartment, and he's now living back in the heart of Neuilly-sur-Seine Paris, hoping the harassment is behind him.

Having given up chasing women long ago, he is now left with the same old void, feeling no sense of belonging. Loneliness is a constant companion, making him feel hollower than ever before. He longs to meet a life partner, a soul mate with whom he can create a future. He wants to love and cherish her, hoping to receive the same in return.

Bored of the same old crowds in the bars and clubs of Paris, Francois has become more selective upon nights out. The same old rifts and jealousy continue within the family, along with the never-ending mixed messages from his uncles. Not knowing whom he can trust, Francois is in constant torment.

Delmare has a new boyfriend, and unfortunately for Francois, history is repeating itself. Jealousy has raised its ugly head again, and it's being directed his way, making it almost impossible for the two of them to get along. Both continually complaining to Delmare about the other, this new man, determined to drive a wedge between Francois and his mother, feels like yet another uncle Gustave.

As a result of Mirabelle having moved south, Francois is spending less and less time at the hotel. He misses Mirabelle dreadfully and feels lost without her.

It's late afternoon on a Friday, and Francois has picked up a pizza on his way back to the apartment. Having just arrived home, he places the box next to his cell phone on the table. As he bites into one of the succulent slices, he decides to call Mirabelle, but after several rings, she doesn't pick up. Finally giving up, he takes the remainder of his pizza into the living room.

After switching on the television, he sits on the sofa to finish his pizza. Then he picks up a copy of *Paris Life* magazine and lies back, flicking through the pages as he occasionally glances at the TV. It's not

131

long before he's bored, neither the magazine nor the television programme satisfying him. Sighing, he tosses the magazine onto the floor and decides to head out.

As he locks his door behind him, his cell phone rings. He decides to take the call back inside his apartment, so he quickly unlocks the door and then kicks it shut behind him.

It's his friend Elijah. Francois is disappointed, hoping it was Mirabelle.

"I wanted to tell you that we're going to Israel for three weeks, so I won't be around for a while," Elijah says. "I'm off to stay with Papa. We're going to see my uncle too. He has moved to Jerusalem."

"Why did he move there?"

"It has a bigger synagogue. He's really happy to begin working there. The previous rabbi retired. He was very old."

"When do you leave?"

"On Monday."

"Okay, well, let's meet up when you're back. Ring me if you can when you're there."

"Okay, my friend. Take care, Francois. See you soon."

After the call, Francois changes his mind and decides to stay in after all. Feeling deflated at not having spoken to Mirabelle, he decides to make it an early night and gets into bed.

He pulls the thick duvet up under his chin and then turns on the radio on his bedside cabinet. A discussion about poetry is underway. Having enjoyed writing many poems himself, the soothing words take him deep inside his imagination, and for a while, as the presenter reads a poem about the beauty of a lake hidden deep within a forest, he is lost in his thoughts.

When the discussion ends, Francois switches over to classical music. Soon the sound of Debussy fills the bedroom, immersing him in the intertwined sound of piano and strings.

Unable to sleep, Francois gets up and wanders into the kitchen. Opening the refrigerator, he takes out a carton of milk. Then he switches on the kettle and makes a coffee. As he sips his coffee, he looks out the window and watches as people make their way home, having been out for the evening.

Back in his bedroom, he opens his wardrobe and takes out his black ninjutsu uniform. He slips it on and then stands in front of the mirror, looking at his reflection.

He goes into the lounge and flips through his vast collection of CDs, looking for one in particular. He finds it, and soon Debussy's music fills his ears once again. As the beauty of the music fills his world once more, he begins to practice his techniques, slow and sure and in ritualistic fashion. He runs through an abundance of skilful moves, executing each one with perfection. His forehead breaks out in sweat, his eyes alert and fixated, his opponent being his shadow on the wall.

The next morning, Francois wakes up early and decides to go to the park. The cool November air flushes his cheeks red, and he adjusts his scarf, trying to keep his neck warm. Having tried to reach Mirabelle again, with no luck, worry has begun to prey on his mind.

When he arrives at the park, it is virtually deserted. Outside a coffee hut, a small group of people are chatting as they wait in line for a welcome hot drink.

Francois sits on an old wooden bench and takes out his wallet. He smiles as he pulls out a tiny black-and-white photograph of him as a young boy, reaching out his arms as he sits on Mirabelle's lap. He pulls out his cell phone to call her again, but before he can, he receives a call.

It's his cousin Phillipe. Surprised but happy to hear from him, Francois smiles.

"Hi, Phillipe. How are you?"

"Francois, I need to tell you something. Are you sitting down?"

"Yes, why? What's the problem?" Francois asks, feeling afraid.

"It's Grand-mamie."

A knot forms in Francois's stomach, his entire body gripped with fear.

"What is it?" Hearing nothing but silence, he starts to panic. "What is it, Phillipe?"

"She died, Francois, and I need to tell you, we already had the funeral. She died two days ago. We thought it would be too much for you. I'm sorry, but she's gone."

"You thought it would be too much for me? And telling on the phone is not?"

"I'm sorry. The family said you're fragile."

"The family is selfish. Died? She died?"

"Yes, Francois."

"No, God no. And nobody told me or invited me to the funeral?"

Not wanting to hear another word, Francois hangs up, his eyes bursting with tears.

Not interested in the when, how, or why, too shocked and angry at not having been told, too hurt at not being invited to the funeral, he feels like he has just been plunged into ice-cold water, and his world turns dark.

"Dead? She's dead?" he gasps, placing his trembling hand upon his chest. Feeling exposed and vulnerable as the news sinks in, he can barely breathe.

As his world comes crashing down around him, he lets out a wail, catching the attention of the people in the coffee queue. They stare at him as tears stream down his red cheeks.

Desperation creeps across his face, his fear of being alone in the world now realised. He stands up and races out of the park.

Skidding and stumbling through the arched gates at the entrance, Francois bolts across the busy street, almost hit by a car, the driver slamming on his brakes. As the driver honks his horn in rage, Francois doesn't even look back. He runs down street after street, desperate to get back to his apartment.

As he turns the last corner, almost home now, Francois doesn't notice a young couple walking hand in hand towards him, and he crashes straight into them. The woman stumbles, and the man falls backwards onto the pavement. Flicking his middle finger at Francois, he yells obscenities at him. Locked in a daze, Francois doesn't even notice, panting and puffing as he continues to run.

Finally arriving home, he fights for breath whilst trying to put his key into the lock, his hands trembling. Finally, he manages to unlock the door. Francois enters his apartment, then slams the door behind him.

Now inside his apartment, he doesn't know what to do next. He drops his keys onto the floor, the only other movement being his tears dripping off his chin. Each beat of his broken heart feels more painful than the last.

"Grand-mamie!" he screams. His voice breaks, like a child snatched from his mother's arms. Then he crumples to his knees, his face in his hands, and sobs. The sound of his wailing cuts through the silence of the empty apartment.

In utter despair, he stays like that for what seems like an eternity. Then he raises his head, his expression blank, and stares straight ahead. His body suddenly surging with rage, Francois stands up and walks into the living room. He stands opposite his cabinet, staring at the array of his possessions littering the surface. Then he swipes his hand across and sends them all crashing to the floor. Racing into the kitchen, he repeats the same action in each room, grabbing whatever he can and trashing his apartment.

In the process, he accidentally injures his face. Blood trickles down his forehead and onto his cheek.

Finally, when there is nothing left to trash, he walks back into the living room and slumps onto the sofa, surveying the devastation with eyes that are red and sore. He doesn't care about the damage. All he cares about is his precious Grandmother, and she's now gone.

CHAPTER 18

Star of David

Now moved to Nice, Francois is hoping to escape the harassment and make a fresh start. Missing his grandmother terribly, he takes comfort in walking past her apartment in the old part of Nice at every opportunity. Summer has arrived, and it's humid outside as the streets begin to fill with the early morning sun.

Blow drying his hair in the mirror, Francois takes a great deal of time and patience as he meticulously arranges his abundance of shiny brown curls. After he sprays his favourite Calvin Klein fragrance upon his neck, the reflection of his handsome face stares back at him, and he smiles. The sun creeping up the building and into his apartment sends dancing sunbeams that reflect in the kaleidoscope of his aquamarine eyes.

Having set up a business with Christophe, the two of them have started buying and selling used luxury cars. Francois is based in the south, and Christophe is in Paris. After spending most of the morning placing adverts online, Francois begins to tire.

Then his mood suddenly shifts. Something triggers the memory of the attacks in Paris, and his thoughts turn from light to dark.

Rubbing his forehead to comfort himself, his hands tremble, and he whispers a few words of Hebrew. He sits down on his bed for a few minutes and looks out the window, waiting for the anguish to pass. The clear blue sky calms him, and he decides to head out in search of something for lunch.

Grabbing his keys and his cell phone, he closes the thick dark wooden door behind him. As he begins to walk away, he stops, then returns to the door, vigorously shaking the handle to ensure it is locked. Satisfied, he leaves, taking the elevator down to the ground floor.

In the lobby, he sees the light from two large chandeliers glistening on the surface of the grey-and-white marble floor. The elegant gold-patterned glass entrance doors slide open as Francois steps onto a red rug outside, then down the sandstone steps.

Boulevard Victor Hugo, upon which Francois now lives, is splendid and beautiful. The long street is filled with tall, elegant white, crème and peach stone buildings, each with its own particular carvings. Some of the windows display olive or crème wooden shutters, with iron railings surrounding balconies, all of them in curved and twisting designs. Striped awnings offer shelter from the summer sun as the residents of Nice sip their morning coffee, looking down from their balconies at the activity on the streets below. As the glorious sunshine dapples the stone, creating flickering shadows from the tall, luscious trees that line the pavement, Francois passes under a palm tree and walks past brightly coloured flowers sitting in large stone pots. The popular location, positioned right in the heart of Nice, is only a few streets away from the famous Promenade des Anglaise, which runs parallel along the beach.

Dressed in a dark blue polo top, black jeans and brown sneakers, with his sunglasses perched on top of his head, Francois cuts through a side street, the familiar route leading to a nearby bakery. When he reaches the end, he turns left onto another street known for its abundance of small delicatessens and pastry shops. Francois buys a freshly made chicken, grape and brie baguette.

"Merci, au revoir."

"Merci, monsieur," the lady behind the counter replies, smiling in admiration of his beauty as he walks away.

Deciding to take a new route back to his apartment, Francois searches in his pocket for his broken phone charger. Seeking a replacement, he turns down a less familiar street. It's quiet and shaded, situated in between two tall buildings, and offers some respite from the heat.

He stops at the first shop on the street, a photography store. It has an array of camera equipment on its shelves.

"Excuse me. Do you know if there is a cell phone shop nearby that sells these?" He holds up his charger. A young man in his twenties, in the middle of assembling a large camera tripod, looks up.

"Halfway down the street on this side there's a cell phone shop," he says. "They're good, not expensive." He smiles at Francois as if to indicate he's shared a secret.

"Thank you," Francois replies and then leaves.

Continuing down the street, Francois keeps track of each sign peering out from above the shops. Finally spotting a sign displaying a cell phone symbol, he makes his way towards it.

As he nears the shop, he sees a group of three men standing on the pavement. One of them is leaning against a car. The other two are standing next to a building.

The first man has short, dark buzzed-cut hair. His arms are heavily tattooed, and he's wearing a tight white T-shirt, khaki trousers and boots. Another with black hair is more powerfully built than the other two. He is wearing sports clothes. The third is an immaculately groomed blonde. His long hair is pulled back into a neat ponytail. His skin is tanned, and he's wearing a short-sleeved violet shirt and tight blue jeans. On his feet are expensive suede shoes, which he's wearing without socks.

As Francois passes by, the blonde draws on his cigarette, then deliberately blows smoke into Francois's face, grinning. Almost immediately an old and unwelcome feeling arrives in the pit of Francois's stomach. Sensing danger, he looks straight ahead as he walks past. A few steps later, he hears a single word.

"Pig."

Turning back, he searches the men's faces, one by one. The blonde leaning against the car is still grinning, whilst the other two merely stare, their expressions menacing as they await a response.

"You heard it," the blonde says. "You Jewish pig!" he sneers, spitting on the ground near Francois's foot. "What's your problem, Jew?"

Before Francois can respond, the man with the buzz cut lunges at him, and a fight breaks out. Francois defends himself using his martial arts skills, as fists and feet fly, three against one.

Losing his concentration for a second, Francois looks down and notices his cell phone charging cable on the pavement. That allows one of the men to kick him hard in the back, causing him to stumble in pain.

As the fight becomes more violent, a brave elderly lady who had been watching from across the street arrives. Francois's first thought is that she has come to call them off, but to his horror she mistakenly assumes Francois the troublemaker and begins raining down blows upon his back with her walking stick as the others look on in laughter. Confused, exasperated and wincing in pain, not wanting to retaliate against an elderly lady, Francois manages to break away. He runs off, crossing several streets before he stops, totally exhausted.

Hurt, angry and confused as to why the elderly lady did not take his side, Francois is devastated. After sitting on a bench for a while, encountering several stares due to his battered and bloody face, Francois heads back to his apartment.

In the bathroom, he inspects the damage to his face, noticing a large graze upon his neck. Puzzled as to how they knew he was Jewish, he touches the star of David around his neck, and the realisation of what just happened becomes clear.

The night is long, and he's unable to sleep, the pain in his right cheek and the rest of his body causing him too much discomfort. Wired and alert, obsessive thoughts race through his mind.

Has he been followed from Paris? Are his attackers from Nice? Who are they? Do they know where he lives?

Reaching for his cell phone, he checks the time. It's 4:00 a.m. His mouth dry, Francois decides to fetch a glass of water. He flicks on the kitchen light and fills a glass left on the drain board. As the cold water fills his glass, Francois enters a trance-light state, staring straight ahead. He does not notice as the water overflows his glass and drips down onto his bare feet. Finally feeling the cold and wetness, he looks down and snaps back to reality, rushing to turn off the tap. Grabbing a kitchen cloth, he wipes the water from his feet and returns to the bedroom.

Early the next morning there's a knock at his door. Francois bolts upright in bed and looks at his cell phone. It's 6:15 a.m. Wondering who could be knocking at his door so early, he jumps out of bed and pulls on a pair of jogging trousers, groaning in pain from his injuries. Fight or flight mode kicks in. His body poised in a defensive posture, he approaches the front door as whoever is out there knocks again, much harder this time.

"Open up. It's the police."

Baffled as to why the police have arrived, he looks through the spy hole and sees five police officers outside his apartment, armed with batons. Scared and confused, Francois unlocks the door. Before he has a chance to ask what they want, three of the officers grab him and pull his hands behind his back. He hears a clicking sound as his wrists are cuffed. Two of the officers position themselves either side of him. Then, holding onto each arm, they march him out of the apartment, locking the door behind them.

"Hey, what do you want? Why have you cuffed me? What's going on?" Francois asks, baffled and frightened, but the officers ignore him as they enter the elevator.

Francois is angry at himself for not protesting harder and instead following their lead. Things have been difficult for so long with so many battles to fight that Francois has grown accustomed to being bullied. Then, recognising that he has become dangerously passive, he finally finds his voice.

"What's the problem? Why have you come? What's going on? Let me go!" His wrists ache in the cuffs behind his back. "What's wrong? Tell me!"

Their continued silence causes him to panic as he tries to shake off the two officers gripping his arms.

"Stop!" one of the officers says as the elevator reaches the lobby. "We'll tell you when you get to the police station."

"The police station? Why are you taking me there?" Francois demands, but the officers continue to ignore him. Left with little choice Francois gives up and stops resisting.

At the police station, Francois is taken into a side room for questioning.

"Sit down here," one of the officers instructs as he exits the room, leaving two police officers standing in front of the door waiting with Francois. Eventually, the station master walks in and sits down across the desk from Francois.

"Mr Ronen, you have been brought here because you attacked an old lady."

"What? Are you crazy? Are you talking about what happened to me yesterday? She attacked me! She didn't realise I was being attacked. It was anti-Semitism. I would never attack an old lady. My grand-mamie brought me up. I love old people!"

"That's not what our witnesses say."

"What witnesses?"

"There were some men who say you launched an attack on them."

"That's a lie! They attacked me. I'm sure it's because they saw this!"

Francois pulls out his star of David from his shirt. "I was attacked by anti-Semitic idiots. An old lady was hitting me, defending them. She didn't know what was happening."

"Come on, Mr Ronen, an old lady was hitting you? How is that possible?"

"I don't know. Maybe she was confused and thought I was the attacker. I don't know."

"Mr Ronen, now come on."

"It's true!" Francois shouts.

"Calm down, Mr Ronen. You don't want to be in more trouble, do you?"

"I haven't done anything! They're lying! I had to defend myself against them. Why haven't you arrested them?"

"Mr Ronen, we understand you have had some stays in a psychiatric hospital."

Francois's face turns red with anger. "These cuffs are hurting my wrists."

"Okay, if we take them off, will you stay calm?"

"Yes, yes I will."

The station master nods at one of the other officers, who takes off the cuffs. Francois sighs in relief, rubbing his wrists.

"As I just mentioned, Mr Ronen, you were in a psychiatric hospital before."

"So, what? What's that got to do with anything?"

"You must have a psychiatric assessment.

"But I've done nothing wrong. I don't need a psychiatric assessment. You're assuming I must be the bad person because I've been in the hospital. That's not fair, and I already told you they attacked me. When are you going to listen?"

"Wait here, Mr Ronen. I'll be back."

The station master leaves the room. He returns with a short, bald man who's wearing a blue-and-white pin-stripe shirt with smart black trousers. His silver glasses are perched on the end of his nose.

"Hello, Francois. I'm Doctor Leclerc. I've come to talk to you."

"I don't need to talk to you, thank you. There's nothing wrong with me. I was attacked. I'm Jewish, and I was attacked. Don't you understand that?"

"What about the old lady, Francois?"

"What about her?"

"Well, what happened?"

"She hit me with her walking stick! I don't understand what she was trying to do. Maybe she hates Jews too. Maybe she made a mistake. I don't know."

"I was told there are witnesses that say you attacked her."

"Are you crazy, Doctor?"

Doctor Leclerc tries to hide his smirk.

"It's not even about her," Francois says. "The witnesses are the men who attacked me. How can that be fair? I had to defend myself against an attack because I'm Jewish. As I already said, I love old people. My Grand-mamie raised me. I adored her, but now she's dead."

"I see," Doctor Leclerc says, observing the sadness creeping across Francois's face.

"Here, look at my scar," Francois says. "I was harassed in Paris for two years, and in one attack I was almost killed. That's why I moved to Nice, to escape them. Now it's happened to me again. Look at my neck, Doctor. What do you see?"

Doctor Leclerc looks at the graze upon Francois's neck. "I see you got hurt, Francois."

"Not that!" Francois retorts, growing increasingly irritated. "It's my symbol. Don't you see? They saw my star of David."

The doctor stares at the symbol for a few seconds, then makes some notes in a file. He looks at Francois again. "Wait here," he instructs and then leaves the room. Francois sits quietly, his hands trembling.

The station master re-enters the room. "Mr Ronen," he says, as Francois looks up.

"You're free to go."

With a huge sense of relief, Francois gets up and walks out of the room, trying to contain his anger.

After leaving the station, he stands for a moment in the sunshine, tears rolling down his cheeks.

"Thank you, God," he whispers. Then, wiping his eyes with his sleeve, he makes his way home.

CHAPTER 19

The Frenchman

It's 2008, and Lori is sitting at her computer. Having logged into Myspace music, she has just created a profile. She lives alone after the breakup of a long-term relationship two years prior, so her time is her own.

She is tall and beautiful with long light brown hair, full and luscious heart-shaped lips, and large honey and green hazel eyes. Having recently turned forty, she immerses herself in a world of musicians and creatives, where she feels happiest.

While nibbling on crackers, she scrolls through profiles, looking for people to converse with. Eventually, she stumbles across a little black-and-white photograph of a very handsome man. His thick, dark, wavy hair appeals to her as reads his profile. He's French, and he's in his early forties. He enjoys music, concerts, reading, and his family in France, Israel and America.

He sounds interesting, she thinks. Reading through his profile again, she notices he's Jewish. Having never met anyone Jewish before, she decides to send him a message.

"Hello! What type of music do you like?" she writes. Then she carries on looking at other profiles.

Deciding to make a cup of tea, she wanders off to the kitchen. Several minutes later when she sets her hot cup beside the monitor, she notices a message waiting for her.

"Hello, my name is Francois. I like David Bowie and many other artists. And you?"

Lori is a little surprised, having not expected him to answer.

"I like David Bowie too," she replies.

"You like Depeche Mode? Me I love them," he says, writing in broken English.

"Yes, they're great," she writes back, noticing he included a kiss and smiles with his last reply. *He seems sweet*, she thinks. Wanting to be cautious, she asks him a few questions.

"So, why are you on this site?"

"I want to connect with people who love music," he replies, adding another kiss.

"You're Jewish?" she asks, not knowing anything about the religion.

"Yes, I love the Jewish religion," he replies. "It's wonderful."

The messaging continues on well into the evening until she begins to feel tired.

"It's late now in the UK," she writes. "I'm going to bed."

"Tomorrow?" Francois replies.

"Yes."

After ending her message with a kiss, Lori gets ready for bed.

Switching off the bedside lamp, she settles down to sleep. The hours pass slowly. Restless and unable to drop off, she switches on the lamp and gets up to fetch a glass of water from the kitchen.

On her way back to the bedroom, she yawns, then stops and stares at her blank computer screen, thinking about her new French friend. Deciding to switch the computer back on, she discovers a new message waiting for her. It's from Francois.

"Goodnight. Sweet dreams," it reads, making her smile.

"Goodnight, Francois," she replies. She is just about to turn the computer off when another message pops up.

"Kisses," it reads, with a small picture of a red rose. Her heart warms as she looks at the message. Happy but tired, she heads off to bed.

Over the next few weeks, the messaging continues, and they get to know each other better. Eventually, Francois asks for Lori's email address, wanting to move from profile messages to a more personal level. They discover they each have a silly mutual sense of humour, typing playful messages to each other.

It's Sunday morning. Lori gets out of bed looking forward to reading a new message from Francois. When she opens her emails, however, there's a message from him she doesn't understand.

"Mauoo," it reads. She stares at it, a confused look on her face.

"Mauoo? What an earth does that mean?" she mumbles to herself. She decides to Google it, but she doesn't find anything. She looks it up on a French translation website, only to realise the word isn't French either.

"What do you mean by 'mauoo'???" she types, then she waits. Five minutes pass, then ten. Still nothing. Becoming bored, she watches some music videos, Kate Bush followed by David Bowie. When there's still no reply, she decides he must be out, so she goes off to make herself some breakfast.

Throughout the day, she busies herself with household chores sighing periodically with disappointment. Later in the afternoon, she takes another look at the computer, but there's still no reply. A wave of emotions washes through her head as she realises, she has become attached to this Frenchman. Several thoughts pop into her head.

Maybe he's chatting with several women. Maybe I need to chat with other men. Maybe he's met somebody special. Why am I worrying and being silly? This is supposed to be a music website.

Feeling sad, her excitement starts to diminish, but she tries to comfort herself. *This man lives in France, and you've never even met him,* she tells herself. *Don't be stupid!*

Deciding to go out and get some groceries, including a little chocolate, Lori heads out.

Evening arrives. Unable to concentrate, she turns on the television and soon finds herself clicking from channel to channel, feeling bored and fed up. Finally settling on a music programme, she tries her best to concentrate, but as she stares at the screen, her mind drifts, and she finds herself daydreaming about Francois and France. Annoyed at not being able to shake off her disappointment and unable to understand why, she turns off the television and gets ready for bed.

Feeling hungry, she goes to get a packet of crisps from the kitchen. On the way back, she avoids looking at her computer screen, not wanting to let it get to her any longer. Then she stops. Letting out a big sigh, she sits down at the computer and looks through her emails. As she eats her crisps, a big smile creeps across her face. At the top of her inbox is a message from Francois. The subject line says, "mauoo." Still clueless as to what it means, she laughs as she opens the email and begins to read.

"Bonjour, Lori, can I have your cell phone number?" it reads. Lori stares at the screen as she struggles to decide what to do.

Why not? she tells herself. *He seems nice. He doesn't know where I live, and he's in another country.*

She sends him her number, and almost instantly her phone rings, making her jump.

"Wow, that was quick," she says, looking at the call display to see the number is from France. She picks up her phone.

"Hello."

"Ello, Lori. It's Francois ca va?"

She giggles at his broken English, instantly loving the sound of his French accent and his deep, velvety voice.

"How are you?" he repeats in English this time.

"I'm fine," Lori replies, feeling her cheeks turn hot and flushed.

"Mauoo," Francois says.

"What is mauoo?"

"What is mauoo, it is a cat of course. Mauoo."

Lori bursts out laughing. "You mean meow!"

"Yes, mauoo." Francois laughs, then emails her a cute emoji of a cat's face.

"You have the same silly sense of humour as I do, Francois."

"It's really wonderful to know you, Lori."

"You too, Francois."

"Listen, do you want to come to France?"

A little taken back by the invitation, Lori decides to ask more about him. "What do you do? What's your job?"

"I sell luxury cars. They're not new; they're seconds: Porchee, Mercedes … I have a business partner in Paris, but it's harder now, with the recession."

"Oh, you mean second hand, used Porsche."

"Yes, Porchee."

Lori smiles. "So, you live in Nice. It must be beautiful there."

"Oui, beautiful. My family is from Paris. My grand-mamie moved to Nice too, but she died, it's warmer here. My uncle lives near Nice too."

"What about your parents?"

"My maman sold the lease on a hotel that my family used to run in Paris and retired to Israel. But she's thinking about moving back soon and buying here in the south of France. My father lives in Belgium."

"Oh, Israel. Sounds interesting. And Belgium. Do you get to see them often?"

Francois doesn't answer the question, preferring to talk about Israel. "Some of my family members are in Israel and some in America. Israel is a wonderful country."

Lori smiles, feeling slightly enchanted by him and the pureness of his words, warming to him further.

"How about you?" he asks. "Your family?"

"Yes, my parents live in small towns near a city named Bristol. They got divorced when I was fourteen. I also have a sister and a brother. I am the middle child. I work in an office. It's very boring, but I have a passion for music. I love to create music."

"Me too. Come, my darling, come to France. I'll help cover the cost of the flight."

"I'll pay too," Lori insists, thinking it best seeing as she's never met him before. "I would love to come, Francois. I have some holiday time due very soon at work, in a couple of weeks, in fact."

"Okay, my love, come. I invite you."

Lori is taken back by his use of the word "love," already feeling flustered. "Okay, okay, Francois I will."

"I go now Lori. I must get food. Speak tonight?"

"Yes, tonight."

"Tonight," Francois repeats. "Kiss you, Lori."

The following day while driving home from work, Lori feels a new sense of happiness. She turns up the volume on the radio as "Ashes to ashes" by David Bowie plays. She looks forward to speaking to Francois later.

When she arrives home, she puts a lasagne in the oven. As she's chopping up a side salad, her phone pings. She picks it up and reads the text. "Bonjour, Lori. Hope u had a good day. Mauoo kisses Francois." Smiling, she texts him back.

After finishing her meal, she tidies the kitchen, then decides to go to bed.

Before placing her cell phone on her pillow, she checks the time. It's 9:15. Just then her phone rings.

"Ello, Lori, my darling, you have a good evening?"

"Yes, it was okay. I was at work today, and I cooked a lasagne when I got home."

"Lasagne, I love it. That's well."

Lori giggles at his broken English, loving his French accent even more than before.

"Why you laugh, Lori?"

"It's your accent. It's sweet."

"Sweet? Why is sweet?"

"It means cute, lovely."

"Lovely. I know this word. Merci, Lori. Yours also."

As they continue to talk into the night, Francois yawns, feeling tired.

"Are you okay? Are you tired, Francois?"

"Oui. It is one hour later in France."

"Sleep if you want to, Francois."

"Not yet. It's okay. Tell me more about your music, Lori."

As Lori begins to talk about the songs she has written, after a few minutes, she is interrupted by a strange noise in her ear. Turning up the volume on her cell phone, she hears the sound of heavy breathing, as it dawns upon her that Francois has fallen asleep. Chuckling to herself, she places her cell phone back onto her pillow and listens for a while. Switching off her bedside lamp, she lies still as the moon shines through a gap in the curtain, lighting up her face. As she continues to listen to

Francois breathing, a feeling of protectiveness rises up within her, taking her by surprise as she senses his loneliness. Eventually, her eyes feel heavy, and she blinks, trying to stay awake. Unable to fight her tiredness any longer, she gives in.

"Goodnight, Francois," she whispers into the phone, then settles down to sleep.

CHAPTER 20

Soul Meets Soul

It's August 2009, and Lori is on a flight from Bristol to Nice to meet Francois for the first time. Looking out the window as the airplane nears the airport, she sees the deep indigo ocean, topped with a scattering of white yachts, dancing upon the aquamarine waves.

As the pilot instructs everyone to prepare for landing, Lori pulls out a small circular mirror and checks her hair and makeup one last time.

After exiting passport control, she makes her way down to baggage claim. Filled with excitement at the thought of meeting Francois, she finally spots her purple patterned case traveling along the carousel. Then she makes her way to the toilets for one last check in the mirror. She looks at the reflection of her short-sleeved satin blouse and royal-blue skirt, which shows off her long legs, as well as her dark blue heeled shoes and smiles. Then she makes her way to arrivals.

As she follows the crowd through the entrance, people shriek with delight at spotting their loved ones. Others hug and kiss all around her. She looks for Francois, his photograph etched in her mind. Several minutes pass, but she doesn't see him anywhere. For a split second, she begins to worry that he hasn't come. Deciding to sit, she waits patiently, listening with fascination to the language of love all around her. As the area starts to clear, she remains sitting. Then she notices a man speaking into a cell phone near the doors, looking over at her every so often.

Is that him? she wonders, noticing his beautiful curly dark hair and handsome face, though he's a little plumper than he was in his photograph.

Eventually, he walks over to her still speaking in French on the phone. He smiles as he hangs up.

"Hello, Lori," he says. The situation seems surreal. Then Lori notices Francois is a little anxious. After then taking the handle of her case, much to her surprise, he takes her hand as she stands up.

"We catch a bus. It's easy," he says, immediately taking charge.

"Okay," Lori replies, feeling a mixture of apprehension and excitement as they make their way out of the airport.

After walking a short distance to a bus stop, he asks if she's hungry.

Lori smiles, loving his accent. "Yes, a little."

When the bus arrives, Francois takes hold of her case. They step on board, and Francois wheels it up the aisle. Lori is happy, noting his gentlemanly gesture as he directs her to an empty seat. Placing her case in front of him, he sits beside her, then turns to her and smiles as the bus pulls away.

As an array of thoughts run through her head, she turns to look at Francois with a feeling of inexplicable belonging. This surprises her, seeing as they have only just met in person. Looking out the window at the buildings lined with tropical trees and flowers, she watches the people of Nice going about their business. Eventually, the bus pulls up at its final stop, and Francois turns to Lori.

"We get off here."

As the bus pulls away, it reveals a wondrous view from across the road. Lori looks at the blue sparkling ocean and the beach dotted with parasols and pockets of people soaking up the summer sun. The smartly dressed people of Nice as well as tourists stroll along the promenade. Brightly coloured mopeds whizz by, darting in and out traffic, the drivers' open-faced helmets revealing locals, both young and old, their light cotton clothing flapping behind them.

"We are going to a petite restaurant," Francois announces, Lori delighting in his accent once again.

"That will be lovely."

"Good. They have wonderful fish there. You like fish?"

"Yes."

"Good. We go."

Soaking up the vibrant energy of Nice, they hold hands, Francois pulling Lori's case as they walk past groups of people sitting outside restaurants, bars and cafes. Brightly coloured flowers tumble down the walls of oat, lemon and pale terracotta buildings with their windows displaying wooden shutters. They arrive at a cobbled entrance leading to an outdoor seating area of a little restaurant, and Francois leads the way to an empty table.

"We sit here?" he asks, and Lori gladly agrees, feeling hungry and in need of a rest.

"The salmon salad is good. You want this?"

"Yes, great," Lori replies. They look at each other, observing each other's expression, their mutual admiration for each other's beauty clear for all to see. Francois raises his arm to get the waitress's attention. An exchange of French words darts back and forth and before long a glass of cool sparkling rosé arrives, laced with ice. Two plates also arrive, filled with fresh leafy green salad, baby potatoes and dark pink salmon draped with basil. Lori takes a sip of the rosé, and the taste is delightful.

"French wine? Very nice," she remarks.

"Yes, French wine good, very good." Francois points to the label, which has a castle on it. "Le Chateau, very good."

They tuck into their meal, each individual flavour fresh and delicious. Before long, both plates are empty.

"We go?" Francois asks.

"Okay, yes," Lori replies, having no care where "go" is. She is on an adventure with her Frenchman, and she is happy.

"This way," Francois says. He takes her hand, and they walk side by side in the sunshine. Cutting through a small park, they pass by the sound of singing birds in tropical trees and chirping crickets amongst the grassy plants. After crossing a few more streets, they finally arrive at the end of a long street, Boulevard Victor Hugo.

"I live up here. Come."

As they walk, Lori realises she has been so enchanted by Nice that she hasn't asked Francois many questions.

"How long have you lived here?"

"Oh, about eight mont."

Lori chuckles at his pronunciation of "month."

"You laugh, why?" Francois asks, looking worried.

"Oh, it's okay," Lori replies, sensing his concern.

"It's the way you speak, your accent."

"What is it?"

"I like it. It's sweet."

"Sweet? Sweet like candy?"

"Yes, like candy."

They both laugh as they continue up the street until eventually Francois stops.

"Here," he says, pointing to an elegant white stone building. Lori looks up. The building is seven stories high, each apartment with its own balcony.

"I live here, one, two, three, four." Francois points up to an apartment on the fourth floor, situated in the middle of the building. "Come, Lori, I show you."

Passing through gold-trimmed sliding glass doors, it suddenly occurs to Lori that she will be alone with Francois, having only met him for the first time in person. Feeling safe, she decides to go with her gut and follows him into the lobby.

They take the elevator to the fourth floor, where they are met by a hallway with a marble floor and two dark wooden doors at either end. Francois directs Lori to the left. As they stand at the door, Francois pulls out his key and unlocks his apartment.

Inside, the floor is a continuation of the grey-and-white marble. The spacious lounge is sparse, with two large expensive-looking floral vases placed on the floor. At one end is a brown leather chair near a music centre with a large collection of CDs scattered around it. At the other is a desk with a tall, elegant gold-and-glass lamp sitting on it, next to a laptop surrounded by cups and pens. Two large bedrooms and a kitchen lead off the lounge. In the bathroom is dark green marble, with a gold-coloured taps and sink. Lori immediately notices the apartment is a little messy.

As Francois slides open the large glass doors to the balcony, a mixed soup of sound floods the apartment. Traffic, tweeting birds, music and voices can be heard. After switching on the television, Francois goes to the bedroom. Lori sits on the brown leather chair, soon becoming immersed in French television, the language and an array of unfamiliar commercials fascinating her.

"I put your case here," Francois says. Getting up to take a look, Lori finds her case on the floor of the master bedroom.

"That's fine," she says, a little surprised to find an unmade bed and the floor filled with discarded shoes and clothes. They look at the bed and then at each other, both of them smiling and not caring about the mess, feeling happy and accepting things as they are. Lori decides she will mention it later and perhaps offer to help him tidy things up.

Returning to the lounge, Francois sits on the chair and invites Lori to sit on his lap. With his arm around her waist, he turns the channel over to music and raises the volume. Then he gets up and dances around a little, and they both laugh. Then he bends down to her as she sits, and they kiss passionately.

"You want to go out, maybe get a coffee?" he asks, pulling back.

"Yes, great. I would love to."

"Show you more of Nice?"

"That would be great."

After leaving the apartment, they head towards a large square full of alfresco diners, each restaurant full to capacity as people enjoy the sunshine. Walking hand in hand, they stop to listen to an old man sitting on a stool, playing romantic French music on an accordion. Continuing on, they eventually arrive at one of Francois's favourite cafes, which sells coffee and delightful pastries.

"Here, the coffee is good," Francois says, pulling out a seat for Lori. "You like cappuccino? It's nice here."

"I like lattes."

"Okay, we have lattes."

Lori giggles.

"You laugh again, huh?" Francois smiles. "How long you are staying? A week?"

"Yes, a week."

"Good, my darling. It's short, but we are together."

Francois's voice is tender, his accent smooth and delightful. Never having felt so deeply important before in past relationships, Lori is blissfully happy. Francois takes her hand in his and then kisses it, taking her by surprise. Liking this wonderful French culture, she looks into his eyes and smiles, enjoying being romanced.

As they sit and chat, two very attractive women walk past, and Francois turns to look them up and down. Surprised by his behaviour, Lori watches as Francois smiles to himself, admiring their beauty. Then she shrugs it off.

After finishing their coffee, they explore the area a little further until Francois suggests they make their way down towards the beach to Promenade des Anglais. As they walk along the promenade, Lori soaks up her surroundings. Eventually, they reach a small port area.

"We go to the market."

"Market?"

"Wonderful food there."

"Sounds good."

Taking her hand, Francois leads Lori across the street to a stone arch. A creeping vine twists around it, intertwined with dark pink flowers. As they pass beneath it, a sweet fragrance fills the air.

On the other side, they are met by a bustle of activity. Surrounding them is a mass of traditional stalls, each with a different coloured canopy selling freshly caught fish, an abundance of fruits, vegetables, pastries and a variety of breads. A delicious mixture of aromas fills the air as crowds mingle amongst the stalls, sampling food and filling their shopping bags.

Francois pulls a crumbled carrier bag from his trouser pocket and leads Lori to a stall he knows well, the fishmonger. Ordering two fresh whitefish from a glass box filled with ice, Francois turns to Lori and smiles, lifting her hand to kiss her fingers.

"Great fish, wonderful."

They watch as the fishmonger wraps the fish in white paper and then hands it to Francois. After he places it in his bag, they continue to walk.

"Come," Francois says, heading towards a cheese stall. Taking a taster on a wooden stick, he places it at Lori's lips.

"It's good. Try."

As the cheese melts in Lori's mouth, she smiles with delight. "Gorgeous. Shall we get some?"

"Of course."

After they continue to explore the market, walking from stall to stall, they decide to leave, heading back to his apartment.

Excited to cook for his new girlfriend, Francois heads straight for the kitchen. Reaching for a bottle of ketchup from the cupboard, he squeezes a large dollop into a small pan. Lori watches as he then takes out a carton of crème fresh from the refrigerator and spoons it into the ketchup. After scattering some fresh herbs into the mixture, Francois mixes it all together, forming a thick pink paste.

"Taste," he says, holding the spoon up to Lori's lips.

"It's good."

"I know." Francois grins, and they both laugh.

Poking his finger into the mixture to taste it, looking very pleased with himself, he places the fish in a dish and turns on the oven. After putting baby potatoes on to boil, he chops some fresh tomatoes, placing them on two plates. Then they make their way into the lounge.

"You will love," he tells her, reaching down to turn on the stereo. The glorious sound of a French male singer fills the apartment with a romantic accompaniment of strings and piano. As they look at each other, the atmosphere turns sensual. Francois takes Lori's hand and leads her to the bedroom, and they make love for the first time. Later, lying in bed, both of them are happy as they hold hands.

"What's that on your stomach, baby?" Lori asks, noticing a long, crude-looking scar.

"It doesn't matter. I will tell you another time."

"Tell me more about your family then," Lori says. Silence falls between them before Francois finally replies, rubbing his forehead as if searching for the right thing to say.

"Not now," he says, leaning over to kiss her. "We must eat."

Leaping out of bed, he rushes to put on his boxer shorts, then returns to the kitchen.

Lori gets up and rummages through her case, taking out a pair of shorts and a T-shirt. She puts them on quickly, eager to join him in the kitchen.

"I love your hair in all directions," Francois remarks, making reference to Lori's messy hair. They both smile as Francois opens the oven door, taking out the hot, bubbling fish. The smell is divine.

"Mmm ... it looks lovely, Francois."

Francois breaks off two large pieces of French bread and places them on the sides of their plates. Then he carries the plates into the living room, setting one on the desk and the other on the chair.

After dinner they decide to stay in for the evening, Lori feeling tired from her journey from the United Kingdom. She sits on Francois's lap as they watch music videos before returning to bed to sleep.

The next morning, they wake early to the sound of the bustling streets of Nice.

"Good morning, my darling," Francois says, leaning over to kiss Lori. After a breakfast of croissants and orange juice, they head on out.

Deciding to take in the shops, they wander from store to store. As they walk, Lori's delight turns to worry as she observes Francois's wandering eye, looking each beautiful woman up and down. Trying to brush it off, after a few hours she becomes irritated and decides to speak up.

"Francois, are you sure you're interested in me?"

"Yes, yes, of course. Why you ask?"

"Well, it seems you're interested in many other women too."

"I don't understand," he replies, his voice serious.

"You keep noticing other women a little too much, and I'm getting fed up with it."

"What mean, fed up?"

"Upset. It's disrespectful."

"Oh, it's nothing, no, not worry."

"Nothing? Well, it's something to me," she snaps, starting to doubt if she has done the right thing in coming to France. Striding on head, she is now totally fed up. "I'm going back to the apartment."

"You're wrong. I did nothing," Francois protests.

Lori tries to make her way back on her own. Realising she's lost, she looks behind to find that Francois is following her. Angry but a little relieved, they walk in silence back to his apartment.

Wanting reassurance, Lori decides to call her sister and tell her what's happening. She goes into the bedroom and shuts the door. About fifteen minutes later, she returns to the lounge to find Francois sitting in the leather chair, a worried expression on his face.

"I'm going back to the UK," she says.

"Why? No, Lori," Francois replies, sounding scared.

"I think you're playing games. I had a long relationship before, and now I've had two years on my own. I realise I don't have time for games or to be messed around with. If you just want to play, well, I'm going to let you."

With that she returns to the bedroom to pack her case. Francois follows her.

"Stop, stop!"

"Why?"

"Come out and sit down."

"I don't want to sit down. You've hurt my feelings, Francois."

"Sit, please," he pleads, pointing to the chair. Lori walks out of the bedroom and sits.

They stare at each other in silence for a few seconds. Then something totally unexpected happens: a tear rolls down Francois's face. Lori is stunned, then deeply moved.

"I was trying to make you jealous," he admits. "I'm sorry, Lori." Silent tears continue to fall.

"You don't need to do that. I like you, Francois."

Realising that this strong man standing in front of her is also fragile, Lori forgives him, and at that very moment, she falls in love.

CHAPTER 21

The Breakdown

It's September 2009. A few months have passed since Lori returned from France. She and Francois have made plans to reunite as soon as possible, and she's looking forward to seeing him again.

While sitting at her computer eating dinner, her cell phone rings. She smiles in anticipation of it being Francois, but before she can utter a word, she is met with the sound of a desperate voice.

"Grand-mamie. Grand-mamie!" the voice wails.

"Francois, what's wrong? Are you okay?"

There is no reply. Then she hears him crying.

"What's wrong, baby?"

Still no answer. Then the line goes dead. Worried, Lori tries to call him back, but the phone won't connect. After trying a few more times, she gives up. Waiting for a while as she tries to figure out what to do next, she finally decides to call Elijah.

"Lori, hi, how are you?" he asks.

"I'm okay, but I'm worried about Francois."

"Why? What's wrong?"

"He just rang me, and he seemed to be afraid. He was crying, and he sounded confused, crying for his grandmother."

"He was? I know he gets very upset about her death from time to time."

"I don't know what to do. The phone went dead."

"I'll try to call him, Lori. I'll call you back."

Lori hangs up, waiting anxiously for Elijah to call her back. Ten minutes pass. She tries to call Elijah, but he is engaged. Then her phone rings.

"Lori, I tried to call Francois a few times, but his phone is dead," Elijah says. "What can we do?"

Lori makes a snap decision. "I'm coming to France, Elijah."

"What? Are you sure?"

"Yes. Something is really wrong. I need to go. I'll call you once I get there."

"Okay, if, you're sure. I'm so sorry, Lori, but my wife, is away in Normandy. I'm looking after the children in Paris. I have called him many times also."

After arranging to take some time off work, Lori books the first available fight, which leaves in three days' time, and continues to try and reach Francois on the phone right up until the flight.

It's late afternoon. Having arrived in Nice, Lori calls Francois's cell phone as she sits in the back of a taxi, but there's still no answer. As she gazes out the window, her eyes half closed and the sun shining on her face, she feels no excitement, her eagerness to find out what has happened to Francois at the forefront of her mind. As the taxi drives alongside the promenade, she imagines them walking there together. Much like a magician shuffling his cards, a flutter of memories returns, momentarily offering her comfort. Then the sound of Francois's desperate voice echoes in her mind as various scenarios play out.

Could his phone be broken? Has he fallen ill? Maybe he's okay now and will be so happy to see me unexpectedly.

Before long she arrives outside his building. After paying the driver, Lori stands there looking up at Francois's apartment. After trying to call him one last time, she decides to walk to the opposite side of the street to get a better look at his place. She notices the sliding glass doors are shut, and the light is off.

After crossing back over and wheeling her case up the sandstone steps to the entrance, she presses the buzzer for Francois's apartment and waits. There is no answer. She tries again. Still nothing. Deciding he must be out, she sits on the edge of the landing and waits.

Time passes slowly, and still there is no sign of him. Lori walks to the side of the building and looks up. For a split second she contemplates climbing up, then dismisses the idea as ridiculous as she thinks about the danger of falling. Walking back around to the front, she looks up at Francois's balcony.

"Francois!" she calls, but nobody answers. "Francois!" she yells as loudly as possible.

But it's no use. Her calls are swallowed by the din of the constant traffic, and she gives up.

Looking at her watch, she realises it is almost 8:00. Feeling hungry, Lori wanders off in search of a bakery. When she returns, she sits on the red mat in front of the sliding glass doors and eats.

Frustrated that no one has left the building yet, enabling her to enter, she is tired and fed up. Then she sees a man coming up the steps, rushing to enter the building. She scrambles to get to her feet, waiting for him to approach her, but he disappears through another set of doors farther up on the left, making it impossible for her to grab her things in time. Only then does it dawn on her that the doors she has been sitting front of on the right are locked. Peering inside she notices a cleaning sign placed on the floor behind the doors. The writing is in French, but the message is obvious.

"Fucking hell!" she yells in exasperation.

Now past 9:00, with no one else having entered or left the building yet and desperate to find a way in, Lori realises it is too late to find a hotel, and she feels utterly miserable. As darkness falls, she resigns herself to sleeping outside. Taking a few items from her case to keep warm, she rests her head against the white stone entrance in front the doors and tries her best to sleep.

The night seems endless, and sleeping is an impossibility as she is continuously woken by a passing traffic.

"Where is he?" she mutters, close to tears.

After nodding off and waking up all night long, when daybreak finally arrives, the welcome warmth of the sun creeps across her body. Opening her tired and heavy eyes, she checks the time on her cell phone. It's 6:20. Her body is stiff and aching as she stretches her long legs, then tries to stand up. Unable to drink all night due to there being no bathroom to use, she gulps down the remainder of her water. After stuffing the extra clothes back into her case, she hears something behind her and turns round. The doors have opened at last, revealing a man in his fifties standing behind her. They stare at each other for a moment, him with an astonished expression on his face. Lori looks him up and down. His work trousers are blue, and on his white shirt is a gold badge that says, "Concierge."

As he begins to speak to her in French, she grabs her case and wheels it inside, feeling tremendously relieved.

"I'm sorry I don't understand what you're saying," she says. "Petite Francais."

"Who you want?" he asks.

"I need to get into my boyfriend's apartment. I have come from England. I think he's ill."

Looking Lori up and down, he scratches his head in confusion. "His name?"

"Francois Ronen. Monsieur Ronen."

"Okay follow me. I see you before long time ago," he instructs, taking Lori by surprise. With a huge sigh of relief, she follows him to the elevator.

Once in the elevator, Lori feels her heart pounding against her chest as various scenarios run through her head about what could be waiting for her inside the apartment. Trying to stay calm, she grits her teeth as they exit the elevator. Standing outside Francois's apartment, the concierge pulls out a huge set of keys. He inspects one after the other, each one marked with a number, Lori tries her best to be patient. Eventually, after finding the correct key, he opens the door.

When Lori steps inside, a shocked expression creeps across her face. The apartment is a mess. Various objects are scattered across the living room floor. Hordes of dirty cups sit in groups next to Francois's laptop, and piles of unwashed clothes are on the floor. Lori goes into the second bedroom, then the kitchen and the bathroom, everything is a mess. Returning to the living room, she finds the concierge still standing there. She doesn't know what to say. Then he points to a key on a table.

"Look," he says, indicating she has access to the apartment now. As he turns his back to leave, Lori senses he knows more than he's letting on, so she decides to try to find out more.

"Where is Mr Ronen?"

He stops, but he doesn't turn around. He merely raises his hands and shrugs as he walks out the door.

"No, wait, please. Please tell me what's happened to Francois," Lori pleads.

Turning around and looking over his shoulder, the concierge looks as if he is about to reveal a secret. "Police, they take him," he says, and then he leaves.

Stunned and confused, Lori closes the door. Then she stands there looking at the mess for a few moments, not knowing what to do next.

Sitting in the familiar brown leather chair, Lori looks out the glass doors leading to the terrace. Then she gets up to open them. To her disappointment, they are locked. After hunting high and low for the key, she gives up. Sitting back down and feeling utterly fed up, she sighs. Then all at once, much like the whistling of an old kettle, out comes all of her steam. The emotional turmoil of the last forty-eight hours coupled with her tiredness from her uncomfortable night catches up with her, and she begins to sob.

A little later, having calmed down, Lori goes into the bathroom to inspect her makeup. As she looks into the same mirror as Francois has done many times before, in her mind's eye she imagines him staring back at her, two tear-stained faces lost in a moment of time. As she blinks to see more deeply, his face begins to fade, making her feel sad. More determined than ever to find him, Lori begins to formulate a plan.

Wheeling her case into the bedroom, she strips the bed, putting on clean bedding. Then she spends the next few hours cleaning the apartment. Finally, feeling hot and sweaty, she takes a well-earned shower.

The hot water is especially welcome, gradually washing away her night of discomfort. Putting on a pair of white jeans and a short-sleeve floral blouse and sandals, she applies her makeup, then blow dries her hair, taking care to style it immaculately into a neat ponytail. Then she places the key in her handbag and heads out in search of the nearest police station.

Standing outside the apartment building, undecided about which direction to take and unable to speak much French, Lori decides to ask the first person she sees, a middle-aged man.

"Excusez-moi, petite Francais, I am English, Anglais. You know where the police station is?"

The man looks at her with a slightly confused expression. "No," he says without stopping.

She asks the same question to an old lady. Looking somewhat surprised, she stops and smiles. "English, yes?" she says, her voice kind. "My cousin lives in England, in London."

"You know where the police station is?" Lori asks her again.

"No," she replies, walking away.

Lori rolls her eyes. Then she notices what appears to be an estate agent a few doors up from the apartment block. Deciding this would be a better option, she goes inside and is met by four immaculately groomed staff, busy at their computers. She asks the man nearest the door, and not only does he know where the police station is, he prints out a map for her and tells her which bus to catch.

As Lori waits for the bus, her mind turns to Francois. She remembers their first meal together at the little restaurant and smiles. Her smile fades, however, when she remembers his fragile broken voice during their last phone call.

Two buses come and go but not the one she needs. A few minutes later, she sees another bus coming.

"At last," Lori whispers.

Remembering the estate agent's instruction to get off the bus after passing a second church, she keeps a careful lookout so she doesn't miss it. When she spots it, eager to get off, she makes her way to the front.

As the bus pulls away, Lori feels a sense of relief that she is about to find out what has happened to Francois and why it involved the police.

The police station is a few buildings up from the church, set back from the street. Upon entering, Lori is met by a queue of people waiting their turn in front of the reception window at the rear of the foyer.

She feels impatient as she listens to tourists from other countries who have gotten lost, pushing maps under the glass panel and asking for help. Meanwhile, the locals register an array of complaints. Understanding a little of what is being said, she sighs, wishing they would hurry up. Eventually, she reaches the front of the queue, only to be met by a stern-looking policeman sitting behind a window.

"Oui?" he says.

"Can you help me? I'm sorry." After explaining her situation in her limited French, Lori gives Francois's full name and age.

"I'm very worried. I understand the police came to his apartment."

The policeman raises his hand. "Wait," he instructs. Then he mutters something in French to another officer at a desk behind him. The second officer looks at Lori and then comes out to the foyer.

"Come," he says, leading her through a door at the rear of the foyer and into a long hall. Lori looks up at the curved oak panelling on the ceiling. On the walls are black-and-white photographs of officers with their various ranks titled beneath on gold placards. Another officer arrives as the other leaves.

"Hello," he says. "How can I help you?"

Lori instantly feels relieved that he speaks English, and his tone more welcoming.

"My partner's name is Francois Ronen. He has disappeared from his apartment. I have come to France to find out what happened to him. He called me before I came over from England, and he was very distressed. I'm very worried about him. The concierge from his apartment building says the police took him. Why? What has happened?"

"Okay, tell me his name again."

"Francois Ronen."

"Okay, wait here. I'll be back soon," the officer says, pointing to a wooden chair in the hall.

Lori waits anxiously for news, and eventually the officer returns.

"My dear," he begins, "he's in the hospital."

"The hospital?" she gasps.

"Yes, the hospital of psychiatrie."

"You mean psychiatry?" she asks, shocked at what she has just heard and wanting clarity on this unexpected news.

"Oui, yes dear."

For a moment she doesn't know what to say. "What is the name of the hospital?" she asks.

"St Maine. It's a little outside Nice. You can take a bus there or a taxi. Now I must go, dear."

"But why is he there?"

"He must be ill. It happens."

The man leads Lori back to the foyer. "Goodbye," he says, closing the door behind him.

Upon leaving the police station, Lori makes her way up the street looking for the nearest taxi stand.

A taxi takes her north to the outskirts of Nice, coming to a stop outside a large group of white buildings, each dotted with small square windows, with various lush flowering shrubs and palm trees growing in between. At the entrance is a small beige security office with a flat brown roof.

"St Maine?" Lori asks.

"Oui," the driver replies.

As the taxi pulls away, Lori makes her way over to the security office and peers through the window, seeing a security guard sitting at a computer. He glances up at her and then turns back to the computer screen, taking little notice. Finding this strange, Lori knocks on the window, but he doesn't move. Annoyed, Lori knocks again, harder this time. He spins around in his chair and, with an impatient look on his face, slides open the window.

"Oui?" His voice is deep and impatient, and he mutters a few more words in French. Lori is flustered, not understanding what he's saying.

"Excuse me," she interrupts. "I am Anglais. Sorry, petite Francais. I need to know where to go. My partner is here. Where is reception?"

The security guard frowns, looking puzzled, and Lori realises he does not speak English. Then, picking up on the word "reception," he nods and extends his arm, pointing.

"La gauche."

"Merci, monsieur."

Lori makes her way up the drive leading into the hospital grounds. When she nears the corner of the first building, she looks up at a tall white building at the top of the circular entrance drive. As her eyes survey every detail, a shocked expression creeps across her face as she realises each window is covered by metal bars.

"My god, it's like a jail," she says.

After rounding the corner of the building, she stops, looking in front and behind, wondering if she is going the right way. Daunted by the size of the grounds, she starts to worry if she is going to be able to find the reception.

"Where is it?" she mutters, trying to find a sign. Towards the end of the building she notices the sun glistening on a pair of double doors, so she walks towards them, passing by various plants and shrubs on her right.

As she approaches the doors, she hears a deep, gravelly voice.

"Mademoiselle, mademoiselle."

Looking down, Lori notices a pair of crossed legs sticking out from the other side of a large shrub. Cautiously walking forward and peering around the other side, she finds a man sitting dressed from head to toe in denim and wearing tatty brown sandals. His deep green eyes are sad, his wavy hair is greasy, and his face displays deep lines from the story of his life. He raises his hand to reveal an empty cigarette packet. His fingernails are long and dirty. He begins to speak in French, talking clearly one moment and mumbling the next. Lori has no idea what he is saying, other than realising he wants some cigarettes.

"No, no cigarettes sorry," she say, as she passes him by. He looks her up and down and grins.

"Okay darling."

Lori looks back, a little surprised to hear him speak English, only to see him wink.

Standing outside the glass doors, she looks back to where the man was sitting and notices he's gone. Just then she finally spots a sign with the word "Reception" written on it just inside the building. Sighing with relief, she attempts to push open the door, only to find it is locked.

"For God's sake," she says, frustrated at yet another obstacle. To the left of the doors she notices a panel with three buzzers, each with a departmental placard in French. She decides to press the top buzzer but then hesitates for a moment, thinking she might disturb an important department. With no idea which one to choose, she decides to press the second buzzer. As she waits for an answer, she begins to feel anxious as her mind turns to Francois. Eventually, she presses the second buzzer again, holding the button down a little longer. Suddenly, a very stern female voice addresses her.

"Oui?"

Slightly startled, Lori gulps, feeling like a child who just got in trouble with the school master.

"Excuse me, madame," she begins in her most polite voice. "I have come to find Francois Ronen. I am Anglais. I am his partner."

"Reception! Reception!" the voice bellows. "Droite! Droite!"

Understanding that word at least, she looks to her right. Beneath a window is a buzzer with a small placard under it that reads, "Reception." Cursing under her breath, Lori presses it.

As she looks through the doors, she hears them click and then notices a woman sitting behind a glass panel waving at her. Realising she wants Lori to push the door open, at long last, she enters the building. As she approaches the woman behind the reception desk, she decides to simplify her explanation for being there.

"I'm here to see Francois Ronen," she says.

"A patient?" The woman smiles. "Ahh you are English, oui?"

"Oui, oui, yes," Lori replies feeling relieved. "Is he here? I have come all the way from the UK to find him."

"Wait here," the woman instructs. Then she goes into the office behind her to speak to another woman. As Lori watches them through the thick dividing window, she tries her best to be patient. Finally, the woman returns. Then she sits down and checks something on her computer."

"Is he here?" Lori asks.

"He is here, yes, but I don't think you can see him."

Lori's mouth drops open, and a knot forms in the pit of her stomach. Every part of her body feels exasperated.

"What, he is, why, why not, can you tell me why not?" she splutters.

"You can try if you want," the woman says. "Go to his building. It's the next one up." She points. "Ring the door and speak to them. You will see what they say, okay?"

"Okay, merci."

The knot in Lori's stomach tightens. Feeling utterly deflated, she makes her way to the next building, hoping and praying that they will let her see Francois.

When she arrives at the entrance, she looks through the square window in a pale blue metal door, only to see a tiny lobby and an identical door on the other side. There is no receptionist. Soon she is met by a feeling of dread, her intuition telling her she is not going to be able to see Francois after coming all this way.

Lori presses a red square button and then waits. A few minutes later, a nurse appears, looking at Lori through the window on the second door. Then the door unlocks, making a low pitch mechanical sound. Dressed in pale blue cotton trousers and a matching short-sleeve top she walks to the left of the door, and her voice appears through the intercom.

"Oui?"

Lori takes a deep breath, fed up at having to explain everything again.

"Bonjour. Excusez-moi, petite Francais. I am English, Anglais."

"Oui, oui," the nurse says, also impatient.

"I am here to see Francois Ronen. Monsieur Ronen."

"Ah, oui, Monsieur Ronen."

"Oui, Monsieur Ronen. Is he here?"

Realising the nurse speaks little English, Lori decides to push a little. "Does anyone speak Anglais?"

"A minute," the nurse replies. She returns through the inner door. Soon an older, more official looking female nurse arrives. She unlocks the outer door and stands looking at Lori.

"What do you want?"

Feeling relief that her English is good, Lori smiles. "Yes, hello, I have come to see my partner, Francois Ronen. Is he here?"

"Oui, he is here."

"Can I see him?"

"No."

"Why not? I have come all the way from the UK. Please, he's my partner."

"Sorry, but no. He has not been here long, and he can't receive any visitors yet. He is ill."

"What's wrong with him?"

The nurse stares at Lori, looking slightly bewildered. "You are at hospital psychiatrie," she replies.

Feeling stupid and utterly heartbroken, Lori feels her eyes well as it dawns on her that she is stuck in France for a week, unable to see Francois. After thanking the nurse, she leaves.

Walking quickly out of the hospital grounds and past the security building, she walks up the road a little. Then she decides to call Elijah.

"Elijah, he's in a psychiatric hospital."

"Oh, Lori, I'm sorry."

"You're sorry? What do you mean? You knew?"

"Sorry, Lori. Francois asked me not to tell you. He loves you so much, and he's a strong, amazing man, but he's also fragile. I'm sorry, my friend."

"They won't let me see him, Elijah, I feel so sad."

"Courage, my friend. He loves you so much, Lori. He called you his angel."

"I'm not an angel. I'm not perfect. I love him too."

"What will you do?"

"I'll have to spend the week in his apartment, then return to the UK. I'm so worried about him."

"I know, Lori, I know."

"I'll call you when I'm back in England. Kiss you."

"Kiss you too, Lori. We'll speak soon."

Crossing over the road from the hospital, Lori finds a small stone seat overlooking a river and sits. She feels all alone, her heart crushed. Then all at once, the worry and stress of the last few days, along with her bitter disappointment of not being able to see Francois, overwhelms her. As the tears roll down her face, wetting the stone floor beneath her, she sits with her with her head in her hands and her elbows on her knees, lost in sorrow.

CHAPTER 22

The Apple

Autumn has arrived, and Lori is on a flight to visit Francois again, having booked herself into a small hotel in Old Nice harbour. She has missed him terribly and decides to go to the hospital straight from the airport. This time determined to fight his corner, she is eager to protect him. She is also impatient to find out what is happening and how long he must stay.

When she arrives at reception, this time she is more confident. After finding out which ward Francois is on, she makes her way there, still pulling her suitcase. After passing three tall white stone buildings, she arrives at a fourth, as instructed.

Looking up between the leaves of a nearby palm tree at the blue sky, her eyes are then drawn to the bars on the windows, the contrast of beauty and ugliness undeniable.

"Why bars?" she whispers, not understanding the need for them at first, then concluding that they were put in place to stop people from falling out—or jumping. She shudders at the thought of Francois in such a place.

Checking the ward's name on the placard outside, her heart beats with excitement. At long last she is about to see Francois again.

She notices a little camera lens looking at her at the top of the panel after she presses the buzzer.

"Oui?" a voice says.

"Hello, I have come to see Monsieur Ronen, Francois."

"Okay come."

The door clicks. Pushing it open, Lori is met by a tiny lobby. On the other side are old, tatty elevator doors. She presses the button and waits. For a couple of seconds, nothing happens. Eventually, a clunking, scraping sound emerges as the elevator descends, and the doors open. Lori presses the top button, and the elevator crawls back up, reaching the third floor. With no idea what to expect, having never visited anyone in a psychiatric hospital before, Lori feels nervous.

The doors crank open, and she is met by the sight of a long lime-green corridor and a waft of cleaning chemicals. She walks to the other end, where she reaches a door with a small window in it. She peers through and looks into the ward.

Feeling as though she has just been catapulted into another world, she notices a couple of patients wandering around as if in a dream-like state. Pressing yet another buzzer, she waits. Shortly afterwards a nurse appears at the window, and the door opens.

"Come," she says. She's dressed in pale blue cotton and wearing white clogs. She gestures for Lori to follow her down a corridor. The corridor is lined with doors, most of which are open. As she passes, Lori glances inside the rooms to see patients lying on their beds. Others are sitting in chairs, and still others are shuffling up and down the corridor.

As she observes this strange, new existence, Lori notices their dead eyes, thinking that maybe the culprit for this is their medication. They pass by a man dressed in a stained grey jogging outfit, and he smiles.

"Bonjour," he says to Lori, his eyes surrounded by deep, dark circles.

Just then a young female patient comes bounding up to them, her hair in pigtails. She's dressed in peach-coloured pyjamas and carrying a giant teddy bear. Overly excited, when she spots Lori, she shrieks. The nurse says something to her in French to warn her off, and the young woman retreats, running back down the corridor, giggling in manic fashion. Unfazed and anxious to see Francois, Lori doesn't care. Just then the nurse stops outside another door, which is slightly ajar.

"Monsieur Ronen," she announces. After looking Lori up and down with an expression of disbelief on her face, she walks away.

Sighing with relief, her heart racing in anticipation of what state Francois might be in, Lori opens the door, closing it behind her. It's a drab room, with pale blue stone walls and two beds, one unoccupied and the other with Francois sitting on the side with his back towards her. Delighted to finally see him, she smiles and walks over to him. Awash with a mixture of emotions as she approaches the bed, Francois doesn't even look up. Lori sees that he is eating an apple and staring at the floor. Lori sits on the other bed, but he still doesn't register that she is there, continuing to eat the apple. Deciding to sit quietly for a few minutes. Then, noticing he is about to eat the core, she speaks up.

"Francois, it's me, my love. Don't eat that bit."

Slowly looking up at her face, he appears bewildered. She notices the same dark circles around his dead eyes, just like the others. He is lost and vulnerable and in his own world.

Feeling extremely sad, her eyes welling up with tears, Lori leans forward and takes the apple core from Francois's hand. He doesn't say a word, just looks at her in silence. Lori turns to look at the bars on the window, then back at Francois, sunshine beaming on his face.

"Francois, it's me, baby. Are you okay?"

Lori sits next to him. She takes his hand in hers, kissing his forehead, then his lips

She glances at the clock upon the wall, frustrated that the hour she has been given is already ticking by. Hearing the voices of excitable and sorrowful patients accompanied by the occasional remark from a nurse echoing up and down the corridor, she gets up to look through the iron-barred window. The contrast between the hospital's drab, miserable interior and the light breeze swaying the tops of the palm trees is even more evident now. Her heart sinks for him and what he must endure, medicated into a zombie-like state. She returns to his side and comforts him until it's time for her to leave.

Catching the bus back to the centre of Nice, she takes out her map, following the route to her hotel. After walking up a short hill from the marina, she arrives at an old, traditional three-story stone building. The windows and their pretty shutters are surrounded by a creeping vine of red flowers. A small, charming garden is located at the front of the hotel. After checking in, Lori goes to her room to rest.

The next morning Lori sets off early, arriving at the hospital optimistic that Francois may be a little more communicative this time. Having been given two hours this time, she is looking forward to seeing him again.

A male nurse beckons Lori to follow him to the ward garden. When she arrives at the garden, Lori sees a rectangle of stone with eight or nine patients sitting at plastic chairs at plastic tables. To the right is a grassy slope with flowering shrubs, along with three wooden benches positioned in between. Another nurse is sitting outside near the door, looking through his paperwork.

"Francois is out here," the nurse says, then he leaves. Lori looks at all the patients and notices the young woman again, still clutching the giant teddy bear. She giggles like a four-year-old as she wanders in between the other patients, causing some to become irritated, and they shoo her away. Male and female patients of varying ages sit and stand, some in silence and others chatting together. Then she spots Francois. He's sitting on one of the wooden benches far from the others, up on the grassy slope. He's talking to an old lady. Lori walks over to see him, and much to her delight, he speaks.

"Baby," he gasps. "Baby, I missed you." His voice sounds hoarse and tired.

"I missed you too!"

He stands, and they embrace, kissing each other on the lips. Then they sit on the bench next to the old lady, wrapped in each other's arms.

Lori decides not to mention the day before, and they talk and talk as the old lady listens intently.

"This is Clementine," Francois says. "Her family put her here. She's old and fragile, and they are fighting for her money."

Lori looks at the old lady and smiles, not sure what to think but pleased at Francois's kindness and for taking her under his wing.

Typical Francois, she thinks, fighting for the underdog being a common occurrence for him.

"Bonjour, Clementine."

The old lady holds out her thin, trembling hand and shakes Lori's hand. She smiles, muttering something in French to Francois.

"She said you are beautiful, my darling," Francois explains, his voice proud. Lori chuckles. Then he takes Lori's hand and kisses it tenderly.

They talk non-stop for the duration of the visit as the old lady looks on, happy to be in the company of two lovebirds.

The week passes quickly. On the last day, Lori is growing short of money. She stops by a bakery and chooses a little square chocolate cake. She cuts it in half, eating her half on the bus and saving the other for Francois.

After arriving at the hospital for the last time before she has to return to England, she makes her way through the hospital grounds to Francois's building when, much to her surprise, she hears someone calling her name.

"Lori! Baby, it's me!"

She looks up to find Francois holding his hands through the bars of one of the top windows, waiting to greet her.

"I'll be up in a minute, baby," she says. Her heart melts with love, then sadness at seeing him like that, the bars troubling her.

He looks like a prisoner, she thinks. *Poor Francois. It's horrible.*

Back in his ward, they sit on his bed, and she reaches for her bag. "I've brought you some chocolate cake. Well, half. I ate the other half on the way here."

She passes it to him and smiles. Francois eagerly opens the bag and looks inside. "You saved half for me?"

"Yes, you needed a treat."

Francois begins to cry.

"Don't cry, baby. It's okay. It's only cake."

"You're my angel, Lori. I love you with all my heart and soul."

"I love you too, my darling. It's nothing."

"It's something to me. I love you, baby."

Lori puts her arms around Francois, and he rests his head upon her breast and weeps.

"It's okay, Francois. I'm going to get you out of here, baby."

"But how?"

"I don't know, but I will. I promise. You've been here too long, my darling. I promise you, I'll find a way."

CHAPTER 23

Trapped

————◆————

It's been fourteen months since Francois arrived at St Maine Hospital, and Lori is getting increasingly worried. Trying to resolve the situation from afar whilst living in England while only being able to speak minimal French is proving to be fruitless. Each phone call to the hospital is no more productive than the last, and with nobody else appearing to be fighting in Francois's corner, his confinement is dragging on and on.

Finally, Lori decides to travel to France to meet the hospital management team to get some answers. After several calls to the hospital, she manages to secure a meeting with the director of patient care. After that she immediately books a flight. She is also given the number for the phone in the ward, so she rings to speak to Francois.

"Oui?" a patient says.

"Bonjour, Francois Ronen, si vous plait."

"Quel?"

"Francois Ronen, Monsieur Ronen."

"Quel?"

"Can you get the nurse?"

Lori hears the phone cable rocking back and forth as the patient leaves it dangling and walks away.

"Hello … hello!"

"Hello, baby, it's me," Francois replies, his voice weary, masked by strong medication.

"Oh, thank God. How are you, baby?"

"Not so good. They're horrible here."

"What has the doctor said? When can you leave?"

"He says another six months. He's crazy. I'm well."

"Six months?"

"Oui, six months."

"The psychiatrist is crazy. Why so long? That's ridiculous, Francois. Why is your voice so weak? I'm worried. Are you okay?"

Now losing the will to fight, Francois's spirit is broken. "Lori, my darling, there's no hope. You must understand that."

Lori sits on the floor, still holding the receiver. There is silence between them for a moment. "Don't say that, Francois. I'm going to help you."

"Lori, I want to tell you something."

"What, baby?"

"Give up on me. Just give up. There's no hope. I'm finished, and you're wasting your life, my darling. Give up on me, and go meet somebody else."

They both begin to cry.

"No, I won't, baby! Don't say that! I don't want anybody else. I'm not giving up on you. I've booked a flight, and I'm going to rescue you. You mustn't give up. I love you, Francois, I love you."

Lori feels desperate, filled with fear and sadness. "Francois, Francois, are you there? Francois!"

She's distraught, her heart broken, worried he has hung up. There is silence, then to her relief, he speaks.

"Are you sure you want me?" Francois asks, tears streaming down his face.

"Francois, I've wanted you my whole life. Yes, I will never give up on you. In three weeks, I have a meeting with someone high up at the hospital. I will find out what's going on. Just give me time."

"Someone is trying to keep me here; I know it."

"I love you, Francois. I can't forget you."

"I love you too. I have to go now though. Another patient wants to use the phone. They say I've been on it for too long."

"Okay, darling. We'll talk again soon, okay? Never give up."

"I love you, Lori. Kiss you."

"I love you too."

Searching for a piece of music on her laptop, she finds "comptine d'un autre ete I-apres midi" by Yann Tiersen, their tune of love. As she listens to the music, she hangs her head and sobs.

It's late morning when she arrives in Nice, taking a taxi to the same hotel near the marina. After taking a shower, she lies on the bed thinking about the coming days. Running through what she might say in her upcoming meeting, she's determined to get a good result for Francois.

Her hair still wet and her cheeks flushed from her hot shower, her phone rings. She looks at the call display, but she doesn't recognise the number.

"Hello."

"Hello, Lori," a lady says with a strong French accent. "It's Delmare, Francois's maman. Elijah gave me your number."

"Oh, hello," Lori replies, not knowing what to say.

"My dear, I have moved back from Israel, and I now live near Nice. We must meet. Can you meet tomorrow?"

"Yes, um, that would be nice."

"You know my son has a mental illness. Can I ask you, are you going to stay with him? It will break his heart if you don't. You know he loves you so much."

"I don't care about the mental illness. I love him too."

"Hotel Negresco is opposite the beach. Do you know it?"

"No but I'll find it. Let me write it down. Okay, what time?"

"Eleven thirty."

"Okay, see you tomorrow."

"Yes, my darling, tomorrow. Goodbye."

Lori dries her hair and applies some makeup. Then she gets dressed and heads out in search of some lunch.

Halfway down the hill from the hotel, she stops and sits on a bench. Taking out her map, she takes a couple of minutes to study the area, then continues on.

While walking around the marina, she passes by the ruins of Colline Chateau. Turning up a side street, she stumbles across a quaint little restaurant. Met by a tantalizing aroma seeping out from the kitchen, she looks at the menu and sees specials for pizza, pasta and seafood salad.

The roof is awash of blue flowers, and the windows are decorated with pale blue wooden shutters. Elegant curved white seats are placed upon the cobblestone, each with varying colours of pretty cushions. Deciding to take an early lunch, Lori sits at a table with two chairs. Soon, a waiter approaches, and upon his recommendation she orders a fresh salmon salad followed by a glass of chilled rosé.

As she waits for her meal to arrive, she closes her eyes. With the warm sun shining on her face, she smiles, allowing herself to relax a little as she listens to the sound of the hustle and bustle around her. Remembering her phone call with Francois, however, her feeling is short lived. When she opens her eyes and looks at the empty chair across from her, her heart sinks.

Following her meal, she arrives at the promenade. Lori remembers Francois walking beside her, and she feels profoundly sad, wishing she could hold his hand. She fights back tears, not wanting to ruin her makeup.

As she nears the hotel, realising she is about to meet Francois's mother for the first time empty handed, she turns up a side street in search of a gift. She stumbles across an old arcade full of boutiques. As she walks through the arched entrance, she notices the lattice of sculpture within the iron roof. The sun shines through the old stained-glass, creating a sea of colour on the white marble floor.

Enchanted by the array of beautiful things, she looks through the windows of the boutiques until she finds one selling women's accessories. She looks through rack and racks of chic belts, tailored hats, silk scarves, designer sunglasses and beautiful pens. One pen in particular catches her eye. It's a fountain pen encrusted with diamond and pearl beads. After getting it gift wrapped, she heads towards the hotel.

As she approaches, Lori looks up at the magnificent white stone building. Its peach-coloured roof houses a circular section with the name of the hotel in large gold letters. With no idea what Delmare looks like, she walks up the steps towards the terrace, as instructed. After surveying the people at the tables for a few moments, she notices two people looking over at her. One is a very attractive lady, smartly dressed with a deep suntan and an immaculately made-up face. Beside her is an older man in crisp white shirt and tailored trousers wearing thick sunglasses.

"Lori!" the lady calls, waving her hand. It's Delmare. "Lori, hello, come."

Lori walks over to join them, not knowing what to say.
"Lori, you're here, my darling. It's good to meet you." Delmare takes Lori's arms and pulls her close to kiss each cheek.

"It's good to meet you too, Delmare."

"You would like a glass of wine?"

"Okay, why not? Yes, please. This is for you." Lori takes out the gift-wrapped pen from her bag and hands it to Delmare. Looking intrigued, Delmare opens it.

"Thank you, my darling. It's beautiful."

Lori notices that Delmare looks genuinely touched.

"This is my brother, Gustave," Delmare says, introducing the man next to her.

"It's nice to meet you," Lori replies, shaking his hand. Delmare and Gustave smile. After conversing in French for a minute, they look at Lori.

"You have come to see Francois?" Delmare asks.

"Yes. I'm going later today. I hope he's okay."

Again, they converse in French. Lori notices Gustave seems flustered and annoyed with Delmare. Unable to understand what is being said, Lori decides to ignore it.

"My son has spoken so kindly about you. You make him happy."

"Thank you, Delmare. I'm so happy to see him."

After chatting for another thirty minutes, Lori finishes her wine and decides to leave.

"I'm going to get the bus now. It was so nice to meet you both."

She stands up to embrace them.

"Gustave brought me here," Delmare announces, appearing embarrassed.

After saying goodbye, Lori heads back towards the city centre. As she walks, she can't help but wonder why Gustave didn't offer her a lift to the hospital or at least ask how she was getting there. Then, remembering the tension between him and Delmare, she brushes it off and continues toward her bus stop.

When she arrives at the hospital, Lori makes her way to the reception area, ready for her meeting with the director. After a long wait, she is taken through the building to an elevator, accompanied by a woman wearing a stern expression. Soon they are joined by another staff member. Lori watches as they exchange a few words in French, the second woman looking at Lori. Noticing a smirk on the woman's face, Lori glares at her as they arrive at the upper level. As the doors open, they are met by a plush office suite. A secretary directs Lori to follow her, and they walk on a luxurious carpet down a short hall decorated with fine oil paintings.

"In here, please," the secretary says.

They enter a large office. Sitting at a big desk is an attractive, immaculately dressed woman wearing a designer suit.

"This is Madame Aubert," the secretary says, "the director."

Shortly afterwards, the other woman from the elevator joins them and is introduced as one of the ward managers.

"Please sit," the secretary says, pointing to an empty chair.

"What is it you want?" the director asks, getting straight to the point.

"I want to know when Francois will be discharged. He's been here so long. What's the plan for him?"

"He is ill, Madame," the director retorts.

"I know he became ill, but he's better now and desperate to leave. He's been here for months and months."

"He and his mother do not get along."

Lori stares at the director, not quite knowing how to respond, having very little knowledge of Francois's relationship with Delmare.

"But he was in his own apartment."

"But now he can't live there, and he wants to live with his mother, but she is delicate too."

Lori frowns in confusion. "Okay, fine, but could you please tell me how long he'll be here?"

"I will look into it, but now I have another meeting," the director replies, her manner unconvincing.

Hugely disappointed, Lori gets up to leave, realising there is little she can do, especially living in a different country. Deciding she can only hope for the best, she thanks the director for the meeting and then makes her way over to the ward to see Francois.

At the ward, Lori follows a nurse who leads her to a large room with what appears to be grooming equipment on a long steel table. Standing next to the table with a male nurse is Francois, having his fingernails clipped. Lori notices he appears vulnerable, his face ashen and his hands trembling. The male nurse does not notice Lori standing in the doorway at first. He speaks to Francois in an impatient manner as Francois holds out his fingers. The nurse glances at the doorway. Surprised to see Lori standing there, he smiles, and his demeanour changes, his voice becoming calmer as he continues to speak to Francois. Lori looks on, making it clear she noticed, waiting until after the nurse has finished.

"Francois," she says, but he does not look her way. "Francois, it's me, my love."

Francois stares at her with a blank expression on his face. Noticing the dark circles around his eyes, she realises he has become conditioned to his environment, and he does not recognise her. She walks over to him, putting her arms around his shoulders.

"Baby, it's me," she whispers, kissing him on the cheek.

"Garden," the nurse suggests, still standing in the doorway. He points to the door. Lori takes Francois's hand, leading him out to the garden. As Francois walks with her, he doesn't say a word.

"I missed you, baby. I love you," Lori says, her voice soft and reassuring.

When they arrive at the garden, Lori leads him up the grassy slope to a bench in the shade, and they sit.

"Are you okay, Francois?"

He looks at her in bewilderment as tears well up in her eyes. Then at last he speaks.

"Yes."

"Francois, it's me, baby. It's me, Lori."

As he looks at her, a smile appears on his face. Now recognising her, he begins to cry. Putting her arms around him, Lori offers him comfort.

"Don't cry, baby. It's going to be okay. I'm trying to get you out of here."

They sit in the garden for the rest of the hour, then it's time for Lori to leave.

Some of the patients are starting to make their way inside for dinner.

"You come tomorrow?" Francois asks as his mind begins to clear from the haze of the strong medication.

"Yes, I will see you tomorrow, Francois."

She kisses him on the lips and then leaves.

The next day after arriving at the hospital early, Lori is taken to a different area within the ward. Told to follow a tall middle-aged male nurse, she is led through a secure door and then into a much quieter corridor with only two doors leading off it. Muttering something in French, the nurse stops outside the second door, indicating Francois is inside. As she watches the nurse walk away, Lori is curious as to why Francois is in this new area.

She opens the door and peers inside. To her horror, she finds him in a tiny, dingy room lying on a plastic bed covered with a thin sheet and a blue blanket. On the floor is a vertical urinating bottle. The window is covered with dense faded plastic that blocks out the sunlight. His trembling is more profound now, and his handsome face is marred by a shaving cut. He attempts to smile to welcome her.

"Francois, what are you doing in here, baby? It's horrible!"

"Don't mind, baby," he replies, his voice hoarse.

"I do mind. Why are you in this horrible room?"

"They've isolated me."

Lori looks around the room. "Isolated you? Why?"

"I couldn't cope with the medicine, and I had an argument with a nurse, so now I'm here."

Deciding to try and cheer Francois up, she takes out her mobile phone and starts to film him.

"You look like Elvis, baby. You look so handsome."

Just then the same tall, miserable male nurse pops his head in the door to check on them. He says something in French to Francois. Francois offers an angry retort, and the nurse leaves.

"What's the matter, Francois? What did he say?"

Francois lies back on the bed. Lori does the same, wanting to comfort him. As they hold each other, they don't care about the drab, miserable room anymore. Intertwined on the bed, they are silent, lost in thought. They're so happy to be together again, they could be lying on golden sands on a beach in paradise.

"He asked what you're doing with me," Francois says.

"That's horrible! What fucking idiot. He can't speak to patients like that."

"They do here, baby."

"Don't worry, sweetie. I love you. It's not his business. What did you say back to him?"

"I told him that, that it's not his business."

They smile.

Their hour passes quickly, and soon a female nurse arrives, informing Lori that she must leave.

Placing her hands on either side of Francois's face, Lori kisses him goodbye. "Be strong, baby," she whispers.

"See you tomorrow."

Feeling sad and finding it difficult to leave him, she forces herself to walk away, giving Francois a little smile as she leaves the room.

The next morning, Lori goes in search of a restaurant closer to her hotel and heads down the hill toward the marina. As she wanders along the quayside, feeling very alone, she thinks of Francois. The wonderful boats and beautiful buildings don't register. How she wishes he was with her to enjoy the day. She sighs deeply at having to endure this cruel separation.

When she reaches the cobblestone street that leads to the restaurants, Lori passes an old stone building and notices a scruffy man sitting on the steps at the entrance. Watching him mutter to himself, she notices his vulnerability, and her mind turns to the patients at the hospital.

She finds a pizza restaurant and decides to eat there. She goes inside and sits at the window. Shortly afterwards, a waiter appears.

"Bonjour, mademoiselle."

"Bonjour." She smiles. Then he continues to speak in French.

"Sorry, I'm English," she says. "I would like a pizza."

"Ah, English, my uncle is there in London. I have been."

"I'm not sure which one to choose," Lori replies, looking at the menu.

"Allow me. You like olives?"

"Yes, I love them."

"Try the Passaladiere, wonderful."

"Okay I will. I'll have an orange juice too please."

While she waits for her meal, she scrolls through her cell phone, reading old text messages from Francois and looking at photographs. She can't wait to see him again.

After finishing her lunch, the waiter arrives.

"You enjoy?"

"Yes, lovely."

"You see I recommend the best. You are exploring Nice?"

"Yes, I am. I have family here." She stops herself from mentioning the hospital, not wishing to explain her business. With a sinking feeling in her stomach, she hides her sadness behind a smile.

Upon arrival at the hospital, she finds Francois in a nervous state. He's naked from the waist up in a shower room, his hair dirty and matted.

"Baby!" he cries. Can you help me?

"Hi, Francois. What's wrong, my love? You look terrible!"

"They won't help me shower. I'm too weak. I'm too weak."

"It's okay, Francois, calm down. I'll help you. Do you have a towel?"

"No, I can't find it, and they won't give me another. Look, I'm trembling. It's the medicine, baby. The drugs are too strong, too strong."

"Francois, be calm, baby. I know. I'm not happy about it. I'll ask the nurses for a towel."

Wandering up the corridor, Lori finds two nurses chatting in one of the medical rooms.

"Excuse me," Lori says. "I need a towel for Francois."

They turn to look at her, not understanding English, then carry on chatting. Impatient and annoyed, Lori goes in search of another nurse. Unable to find anyone, she heads back to the shower room to check on Francois.

As she enters, she finds Francois with a very frustrated male nurse. Lori watches as he slings a towel at Francois. Wanting to tell the nurse off, she's frustrated at her limited knowledge of French. Instead, she scowls at him as he walks past, leaving her and Francois alone.

"They're horrible here," he says.

"I know. I can see that. Don't worry, baby. You won't be here much longer. I promise. Come on, take off your shorts. I'll help you, Francois."

After he struggles to remove his shorts, she eases him into the shower cubicle. Gently rubbing shampoo into his hair, she washes his face and body, feeling sad to witness him trembling throughout. After helping him out of the shower, she pats him dry, wrapping the towel around his head, then kissing his nose. After retrieving his shorts, between them they pull them up, then make their way to his bedroom.

"Francois, my love, you know this is my last day here."

"I know. I'll miss you so much." Francois begins to cry.

"Don't cry, baby. I promise I'll come again soon."

Wrapped in each other's arms and kissing, they sit on the bed in silence, both of them periodically glancing at the clock until the time comes for Lori to leave. A nurse arrives at the bedroom door to accompany her to the elevator. They kiss again, both of them torn at having to say goodbye again. A tear rolls down Lori's face, and she stands.

"Bye, Francois. I'll call you tomorrow."

"Bye, baby. I love you so much."

"I love you too."

As Lori makes her way out the building, she hears Francois say her name. Turning around, she looks up to see him standing at the window on the top floor, his hands gripping the bars. Her heart skips a beat, filled with sorrow at the sight of him.

"I love you, Lori!" he cries.

"I love you too!"

"Bye, my love."

"Bye, Francois."

Her voice breaks, unable to say anything more. She forces herself to walk away, glancing back at him several times until she turns the corner of another building and he is out of sight. Only then does she finally allow her emotions to come rushing to the surface. As she cries, the thought of him standing at that barred window like a prisoner is simply too much to bear.

CHAPTER 24

A Sense of Home

Francois has finally been given leave from the hospital. Having already arrived in Nice, Lori arranges to meet him at her hotel room the following morning.

As the warm sun creeps up the building, casting dappled silhouettes from the olive trees, Lori is awoken by the sound of her cell phone ringing. Her eyes half open, she searches under the bed cover as it continues to ring. Then, spotting it on the floor, she stretches down to retrieve it. When she looks at the screen, a smile appears across her face. It's Francois.

"Baby, I come. I'm on the bus." His voice, childlike with excitement, causes Lori's face to light. up.

"Hi, baby. What time do you think you'll be here?"

"Maybe ten."

"What time is it now?"

"It's gone nine, my love."

"Oh! I thought it was earlier. Okay, I need to shower. I can't wait to see you, Francois."

"Me too, my darling."

"You know where to come?"

"Yes. I have the address. See you soon, I'm going to ring Elijah."

"Okay. Bye. I love you."

"Bye, my love. I love you too, Lori."

After taking a shower and styling her hair, Lori searches through her clothes, opting to wear shorts and a blouse. Applying some pretty shimmering makeup, she looks into the mirror, satisfied, then puts on her sandals. Shortly after that her cell phone rings again. It's Francis. He sounds breathless.

"Hi, baby. I'm walking up the hill."

"Are you okay?"

"No, my feet are bleeding."

"Bleeding!"

"Yes, I'm here now, at the hotel."

"Okay, hold on. I'll come down."

Lori finds Francois sitting on the small stone wall surrounding the garden.

"Francois, let me see your feet."

Lori looks at the bottoms of his feet and gasps when she sees broken, bloody blisters.

"I got them at the hospital. They've all popped," Francois says, wincing in pain.

"Oh my god, baby. Come in. I'll ask the owner for some plasters."

After being given a handful of plasters, they make their way up a short flight of stairs to Lori's room.

"Baby, leave your flip-flops on the floor. Come in the bathroom, and we'll wash your feet. You'll feel better."

Standing in the shower and wincing in pain, Francois waits patiently as Lori holds the shower head over the soles of his feet. After all the blood and grit is washed away, he sits on the bed as she dabs them dry with toilet tissue, then applies the plasters.

"How's that?" she asks. "Are they less painful?"

"Yes, thank you."

They look at each other for a few moments, their love profound, not needing to say a word to each other.

"You suffered to get here."

"I wanted to see you. I love you, Lori. So strongly, so intensely."

"I love you too, Francois."

Sitting together on the bed, they kiss tenderly, wrapped in each other's arms, so happy to be together.

"I'll have an apartment soon," he says. "I'll be discharged next month. I'm moving in with Maman first. Then after that the apartment."

"Wow, that's great! I'll come again then. Will your maman be happy for me to visit at her house?"

"Yes. I told her you are like a wife to me, that you are the one. She is happy you make me happy. She has never let a girlfriend stay at her house before, but with you it's different. She says you have changed me. You are my true love. I've missed you so much, Lori. They took me to see the apartment. It's very petite."

"But you'll be free!"

"Free without you?"

"Do you want to stay in France? Maybe in the future I could move to France."

"I hate France."

"Why? It's so beautiful."

"I don't feel safe here. Anti-Semitism is not good."

"I'm angry about that. Who the hell do these people think they are? It's your country. You can live wherever you bloody wish, baby!"

"Bloody? What is bloody?"

"It's a British swear word."

"Oh."

"Francois, please tell me what happened to you." Lori gently places her hand on Francois's face. "What's that scar on your stomach? How did you get it? You mentioned something about your apartment in Paris too, something about an attack."

"Now isn't a good time."

"Francois, I want to know. I need to know. Why do you get anxious? Why do you get ill? Why do you get depressed? I really want to help you. Please tell me what happened to you. Please, Francois."

Francois looks into her eyes for a moment, then turns to look out the window. "Okay, okay."

As he navigates his memories, Francois's demeanour changes, and his anxiety evident, his hands trembling. Periodically as he speaks, he stares into oblivion. He is close to tears as he relives each harrowing event as if in real time. In the depths of his soul, he is taken right back there as he reopens doors he has fought so hard to seal, time and time again.

Lori listens intently, hanging on his every word. She needs to know the truth about what triggers his fragilities. Hiding her shock as each disclosure is unravelled, she clutches his hand, offering solace and understanding.

"I'm so sorry all these things have happened to you, Francois. It's terrible. I want you to know it's never going to happen again, okay?" Lori pulls him closer, trying to comfort him. "I want you to know you're safe now. Tell me everything. I'm here for you."

Francois smiles, happy he has finally found someone who cares so deeply about him. Taking her hand as they lie down on the bed, he kisses it. Lori lays her head on his chest and listens attentively as Francois lets her in. Out it pours, one traumatic event after another, until finally he stops, with nothing more to say. As he weeps, she kisses him, pulling him close, and for the first time for a long while, he feels loved.

"Thank you for telling me, Francois. I had no idea that Jewish people still have this problem. I'll protect you."

They lie in silence for a while. Then he smiles at her, and they kiss.

"I like England," he says. "It's safer there."

"England? Well, maybe. I don't hear about it, really, but are you sure? France is wonderful."

"Wonderful for you but not for me anymore. I want to go."

"Francois, are you saying you'd like to live with me?"

"Yes, I would love to live with you."

They smile at each other, happy that they now have a plan.

Over the course of the week, Lori visits Francois in the hospital, again. Then he is given more leave, and they excitedly discuss their future together, both looking forward to when they will be living together.

Late one evening when she's back in England, Lori receives a call.

"I'm out!"

"Out?"

"I've moved in with Maman until my new apartment is ready."

"That's great! I can't believe it. Finally."

"Maman says you can come to stay. She has never let a girlfriend stay before, but she respects you, and she knows how much you've helped me. But first I'm going to come to you at the beginning of December."

"Wow, amazing. Yes, come."

Now renting a house in a small market town in Hampshire, Lori has begun to search for an apartment to buy. She has sold her house in south Wales, and she wants to put some distance between her old life and her fresh start.

Standing at arrivals at Heathrow Airport she is ecstatic as she waits for Francois to appear. Before long he arrives along with a crowd of other people. When he spots Lori, he trudges over to her, his head down. Confused at his lack of enthusiasm, Lori is disappointed.

"Francois! Hello, baby. What's wrong?"

Francois looks down at her feet. "I don't like them."

"What?"

"Your boots, baby."

"Oh my God, Francois, is that why you're looking glum? Wow, French men are fussy!"

They both smile, then they kiss and embrace.

"Come on, let's go," she says. Holding hands, they make their way out of the terminal to the carpark.

Back home, they eat dinner, then go to bed early. After making love, they fall asleep in each other's arms.

The week is busy as they explore the town and go out to eat, so happy to be together again. They try not to mention the day that Francois must return to France until the night before.

Driving to the airport, both of them are sad. Francois places his hand on top of Lori's periodically.

"I'll miss you, baby, so much. I love you."

"I love you too, Francois. I'll be buying an apartment, and soon we can be together."

When they arrive at the airport, they go to buy a coffee. Then they wait, holding hands across a table. With the noise from the busy airport washing over them, they are locked into each other's thoughts.

As they walk towards the departures area, their eyes filled with tears, they each find it difficult to let go. They whisper sweet sentiments, each trying to comfort the other.

When they finally reach departures, their hearts sink. They kiss and hug, both of them profoundly sad at having to part from each other again. Having found their soul mates, they feel lost without the other, dreading the prospect of having to wait until they can be together again.

Lori watches as Francois walks away. He looks very handsome in his long black wool coat. As he enters the middle of the walkway, he stops and looks back at her. Lori wants so badly to run to him, but she stops herself, not wanting to make the situation any more difficult for him. Instead, she tries to smile.

"He doesn't want to leave you," a warm, elderly voice says. Looking to her left, Lori sees an elderly lady smiling at her. She smiles back.

"No, he doesn't," Lori replies. They watch as Francois finally turns and disappears down the walkway.

Her heart feeling heavy, Lori makes her way home.

Chapter 25

Sun, Fun and Romance

It's March 2010, and Lori and Francois are about to be reunited again. As she waits at the airport in Nice, Francois arrives in a silver Mercedes. Lori watches him get out of the car and smiles, admiring how handsome he looks wearing his black designer jacket. After kissing and hugging, they hold hands, and Francois wheels her case to the car.

When they arrive in Villeneuve Loubet, they make their way up a hill to Delmare's house, both of them blissfully happy to be together again. Listening to French music as they chat excitedly about the days ahead, for the first time in their lives they are two halves of a whole, equally as ease with each other's company.

When they arrive at a gated entrance to a modern development, full of beautiful white apartments and houses spread across three hills, they are waved on by a security guard. Set amongst a variety of flowering tropical plants, the immaculately kept lawns are dotted with an array of trees. Among them are palms, firs and the deep, fresh fragrance of pine. After driving past swimming pools, tennis courts, a restaurant and a delightful food shop set in a cobblestone courtyard in the heart of the village, they arrive at his mother's house.

"We're here."

"It's beautiful."

Francois wheels Lori's case down a few steps until they arrive at a white wooden gate. When they open it, they are met by a large olive tree to the left, and opposite is a white flowering jasmine tree, its sweet smell filling the air.

"Maman!" Francois calls out as he opens the front door. Sitting on a red sofa is Delmare. She looks very pretty in a brightly coloured long-sleeve top and smart blue jeans. Her hair is shoulder length and wavy, and her face is immaculately made up, her fingernails red. Francois and Delmare have a short conversation in French. Then Francois wheels Lori's case into the bedroom.

"Lori, come and sit with me," Delmare says. They embrace, and Lori kisses her on both cheeks.

"You don't know any French?"

"Very little, I'm sorry."

"My son loves you very deeply. He says you are his jewellery; you make him happy."

"Thank you. I love him too."

"You know, I never let a woman he has dated stay with me before, but with you it's different. He has changed, and you have changed him."

"Thank you for inviting me to stay."

The following evening Francois takes Lori to a nightclub next to the promenade in Nice. As they dance and have fun, they whisper sweetness and sentiments into each other's ears.

After leaving the club, they arrive at a bar and listen to a man playing guitar. Then Francois takes Lori's hand and kisses it tenderly. She is so happy to be romanced and loved.

The days pass quickly. On the third evening, Francois invites Lori to eat at a wonderful restaurant. Both of them are dressed up. They arrive at a classy white building with a large half-moon terrace lit by several pale pink lights. They approach a table with ample space around it, and Francois pulls out a chair for Lori.

As they wait for their meal, they sip rosé while looking up at the stars that fill the night sky. For the next hour Francois tells Lori more about his life, including his ninjutsu training, as she listens intently.

The next morning, they wake early, Francois's arms wrapped around Lori as they lie in bed together. They make their way to the terrace, where they sit with Delmare and eat breakfast.

"You know, my dear, Francois needs to take a medication."

"What do you mean?"

"To stop him from becoming ill."

"But I don't want Francois to be on strong medicine."

"But how will you stop him from becoming ill?"

"Stop, Maman, stop."

"But she needs to know!"

"You take it, you."

"Francois, my son, I'm trying to help you."

"Don't."

Lori and Francois return to the bedroom.

"Do you need to take a pill each day?"

"They make me ill. She needs to take a pill, not me."

"Then don't. Maybe all you need is therapy."

"I have a surprise for you, baby."

"What is it?"

"We're going to meet a very good friend of mine. His name is Gubear. He was in the hospital with depression. His father-in-law is Italian and has an apartment in the hills in the south of Italy. I have arranged for us to stay there."

"Wow, I can't believe it. When are we going?"

"Today, after breakfast."

"Thank you, baby. How exciting."

"We will go by autoroute, then stop to meet Gubear in Menton. It's the last town before Italy. Then we'll follow him to his father-in-law's house to get the keys. It's not far from the border. After that we will follow Gubear to the apartment."

"How long will we stay?"

"Three nights. Then we'll come back to Maman's."

Setting off after breakfast, before long they reach the autoroute. As they drive, Francois puts on a CD.

"I want you to listen to this band," he says. "They're great."

"What are they called?"

"Eskobar."

The first song is "Someone New."

"I love it," she says, "but the words are sad when he sings you're going to find someone new."

"Yes, but he also sings, 'I adore you.'"

Francois glances at Lori, and they both smile.

"Oui."

Francois takes her hand in his, both of them absorbed in each other's presence as the music plays.

"We just passed Monaco, baby."

"Yahoo!"

Eventually they reach Menton, stopping at the rear of some buildings that line the seafront. Francois switches to the radio, and the sound of a female French singer can be heard as they sit and wait for Gubear to arrive.

"It's lovely here. I love it. It's magical," Lori says, looking up at the multi-coloured buildings with their warm tones of pink, coral, lemon and red, some with olive-coloured shutters, others with balconies. In between the buildings is a peek at the palm trees that line the golden sands along the aquamarine sea. The small, romantic town is perfect for lovers. Francois puts his arm around her shoulders as they look at the view.

"Look that's Gubear's car," he says. "Here he is."

A car pulls up beside them, and out gets a tall, willowy man in his sixties. His glasses hang on a chain, resting against his white cotton shirt. Francois gets out of the car followed by Lori, who looks on as Francois and Gubear kiss each other's cheeks and embrace. Speaking in French, they both look at Lori and smile. Lori senses they are talking about her looks.

"This is my friend, Gubear, my darling."

"Hello." Gubear kisses Lori on both cheeks. "England, I love England, but it's cold sometimes. Great history. There's an outdoor market here today in Menton. You wish to visit, Lori? It's ten minutes' walk from here before we go to my father-in-law's apartment for the keys. What you think of the royal family?"

"Yes, sounds good, they're okay, yes," Lori replies, chuckling as she answers all of his questions.

Francois takes her hand as he and Gubear begin to chatter in French. Lori only catches the occasional word, but she doesn't care; she is happy.

When they arrive at the street market, they wander from stall to stall, stumbling across an olive grower. The fresh, plump juicy olives are irresistible. Each woven palm-leaf bowl displays a pyramid of each variety, along with wooden picks to taste. Francois takes an olive and lifts it to Lori's lips.

"Try it, my love."

It's drizzled in oil, with a scattering of red pepper flakes. Lori takes a bite. After licking her lips, she discreetly takes the stone from her mouth.

"Delicious. They're great, Francois. You try one."

She takes a pick, choosing a pale green olive surrounded by tiny cubes of cheese, then places it in Francois's mouth.

"Careful of the stone," she warns.

"I know, I know. I'm French!"

They both laugh.

"I'm going to look at those books over there," Francois says. "Did you see where Gubear went?"

"No, but he must be around here somewhere. I'm going to look at that stall at the back."

Lori wanders towards a curiosity stall at the rear of the market, casting her eyes over a variety of old and interesting vintage items, many of which are military collectables. Then something then catches her eye. Gasping in shock, she discovers the trader is also selling Nazi memorabilia—medals, badges and placards, each displaying a swastika and some with an eagle. Horrified, she turns to walk away, only to discover Francois is standing right behind her.

"Hi, baby. What are you looking at?"

"Nothing. Let's find Gubear."

As they walk away, Francois glances at the items on the table. Then he stops, a shocked and angry expression on his face.

"Fucking asshole," he says, looking at the trader.

"Don't worry, Francois. Let's go."

Lori takes his hand, and they walk away in silence.

"Don't worry about that idiot," she says. "Who would want to buy that shit anyway."

"People do, Lori."

"Well, they're horrible if they do. Let's go."

After buying lunch, they eat on route as they follow Gubear out of Menton. They reach the Frontiere St Ludovic Post and then finally enter Italy.

When they arrive at the nearest town to the border, Ventimiglia, they go to Gubear's father-in-law's apartment for coffee and to pick up the keys. Continuing on, they head up into the mountains.

After an hour or so they arrive at a tiny village full of quaint old stone buildings, with wooden shutters on their windows, set amongst thousands of pine and cedar trees that cover the mountains. In the centre of the village, a bumpy stone street twists off to the right, running slightly uphill. There's an old-fashioned pizza restaurant on one side and a café on the other. At the top of the curve stands a quaint old church, along with its white flaky paint and pictures of Mary holding Christ set back in alcoves.

They pull up outside an old wooden building, parking behind Gubear. Lori and Francois are eager to see the apartment, so happy to know that later they will be able to spend time with each other.

They follow Gubear up some steep steps, where he unlocks an old-fashioned wooden door. As they enter the apartment, they are met with delightful dark wooden floors and walls. Hanging on the walls are oil paintings depicting scenes of the Italian mountains. In the bedroom is a wooden bed along with a chequered blanket. The charming apartment is dreamy and picture postcard perfect.

"Come," Gubear says. Lori and Francois follow him into the bedroom, where he pushes open the shutters. The fresh scent from the trees fills the room, the view revealing the stunning beauty of the lush tree-covered mountains.

"What an amazing view," Gubear says. "Look, Francois."

"Yes, thank you, my friend."

"Thank you, Gubear," Lori adds. "It's lovely."

"Let's go eat at the pizza restaurant," Francois says. "Gubear has to get home soon."

"Yes, great," Lori replies.

Sitting in the sun, they enjoy three delicious pizzas topped with local herbs, vegetables and Italian cheese. As they eat, the tranquillity of their surroundings is magical. They chat and laugh, mixing with the locals.

"Time for me to go," Gubear announces, standing up. Francois and Lori kiss and embrace him. Then they wave him off as he drives away.

"Thank you for arranging for us to come here," Lori says.

"I did it for you, baby."

"Shall we go back to the apartment now? You look tired."

"Yes. It was the drive. Let's lie down for a while."

They make their way back to the apartment, where they fall asleep in each other's arms. Evening comes, and before long it's ink black outside with nothing to be heard but the sound of chirping crickets and the singing from the night birds amongst the trees.

At dawn, after making love they shower together. Then they dress quickly, excited to explore the village.

As they walk towards the centre, they discover they are near a deep, fast-flowing stream, along with a few people are sitting on rocks, dangling their feet into the crystal-clear pale blue water. Lori encourages Francois to do the same. The sight of the river is a welcoming respite from the heat. Lori climbs onto a rock, then steps across the river and sits on top of another. Francois hesitates, looking worried as he senses his vulnerability. She stands, reaching out her hand.

"It's okay, Francois, you can do it. It's shallow. Step over, take my hand."

Unbeknownst to Lori, this moment in time will be etched into her memory forever. Francois cautiously steps across the water, sitting next to her upon the rock. He takes off his tennis shoes, and they dangle their feet in the water, cooling off together.

The next day after deciding to take a coffee in the café, they venture out, exploring the village further.

Along the way they come across an old cobblestone square that appears to be lost in time, having never changed. Old Italian men dressed in black sit and chat, some playing board games others taking refuge from the heat in shaded corners. Brightly coloured flowers of deep red and pink cover some of the old stone buildings overlooking the square. Francois and Lori wander around the village hand in hand, taking in their surroundings.

After returning to the pizza restaurant for dinner, they head back to the apartment to rest. As they walk, they pass a little white church, and Lori is enchanted by its charm.

"Let's look inside, Francois."

"I can't. I'm Jewish."

"It doesn't matter if you're Jewish, baby. It will be interesting to look inside."

Lori goes into the church, but Francois hesitates, waiting outside.

"Come on, baby." Lori takes his hand, leading him inside.

They are met by the smell of old oak altars and sunbeams glistening through the tiny windows. Around the church are various artifacts of Christ and Mary. The white walls with flaking paint display paintings of landscapes, depicting the surrounding area.

Francois looks around in silence. "Come, Lori, let's go," he says finally.

As they leave the church, they are met by a parade of villagers following a priest dressed in a black robe carrying a large gold cross upon a black cane. They stop and kiss in the street as they watch them pass, witnessing a time-old tradition of this hidden gem in the mountains. After the parade passes, they make their way back to the apartment to rest and take shelter from the heat.

Opening the shutters in the bedroom, they gaze out the window, soaking up the breath-taking view of the tree-covered mountains, a vision buried deep in their hearts for ever more.

CHAPTER 26

The Rescue

It's early Autumn 2010. Lori has arrived in Nice. Francois has now moved out of Delmare's house and taken an apartment in central Nice. Looking out the window of the bus, Lori spots Francois waiting for her on the pavement wearing a rucksack on his back. She waves at him, then gets up to disembark. She has just arrived back in France, and they are delighted to see each other again, both of them with huge smiles on their faces. After embracing, they kiss.

"I missed you, my darling," he says.

"I missed you too."

Taking the handle of her case and then her hand, Francois leads the way.

"My apartment is in a Bonnifassi."

"Where?"

"It's a street stopped at the end not far from the city centre. The apartment, it's petite."

"Oh, you mean a cul-de-sac. It doesn't matter if the apartment is small, baby; we will be packing your things and leaving in a few days."

When they arrive at the centre of the city, they hop onto a tram that takes them up Boulevard Gambetta.

"We need to get off," Francois says. "It's two streets from here."

At the entrance to Impasse Bonnifassi, Francois leads Lori through an old cobblestone courtyard and into a wide stone building. The entrance hall, with old grey marble floor and dark oak doors, looks charming and elegant. Francois cautiously turns the lock in the door. Lori looks on, puzzled by his hesitancy.

"What's wrong, Francois?"

"Wait."

Putting his hand out to stop her from entering, he reaches up, edging his fingers along the top of the doorframe, feeling for something. Only then does Lori notice a cotton thread crisscrossing the door.

"What's that for, Francois?"

"It doesn't matter."

Realizing his ever-present fear of being attacked, due to the trauma of his past, is still haunting him, she feels sad, she decides not probe any further.

The snug, functional apartment will do for now, she thinks as she pokes her head around the corner.

"Petite, huh?"

"It's okay, baby. We're together."

"I'll be happy to live in England."

"Are you sure, Francois?"

"Yes, I love you, and I hate it here."

"I love it here, but I understand it's different for you," Lori replies, slightly disappointed that she will experience the beauty of the south of France less often. "Anyway, we'll be together, and you'll feel safer."

"Are you hungry?" Francois asks.

"Yes."

"Then let's go."

Deciding to make a salad, they purchase a hot cooked chicken, luscious plump tomatoes and vibrant leafy greens from a small delicatessen. They also stop by a wine store and pick up a bottle of cool rosé. Then they make their way back to the apartment.

Sitting at the small circular dining table, they eat in silence, each of them occasionally glancing out the window and smiling at each other in between eating and sipping their wine. After lunch they laze the afternoon away listening to music, stretched across the bed as they excitedly plan their future together.

With only two days left before they fly to England, they spend their time visiting the beach and the shops, gradually saying goodbye to Nice.

On the morning of the flight, Lori helps Francois to pack his case.

"I have a bit of room in my case. Put your shoes in there, baby," she says.

Kneeling side by side on the floor, they squish as many items as possible into their luggage.

"I'll put my laptop in my rucksack," he says.

"Okay. I can put your jacket in mine. It won't fit in your case. We need to go," she says. "We have to be there by ten. The flight's at eleven forty-five, remember?"

"Okay, baby. Let's stand outside and wait for the taxi."

Taking one last look at the apartment, they kiss and then leave, locking the door behind them.

As they sit in the back seat of the taxi, they hold hands in silence on their way to the airport. Watching the world go by, both of them are ready for the adventure ahead, this time together.

"Goodbye, Nice," Lori whispers, filled with a mixture of emotions, not knowing when she will see that beautiful city again. But now she feels a new sense of excitement with her love by her side. She has Francois coming with her this time.

As they make their way through departures, they both feel anxious, wanting to get seated on the plane as quickly as possible. Feeling as though they are doing something wrong, that maybe they should have informed somebody, they hurry through the crowd, worried they may be stopped.

When the plane finally takes off, they both sigh with relief. No one can stop them now.

Francois grips Lori's hand, their fingers intertwined, as a sense of inner peace seeps up through his body. For the first time in years, he dares to feel safe.

CHAPTER 27

Joy to Sorrow

Now living in Hampshire England, things are going well. It doesn't take long for Francois to settle into his new life. As the months roll by, they spend their time getting to know the other's likes and dislikes as they cook together and eat out.

Gazing into each other's eyes, their faces lit by candle light across restaurant tables, they hold hands, two foodies excitingly exploring various cuisines. In the mall they check out the clothing stores, Francois insisting on buying Lori elegant garments.

As Lori continues to work at an office a few miles away, Francois tries to keep his business going, selling used luxury cars with his contact in Paris. It's a struggle, having been bitten by the recession of a few years before.

Lori encourages Francois to work out, and they join a gym, taking turns choosing their favourite CDs on the journey over. Both of them love David Bowie and Kate Bush. They smile at each other as one strides on the treadmill and the other lifts weights.

Relaxing at home, they make love whilst listening to music, Lori having been introduced to all of Francois's favourite French artists. Francois shows off his ninjutsu skills, impressing Lori with his knowledge and abilities. They drive into the countryside, strolling hand in hand, enjoying the hot summer sun and exploring the surrounding villages and the woodlands.

Having arranged to meet Elijah in London, Lori and Francois take the train there, and Francois proudly introduces Lori to Elijah in person for the first time. They spend their day wandering around Covent Garden, relishing the delights of the indoor markets and cafes before deciding upon a restaurant to take some lunch. The three of chat and laugh together, having a lot to catch up on. Before long it's late afternoon, and Elijah makes his way to the train station to catch a connecting train to the Eurostar, then back to Paris. On the way back to Hampshire, Francois and Lori stop in the town of Reading, where they visit a host of live music venues, soaking up the evening's entertainment.

All that they have ever wanted has become a reality. At last they are together, having waited so long. They are deeply in love and content. All is well, and they are living in sweet harmony, until one particular morning.

"Baby, why do you keep looking out of the window?" Lori asks.

Francois doesn't answer, but when he goes to look out the bedroom window, Lori follows him. He turns around to look at her, a worried expression on his face.

"Francois, are you okay?"

"No, we're not safe."

"Safe? Safe from whom?"

Lori realises something isn't right with Francois, and she moves to stand next to him. "You see, baby? There's no one there, just trees."

"No, they've followed me."

"Who, Francois?"

"The extremists, the neo-Nazis."

"Baby, no one is interested in following you. Don't be silly. Come and sit down, love."

Francois doesn't answer. Instead he starts to breathe deeply, sweat appearing upon his face. He checks the lock on the front door again and again. Looking on, Lori waits patiently, hoping he will calm down and unsure of what to do.

Unfortunately, he does not calm down, and soon he is locked into a ritual of continually checking the windows and doors, edging towards a state of panic. Lori has no choice but to try to help him.

"Francois, let's go to the doctor."

"Why?"

"Just come. I don't know what else to do."

Taking his hand, she manages to persuade Francois to leave the apartment and get into the car. They arrive at the health centre and are eventually called in to see the doctor.

"Hello, Doctor, this is Francois. Sit down, Francois. He's very anxious," she whispers. "I'm not sure if it's his mental health."

"I see. Have you called the crisis team?" the doctor asks.

"The crisis team? Who are they?"

"They will help you. Go home and call them. It's the best thing you can do. Here's their number."

Lori takes Francois back to the apartment and calls the number as Francois continues to pace up and down, becoming increasingly afraid. Eventually, there's a knock at the door. The community psychiatric nurse has arrived.

"Hello, I'm Norman. Is this Francois?"

"Yes, come in," Lori replies, then she explains what has happened. The nurse persuades Francois to sit down and asks him to stick out his tongue. Francois obliges, and the nurse squeezes some drops of medicine onto it. Eventually, Francois calms down somewhat, and the nurse leaves.

Another week passes, but Francois still isn't right. Lori calls the crisis team again, and they suggest taking Francois to the local psychiatric hospital.

When they arrive at the hospital, Lori is taken into a room by a nurse to meet the psychiatrist, Doctor Foy. Lori is immediately taken back by the hard, cold edge of Doctor Foy's character and her dismissive view of Francois. Her strange and inappropriate questioning takes Lori by surprise.

"Being a French national, how is he going to pay for his treatment?"

"Why would he have to pay?" Lori asks. "He's French. He's from Europe."

Lori is annoyed at this odd and rude remark, its hypocritical undertones coming from a doctor with an obvious foreign heritage herself.

"He's Jewish, correct?"

"Yes, he's Jewish. He has suffered a lot of trauma. He has been a victim of anti-Semitism, attacked by extremists, neo-Nazis I think. He has had many traumas in his life."

"How do you know that?"

"Know what?"

"About the neo-Nazis?"

"I don't need to know; I believe him. He has a massive scar on his stomach. It's very crude, from a knife attack. He was ambushed by extremists in Paris."

Doctor Foy glares at Lori, her eyes full of distrust. Her long years of being amongst people in an unwell state of mind feeds her cynical and disproportionate mistrust of others.

"I'm worried about the medication," Lori says. "It won't be too strong, will it? Antipsychotics are very toxic."

"It will be what he needs," Doctor Foy snaps. She asks Lori to wait in another room as Francois is assessed. Before long he winds up sectioned, and Lori is sent home, instructed to ring in a few days.

When she arrives at the hospital after finally being allowed to see Francois again, a nurse comes to collect Lori and takes her along a pale grey hall with several doors leading off it. As the familiar smell of a chemical cleaner comes wafting up, Lori recalls the hospital in France, and her heart sinks. It's that same awful smell, like the washing away of the human will, as they walk towards his room.

"He's in here," the nurse says. "I'll have to come in with you and stay."

"Okay."

They enter the room together. Francois is sitting on the bed, staring at the floor. Lori notices he's trembling.

"Francois, it's me, baby. Are you okay?"

She sits down next to him. He looks up momentarily with a bewildered expression. She notices immediately that his left pupil is dilated, and he is dribbling.

"What's wrong with his eye?" she asks.

"I don't know," the nurse replies.

"Well, it can't be normal. He has one dilated pupil. He seems very drugged. I'm not happy about that."

"I'll speak to the doctor about it."

"Please do, or I will."

Lori writes a letter of complaint to the health trust about Francois's physical state, but it doesn't come to anything.

Francois's section is short, ending a few weeks later, and he is able to return home. Things begin to settle down again.

It's September, and Francois is starting to come to bed later and later.

"Francois, are you on that computer again? It's past midnight."

"Okay, okay."

"What are you doing?"

"Nothing."

Fed up and unable to sleep, Lori gets up and peers around the corner into the lounge. She sees Francois at the computer. As she walks over, she sees he is about to send an email. Noticing her standing behind him, he quickly clicks "send."

"What do you want, baby?" he asks. Lori instantly feels that something is not right and that he's hiding something.

"Who did you just email?"

"Nobody."

"Why are you being so secretive?"

"I'm not, baby."

"Yes you are."

She opens the email. It's in French.

"Leave it," he says.

"No."

Scrolling down she notices a few conversations between Francois and another person.

"Who is that?"

"Nobody."

She copies the words onto a translation website, her heart pounding, sensing she is not going to like what she sees. She presses "translate," and her mouth drops open as she reads the words.

"I still love you, Francois," the message from another woman says.

"How are you, my darling?" Francois has replied, following by some sexual innuendo and, "What about your husband?"

Lori stares at Francois, her face red with anger.

"What's wrong, baby?" he asks.

Feeling both devastated and furious, she walks over to him, unable to stop her immense feelings of hurt and betrayal.

"What the fucking hell are you doing?" she asks. "Who is that?"

"It's my ex-girlfriend. She won't leave me alone. I'm just teasing her. That's why I didn't stop you from reading it."

"Teasing her? You should be telling her to fuck off. You're putting loads of pictures of women on your social media as well. You're a fucking idiot."

"She's married, but she's still obsessed with me."

"You're encouraging her, saying sexual things, you fucking idiot."

Francois stands up, and they continue to yell at each other. He grabs the back of the office chair and pushes it across the room towards her. The wheels slam into her feet. She pushes it back at him, catching his toe.

"Ow!" he yells.

Francois pushes it harder this time, and it bangs into her leg. Furious, and without thinking, she runs forward, holding onto the back of the chair as she pushes it across the wooden floor. Francois jumps out the way and onto the sofa. Wearing only socks and unable to stop herself, she slides across the floor and crashes into the wall, causing the chair to flip and smash into her face. The metal mechanism under the seat gashes her forehead open, and she screams in agony.

"My head! My head!"

"Lori!" Francois screams. "Are you okay? Oh no!"

Sitting up, Lori looks stunned as blood trickles from her forehead and down her face. She looks at Francois, who is still standing on the sofa, frozen in shock, his face white. Lifting her hand to touch her face, she realises there's an open wound. She stumbles to her feet and goes to the bathroom to look in the mirror. To her horror, she sees a gaping vertical cut running through her eyebrow, and she begins to cry.

Francois runs into the bathroom.

"Baby, I'm sorry."

Lori doesn't answer.

"Baby, I said I'm sorry, my darling. I love you."

"You hurt my feelings, emailing your ex-girlfriend. I've done so much to help you. I need to get to the hospital. Now, Francois."

"Okay, baby, I'm stupid."

Close to tears, Francois becomes anxious, his hands trembling.

"You don't need to be in contact with any women on the computer," she says. "What do you want? If you don't want me, go back to France."

"I do want you. You're the most amazing woman I've ever met."

"Francois, you're in your forties now. Stop trying to be the handsome playboy. It's fucking stupid."

"I know, baby. I was just teasing them."

"Well, stop! We have to go. Put away your ego."

"Okay. I'm sorry, baby. Come on, let's go. You're bleeding."

Forgetting their argument for a moment, Lori drives to the hospital. Francois's trembling hand holds a tissue to her wound throughout the journey.

At the hospital, Lori is taken into a cubicle alone, and Francois is told to wait outside. A nurse questions Lori about what happened. Feeling embarrassment and not wanting to say too much, Lori tells the nurse that they had an argument. However, the nurse writes down that this might have been done deliberately and that Francois may have attacked Lori's face. With the innocence of her confession, Lori is blissfully unaware that this disclosure will come back to haunt her.

It's now November, and with Francois having agreed to give his ex-girlfriend her marching orders, things are good again. Sitting in bed together, they discuss the future, and the topic of children comes up.

"I would love to have a baby with you, my darling," he says. "I've never felt like this before. I want to marry you, Lori. You're the only one I've ever really loved. I've been stupid. You're my angel."

"I love you too. You're the only person I have ever felt that way about. We need to start thinking about a baby. We're not young, so we should try soon. What do you think?"

"Yes, before it's too late."

"Yes, let's make love."

Francois smiles. "You want to try right now?"

"Why not?" she replies. "I'm forty-three years old, Francois."

Lori waits a week and then buys a pregnancy test.

"What does it show, baby?"

"Negative, not pregnant."

"You'll be pregnant soon," he assures her, "and it will be a boy."

Lori chuckles. "How do you know?"

"I feel it."

They spend the next few nights making love and listening to music. Then they go to the pharmacy to together purchase another test kit.

Lori goes into the bathroom.

"What's happening, baby? Are you pregnant?"

"Hold on."

"Lori, what does it say?"

"Francois!"

"You're pregnant."

Lori rushes out the bathroom, showing Francois the result. They both look at the two blue lines on the stick.

"Yes, I can't believe it!" she says.

"Wow, we're going to have a baby."

"I didn't think it would be so quick at our age. I'm so happy."

"Me too, Lori. I'm excited. You're the only person I ever wanted a baby with."

Hugging and kissing, they sit on the sofa together, excitedly discussing names, the sex of the baby and what he or she will look like.

"It's going to be a boy," Francois insists.

"You keep saying that. How do you know?"

"I told you; I feel it."

Before long, Lori is five months pregnant. It's late morning, and she is enjoying a steaming bubble bath.

"Look Francois, the baby's kicking. Come and look!"

Sitting in the hot soapy water, Lori is in seventh heaven, watching in delight as her stomach moves, being pushed in all directions by a little hand or foot.

Francois comes into the bathroom, looking worried.

She looks at his face. "What's wrong?"

"The bath is too hot. You're burning."

"No I'm not."

Francois rushes to pull the plug.

"Francois, I'm fine." Lori notices his hands are trembling. "Are you okay?"

"This boiler is dangerous, baby. We're being gassed."

"It's a gas boiler, Francois, for heating the water. We're not being gassed!"

After getting out of the bath and putting on a dressing gown, Lori notices Francois is pacing up and down the lounge.

"It's the Nazis. It's gas."

"Francois, what are you talking about? That was World War Two!"

Francois continues to tremble.

"Francois, baby, are you okay?"

"No, they're outside. I know it. I know it!"

Beads of sweat form on Francois's forehead as he continually goes to look out the window.

"Francois, there are no Nazis here. This is a small town."

Francois begins huffing, becoming more afraid, returning to the window again and again as he paces back and forth.

"They know I'm here. They know."

His voice becomes panicky, afraid.

After a while Lori realises that Francois has become ill again, and he's in the midst of a breakdown.

"Are you okay, baby?"

"Yes, I'm okay. No, I'm scared."

"Is it to do with the past?"

"Yes, sorry, sorry."

Francois becomes a little weepy, and he goes into the bedroom to rest. Lori follows him.

"It's okay, Francois. I want you to know that you're safe here. You must be traumatised, but you're safe here, Francois, I promise you."

"Okay, okay, I know. They say I have a mental illness, but it's a trauma disorder."

"I believe you, baby. It's okay."

"They gave me really strong medicine in France. It made me feel ill. I can't cope with it."

"I won't let them give you really strong stuff, baby. Maybe you just need something milder."

As the hours pass, and with much reassurance from Lori, Francois begins to calm down, and they resume their daily lives again.

It's Saturday morning, and Lori is making breakfast when she hears a commotion coming from the bathroom. Francois has become anxious again, convinced he's not safe. Lori finds him in a panic, continuously flushing the toilet.

"Francois, what are you doing?"

"I have to get rid of it."

"Get rid of what?"

Peering into the toilet, Lori is horrified to see Francois's gold chain staring back at her, complete with a Star of David pendant. Shocked to see it there, she grabs his hand to prevent him from flushing, trying to break his iron grip upon the toilet handle.

"Francois, why have you thrown your chain in the toilet?"

"I don't want to wear it. I give up."

"Give up? Give up what?"

"Showing I'm Jewish. It's not safe for me to be Jewish. I'm not safe wearing it."

"But why? You can't. You're Jewish. Don't say that, baby. You're making me sad. You were born Jewish."

Francois begins to cry. "I'm not safe."

"You are, Francois, you are. It's just trauma. You mustn't say that, baby. You're safe here. We're in England."

"No I'm not. They'll follow me."

Francois goes into the bedroom and sits on the bed. Grabbing the opportunity, Lori gets a rubber glove from the kitchen and then returns to the bathroom, only for Francois to come rushing back in.

"What are you doing?"

"I'm going to save it."

"No, you must not!"

They wrestle with each other, each trying to hold onto the toilet handle.

"Francois, you're Jewish! Be proud. You can wear it if you want. Never listen to anyone!"

Francois easily overpowers her, and she loses her grip on the handle, unable to stop him. Feeling exhausted, she gives up. They both peer into the toilet, which reveals that the chain is gone. Feeling sad and angry with the people who attacked him, time and time again, Lori goes to lie on the bed.

It's evening, and there has not been any improvement in Francois's condition. Full of anxiety, he weeps and trembles as he continues to pace. Lori looks on, unsure what to do next. She continually tries to reassure him that everything is okay, but it is not.

"I want to go to the hospital. I'm not safe."

"No, Francois. Let me call the crisis team first."

"No, no take me, take me."

"You don't know what you're saying, Francois. You hated it there, and I'm worried they over drugged you. Would it help if we went to the park? Maybe some fresh air will help calm you."

"I don't know."

"Let's try. Come on, Francois. Let's go."

When they're almost at the park, Francois begins to hyperventilate. "I want to go to the hospital!"

"But that doctor was horrible to you. Are you sure?"

"I can't breathe! I can't breathe!" Francois begins banging the dashboard with his fist in a state of panic.

"Okay, okay, Francois, we're nearly there."

When they arrive at the psychiatric hospital, Lori tries to convince Francois to take some pills at home instead. Eventually, she gives in, realising he has become far too ill for her to help him. Scrambling out of the car, Francois races into the hospital, Lori running after him.

"Francois, please, wait, love."

"No, no, I'm not safe!"

Francois's mind is not his own. Confused and afraid, she has to let him go, knowing full well he will not be in good hands. But being five months pregnant, there's little she can do now apart from follow him inside.

Sweating profusely, his anxiety is even more heightened than before. His past has come back to torment him yet again. He is lost, gripped by fear. The damage caused by all the darkness he has experienced from child to man has become too much to bear. Rising to the surface again, each untreated trauma snowballs into the next, causing him to lose his sense of where he is and what he's doing.

Sadly, his insistence on returning to what he hates most, restriction of his liberties, along with the toxic medication, is something he will regret terribly.

Francois runs past the receptionist. She calls out, asking him to stop, but he continues to one of the wards. He knocks on the window of the double doors at the entrance. A psychiatric nurse arrives. Realizing he is in a panic, she peers through the window and then comes out to see what the problem is.

"Can I help you?"

Francois doesn't answer.

"His name is Francois," Lori replies. "He was on this ward before for a short time."

"Hold on," the nurse replies. "I'll be back soon."

Before long she returns, accompanied by another nurse. After Francois is admitted to the ward, a ward manager arrives, and Lori explains what happened that morning.

When she returns to her car, Lori feels sad, defeated and very alone.

Over the next few days, Lori continues to call the ward for updates, only to be told that Francois doesn't want to come to the phone. Thinking this out of character for him, despite him being in hospital, she decides to bring in a cell phone for him to use, hoping it will prompt him to want to speak to her.

Over the coming days, Francois answers the cell phone, engaging in conversation for short periods of time, much to Lori's relief. His vulnerability causes him to weep from time to time as he begins to make sense of his situation. With each conversation, flickers of light begin to switch back on in his mind, offering more clarity as he begins to recover, much to Lori's relief. Eventually, she is allowed back to visit him. The dull, boring confinement of the ward is driving him mad as he tries to find something to fill his days. Lori tries to be supportive, accompanying him to the hospital garden, watching videos, or helping him colour his hair. Meanwhile, her pregnancy is progressing, and it won't be long before their, baby enters the world.

Late one evening in the darkness, Lori is awakened by the sound of her cell phone ringing. It's past 10:00, and she wonders who could be calling her so late.

"Hello," she says, her voice croaky and tired.

"Hello. It's Doctor Foy."

"Oh, hello," Lori replies, shocked as to why she would be calling her so late.

"It's about Francois. I'm ringing to tell you we've made a decision, and he is going to have to have ECT administered. He's not drinking enough fluids."

"What is ECT?"

"Electroconvulsive therapy, sending an electrical current through his brain."

"What do you mean? Shocking his brain? No! Absolutely not. He's drinking more now. Don't you dare touch his brain!"

"If you're going to get emotional, I'm going to hang up," Doctor Foy replies, her voice ice cold. Before Lori can say another word, the line goes dead.

A rush of emotions surges through Lori's body as she's gripped with fear, disgusted and horrified at the suggestion of shocking Francois. Then for the first time she feels vulnerable herself, heavily pregnant and afraid. Unable to do anything, she weeps for hours, the very thought of it repelling her. Eventually, feeling utterly exhausted, she drifts off to sleep, spending the remainder of the night having nightmares about Francois being shocked against his will.

When morning finally arrives, despite feeling drained, Lori calls the hospital, requesting a meeting with Doctor Foy, only to find out she has the rest of the week off. Instead, an arrangement is made for her to meet the ward manager to discuss the ECT.

Waiting anxiously in a meeting room, Lori looks up as the door opens. In walks the ward manager. He is tall and thin and wears black glasses. He is of South Asian origin. His face is expressionless as he looks at her. She realises his lack of warmth means he is on Doctor Foy's side.

"Hello, Lori, my name is Ajay. I want you to look at this." He hands her a booklet that explains what ECT is. "Take a look. I'll be back in ten minutes."

Before Lori can reply, he leaves the room. She picks up the booklet and glances through, then sets it back on the table, not the least bit interested in it. Soon the door opens, and Ajay returns.

"Did you read the booklet?"

"I'm not interested in your booklet. I do not give you my consent to give my Francois ECT."

"Can I ask why not? Do you understand that it's therapeutic?"

"Therapeutic? Are you joking? Going to the spa is therapeutic, not shocking someone's brain."

"You really don't understand, Lori."

"I don't want to understand. You'll never convince me. Sorry, but I'm entitled to my opinion. I forbid you to do it to Francois."

"I'm sorry, but you're too late."

"What do you mean I'm too late?"

"Doctor Foy has authorised it, along with another psychiatrist, and Francois will begin ECT on Monday. I'm afraid there's nothing you can do to stop it, Lori. We have legal authority over you."

"I want to see Francois now."

Lori is taken to the ward. She hugs Francois, tears in her eyes, too worried to say anything about it for fear of scaring him. She notices one of the nurses on the ward whom she trusts, a French speaker, and she discusses the situation with her.

"I know, Lori. I don't agree either," she whispers. "Please don't say anything, but ask to check his heart records."

"I won't say anything, and don't worry, I will check them."

On Monday, Lori takes a day off from work, unable to concentrate, continuously worrying about the ECT. She rings the hospital to speak to the head nurse on the ward.

"I want to know how Francois is."

"He's had three lots of ECT so far. He's due another later today."

"Three? I thought it was only going to be once."

"No, the doctor wants between six and twelve sessions."

"Six and twelve? That's not necessary. How's his drinking? I felt his drinking was already improving before this ECT."

"Are you coming in this afternoon, Lori?" the nurse asks, changing the subject.

"Yes."

When she arrives at the ward, Lori is relieved to find that the nurse they trust is in again.

"How is he?" Lori asks.

"They've given him three lots of ECT. Come on, he's in the small television room. Let's talk there."

Lori follows the nurse into the television room, where Francois is watching a movie.

"Baby," he says.

"Hi, Francois. How are you, sweetheart?"

They kiss and embrace. Lori sits next to him on a small sofa, and the nurse sits in the other chair.

They begin to discuss the ECT in French. Then the nurse and Francois explain to Lori that Francois is not supposed to drink beforehand, so the nurse advises him to drink lots of milk.

"After the doctor found out I had drunk this morning, the ECT was cancelled for today," Francois says, looking delighted.

"I want you to know I don't agree with it either," the nurse confides. "He was beginning to drink enough." Confides the nurse.

Lori puts her hand upon the nurses' arm. "Thank you so much."

Determined to put a stop to the ECT altogether, Lori makes contact with a charity online that raises awareness about the dangers of over medicating patients in psychiatric care and ECT. After a long discussion, they offer to write to Doctor Foy about her worries regarding Francois. After a long wait, their efforts are to no avail, as the hospital does not respond. Undeterred and feeling more confident now after the help from the charity, Lori writes a letter of complaint about the ECT.

She is blissfully unaware that this further letter of complaint starts a secret revenge plot from Dr Foy that Lori will never be able to prove. In the not-too-distant future, a deep dark cloud will come to torment her.

As the days pass, Francois makes further improvements. At times he becomes irritated, feeling trapped in the ward. He continuously complains and asks to be discharged, only to be told that it's too soon.

One day breakfast is late, and Francois is becoming hungry. He starts to feel claustrophobic, stuck in his room and unable to wander around freely. Still under observation, he's being monitored in a two-to-one ratio with the nurses. His desperation grows as he asks repeatedly to go to the garden. Two of the three nurses on day shift constantly check on him, one of which Francois dislikes immensely. She is stern and sarcastic with large masculine shoulders and has a reputation of treating the patients with contempt. Her belittling attitude upsets Francois often, making it impossible for him to relax. Dismissive and disinterested in his frustration, she continues to tell him to wait and return to his room, making him feel like a child. Unable to hold his tongue any longer, he marches up the ward to confront her.

"I want to go to the garden!"

"I told you no, you're too stressed."

"You're making me stressed. I need to get outside. I can't breathe."

"Return to your room," the nurse snaps.

"You fat cow!" he yells. Suddenly, the nurse rushes into the office and presses the alarm. Within minutes three other nurses, two of which are male, come running towards her and Francois.

"He's being aggressive," she claims. Before Francois can say another word, he is grabbed and pinned to the floor, face down. In a panic, he lashes out, his mind racing with fear.

"Get off me! Get off!"

He screams and thrashes about, kicking his legs and thrashing his arms. Suddenly, one of the male nurses yelps in pain.

"My rib! He's hurt my rib!"

Another male nurse arrives in response to the alarm, and between them they manage to drag Francois into the isolation room.

He is trapped. The room is small and spartan with a mattress on the floor and a stainless-steel toilet and sink. Francois starts to panic, his heart racing.

"I'm suffocating. Let me out. Let me out!"

He bangs on the door, looking through a small, reinforced glass window, but nobody comes. In protest he pees upon the floor, then slings the mattress at the door, furious. He yells and screams for another thirty minutes, banging on the door until a nurse finally arrives.

"Francois, if you don't stop, we'll have to inject you."

"Just fucking try it!"

"Stop yelling."

"Fuck off. You're all dead."

Francois immediately regrets those words, but his anger is fuelled by his fear. Within ten minutes four nurses arrive at his door. They enter the room and surround him. Sweating with fear, Francois falls back upon his instincts, and he assumes a defensive ninjutsu pose, forgetting he is weaker now and overweight, and the medication is making him breathless. The four nurses easily overpower him, and before long he is injected with a powerful drug. Bit by bit they watch as he drifts off to sleep. They set him on the mattress and then leave the room, locking the door behind them.

Lori arrives at the hospital to visit Francois, only to be told she can't see him. They tell her to ring the following day for news.

During the call, one of the nurses conveys to her Francis has been aggressive. Unaware of the full picture, Lori is saddened and disappointed. She spends the rest of the day in bed, worries about Francois and how long he will be in this situation. Her strong desire to be together is on hold yet again, and she is crushed.

Early the next morning, Lori rings the ward to get an update on Francois.

"Hold on," a nurse replies.

Lori huffs, rolling her eyes, frustrated by all the secrecy.

"He's off the ward," the nurse informs her when she returns.

"What do you mean?" Lori asks.

"I'm afraid he's not here anymore."

"Not there? Well, where is he?"

"Because he was aggressive, he has been sent to another hospital in London."

"London? He's not an aggressive person; he's a vulnerable person. He was probably frustrated. What happened?"

"It was an incident with one of our nurses."

"Yes, and I bet I know which one. He's complained to me about her before."

"I can't say, Lori. Ring tomorrow, and we'll give you the details of the new hospital."

"Forget it!"

Lori slams down the phone. As bitter tears roll down her cheeks, she sits on the sofa, feeling utterly powerless. She turns on the television, in a daze as the noise of the programme washes over her. Staring at the screen, she shakes her head as she cradles her swollen belly. She feels lost, with no desire to move.

CHAPTER 28

The Baby Snatchers

Now seven months pregnant, after finding out their communication has been restricted, Lori keeps in contact with Francois through a succession of sporadic phone calls to the ward at the new hospital.

One morning she receives a letter. As she reads it, a frown crinkles her forehead. She reads it again, feeling shocked and confused as to why she has been sent such a letter. It's from Children's Social Services. Feeling baffled and insulted, she decides to ring them immediately.

"Hello, my name is Lori Avery I wish to speak to Roger Mac. I have a letter stating he's a social worker, and he wishes to make contact with me, why?"

"He is not in today," a nasal voice replies.

"Well, I received a letter that says he wants to meet with me. Can you tell him I don't need any help? I'm more than capable of looking after myself and my baby in the future, so please tell him I'm not interested. Thank you, bye."

Lori spends the rest of the day mumbling to herself about the outrage of receiving such a letter.

The next day, Lori receives a phone call from Roger Mac.

"I would like to see you," he says.

"Why? I already told you I don't need any help."

"I know. I wish to speak to you about Mr Ronen."

"He is in the hospital."

"I know. When can I come?"

Wondering if the better option might be to meet with him, to reassure him she's fine, she agrees to a meeting.

"Okay, come tomorrow morning, but there's nothing to tell you."

After a sleepless night, she wakes up tired but keen to get the meeting over with, annoyed with herself for having agreed to it in the first place.

There's a knock at the door. When Lori opens it, she is met by a tall blonde man with a serious expression on his face. He sits down and asks Lori a series of questions about Francois's history and how long they've been together. After an hour he finally gets up to leave. Relieved that the meeting is over, Lori gladly closes the door behind him, thinking the matter has been dealt with.

Two days later another letter arrives, this time of a slightly more serious nature. It states that Roger Mac would like Lori to come to their offices for another meeting. Not understanding the gravity of it, Lori rings their office, stating she doesn't wish to come. They put her through to Roger Mac.

"Lori, you need to come to our offices. It's not a choice."

"Why do I need to come? We already met."

"If you don't come it could be very grave for you and your baby."

"What do you mean?"

"I'm free this afternoon. I'll see you at about two o'clock. Goodbye, Lori."

Suddenly realising things have become a little more serious but unable to understand why, that afternoon Lori arrives at the building. After being directed to a row of plastic seats by an overly chatty receptionist, she sits, waiting anxiously.

"They are horrible here," says a woman waiting to her left. Lori looks over at her and notices she's been crying.

"Why are you here?" Lori whispers.

"They took my kids. I'm trying to get them back."

"Why?"

"I was smoking weed, me and my husband. The neighbour reported us."

Feeling the woman has behaved stupidly, Lori doesn't know what to say. However, feeling sorry for her, she smiles. "I hope it works out for you."

"Thanks," the woman replies, sniffing as she wipes away a tear.

Shortly after that, Roger Mac arrives and asks Lori to follow him.

Lori stands up, feeling annoyed at being made to feel like a schoolkid just spoken to by the headmaster.

She follows him down a short hall and into a meeting room, where he directs her to sit. A few seconds later, a woman enters the room.

"This is Steff Butler, Lori, my manager," Roger says.

Lori looks up at her. She is tall with broad shoulders and short bushy brown hair. She is wearing black-rimmed glasses. Looking down at her Doc Martin boots, Lori feels intimidated by her aggressive-looking attire. She instinctively places her hand across her growing, baby bump. As Steff begins to speak, Lori senses a cold, hard vibe coming from her, and she knows this is not going to go well.

They begin a series of endless questions, like a barrage of bullets fired one after the other, and the intensity in the room heightens. Pushing harder and harder, they want to know more and more about Francois, including his background, his mental health and his behaviour. Out of her depth, Lori becomes their prey.

"We're concerned about the baby and Francois becoming mentally unwell," Steff says.

Trying desperately to explain to them over and over again that Francois is not aggressive or a risk to her or the baby, Lori tells them that he's vulnerable and loving towards her. She also explains that she sought help from the local doctor's surgery, taking him there when he became ill. Roger and Steff appear unimpressed, not wishing to recognise her taking responsibility and being proactive. Lori also explains that she is in contact with the crisis team, showing them that she has taken initiative. But her explanations fall upon deaf ears. She feels exasperated as they continue to point out they are not the least bit interested.

"He's aggressive. He injured you, your face," Steff says.

"No he didn't! It was a stupid argument about an ex-girlfriend, and we both regretted it. It was long before the pregnancy. I slipped under the chair. It was the mechanism of the chair, an office chair. We've never been so stupid again. We love each other. He is traumatised and has had many anti-Semitic attacks in the past by neo-Nazi types. He's vulnerable, not violent. It's not a violent relationship!"

"We think it is," Steff says. "We received a letter from Doctor Foy about him. Lori, he's a risk."

"A risk! A risk to whom?"

"You and the baby."

"But he has never harmed me, and he would never harm me or our baby. I called the crisis team when he got ill. I've acted responsibly."

"We disagree."

"He's had many traumas. Dr Foy is angry with me because I wrote two letters of complaint about her to the health trust. She over medicated him and gave ECT when I believed it was unnecessary. She has written to you because of that. Yes, he gets frustrated in the hospital, but at home he is loving and romantic."

Lori starts to get emotional, her fruitless attempts to get them both to understand failing miserably. She is worn down, hormonal and heavily pregnant, feeling vulnerable herself, and she feels like giving up.

"We're going to leave the room, Lori, and we'll return in fifteen minutes, by which time we will expect you to listen," Steff says.

They both leave. Close to crying, Lori struggles to hold back her tears. She is terrified, confused and feeling totally out of her depth.

As she sits there wringing her hands, they finally return, their faces stony.

The next hour feels like an interrogation. Relentless in their questioning, they turn up the pressure as they begin to pick her apart, accusing her of believing false things about Francois. Their questioning becomes more intrusive and personal. They even begin to dissect her own history until the whole miserable experience comes to a grinding halt. Lori's head is spinning, her mind shot to pieces. She is trapped in a nightmare, much like a hostage.

Roger Mac slides a document across the table to Lori.

"We're serving you with a section forty-seven," Steff informs her.

"A what?"

"You will find out soon enough. You'll be requested to come back for another meeting."

Only then does her instinct kick in as it finally dawns on Lori what is happening.

"Are you trying to take my baby?"

"Not at the moment," Steff replies, her voice void of emotion.

Lori's blood runs cold. As she gets up and makes her way out of the room, her hands are trembling. Eventually, she reaches the car park. She sits in her car for a moment, sobbing. Then she drives home.

Back at her apartment feeling totally overwhelmed, Lori doesn't know what to do. She's deeply in love with Francois and has never experienced any danger from him. She is rigid with stress, knowing she can't just walk away from him.

"He hasn't done anything wrong," she mumbles to herself. Then, after concluding that the whole thing is ridiculous, she goes to bed.

As nightfall arrives, however, she can't sleep at all. She's haunted by horrible dreams of hollow grey hands from several faceless people pulling away her baby. She begins to sweat from head to toe, restless and locked in a terrible nightmare, watching herself struggle to pull them off. Back and forth they go as she becomes more and more desperate to break free of them. Then, like a bolt of electricity shocking her body, she wakes, gasping and afraid and with intense pains in her stomach. Switching on the bedroom lamp, she feels dampness between her legs. She rolls back the duvet and sees blood.

"Oh my god!" she cries. She calls the hospital for support and is advised that any more blood loss will mean she must come in. She lies back down, unable to sleep as she waits for morning.

The next day Lori calls Francois to explain what's happening.

Horrified, he is frustrated at his hospital confinement, which makes it impossible for him to help her. He pleads and argues with the nurses, wanting to telephone Lori more often. The lack of support from them causes his mental health to suffer further. With no one to comfort him, he is continually put into isolation, shouting and lashing out, worried sick about Lori and their unborn baby.

The no-nonsense approach of the male African nurses in the hospital makes them very unpopular with the patients. The constant abuse of their power makes Francois feel increasingly isolated. With the only male nurse that Francois is able to confide in working only two days a week, he has no escape, and he feels trapped and overwhelmed.

"Francois, I love you."

"I love you too, baby, I can't get out of here. The nurses are horrible, and so are the assistants. Someone died here in their bed."

"What? Oh my God. They don't want us to speak any longer. They want us to end our relationship. Why should we? What have we done wrong, Francois? Nothing."

"I haven't done anything wrong," he says. "Don't end it, baby, I love you."

"I love you too."

Lori hears the voice of a nurse nearby.

"Did you draw on the wall?" the nurse asks.

"No. What do you mean?" Francois replies.

"It was you. Hang the phone."

"No, go away."

"Hang the phone," the nurse demands again.

"Francois, who is that?"

"It's the nurse manager. They're abusive here, baby."

"He's talking to you like a child."

"I know."

"I said hang the phone!" the nurse manager shouts.

"Fuck off," Francois replies.

There is the sound of a struggle and then the phone goes dead.

"Francois, Francois, are you there? Francois!"

Lori listens for a few more seconds, then hangs the phone. She goes into the bedroom to lie down, totally at a loss. After putting off telling her family for as long as possible what is happening, not wanting to worry them, she decides to call her sister.

Her sister and mother travel to Hampshire after being invited to a meeting with the local authority, only to be met by a barrage of threats and intense questioning.

"We don't mess about," a social worker says finally. "In six weeks we go for adoption."

Traumatised by this nasty and unprovoked attack, they realise they have a huge fight on their hands.

Before long Lori is forced to undertake psychiatric and psychological assessments, which she passes with flying colours, much to the annoyance of the local authority.

After reading several documents written about her conduct during their meetings, she notices they are trying to portray a false narrative of her being mentally unwell. Angry at their lies, this makes her more determined than ever that the authorities will never win.

Word spreads quickly within the family, and as the day approaches for an important meeting with the local authority, Lori's brother and sister come to support her.

During the meeting, Lori feels totally overwhelmed. Representatives from several agencies sit in, including reps from the police, social services, mental health, midwifery, health visitors and social service management.

As people introduce themselves around the table, Lori looks at each face in turn, still totally confused as to why this is happening to her. She feels like she's having an out-of-body experience, trapped inside a bad dream. Knowing how happy she is with Francois and how much they love their unborn baby, she doesn't understand why they're not concentrating on abusive parents, and she tells them so.

"I don't want Roger Mac coming to my house again or that Steff. They were aggressive with me."

"This is Juliette Brown, another social worker," the case manager says. "She will be working with you now."

The manager is an older heavily made-up woman with dark red nails and a scowl on her face. Lori looks across the table at Juliette, a short, thin sour-faced woman with short dark bobbed hair and glasses. She offers Lori a weak and insincere smile.

The case manager asks if Lori has anything to say and if she will agree to break off her relationship with Francois. This line of questioning is repeated over and over again, followed by a shotgun of psychological attacks designed to break her. At the end comes a vote to decide Lori's fate.

"Everyone, please raise your hand for an interim care order for this unborn baby if in agreement."

One by one they all raise their hands, the only hesitancy coming from the two midwives, but soon they also follow suit. Lori is dumbstruck, humiliated and frightened. She begins to cry.

"You don't even know him," she says. "You keep talking about risk, but he's not a risk. Life is a risk. Everything is a risk. He has never harmed me, nor would he ever harm me or the baby."

But it's too late. The desensitised cynicism present in all of those around the table shows her that they are unwilling to consider that they might be wrong. Their only interest is to steamroll their agenda through. Unfortunately for Lori and Francois, they are now caught up in a tidal wave of paranoia after recent media coverage of Children's Social Services failings. Unbeknown to Lori, this outcome was decided long before the meeting.

Over the coming weeks, a stream of letters from social services arrive, informing Lori of further meetings to attend and forms to fill in as things turn uglier and uglier. Their tactics are relentless, designed to confuse and overwhelm until it all becomes too much, hoping she will give in.

It's now July 2012. Lori's pregnancy is almost full term, and she's trying to look forward to the birth. One afternoon, feeling particularly exhausted, she sits on the sofa and looks out the window, watching the leaves fluttering on the trees, their dappled shadows dancing upon the wall of her lounge. But the sunshine offers no relief from her torment, the words of the authorities swirling around in her head.

"Are you going to put ''Francois' on the birth certificate? We don't think you should."

"You need to end the relationship."

"He's a risk."

"Most of the people we see give up the baby and choose their partner."

"We don't not believe all that happened to him. We feel he's delusional."

She has to dig deep to retrieve her hidden determination.

"They will never win," she vows. They are only making her love for Francois and their baby stronger.

Unable to give up her soulmate, knowing that their baby was made from their love for each other, she begins to caress her baby bump. She is torn, realising she may have to part from Francois for a while, the thought of losing her baby too much to bear.

It's nearing dinner time, but Lori doesn't feel like preparing anything. Unable to relax or enjoy anything, she decides to call Francois.

"Baby, this place is terrible," he says. "They won't discharge me, the nurses are all horrible, they're all from another country and they can hardly speak English."

"Francois, stop, wait. I need to talk to you. Please don't get upset, but we might need to stop being together for a while."

Francois's face flushes with fear. "Baby, don't leave me. I love you so much, Lori. Don't let them bully you. They're crazy."

"I know. I love you so much too, Francois. Of course I don't want to, but we might have to for a while. Otherwise they'll take the baby."

Francois's eyes fill with tears. "Lori, you know I love you with all of my heart and my soul."

"I love you too, Francois, so much."

Knowing he is vulnerable, Lori feels bad for making him feel even worse, but the baby growing inside of her is more precious than them both, and her hands are tied.

Deciding to take a bath, she leans down to turn on the hot tap when a deep, throbbing pain shoots through her pelvis, causing her to gasp. Turning the tap off, she goes to lie down on the sofa. Tears roll down her cheeks as she worries about the baby. Then, much to her relief, the pain begins to ease. Falling into a deep and much-needed sleep, she doesn't wake until morning.

She puts some bread in the toaster, then returns to the lounge. As Lori sits, the throbbing pain shoots down her pelvis again, this time more intense, and it continues on and on. Only then does she realise that she's experiencing contractions.

Taking out her cell phone, she calls her mother.

"Are you having contractions?" she asks.

"Yes, yes. It's so painful."

"Okay, love, I'm coming. I'll be there in a couple of hours. I'm leaving Bristol now."

When they arrive at the hospital together, they are put into a birthing room. As the gaps between contractions shorten, day turns into night.

A few minutes past 3:00 a.m., with her mother by her side, Lori gives birth to a healthy baby boy.

"What are you going to call him?" the nurse asks.

"Milo. I knew I was having a boy. I asked at one of the scans."

"He's lovely, and that's a lovely name."

Lori is mesmerised and head of heals in love as she stares at her newborn, unable to stop smiling.

"He's wonderful Lori," her mother says as she gives him her first cuddle.

As the night wears on, they begin to tire. After giving Milo a few more feeds at her breast, Lori settles down to sleep, and her mother returns to Lori's apartment for some rest.

"I will see you at around ten tomorrow morning, my love," her mother says as she bends down to kiss Lori on the cheek.

"Okay, Mum. See you soon."

Lori smiles as her mother leaves the room.

The next morning Lori rings Francois at the hospital, overjoyed with the news that their baby boy is safe and well. Francois is proud and delighted to be a father, getting emotional.

"I'll call you again later, baby," Lori says.

"Okay, Lori. I love you. Are you both okay?"

"Yes, speak later."

After breastfeeding and cuddling Milo, she rests in bed, gazing proudly at her newborn baby boy in his cot. She looks at the clock. It's 9:45, almost time for her mother to arrive. Looking forward to seeing her, she sits up in bed.

The door to the room opens, and Lori smiles ready to greet her mother. Instead it's two social workers, Juliette Brown and Mary Troy. Lori's smile vanishes, replaced by a confused expression.

"Hello, Lori. We're here for Milo," Juliette says.

"What do you mean?" Lori asks. "What are you doing here?"

"You need to hand him over."

"What? No way! Why? What are you doing? Get out!"

"We're serving you with a section twenty. You need to sign this paper."

"What! no way, I'm not signing anything. Get out! Get out!"

Lori picks up Milo from the cot beside her bed and holds him close to her chest.

"If you don't hand him over, we'll call the police," Juliette warns.

"Call the police? What for? No, I won't!"

"Then we go to court today at two o'clock," Juliette replies, her cold voice exact and threatening.

Suddenly, Lori's mother arrives. Noticing Lori is crying, then seeing the two social workers in the room, she asks what's going on, then sits next to Lori on the bed. The child protection lead midwife also enters the room. She already told the two police officers who were waiting there to leave, after having scolded the two social workers before they entered Lori's room, telling them that having the police there was ridiculous and their decision-making baffling.

"Lori, Lori, listen," she says.

Lori begins to sob still, holding onto Milo. "Please help me. They want to take my baby."

They both look over at the two social workers, who appear unfazed by Lori's tears. The midwife asks them both to leave. After they're gone, she hands Lori a list of solicitors to call.

"I know this is a very difficult situation for you, but you must ring a solicitor. They're going to court today to try to take your baby."

Calling the first solicitor on the list, Lori begs for help. A barrister is sent to the magistrate's court, but she can do nothing to defend Lori other than represent her. With no knowledge or time to prepare for the case, the magistrate grants an emergency protection order. This unfair and corrupt strategy, certain to favour the local authorities, ambushes Lori with no warning, leaving her with no time to prepare a defence. It's a certain win for them, and Lori is powerless to stop it.

Having to resort to visiting her baby in the maternity ward, she is only allowed to see him for a few short hours each week. Each visit is filled with joy to see her baby again, mixed with profound sadness and bewilderment at the utterly ridiculous and cruel nature of the circumstances in which she finds herself.

The arrangement becomes vital in buying her more time to prepare for the onslaught from the local authorities, with their endless, desolate treadmill of meetings and court appearances.

"This way," a maternity nurse says in her warm, welcoming voice as Lori follows her along the ward and into a room with a plastic transparent cot containing Milo. Lori's heart sinks upon discovering his only companion is a little radio at low volume, playing music.

"It should be me," Lori says. The nurse smiles in compassion. "Milo, Milo, I love you, sweetie," Lori whispers, able to pick up her baby again at long last. She is in seventh heaven.

The visits go quickly, and the days in between are painfully long. During each visit, Lori is accompanied by a scowling member of the social services contact staff. They deliberately write unhelpful and unnecessarily negative comments for their report whilst Lori tries to breastfeed Milo and care for him.

Encapsulated within the emotional turmoil along with Lori are her brother, sister, mother and stepfather, all of whom are trying to support her. The whole thing becomes tiresome and heavy for each one of them.

As if things weren't bad enough, out of the blue the children's services management decides Lori must leave the county she lives in. This wildly erratic and illogical decision baffles the family. At a meeting just before a court appearance, Lori's barrister tries to argue with the barrister representing the local authority, saying this will prove impossible for Lori. It will also put her at risk, travelling up and down the motorway three days a week from Bristol to Hampshire to see Milo. But her argument falls upon deaf ears. Lori and her sister decide to stay at a hotel to be as near to the hospital as possible. It all takes a heavy toll on Lori, and without any after-birth care, she finds the experience so devastatingly stressful that she develops diarrhoea and vomiting.

Another court date arrives, and for the local authority it's another win. The female judge, blatant and biased, is clearly on their side. She appears void of interest, as Lori tries in vain to state her case, only to be told after that her baby will be taken into foster care the next day. After the hearing, Lori's wails of despair swirl around level three of the court building, hitting the ears of all within.

The family relays the terrible news to Lori's mother, who is waiting at Lori's apartment alone with Milo. Faced with the grim and heart-breaking task of having to hand over her baby grandson to a social worker, she is utterly devastated.

The family stops at a service station on the way back to Bristol. No longer able to hold it together, Lori gets out of the car to call Elijah.

"Elijah, they're taking our baby tomorrow!" Lori screams into the phone, her sorrow overwhelming her.

"Lori, my darling, I'm so sorry. What can I do?"

"Nothing, Elijah. There's nothing you can do."

"I'm so sorry, Lori. I'm here if you need me. I love you, my friend."

"I love you too. I have to go."

Later that evening after the family reaches Bristol, Lori calls Francois to tell him the news. Devastated and angry, he begins to cry.

"We'll get him back, my love, I promise you," he whispers.

The following day, exercising his right to call a family solicitor practice to represent him, Francois encounters resistance from the treating psychiatrist, who feeds him the false narrative that he does not have the capacity to do so. Francois argues with him, making it clear he knows the law and that this lie will create a problem, as he threatens to sue the hospital. Finally granted permission to contact a solicitor, he secures a meeting, instructing a barrister to help him and their baby.

The barrister attends court, keeping Francois informed of the ongoing events, but gradually it becomes too much for Francois to bear. Stuck in the hospital and unable to help Lori, he becomes incredibly frustrated. After getting into an argument with the unsympathetic staff, he ends up in isolation yet again.

As time goes on, Francois discovers that Juliette Brown has been sabotaging his opportunities to go to court. Francois instructs his solicitor to put a stop to it, and she is warned off, after being told that what she is doing is harassment.

A few weeks pass, and at last Francois is allowed to leave London and the tortuous experiences of the hospital behind him. He is transferred to a low-security psychiatric hospital in South Hampshire. Much to his relief, his new doctor is more favourable toward him, and the staff is more humane.

Less than a week later, Lori and Francois have an intense and painfully sad telephone conversation, deciding they are left with little choice but to break off communication and end their relationship to try to help the situation. They both know in their hearts that it could never be forever. As for the family, they continue attending court with Lori and supporting her fight to get Milo back.

During the proceedings, Lori is only able to see Milo at a contact centre run by the local authority. When she's given only three, three-hour meetings per week, she writes a letter asking for more time with him, but her request falls on deaf ears. Weary, frustrated and furious, knowing the whole situation is totally unnecessary, she bides her time, biting her tongue, anything to get Milo back.

As if the torment of not being with her baby wasn't bad enough, she also has to endure a continuous barrage of nasty, cutting comments from the social workers each time she turns up at the contact centre, which only makes her hate them even more.

It's Monday morning and after a sleepless night of fretting and missing her baby, Lori arrives at the contact centre to see him. After only having been with him for five precious minutes, she is asked a question of the most inappropriate nature, implying a secret undertone of permanent separation.

"Shall I take a photograph of Milo for a memory?" one of the contact workers asks.

"Why do you want to photograph him?" Lori asks. "You're not going to keep him!"

She's flabbergasted at this woman's lack of compassion and her stupid question. She glares at the woman, silently hating her and everyone in the building.

In between nursing and cuddling Milo, Lori glances up occasionally, noticing the contact worker is continually watching her. Angry at being treated like a criminal, she does her best to swallow her feelings and says nothing, not wanting to give them any more ammunition to use against her. Having already faced their wrath a few times after speaking out, she has learnt that some take pleasure in criticising her, writing exaggerated self-opinionated comments, without foundation. Much like a vulture circling its prey, devouring every piece of flesh, they pull her mothering skills apart at every opportunity. They never compliment her, knowing full well that snatching her baby will give her no time to learn, making her unfamiliar with how to care for a newborn. Lori tries her best to ignore them and muddles through, cherishing every moment with her beautiful baby boy, biding her time.

One afternoon, having just handed Milo back at the end of the session, as she leaves the room, she is met by the sound of giggling. Turning around, she spots two social workers, one of whom had accompanied Juliette to an earlier court appearance. Lori is so traumatised at having her baby taken and the relentless toll the situation is taking on her wellbeing that she has forgotten to change her sanitary towel. She notices upon arriving home that her skirt is bloodstained at the back, which is why the women were laughing.

One morning Lori receives a call from Juliette saying that Milo has been placed into foster care, driving yet another dagger into her heart.

"The foster carer is taking Milo to the hospital today for a check-up, and we're letting you go there to meet them."

Struggling to stop herself from swearing, Lori writes down the details and then makes her way there. Having to put up with only being an observer of her own baby at the check-up kills her inside. She feels utter humiliation and hurt as she watches with gritted teeth while the foster carer touches and handles her baby. The only thing keeping her together is her sheer determination to get Milo returned to her care. Trying her best to stay strong, she says nothing.

After spending many dark and lonely nights longing to hold her baby, one night Lori wakes up more anxious than usual, a mixture of horrible fears running through her head. Switching on the light, she looks over at the beautiful powder-blue Moses basket that her mother bought. She gets out of bed and sits on the floor, stroking the soft cotton covers and staring at the basket as a thousand thoughts rush through her head. She's unable to make sense of her terrible situation, trapped inside a never-ending nightmare. She begins to weep. Then, unable to keep her eyes open any longer, she gets back into bed and prays.

"Please, God help me. Please help me get Milo back."

She sobs into her pillow until she finally drifts off to sleep.

One afternoon during a contact visit, Lori and her mother notice that Milo is looking unwell. He coughs profusely, and he is pale, limp and sweaty. Her mother, who is a trained nurse, knows instinctively that he has whooping cough.

"He needs to go to the hospital today," she says to the contact officer.

As the visit progresses, Milo continues to cough. Afterwards, he is admitted to emergency.

Milo ends up needing to stay in the hospital for nine days. During his stay his health deteriorates further, and he requires oxygen. He is unable to pass stools, and his heart is racing. Meanwhile, the local authority spins a story that it was their idea along with the foster carer to send him there. The situation becomes a carefully planned and distorted version of the truth as to who acted first. Eventually, the local authority makes a cynical attempt to manipulate a report to make it appear that they had acted swiftly in suggesting that the baby go to the hospital when, in fact, he was left to deteriorate for far too long.

Lori is furious that their delay to act has caused Milo to require a hospital stay, but once again she must bite her lip. Upon finding out that a new judge has been assigned, she bides her time for her day in court. She's devastated for Milo, knowing that what they are doing is wrong, their decision-making bewildering. For the first time she begins to keep a diary of all that is happening, which is a good thing, as the situation is about to get worse.

The Local Authority now states that Lori must leave Hampshire, as they are assessing her "risk" level. This strange and random idea baffles the family and their barrister alike. Furious, the family tries to argue the instruction is beyond ridiculous, as Lori is no risk to her own baby. Trying in vain to convey their worries, they explain that Lori needs to continue her contact visits, so living near the hospital is vital.

The family's barrister tries to reason with the local authority, repeating to them Lori's life could be at risk travelling back and forth upon the motorway for her contact visits. Hoping to make them see sense, she discusses the situation with their barrister as well, pleading that the situation is unsustainable. But the local authority manager holds firm, as does her boss, the area manager. Their years of cynical distrust of any parent blinds them to any innocent parent, and the pleas fall on deaf ears.

Francois makes three attempts to come to the court, but each time his requests are denied. Soon, he discovers that the local authority had been interfering. Juliette has cleverly manipulated and influenced the mental health social worker at the hospital. Together they hatch a plan to prevent Francois from attending court, writing to the judge and stating that he is still far too ill to attend and has no capacity.

Upon hearing this, Francois's solicitor intervenes to put a stop to it, warning the local authority not to harass his client. Then, miraculously, at the last hearing, Francois's new treating psychiatrist gives permission for him to go to court to help fight for their son, sending a letter to the judge to tell him so.

The day of the final hearing arrives. All eyes are on Lori and Francois. For the first time in a long while they are together again, if only in a court waiting area. They are unable to sit near each other, both with their own barrister and the local authority and the child guardian with theirs. Secretly, both of them are delighted to see each other again, even in the most tragic of circumstances. They exchange glances and smile at each other whilst the social workers and the child guardian look on like scowling cats.

When the local authority team disappears into a meeting room with their barrister, Lori turns to her barrister. "Are we allowed to speak?" she asks, wanting to say hello to Francois.

"Yes, why not?" her barrister replies.

"Hello," Lori says, looking over at Francois.

"Hello. How is Milo?" he asks.

Unable to relax with the pressure of their situation and what they're about to endure, both are careful as they enter a short discussion about baby clothing, Lori reassuring Francois that Milo has everything that he needs.

A member of the court staff announces that it's time to go into the room. Just as she is about to stand, Lori notices the barrister representing the local authority is standing by her side.

"I think you've been treated appallingly," the barrister whispers.

Lori is pleased that even the opposition's representative can see through their madness. Though immensely grateful for this honest and risky admission, Lori says nothing.

Having studied law, Francois is comfortable instructing his barrister. Despite the fact he is still on a committed at the psychiatric hospital, he proves the local authority wrong during the hearing. Sitting quietly and attentively, his demeanour is normal, much to the social workers' dismay. Their bare-faced lies, exaggerations and poor decision making begins to fall apart, the wise judge seeing straight through them. Smokescreens of manipulation and the inaccurate picture they painted of this mentally unwell "monster" of a man begin to crumble before their eyes. This new judge sides with the family, telling the local authority on no uncertain terms to return Milo to Lori the following day, and after four long months, the wretched nightmare finally comes to an end.

Feeling brave to speak out, Lori makes a final comment at the hearing, turning around to look at the miserable face of the social worker manager, Bridie Holmes.

"I'm going to sue you," she says through clenched teeth.

A few weeks after Milo is returned to her care, Lori makes good on her word and issues proceedings to sue the local authority for taking her baby unnecessarily.

Over the course of the next two years, she fights hard for justice, tirelessly overcoming every obstacle and trick the local authority pulls to strike out and diminish her claim. After four separate court hearings in Bristol all go in her favour, she emerges victorious.

CHAPTER 29

Bristol Life

Never wanting to return to Hampshire again, Lori decides to rent out her apartment, eager to move away from the nightmare she and her family have endured. Packing the last of her belongings, she can't leave the area soon enough.

After moving to Bristol to live with her mother and stepfather temporarily, she focuses on Milo as she tries to piece her life back together.

As for Francois, he is eventually able to relocate to a hospital in Bristol for the remainder of his section, and at long last he is able to be near them both.

After being invited to a meeting at the new hospital with his treating psychiatrist, Lori and Francois are relieved to discover that she believes he is not any risk to Milo. She is supportive of them living together as family as long as they access mental health support immediately if Francois becomes unwell.

After an offer from Delmare to pay their rent until they get on their feet, they search for a property. Lori is a little apprehensive at first, feeling that the rent is more expensive than she expected, and she's worried about the possibility of the payments stopping. But after Francois reassures her that the rent will be covered, they sign a lease. They're full of joy at finally being able to settle into family life, all three of them together at last, in their new home.

The coming months are blissfully happy as they spend their days relaxing in the garden, eating out, and taking Milo, now a toddler, for days out. Lori starts in a new office job whilst Francois stays at home. Unfortunately, their joy is about to be pulled out from under their feet yet again.

"Francois, the rent hasn't been paid this month," Lori says.

"Maman is paying it."

"No, it hasn't gone through."

"What? I'll ring her."

He calls his mother on his cell phone. "Maman, the rent hasn't been paid."

"I can't pay anymore. It's enough," Delmare replies.

229

"But Maman, you said you would help for six months."

"I can't, I tell you!"

The phone goes dead.

"What are we going to do, Francois?" Lori asks once he informs her of the situation. "It's expensive here. I thought we would only have to start paying in six months."

"I don't know. I don't know."

"You have to do something, love. I can't pay it all."

"Okay, okay."

As the days wear on, several arguments break out between Lori and Francois as the worry about their situation becomes suffocating. Francois gradually becomes increasingly anxious. Lori is oblivious to the fact that Francois's low threshold for stress will not bode well, especially with the sudden arrival of a major problem.

Francois's vulnerability starts to spill overboard as he continually paces up and down the living room. Close to tears and not knowing how to resolve their problem or who to call, he is at a loss. Lori takes Milo to her mother's. When she returns, another argument breaks out. Needing a secure environment for Milo and needing to know that the rent will be paid, she moves in with her mother for a while, leaving Francois to sort it out alone.

Francois's mental health begins to deteriorate, his life events making him fragile, and without Lori he is devastated. With no supportive parent to ring for advice, in desperation, he makes a flurry of phone calls to friends and distant relatives asking for a loan, but most can't or are unwilling to help. In his desperation, his mental health declines further.

"Please, God, help me," he says, then he prays in Hebrew,

As the days pass, Francois does not venture out. Soon, hunger gets the better of him, and with the cupboards running low, he forces himself to go to the supermarket. As he walks, he doesn't feel the hot sun on his face or hear the birds in the trees as he passes, his mood blue.

Staring at a shelf full of packets of food, he feels very alone, not really taking in what he is looking at. Without Lori his world is empty, his heavy heart turned to stone. Unable to stop himself, he begins to weep. Soon, a friendly store assistant approaches, a concerned look on her face.

"Excuse me, are you okay?"

"My partner has left me."

"Oh, I see. I'm sorry. Here, come on, love. I'll help you with your shopping."

After leaving the store with two full bags of groceries Francois wanders back to the house. He eats a little, then sits on the sofa, trying to calm the swirling thoughts in his head.

As evening arrives, Francois is not only blue but anxious again, the old fears creeping out from far corners of his mind. He is now in the early stages of another breakdown.

Leaving the house again, he wanders the streets in the dark for several hours, not knowing what to do. Finally, he returns home. It all becomes too much as his fragility starts to engulf him, the pressure of trying to find a way to come up with the money becoming a trigger for his past. As all of his fears and traumas rear their ugly heads once more, he spends most of the night fearful of being followed by neo-Nazis.

Wailing for Lori, feeling scared and alone, with his soulmate gone, the very person who believes in him, his confidant, his supporter, he begins to imagine he is surrounded by danger. He runs from window to window, checking that the front door is locked. Over and over again he twists the handle back and forth, his face red and sweating, his heart pounding out of his chest and his eyes wild, now in a full-on breakdown.

Before long the neighbours hear, and the police are called. Mental health services steps in, and Francois returns to the very place he hates the most, the psychiatric hospital.

Having not heard from Francois for almost two days, the knot in Lori's stomach won't shift. Anxious as to what might have happened, still deeply in love with him, she knows something is wrong. She tries ringing his cell phone, but each time she discovers it's still switched off.

Later that evening after asking her mother to look after Milo, she goes to the house. Opening the front door, she is met by a mess. As she walks from room to room, she sees many of their belongings covering the floor. She goes into the garden to try Francois's cell phone again, hoping he'll answer this time. She's just about to dial when she hears a voice.

"Are you looking for your boyfriend?"

Lori looks up to see a woman looking over the fence from next door.

"He's gone," the woman says. "The police took him."

Hearing an underlying tone of sarcasm from the woman, Lori decides not to answer. Once she's back inside, she rings the police, only to discover that Francois has been hospitalised again.

Feeling profoundly sad, alone and worried, despair sets in. She cleans the floors and tidies things up. Then she heads out. A few days later, she returns to collect their belongings.

After living with her mother and stepfather for five months, Lori decides to rent an apartment for herself and Milo not far from them.

On her days off from work, she visits Francois in the hospital. When she arrives at his ward, she feels a sense of déjà vu. She presses the buzzer and then waits. After a few minutes, the door catch release is activated, and she enters.

"Hello. I've come to see Francois," she tells the nurse on the other side of a glass screen.

"We'll go get him."

"How is he doing?"

"He's okay. Really fed up with being here and desperate to see you."

"Okay, thanks."

A few minutes later, Francois appears, wearing a big smile on his face. As the door opens, he flings his arms around Lori, and they kiss.

"Hi, baby, I missed you," he says. Lori notices the dark circles around his eyes and his trembling hands from the medication. Her heart sinks a little, this familiar sorrowful sight returning to torment her yet again. Knowing there is little she can do to stop it, she tries to ignore it.

"Do you have leave, Francois?"

"Only the garden at the moment."

"Okay. Let's walk around the garden."

The nurse releases the security door, and they walk hand in hand in silence down the sloping path and into the sunshine. Turning right, they walk up a path surrounded by trees and shrubs. Suddenly, Francois becomes confused, and he stops. As Lori looks on, he weeps in silence, each bitter tear streaming down his face a symbol of his torment at having been hospitalised yet again, along with the forced medication he has had to endure, haunted by the ghosts of tortured memories buried deep in his soul. He can't believe he's there again, alone and lonely. Lori offers what comfort she can, putting her arms around him.

"It's okay, baby, it's okay," she whispers.

As the days pass, little by little Francois begins to improve. Soon he is able to take leave away from the hospital, having days out with Lori and Milo. Then, much to their delight, a couple of weeks later, Francois is fully discharged.

The morning arrives for Lori to collect Francois. Having discussed him moving back in with her and Milo again, she looks forward to picking him up. When she drives up the slope to the ward, she sees him outside chatting with a male nurse. By his feet are four plastic bags full of his belongings. Pleased that they will be together again soon, Lori can't help but feel a little sad to see the plastic bags, knowing how his life started out at the hotel in Paris.

She parks, and Francois walks over to the car with a big smile on his face.

"Hi, baby."

"Hi, Francois."

"This is Phil," he says, introducing the nurse.

"Hi Phil," Lori says.

As they place his bags in the car, Lori is eager to go, wanting to be settled into family life again, having missed her man. Soon, they are driving away from the hospital.

"How's Milo?"

"He's okay. He's with Mum. What's that, your medication?" Lori remarks, noticing Francois clutching a white paper bag.

"Yes. But I'm not taking all these. They're too strong."

"Well, take something, Francois. I don't want you going back in there again. It's really hard on you and me, with you going in and out of that place like a washing machine cycle. I know it's difficult, but try to take just one pill a day, a low dose or something to keep you from getting ill. Not too strong but just a little please. I want us to be settled for Milo."

Even as Lori pleads with him, she feels torn, knowing that the toxicity of the medication is damaging his body, coupled with the realisation that if he takes nothing, she will lose him to the grip of psychiatry again. As she listens to her own words, even she is not convinced of what she's saying.

After unloading the car and checking out the apartment, Francois sits on the bed as Lori unpacks his clothes, showing him the empty shelves she has saved inside their wardrobe, trying to make him feel welcome.

They put all that they have experienced to the back of their minds once again, this familiar routine they decided on long ago. As sad and frustrating as it is, they have come to accept it for now. They yearn to be together again, to forget all that's been for now. They smile at each other, able to breathe again, both of them longing to be a family unit.

"I'm off to collect Milo," Lori says. "See you soon."

"Wait, baby." Francois gently takes hold of Lori's face in his hands. "Lori, I want you to know, I'm going to fight, baby, fight for us, our son and for our future, okay?"

Lori smiles. "Yes, I know, Francois. We'll be okay."

"I want us to have a good life. I really do, Lori."

"I know, baby. I love you. You're strong, and you've been through so much. I believe in you, Francois. If you can stay well, we can make it. See you soon. I won't be long."

Francois watches from the kitchen window as she waves while making her way down the steps to her car.

Going into the lounge, Francois sits on the sofa and sighs. He looks around the room and finally allows himself to believe for a moment that this wonderful feeling of being with his family, of being wanted, which he has searched for his whole life, will last forever.

Days turn into weeks and then into months. Life is good for their happy little family.

"Daddy, play with me."

"Come on then, my little king, come and play."

Pleased to have his father back, Milo laughs as they play together with his toys. With his bedroom positioned at the end of a long hall, Milo is afraid to sleep alone, having spent long periods of time without Francois. He has become accustomed to snuggling into his mother's warm body, feeling safe with her arms around him.

With Lori still needing to work and unable to get Milo to sleep independently, she asks Francois to sleep in Milo's bed until they can work out what to do. Though disappointed, Francois accepts the arrangement—until he doesn't.

"I'm fed up with sleeping in Milo's bed," he says. "I'm lonely, baby."

"I'm sorry. It's because you've been away a lot, Francois. I can't get him to settle in his own bed. I have to get up so early for work, and I'm too tired to keep trying to get him to settle in his bedroom."

"But my place is with you."

"Francois, I know it's difficult. I agree with you, but just be patient. It's hard for me too. I have to do everything. He won't sleep in his own bed, and I don't know what else to do."

Over the next few days, they begin to bicker, Lori complaining about the responsibility on her shoulders and Francois about feeling unloved.

"I love you, Lori."

"I love you too, but it's difficult."

As the days pass, Lori notices Francois's mood change, wavering between anxiety and tears.

"I feel blue, baby."

"Francois, are you going to be alright?"

"Don't worry; it will pass. I just need more love from you."

"I'm sorry. I'm doing my best. I have a lot to do with Milo and worrying about you. Francois, please tell me you're going to be okay.

Please don't get ill again. Take a pill that's not too strong, just to tide you over."

"I can't. They make me feel ill."

"But I'm worried if you don't take anything, you'll have to go to the hospital again. I agree with you, but what can we do? We can't afford therapy."

"I'll be alright."

After dinner, Francois becomes tired and decides to go to bed early, Lori remains in the living room playing with Milo. As Francois lies in Milo's bed surrounded by fluffy toys, he stares up at the ceiling and rubs his head, feeling anxious and unable to relax.

Soon a deep, dark fear comes knocking at the entrance of his mind. His eyes widen as if recalling buried memories. Then a grey mist appears before his eyes, and it turns into the face of the Syrian, his sinister smile mocking him. Then it turns into the face of the neo-Nazi holding the knife. Francois watches as the blade glistens. Back in the grip of his past once again, he relives that horrifying moment as the tip of the knife pierced his skin, and he gasped in terror. He also remembers the mixed messaging, the jealousy and the in-fighting of the family, his feelings of confusion and isolation and of not knowing who to trust. It all begins to close in on him.

Putting his hands up to defend himself, he swipes at their faces, trying to make them go away. He begins to hyperventilate, his face soaked in sweat. He is close to screaming, but then, one by one, their faces disappear, each taking the memory far away with them, and soon all is still. Leaping out of bed, he looks out of the window.

Upon hearing a thud coming from the bedroom, Lori makes her way upstairs.

"Mummy!" Milo shouts, wanting to continue their play. Lori returns to the living room.

"Here I am, love."

Francois continues to look out the window for a while, checking that no one is outside to harm him. Finally feeling exhausted, he returns to bed. He fights to keep his heavy eyes open, but within a couple of minutes he drifts off to sleep.

Once Milo is occupied playing, Lori goes upstairs and pops her head into the bedroom to check on Francois. Seeing that he's sleeping, she assumes all is well and goes to run a bath for Milo.

A little later, Lori and Milo go to bed. Unable to sleep, she lies awake worrying about Francois. After Milo has fallen asleep, she creeps back down the hall to Milo's bedroom. Sitting on the carpet, she watches Francois sleeping for a couple of minutes before she returns to bed.

It's just after midnight when something disturbs Lori. She wakes to find Francois's silhouette at the entrance to the bedroom.

"What's the matter, Francois?" she whispers. He walks into the room and sits at the foot of the bed.

"I trusted you. I loved you so much." He stares at her for a few moments, his expression like that of somebody looking at a stranger, his voice hoarse and despairing.

"I gave you my heart, Lori."

"I know, baby. I love you too. What's wrong?"

Lori's heart sinks as she holds onto every ounce of hope that Francois has not become ill again.

"You told them I'm here. Why did you do that? Why? I loved you so much. I trusted you."

Lori looks at Francois's face, in a state of panic.

"Who?"

"The Nazis, the extremists."

"Baby, I didn't tell anyone you're here. There are no Nazis in this small town. You're safe, Francois. Shhh ... don't wake Milo. Nobody is interested in you, darling."

"I'm not safe. I loved you so much. Why did you do this to me, Lori?"

"Francois, I love you too, but you don't know what you're saying. Hold on. Let me come out of the bedroom. Let Milo sleep."

They go downstairs to the lounge and sit. Francois's hands are trembling as he looks at Lori, his expression full of distrust.

"Francois, I can absolutely assure you there are no neo-Nazis in this silly little town. You're in the United Kingdom, where we don't have many. Even if we did, they would be in a different part of the country, and the police would arrest them. We don't put up with that in this country, baby. I haven't told anyone you're here. Why would I? I love you and want to protect you."

As they sit in silence, their arms around each other, bit by bit Francois begins to calm. Eventually tiring, they return to bed.

The following afternoon, having collected Milo from school following work, Lori opens the front door and is met by a mess leading to the kitchen. Cautiously, she steps over the array of items scattered on the floor and peers into the lounge, asking Milo to wait behind her. She discovers Francois pacing back and forth, sweating and in a state of panic, surrounded by more mess. She sees that the window is open, and something is hanging from it. She looks behind her and sees Milo playing with some of the items on the floor. Walking over to the window, Lori discovers Francois has hung his Krav Maga T-shirt from it. Only then does it dawn on her that Francois has become ill again.

Knowing she has to leave before Milo notices his daddy has become ill, Lori takes Milo's hand and creeps down the hallway to the front door. She plans to drop him off at her mother's. Despite feeling bad at leaving Francois in a state of vulnerability, she goes out.

After dropping Milo off, Lori parks near her apartment to make a call. Wracked with guilt and worry, she dreads what she is about to do and hates herself for doing it, but she calls the crisis team for help. Her betrayal of Francois is at the forefront of her mind, knowing how much he hates psychiatric hospitals and how ill the medication makes him feel. Her heart is broken. Despite her fears of the damage the medication is doing to his body, she is left with little choice, not wanting him to deteriorate further.

Returning to the apartment, feeling terrible at having made the call, she sits in the armchair opposite Francois. He makes frantic phone calls for help to random numbers, not really knowing what he's doing. Witnessing this sad and surreal situation as if in slow motion, she notices his hands are trembling terribly. This pitiful site is not the man she loves so deeply but the fragile little boy within, damaged by the cruel world for his love of his faith.

Looking at Lori, Francois stands. "The darkness is coming," he says, his voice hushed and afraid.

After several delays whilst waiting for the crisis team staff to get organized, the delay only makes matters worse. As she sits in the lounge watching Francois, the immense guilt almost consumes her. Lori sadly witnesses another frantic forty-eight hours of Francois deteriorating further and further into an even more vulnerable state.

Lori is upset to discover that due to a lack of mental health staff, the police will have to pick him up. Shortly after she learns this, the police arrive, and Francois is once again on his way to the place he dreads the most.

CHAPTER 30

Trials, Tribulations and Love

It's now 2018, and a difficult decision has been made, a decision causing the searing of two hearts. Having found each other after recognising a mutual sense of belonging, they feel at home when they are together. After discovering a deeper love than they could have imagined, having spent half their lives searching, these two souls are about to be forced apart.

Life's cruel hand has dealt them another blow, tearing them apart. After having a discussion about what is best for Milo, Francois decides that despite Lori having acted responsibly each time he has become ill by seeking help from the crisis team, the situation has become unfair to her. Together they decide that the onus is now upon Francois to seek professional help. It's time to find a therapist to help him overcome his demons.

They decide to live apart until Francois can find a pathway to heal. As sad as they are, they continue their relationship in separate homes, trying to make the best of a difficult situation.

Now discharged from the hospital and with no money to fund his own accommodation, Francois reluctantly accepts government funding and moves into a shared house with four other men, all having come from a similar situation, vulnerable and with a background of mental health problems.

Unable to settle, having been so independent in his younger years, Francois becomes frustrated, feeling like the support staff are treating him like a child. Eventually, he moves out, finding himself in yet another household of supported accommodation in central Bristol. Feeling even worse than before, unsafe and more unsettled, longing to be with Lori and Milo but unable to afford to rent a decent apartment for himself, he is becoming disillusioned and is losing hope.

Each weekend Lori picks him up and takes him for a day out with her and Milo, but this continual cycle of disconnection is becoming more evident.

"Baby, where are you? You're late!"

"I know. I had so much to do. It's difficult. We're outside Bristol, remember?"

"I've been waiting a long time."

"Well, wait inside!"

"Don't shout at me."

"Don't pressure me. If you had taken the pills, you would be living with me, but you couldn't do it, could you? You're selfish. I'll be there in twenty minutes!"

Feeling tired and frustrated at being in the same situation yet again and the ongoing responsibility always at her door, Lori is growing tired of the continuous trips, forever having to do the running round. However, shortly after hanging up, her anger begins to subside. She regrets what she said, her love for him stronger than her annoyance at having to be the strong one. Deep down she knows that since meeting Francois, for the first time in her life, despite the difficulty, she feels safe to test his love, knowing he will never leave her or her him. He's the only man she ever felt she could be herself with, and this secure feeling keeps her running to him, to save him.

After getting stuck in traffic, she finally pulls up at the tatty-looking white stone house. She sees Francois standing outside, waiting as usual, desperate to see her and Milo. It's his only escape from the loneliness and boredom of his situation. After he gets into the car, they kiss.

"Hello, darling. I'm sorry. Hello, Milo, my darling. How are you, my little king?"

Milo giggles. After a brief discussion about what to do, they settle on the idea of visiting Gloucester Road, a favourite of theirs with its abundance of independent coffee shops and offerings of international cuisine, followed by a visit to the park, so Milo can play.

When they arrive at St Andrews Park, they sit on a small wall surrounding a children's sand pit watching Milo play with the other children. Francois reaches out his hand, taking hers.

"I love you, baby."

"I love you too."

Their combined mixture of love and sadness at not living together anymore feels isolating as they listen to the chatter and laughter of the other parents around them.

Finding the current rent on the apartment too expensive, Lori and Milo move farther out of county to Wotton-Under-Edge, a pretty little market town on the perimeter of a vast area of natural beauty known as the Cotswolds. The charming old stone buildings lining the sloping high street look like a chocolate box lid.

Having moved above one of the shops, life is not easy as Lori juggles driving Milo back and forth to his school, which is farther away, working several miles away and visiting Francois in central Bristol. Now that she's even farther out, the journey is even longer, making things difficult, and they begin to argue. Francois complains about the lack of affection and the infrequent visits. Lori complains about his lack of understanding. Both of them are lonely without the other.

One night Lori receives a worrying call from Francois. Already concerned that his current accommodation is far from suitable for a vulnerable person, the inevitability of Francois becoming ill from the stress of it is almost certain.

"Baby, it's me. Did I wake you?"

"Yes, but it's okay. It's past midnight. Are you okay?"

"No."

"Hold on. I don't want to wake Milo. I'll go into the lounge."

"Okay."

"What's wrong, Francois?"

"Somebody put razor blades at my window."

"What? What do you mean? Where, outside?"

"Yes, I'm worried."

"You mean on the window sill?"

"What is a sill"

"The stone shelf outside your window."

"Yes, there."

"That's weird. Maybe it was someone on drugs. You are in the centre of Bristol."

"I don't know. I'm worried. I think they were put there as a warning to me."

"I'm sure they weren't, baby. Don't be worried. It'll be okay."

Hearing the fear in Francois's voice, but feeling tired and with work the next day, she tries to reassure him, speaks gently and slowly in a warm tone, helping him feel safe. Fearing that she may provoke a reaction that could lead to him becoming unwell again, she tries to calm him, but in the back of her mind she is worried not only about the razor blades but also by the sound of his voice.

"Francois, I'm sure it's nothing. Go back to sleep. We'll speak about it tomorrow."

"I can't sleep."

"But Francois, there's nothing I can do, darling. It's the middle of the night, and I have Milo."

"Okay, tomorrow."

"Okay. I love you. Don't worry."

"I love you too."

Lori tries to get back to sleep, but she can't, knowing the razor blades were probably not anti-Semitism but were probably dumped by some unsavoury junkie, she worries about the effect it will have upon Francois's mind.

After dropping Milo at school, she makes her way to work. Yawning periodically while listening to the radio, she pulls over to make a call to Francois before entering the car park. Surprisingly, it goes straight to voicemail. Having not received a call from him before leaving the apartment, as she always does, a pit forms in her stomach, her gut instinct telling her all is not well.

Throughout the day each time Lori visits the bathroom, she tries to call Francois, but there is no answer. She tries ringing him several times throughout the evening, but he doesn't answer. With few other options, she decides to call the crisis team for help. Unable to do anything straight away, they suggest the police visit him for a welfare check. Lori contacts the police, and they offer to go that evening and then report back to her.

It's late evening when, much to Lori's surprise, she receives a call from the police to inform her they have checked on Francois, and he told them he is fine. Dissatisfied with their explanation, knowing he can't be "fine" due to him uncharacteristically not calling her, she decides to contact the crisis team again, telling them that they must go see him.

During their visit they contact Lori telling her that Francois has been found to be very anxious with dry, bitten lips and not feeling safe at all. Shortly afterwards they contact her again, informing her that they have decided to take him to hospital for an assessment, as it is clear to all that Francois has become ill again.

Early the following morning, Lori is sitting in the kitchen staring out the window feeling heartbroken and bitterly disappointed. So desperately wanted him to do well, but now that his fragility has gotten the better of him yet again, she's upset and frustrated that she was unable to do more.

"Mummy, can you play?" Milo asks, a welcome distraction at that moment.

"Yes, sweetie," Lori replies, and they go to play together in the lounge.

A week passes, and Francois has been sectioned for twenty-eight days. Lori calls the ward for an update every couple of days, only to be told Francois is unwell and distressed. Finally, however, she is able to reach him on the phone.

"Hello, baby, how are you?"

"I'm okay. Why did you call them, Lori?"

"Francois, I had no choice. I'm sorry, but you weren't drinking, your lips were dry, I had to do something. That house you were living in was terrible. We need to find somewhere better for you."

"I didn't feel safe there."

"I know, sweetheart. I really didn't want to call the crisis team again, but you had become ill, love. Don't be angry with me. I'm on your side, Francois."

Lori listens intently to Francois's voice, noticing he's more breathless than usual.

"These drugs are going to kill me. They're too strong, too strong."

Hearing the phone rattling in Francois's hand, she realises the medication is causing his hands to tremble. She feels anxious and worried about his heart.

"Have you spoken to Dr Hing?"

"Yes, but he doesn't listen. I'm fed up, fed up. It's not a life."

"Please don't give up, Francois. We'll find a way."

"I love you, Lori."

Francois begins to cry, the torment of the medication making him miserable, and the relentless cycle of becoming ill yet again frustrating him. Stuck in the hospital again, missing being with Lori and Milo, it's all too much.

"Francois, don't cry, my love. The nurse said I can visit now. I'll come on Wednesday when Milo is at school. I have to go now, my love. I have to make dinner. Milo is hungry. Bye, Francois. I love you."

"I love you too."

Lori goes into the bathroom and closes the door, sighing deeply. She stares into the mirror, feeling lost, her heavy heart weighing her down as a rush of emotions pip at the surface. She feels trapped, sad, frustrated and helpless, all at the same time.

Is this what my life has become? she wonders. Her guilt for worrying about life in the future is a constant but unwelcome companion now. This is the man she dreamed of, her soulmate. She's so deeply in love that she can't see a way out. Worried by her own thoughts, she dares to think that the only way she can be free is without him, if only he would disappear, but that thought is too much to bear. Her love for him stronger than ever before, she begins to weep.

"Mummy," Milo says.

"Just a minute." Turning on the cold tap and splashes her face, then checks it in the mirror.

"What is it, Milo?"

"Are you coming out, Mummy?"

"Yes, hold on."

Unlocking the door, she kisses Milo on top of his head, then begins to prepare dinner.

Wednesday arrives. After dropping Milo off at school, her initial feelings of dread to be driving to the hospital yet again start to diminish. Soon her heart begins to warm, and she begins to look forward to seeing Francois again.

As she turns up the radio to alleviate the boredom of the familiar journey, a collection of scenes shuffles through her mind, things they have done, words they have spoken, and soon a smile replaces her earlier serious expression.

After driving up the slip road towards the building's entrance, she parks and then approaches the door. A nurse recognises her through the window and presses the security release button. As she waits in the small foyer for Francois to arrive, she feels excited to see him, her love having replaced all negative emotions.

Having been told a few days prior that Francois is dreadfully in need of a haircut and a shave, she has booked him into an up-market barber, who offers a traditional shave and a hot towel pampering. When Francois appears at the glass door, Lori is taken back to see he now has a beard, and his hair is scruffy and long. Although she feels sad to see him looking unkempt and vulnerable, she tries to hide it as he smiles through the glass at her.

As soon as the door opens, they lock eyes. The nurses watch through the window in the office as they embrace. Gone is Lori's astonishment at his appearance. She's now keen to transform him back into her handsome man, wanting him to feel proud of himself again and to feel wanted.

"Hi, baby, are you okay? I'm going to take you to get a shave and a haircut."

"Hello, baby. I missed you, Lori."

She kisses him and then they leave the building. As they walk to the car, he takes her hand.

"I know a great place," she says. "Let's get you sorted."

"Okay, baby."

Her warmth offers him a sense of security again. Feeling wanted and loved, he is happy to go along with it.

Unable to park outside the barber's or to find anywhere nearby, they have to settle for much farther away, at the top of a hill. As they make their way down, Francois becomes breathless, having to stop several times. He holds his chest, struggling to breathe. Lori becomes a little impatient, putting it down to him being overweight.

"Come on, Francois, we need to get there."

"I can't breathe. It's the medicine."

"I'll get the car later when I take you back. You can wait where you waited before. Don't worry."

At the barber's, an immaculately groomed middle-aged man shows Francois to a chair, then returns with a large bowl of shaving foam and a brush. As he gets to work on Francois's beard, Lori sits watching the stubborn whiskers fall to the floor. She feels relieved and happy to see him being tidied up, gradually transformed back to his old self.

Francois looks in the mirror and smiles at her face reflected behind him. A hot steam towel is placed over his face. Worried that he might panic, Lori asks him if he's okay. When he responds with a satisfied groan, she relaxes back into her seat. A haircut follows, and Francois looks handsome and more confident again. After thanking the barber for his kindness and patience, Lori pays and then they leave.

After having lunch, they spend their few precious hours together wandering in and out of shops. Before long it's time for Francois to return to the hospital.

"After we take Milo out on the weekend, we can come up here again next Wednesday," she says.

"Okay, baby."

They kiss and hug and then Francois reluctantly gets out of the car, both of them sad at not being able to drive home together. As Lori leaves the hospital grounds, she sighs, fearful that this pattern of yearly hospital stays knows no end. She feels torn, so badly wanting to live a normal life with Francois and Milo but unable to find a solution to keep Francois well. She's frustrated that he is in the hospital yet again, worried that the medication is making him balloon in weight. She fears not only for his mental health but his physical health as well.

Having sold her apartment, Lori has taken an office job and is keen to buy a house. Having to satisfy the mortgage lender, she has no choice but to work full time. That evening she calls Francois to give him the news.

"I got the job."

"Well done, baby. That's great."

"The problem is, next Wednesday is the last time we can meet during the week. The job is full time, so we'll only be able to meet on weekends until you're discharged."

"Full time? Why did you take full time? I'll hardly see you."

"Francois, I need to buy a house now that the apartment has sold. I can't keep wasting money on rent."

"But I'm alone, baby. I miss you."

Unable to hide her frustration at his lack of understanding, they begin to argue.

"But you can't help me, Francois. You keep getting ill. All the pressure is on me. I need to buy a house. I can't keep renting this flat. It has lots of stairs, and the shopping is heavy. I'm also far from Milo's school. My life is difficult, and I have to keep coming to the hospital!"

"Have to?"

"I don't mean it like that. I have to keep moving forward, Francois. Don't be selfish. I do everything!"

"I can't help it. When Maman returns the money she owes me, we can buy a house together."

"I know, but that could take ages. Try to understand my situation."

"I'm alone!"

"I'm fucking alone and tired Francois."

"Okay, so you swear, baby. You're cold with me. You used to be so tender. I really don't know if you love me anymore."

"I do! In the future after you're able to afford therapy, things will be better."

"I don't think you love me, not like you used to. You say I don't have any money."

"I do love you. It's just very difficult for me, so difficult, Francois, with you going into the hospital all the time."

"I understand."

"I'll see you on Saturday. Let's take Milo to Victoria Park in Bath."

"Okay. See you then. Bye, baby. Speak to you tonight."

"Okay, bye/ I love you."

Later that evening, Lori tries to get Milo to sleep in his own bed, but he's too accustomed to sleeping with his mother, so she gives up. After tucking him in next to her, she watches his eyes get heavier and heavier as he drifts off to a land of innocent dreams. Smiling as she studies every detail of his angelic and beautiful face, she hears her phone ring. It's Francois.

"Hi, Francois."

"Hi, baby."

"I miss you."

"I miss you too. It's difficult for me too, Francois. Try to understand."

"I know, baby. Is Milo sleeping?"

"Yes."

"Kiss him for me."

"I will."

"You would miss me if I was gone."

"What do you mean?"

"If I died."

"Don't say that. That's horrible."

"You would though."

"Francois, don't, baby. Don't say something like that. You make me sad and worried."

"I'm sorry, baby. Goodnight, Lori. Kiss you, I love you so much. I adore you, Lori."

"Kiss you. I love you too, baby."

"Tomorrow."

"Yes, tomorrow."

Saturday arrives, and after a busy week, Lori welcomes the chance to get out in the fresh air. On her way to pick up Francois from the hospital, she looks forward to the day ahead.

They arrive at Victoria Park and smile as Milo runs ahead of them, making for a carousel ride of vehicles.

"Mummy, Dada!" Milo stands by the ride, excitedly waiting for them to pay.

"You want to go on here, my son?"

"Yes, the bus."

Francois pays, then lifts Milo up, placing him inside a little red bus. Delighted, Milo spins the steering wheel, pretending to drive as Lori films him on her cell phone.

"He's so sweet."

Francois nods. "Our little king."

After the ride they make their way to a climbing frame situated within a sand pit. Lori and Francois sit in the sunshine watching Milo go up and down the ramp carrying a plastic cup full of sand, each time tipping it down a tube. Milo peers through the tube each time to watch as the sand seeps through to the end. He repeats the action over and over again as Lori and Francois keep a watchful eye on him.

Beginning to get hungry, they discuss what to eat, then they get up to take Milo to the café in the park, only to discover he's not there. Gripped with fear, their hearts begin pounding as he is nowhere to be seen.

"Where is he?" Lori cries.

"I don't know. I'll go this way. You look over there."

They split up. As Lori runs around in a daze of panic, an all too familiar feeling of fear rises up deep within her, like Hampshire repeating itself all over again, putting their vengeful hands upon her baby, then taking him. Trying to stop herself crying, and with other parents in the busy park oblivious to her plight, she searches left and then right, tortured with the thought that her child is now in the grasp of a pervert. Then at last, several minutes later, she spots him waiting his turn to go down a tall slide halfway across the park.

"Milo!" she cries out with relief. "Are you okay?"

"Mummy, I'm going down the big one," he replies with delight.

Shortly after that, she notices Francois close by. "Francois! Francois, come! He's here!"

Francois rushes over to her, looking exhausted.

"Look, baby he's up there."

"Thank God," Francois replies.

Their last Wednesday together for the moment has arrived. Choosing to spend the day in their favourite area of Bristol, they head for Gloucester Road in search of some lunch. As they walk hand in hand, Francois begins to feel breathless again. Finally, they arrive at a rustic-themed coffee shop. Deciding to sit at the rear where it's quieter, they order coffee and lunch. As they sit and wait, a gentle flavour of jazz plays in the background. Francois takes Lori's hand and holds it across the table. It takes her back in time, and she remembers the first time he ever held her hand in a bar in Nice, just off the promenade. Then something awakens within her from long before any of the problems. She rediscovers his handsome face, fuller and more aged than before. But she doesn't care as she looks into his beautiful pale blue eyes. They flicker and then widen, making her heart pound as she feels a deep connection to him again, like she has just seen into the depths of his soul. For that precious moment they recapture their old romance. Lori has no idea of the significance of this precious memory and how it will repeat itself for her again and again in the future.

"I love you, Lori."

"I love you too."

Their meal arrives, and they eat in silence, glancing occasionally at each other and smiling, each sensing the other's happiness to be together.

They spend the rest of their time looking around several shops. Before long it's time for Lori to take Francois back to the hospital and to pick up Milo from school.

As they make their way to the car, a sense of sadness falls between them. Lori thinks about the job she will soon have to start in order to secure the house she will buy, which means she will have less time for Francois.

CHAPTER 31

Goodbye, Darling

It's nearing the end of 2018, and Christmas is just around the corner. Sitting on the floor of the living room, wrapping presents, Lori looks on as Milo decorates the Christmas tree. The phone rings. It's Francois calling from the hospital.

"Hi, baby. They want to know if I'm staying with you on Christmas Eve."

"You can stay?"

"Yes, wait. Speak to the nurse."

"Can he stay over with us on Christmas Eve?"

"How do you feel about that, Lori?" the nurse asks. "If you're happy, we're happy to let him stay two nights."

"Yes, I'm fine with it. Great."

"Hi, baby, it's me again. Great, eh?"

"Yes, love. It will be so nice to be together."

Christmas Eve arrives. Lori collects Francois from the hospital. After putting the turkey in to roast, they chop up vegetables in preparation for dinner. Lori smiles at Francois. The settled family feeling is refreshingly welcome. Knowing he must return to the hospital two days later, she puts it to the back of her mind, not wanting to think about it. She pours them both a glass of wine.

"Happy Christmas, baby."

"Happy Christmas."

"Happy Christmas, Milo."

Francois returns to the lounge and sits on the floor, leaning against the sofa. Milo climbs on top of his legs. Francois wraps his arms around him as they watch a movie together.

When they sit down to eat, Francois places a hand on Lori and Milo's heads and recites a short prayer in Hebrew. After pulling Christmas crackers, they tuck into their Christmas dinner.

The following week, having started her new job, Lori is beginning to feel tired. Worrying that all the pressure is seemingly on her shoulders again, she is unable to help herself from feeling impatient with Francois's continued complaints about her lack of calls or his loneliness.

Her resentment at having to be the main breadwinner yet again, coupled with trying to buy a house to enable stability has caused her to stop laughing at his formerly amusing quirky ways and his jokes. Francois's lack of understanding regarding her situation only perpetuates her fears.

While driving to work one morning, she receives a call from Francois. He tries in vain to make her laugh, putting on a silly voice. Fatigued and irritated, she is not amused.

"That wasn't funny."

"Baby, you're cold with me."

"I'm tired, Francois."

"Do you still love me?"

"Yes."

"You're not the same. I help with money too. I only get government money now."

"I know, Francois, and I'm grateful, but it's not enough. Listen, I'm almost at work. I'll call you later."

A little later that day, Lori receives a call at work. Much to her horror she is told Francois is in a general hospital with heart problems. Having been reassured that it's not life threatening, she waits until after work, asking her mother to take Milo, before travelling to the hospital to visit Francois.

When she arrives at his ward, she finds him hooked up to a drip, looking ashen and feeling breathless.

"Hi, Francois. Are you okay, baby?"

"I have water around my heart."

"Around your heart? What do you mean?" Lori sits in a chair next to his bed.

"My heart is not good, Lori. You need to marry me, baby."

"Why? What do you mean?"

"My heart is weak. You'll inherit from my maman. It's all I have, her house."

"I'm not going to marry you just because you're ill. Don't say that, Francois. You're making me sad. I'll marry you because I love you and when we can afford it, not because you're ill."

"Don't tell my maman. She'll worry. I told her I'm okay."

"But she should come to see you."

"No, baby, don't worry her."

Lori notices Francois's legs are swollen.

"It's the meds," he says. "I told you they're destroying me. They're too strong. They're dangerous for my heart."

"I know, Francois, but I don't know what to do. I think they're too strong too. What's happening? Are they going to reduce them?"

"I have a second opinion psychiatrist coming next week. I'm going to try to reduce them or come off them."

"Okay, baby."

Worried but not wanting to make him any more anxious, Lori takes his hand, then leans over and kisses his cheek. She stays for two more hours. Desperately wanting to stay longer, she is torn. Her mother is now in her late seventies, and Lori knows that she will be tired, so she must return to pick up Milo.

"Francois, I'm so sorry, but I must go. I'll come tomorrow with Milo. It's Saturday, and we can come together."

"You have to go?"

"Yes, baby."

"Okay. You'll come tomorrow?"

"Yes. See you tomorrow."

They kiss. As Lori leaves, her heart feels heavy. Seeing him like that, knowing that there's nothing she can do, trapped in her situation, she's angry at the world for a moment as thoughts of rage run through her head.

I have no time, no choice, and I'm unable to help him. Where is the help and support from France? Doesn't anybody but me care about Francois? It's just so cruel and difficult.

The following week, Lori visits Francois again after work, after which she makes the same journey down the long pale green corridor that leads back to the elevator. As she walks, her cell phone rings. It's Francois.

"Hello, baby."

"Hello, Lori."

"Are you okay?"

He doesn't answer.

"Francois."

There's a long silence.

"I'm going to die, Lori."

His words cause her to stop in her tracks. Her heart leaps with fear. Not knowing what to think and not wanting to believe it, she feels afraid. Her first instinct is to comfort him.

"Don't be stupid, Francois. Of course you're not going to die. You have heart pills. You'll be okay. Don't say that." Lori can hear her own voice tremble.

"You should have married me, Lori."

"Francois, stop. You'll be fine. I love you."

"I love you so much, my Lori, with all my heart and my soul. You're everything for me."

"I love you too. I'm so sorry, Francois. I must go. Mum's waiting for me. She's tired. I'll speak to you later, love. Don't worry; you'll be fine."

Stepping into the elevator, Lori feels crushed. She drives back to her mother's house feeling utterly alone, tears streaming down her face.

The following evening, Lori decides to ring Delmare despite what Francois said, knowing that if anything happens to him, Delmare would never forgive her.

As she waits for Delmare to answer the phone, she can't help but feel angry that no one else cares about Francois. On top of that, Delmare's new Dutch partner is a constant annoyance, always at her home. He's yet another person who is jealous of Francois, constantly interfering with his continuous influence over Delmare.

"How is Francois?" Delmare asks.

"He has water around the heart."

"What? He has what?"

"Water, water around his heart."

"It is grave?"

"Well, he's ill, but it's not grave," Lori replies, not wanting to worry her. She hears a muffled voice in the background and knows it's Delmare's partner. Lori is irritated, unable to say anything much about Francois with him there.

Although she wishes Delmare would come to England to offer some support, she continues to play down the gravity of his situation, careful not to send Delmare into a deep depression. She knows Delmare is fragile, and she doesn't want to make the situation worse.

"I can't speak for long, Delmare. I have to get Milo to bed."

"Okay. Keep in contact though."

"Okay."

Lori hangs up full of frustration, wanting nothing more than to tell Delmare to book a flight to be with her son. However, knowing her manipulative partner is a dividing influence, driving a wedge between them all, Lori decides there is no point in trying to persuade Delmare to come. She retreats, not wanting to cause an even wider division between Francois and Delmare.

She gets into bed, trying not to wake Milo, and soon settles down to get some much-needed sleep.

It's Monday, and the last place Lori wants to be is work. Having dropped Milo off at school, she makes her way to the office. Francois calls several times during the day, but she is unable to answer until late afternoon. Having to attend yet another dull sales meeting, she zones out, her mind fixed on only one thing: Francois.

Finally, when break time arrives, she makes her way to the ground floor to ring him back. Before she calls, she listens to her voicemail.

"The second opinion doctor visited me in the hospital. We agree that the Clopixal is not right for me. He wanted to talk to you, but you didn't answer. I guess that's life."

Feeling guilty and frustrated at having missed the opportunity to speak to the psychiatrist, she calls Francois to explain why she couldn't take his calls.

As she drives home after work, Lori feels dreadful for having let him down. She has no choice but to work a full week now, so she can buy the house she so badly wants. Her burning desire to feel settled puts her in a no-win situation.

Nearing the end of January 2019, Francois returns to the psychiatric hospital. After being told that he will be discharged in one month, he is pleased to finally be near the end of his stay.

When he arrives at the hospital, he is met by yet another challenge. The treating psychiatrist has stated that he must have the same medication as before. An argument breaks out between him and the nursing staff as Francois becomes afraid. Knowing his heart is weakening, he is furious, viewing the decision as putting him at more physical risk.

A team of five nurses surround him, one holding the syringe.

"Don't come near me, or I'll punch you," he warns.

"Come on, Francois, you must take it," the head nurse replies.

"I have just returned from the hospital where I was treated for a heart problem, so, no way. Fuck off."

"Francois, please calm down," another nurse says.

"No way. Stay away from me."

They surround him. Weaker now than he was in the prime of his ninjutsu days, that distant man has faded, forever lost in the sea of a past life. Now fifty-five years old, he is broken and bloated with less fight in him.

They pin him down as their poison arrow does its job, sending its dose into the depth of his veins, zooming through his body with every beat of his tired heart.

Francois screams, and then suddenly it's all over. Releasing him, they lay him on the bed and then leave.

Two days pass, and Francois is still upset. Eventually, it's decided that he is to be transferred to the acute ward for the remainder of his stay.

Over the coming weeks, Lori grows increasingly worried about Francois's appearance. His face is ashen, and he's constantly out of breath. On top of that, he reveals that he has had two nose bleeds, and he's having trouble urinating. When she rings the ward with her concerns, she's told not to worry, that staff are monitoring him and that he's fine.

It's Monday, February 4, and Francois has begun to send videos to Lori's cell phone of French and English music. Nine videos arrive, one after the other. While sitting at her desk at work she sends him a message: "Francois, don't send any more. I have no time to listen." She follows up the message with a kiss emoji.

Another video arrives, and she sends another message: "Francois, stop. I have no time." It's followed by another kiss emoji.

Little does she know how significant her last part of her message is: "I have no time."

On February 6, more music videos arrive, followed by a pulsating heart emoji. Lori replies with the same emoji.

On February 13, much to Lori's surprise, the hospital allows Francois to view a flat in preparation for his upcoming discharge. He sends her another music video, followed by a call. Unable to take the call at work, she listens to her voicemails while on her break.

"Love, I just got back. The apartment is nice."

After work that evening, they discuss the apartment. Francois is pleased with it, but he wishes he was going back to live with Lori and Milo. Although both of them feel sad, they reassure each other that it's only temporary. Two more music videos arrive on Lori's cell phone, one in the afternoon, and one in late evening.

The next day is Valentine's Day. Lori is at work. At 10:20 a.m. she sends a message full of funny emojis with hearts in their eyes to wish Francois a happy Valentine's Day. She notices he has read it, but he doesn't reply. Instead, a little later her phone rings. She looks at the caller ID and notes that the person's identity is withheld. She's just about to start her lunch break, so she decides to answer it.

"Hello, is this Lori?" a rather serious female voice asks.

"Yes."

"Hello, Lori, I'm Doctor Upping."

"Oh, hello."

"I'm calling about Francois. I'm very worried about him."

"What's wrong?"

"He is very unwell. I'm concerned he has pneumonia or even possibly septicaemia."

"What? Really? He said he's had two nose bleeds. Oh my God."

"I asked the staff to call an ambulance, Lori, but he turned it away. He doesn't want to go into the general hospital again. I'm ringing you because perhaps you can talk to him."

"Yes, please put him on the phone now."

"Hello, baby," Francois says, his voice weak and breathless.

"Francois, you must go into the hospital. It's serious, baby. You must. You can die from septicaemia. Do it for me. Go!"

"Okay, Lori, I will."

"Put the doctor back on."

"Hello Lori. It's Doctor Upping again. We have called the ambulance. I must go."

Lori waits a few minutes, then calls Francois's cell phone. She immediately hears the sound of the monitoring machine in the ambulance, and the seriousness of the situation becomes even clearer. She is frozen, her body rigid and ice cold. Terrified, tears appear in her eyes, and she doesn't move.

"Francois, it's me. Are you in the ambulance?"

"Yes, baby. I can't really talk much," he replies, his voice breathless.

"Francois, don't leave me, baby. I love you. Don't leave me. I love you, Francois."

"Okay, baby."

The phone goes dead. As if a giant's hand is gripping her heart, the pain in her chest is pumped with fear. Lori rings the office to tell her boss what has just happened. Then she drives home and, as instructed by the hospital, waits for more news.

Once she's at home, she continuously checks the time on her cell phone. Too anxious to wait any longer, she rings the hospital to see what's going on. Lori is shocked to learn that Francois has been put into an unconscious state, as he was panicking too much at not being able to breathe. They advise her not to come in. Instead, she arranges to see him the next day.

The night is long. Unable to sleep, all sorts of emotions run through her head. Lori stares into the darkness. Trying hard not to enter any forbidden entry gates, leading to fears of losing him, she tries to focus her mind elsewhere, telling herself that he'll be okay.

The following day she rings the hospital again and is profoundly sad to discover that Francois is now in the intensive care unit. After arranging for her mother to pick up Milo from school, Lori goes to the hospital.

When she arrives at the entrance to the intensive care unit, the seriousness of the situation dawns on her even further. After pressing the buzzer and waiting to be allowed in, she reads the instructions, which clearly emphasize this is no ordinary ward. It is a ward for the seriously ill. Eventually, an assistant opens the door, a sympathetic expression on her face. She asks Lori to wash her hands and then to wait in a small area just off the ward. Lori does as instructed, not knowing what to expect.

Ten minutes later the assistant takes her through another set of double doors and onto the ward. They pass the occasional patient on their way towards the rear of the ward. She finds out later that this is where the most seriously ill patients are situated.

She finds Francois unconscious with a tube inserted into his throat and encircled by life-support monitors. Sitting next to him is a Mediterranean-looking male nurse who introduces himself in a soft and welcoming voice. He offers her a chair, then asks if she would like a hot drink. He goes on to explain what's happening, pointing to the various machines.

"How is he?"

"He's stable at the moment," the nurse replies.

"Will he be, okay?"

"I'm sorry, Lori, but I can't tell you that. The doctor will come to speak to you soon."

Lori sits, wanting so badly to hold his hand and kiss him but having been advised not to because of the septicaemia. All she can do is look at him. She finds it hard to fathom how he could be in an intensive care unit seeing as she spoke to him only a day ago. Looking at his handsome face, she sees beauty in him even now as he lies surrounded by a surreal jungle of wires, machines and monitors. This sorrowful site only increases her love for him, more intensely than ever before.

She thinks about his emotional fragility and the countless times he has told her he loves her. An overwhelming sense of protection fills her heart, and she sees him as a child, so vulnerable. Soon she begins to feel angry that in his hour of need there is nobody but her. Does anyone in France care about him?

Her eyes well up at the bitter thought of him being alone yet again. She knows how he just wanted to fit in, but he didn't feel wanted or a welcome part of his family after his grandparents died.

"Poor Francois. I love you, baby," she whispers into his ear.

A doctor arrives and asks Lori to come to a side room on the ward. A nurse is already waiting in the room.

"Hello, Lori, I'm Doctor Feilding," she begins. "I need to talk to you about Francois."

"Is he going to be alright?"

"Lori, I'm sorry, but I really can't tell you at this moment."

Gripped by fear, Lori's eyes widen, and her mouth falls open with shock. "You mean he might die?"

"Yes, Lori. Francois is very ill. I'm sorry, but I have to tell you the truth regarding his condition.

"Oh my God." Lori begins to cry. "Oh my God, but he's so lovely."

"We're doing all we can. We have changed the antibiotic in the drip, as the other wasn't working. I'm sorry, Lori. I can't tell you what will happen. This area of the intensive care unit is for the very sick, I'm afraid. At the moment he requires a lot of oxygen, and we have him on kidney dialysis too, as his kidneys are failing, and we need to drain the water from his lungs. His blood pressure is too high too."

"Please don't give up on him," Lori pleads. "Please."

"Of course, Lori. We'll do everything we can to help him. Rest assured, Lori, we will."

Lori returns to Francois and cries.

"You know he can hear you," the nurse says. "Feel free to continue to talk to him."

Lori stays until the evening, when the nurse advises her to go home. She also notes that Francois could be in this state for weeks.

Not wanting to leave him, but with tiredness getting the better of her, she eventually takes the nurse's advice and returns home.

When she returns to visit Francois again on the ward, Lori is told there has been some improvement in his condition. He requires less oxygen, and they have been able to reduce his blood pressure medication.

"You mean he'll be okay? That he'll survive?" Lori asks.

"It could go either way," the doctor replies.

Lori allows herself to feel a little more hopeful as she drives home that day, thinking that Francois might pull through.

The next morning, Lori receives a call from the doctor asking for her consent for Francois to be fitted with a tracheostomy. Unsure what to do, Lori agrees, telling the doctor she will be in later that day.

When she arrives at the ward, Lori sees the tracheostomy going into Francois's neck along with the feeding tube entering his nose. Even in the midst of this surreal and harrowing situation, she notices his abundance of beautiful curls. He seems so peaceful, and she can't believe that he is barely clinging to life.

Not sure she made the right decision to consent to the tracheostomy, she feels profoundly sad and alone. But after listening to the nurse's gentle explanation of its purpose, she realises that if it can be of some help to Francois, agonising over her decision is pointless.

After staying for several hours, she starts to tire, knowing she has to get back to Milo.

"Go home and get some rest," the nurse says. "Remember, he could be like this for weeks."

"But I don't want to leave him."

"We'll ring you if there's any change. He's stable at the moment, Lori. You must return home to your son."

"Yes, I must. He's at my mother's house. He'll be worried. The doctor said Francois might die. I can't believe it."

"Lori, be a little careful," the nurse whispers. "The sense of hearing is the last to go. We really can't reassure you either way. He is very ill."

Standing up, Lori leans down to speak into Francois's ear, tears rolling down her face and her heart breaking. "Fight, Francois. You always tell me you're going to fight. Well, fight now, baby. Fight now. Don't leave me, baby. I love you."

Looking down, she notices a tear running down his cheek. Unsure if it's a reaction to her words or from being so ill, the moment is captured in time, locked deep in her memory.

Wishing so badly she could stay with him all night, she reluctantly makes her way out of the ward and returns to her mother's house.

Halfway through the second week, after a worrying few days, Lori is given fresh hope. Francois has stabilised again and can finally be taken off dialysis. Lori feels momentarily relieved.

However, after another meeting with the doctor, she is gently reminded to be cautiously hopeful.

"Things can go either way in this unit," the doctor warns.

On her next visit, a nurse hands Lori details regarding the hospital chaplain.

"We understand Francois is Jewish," the nurse says.

"Yes, that's right."

"The chaplain will help you contact a rabbi, if you so wish."

"Thank you, yes. I'll ring her."

As Lori approaches Francois's bed, she is stunned, the reality of the situation hitting home yet again. She feels anxious at the thought that she may need to contact a chaplain and what that must mean. Not daring to think she might lose Francois, she puts it to the back of her mind for the moment.

A few days later, Lori changes her mind and arranges to meet the chaplain for coffee in the hospital café. During the meeting, she gives Francois's details, to be passed on to the rabbi of Bristol. The rabbi makes contact with Lori later that day. After a quick introductory conversation, he arranges to come in the following day and to pray for Francois.

The next morning, Lori sits waiting in the family area off the ward for the rabbi to arrive, not quite sure what to expect. Eventually, a slim bearded man in his thirties with black-rimmed glasses walks in, wearing a smile. He's wearing a black suit with white cotton tassels down one leg and a black Borsellino hat.

"Hello, Lori."

"Hello. Thank you for coming," Lori replies, relieved to see him. She explains how ill Francois is and provides a bit about his background. She also says how she is hopeful that his prayers will help Francois.

The rabbi stands to the left of the bed and then puts a kippah on Francois's head. Placing his hands on Francois's head, he begins to pray. Lori looks on, feeling very emotional, and begins taking photographs, wanting to show Francois what happened, hopeful he will pull through and make a recovery.

That night Lori rings Delmare again to tell her how serious the situation is and that she must come to England, encouraging her to take the earliest flight possible from France.

"You mean he could die?" Delmare asks.

"Yes. I'm sorry, but yes. Please, Delmare, you must come. Please."

"I'll come, I'll come."

Suddenly, Delmare's voice becomes muffled. Lori listens intently, thinking that Delmare's partner is trying to influence her otherwise, and she is filled with rage.

"Delmare. Delmare. Hello, hello!"

"Hello, Lori. He's booking a flight right now. I'll be with you tomorrow."

"Good. I must go now."

As Lori hangs up, she can't help but think that only now is Delmare's partner being helpful, right when Francois could be near to death. She is disgusted at the inhuman selfishness of the situation.

Delmare's mind is muddled and fragile. She does not fully grasp the seriousness of the situation, her mood blue and her mind numb from medication. Even after her ticket is booked, her partner and her brother try to convince her that she will not be able to cope and that she should not go. Both of them heap their bad advice on her, motivated by jealousy and selfishness, as they both profit from her numbness.

Somehow, she manages to ignore them, putting aside her own fragility, and the next morning she arrives in England.

After taking Milo to school, Lori and Delmare go to the hospital. The assistant informs them that only one of them can visit the ward at a time. They decide that Delmare will go first, having not seen Francois yet. As Lori sits in the waiting area, she texts Elijah to update him on Francois's condition.

After an hour or so, the assistant returns, telling Lori that Delmare would like the two of them to be together with Francois for a few minutes before she returns to the waiting area. Following the assistant through the ward, Lori finds Delmare with her hand on Francois's hand, looking dazed and devastated.

Lori decides to capture this moment by photographing them together on her cell phone. Later, she will look at this image and discover, to her amazement, that Francois knew his mother was there. At the time, she did not notice that his eyes were open. But locked into an induced coma, he was unable to communicate his feelings.

They drive home together in silence, only speaking over dinner. They're both worried. Lori's reassurances feel hollow as she tries to lessen the burden on Delmare's mind, adopting a supportive role.

On Saturday morning, after a discussion about Milo needing a day out, Lori and Delmare opt for the zoo. Despite the ongoing uncertainty and their constant worry about Francois's situation, they try their best to enjoy the day, keeping in contact with the hospital.

When Sunday evening arrives, Delmare is in a panic.

"Lori, I have a big problem."

"What's wrong?"

"I haven't brought enough medicine."

"What do you mean?"

"I don't have enough. I need more. I won't be able to cope with this situation with Francois. I'll become ill, very ill."

"Can you get it here?"

"No, only in France. I'm so sorry, Lori, but I must return. I must." Delmare starts to tremble.

"Don't leave me, Delmare," Lori pleads. "I need you here."

"I'll return. I promise you, Lori. I promise."

"If you really must go, then okay. I'll arrange for some support at the airport for you. I'll explain the situation."

Once Delmare returns to France, Lori feels very alone, worrying about Francois all day long.

After being given the number of a female rabbi based in Cardiff, Lori arranges for her to visit on Wednesday, again hoping that her prayers will help Francois.

On Tuesday, Lori is at the hospital and has just been taken to see Francois. Noticing that the female nurse does not smile on her arrival, she knows something is wrong.

The nurse informs Lori that Francois has taken a low dip and is not doing so well. He's back on dialysis. Lori is crushed to discover that his blood pressure has also gone backwards, with the medicine having to be increased even higher than before.

Lori places her hand on Francois's legs. Even though he's wearing pressure stockings, they're as cold as ice. Just then a vice-like grip of fear coupled with profound sorrow tightens around her neck and body. Unable to breathe for a second, at that moment it hits her like a dagger through her heart.

He's dying.

It's then that she notices the watery sand-coloured paste that the feeding tube is sending up his nose is trickling out the other nostril and down his neck.

A few minutes later, a senior consultant arrives and stands on the other side of the bed. Lori hasn't met before. A small group of people are gathered behind him. In a daze, Lori is unaware they are student doctors, but she doesn't care. Time stands still as he introduces himself. His words don't register fully as they wash over her. All she understands is that he's in charge of the other intensive care doctors. Suddenly, she hears herself speaking.

"He's dying, isn't he?"

"Yes, Lori. I'm sorry. Everything is at maximum level, and he's not improving. It's unkind to keep Francois like this."

Not knowing what to say, Lori blurts out the first thought that enters head. "But he's a really nice person." Her voice is broken and soft.

"We can't save him, Lori. He's not going to survive much longer. It's kinder for Francois to be dignified and to switch off these machines."

"But are you sure he's dying?" Tears roll down Lori's face.

Giving Lori a sympathetic look, the consultant and the team walk away, leaving Lori alone with the nurse.

"When you're ready," the nurse says. "Take your time."

Lori feels scared as she looks at the black circles around Francois's eyes and his pale, clammy skin, realizing how different he looks from even a few days ago. There is no denying that Francois is slipping away.

Realising that nothing more can be done, this huge, lonely responsibility that's been placed on her shoulders of having to make decisions for him alone has now been taken away from her as Francois moves nearer to the end.

Feeling that it is kinder and more dignified and wanting the very best for him, she takes a deep breath and then gives the nurse permission to switch off the machines.

Telling the nurse that she wants to be alone, Lori stands there looking up at the heart monitor. Just like in the movies, she watches as the peaks and beeps begin to flat line. Then she sits and looks at his face, watching as his skin turns from peach to white as his life slips away, and then he is gone.

At that moment hundreds of images from their ten years together flutter through her mind like a pack of cards being shuffled, just like they did years before when she left him in the terrible hospital in Nice. Each card contains a moment from their days together, ten years cruelly snatched away, gone in a moment, never to be recovered, never to return, his light blown out, like a candle's flame, their love now lost. She begins to wail.

Lori's heart is broken. Her screams and cries echo around the ward. Her one and only true love is gone. The bitter pain of not being able to save him fills with sorrow and regret. Her Francois, the only man who ever understood her just as she understood him. Then, wanting to set him free, she bends down to whisper into his ear.

"Francois, my darling, you can go to be with Grand-mamie now. Go, my darling, go. I love you so much."

Sitting in silence, she photographs him, not wanting to miss her last chance to see his face. The nurse reappears, suggesting she might like to cut a piece of his hair for a memory, and she passes Lori a small plastic bag and a pair of scissors. She snips a few pieces of his dark beautiful curls, then puts them into the bag.

Sitting on the bed, she lifts his lifeless arm and places it around her waist for the last time, knowing she will never feel him hug her again. She wants nothing more at that moment than to be with him.

A little later her sister arrives to offer comfort, followed shortly by the female rabbi. The rabbi was not aware that Francois had already died. She offers some kind words and then prays for him in Hebrew as Lori and her sister look on. The rabbi offers Lori her contact details, suggesting that, when she is ready, she is welcome to join the Jewish community centre she runs. She tells Lori that it doesn't matter that she's not Jewish. Lori thanks her for coming, and then the rabbi leaves.

Lori's sister says her own Christian prayer for Francois. She stays a while longer as they sit in silence together.

"You can go now, if you wish," Lori says. "I want to be alone with him before I leave."

They embrace, and then her sister leaves.

Lori sits looking at Francois's face and body, knowing it will be the last time she sees him. She weeps, not wanting to leave him alone, knowing he felt so alone too many times before. She wants to comfort him even in death, but she is unsure of what to do. Eventually, it dawns on her that she will have to leave at some point. The pain of leaving him is unbearable. Even now she still wants to be with him forever.

Using all of her inner strength and courage, she stands and gathers up his belongings, the only things she has left of him now. Looking at him one last time, holding two large bags of his life, one in each hand, she walks away from his bed, each step more difficult than the last. As she forces herself to move, she is broken and numb. She passes by a sympathetic male nurse on the way out, and he tells her how sorry he is.

As she heads toward her car, carrying the two plastic bags, her heart breaks further. She looks up and down the street, which is full of traffic and busy people going about their lives. Meanwhile, her life has stopped still, her soul weeping.

Driving past the small town where she lives, she makes for a country track as far away as possible from any house. She wants to be away from everyone and everything. She parks opposite some fields.

Turning off the engine, she is totally alone, with only the sound of the tweeting birds. She breaks down, screaming for Francois over and over again.

"I love you so much! I'm so sorry, so sorry, I couldn't save you. You wanted to be wanted. You felt unwanted. Well, I wanted you. I wanted you, Francois. I wanted you, baby. I wanted you ..."

Then, sitting in silence, her face red and tear stained, cried out and exhausted, she calls her mother to tell her she is coming back to her house. She knows she will have to explain to Milo that his daddy has passed away.

CHAPTER 32

Peace with Maman

Having been told by Delmare about Jewish traditions when it comes to funerals, Lori knows that the deceased are to be buried quickly; in fact, the very next day. Alone and without any help to organise it, this proves impossible.

Wanting to do the very best for Francois, she gets in touch with a Jewish charity for some advice, then contacts the rabbi in Bristol again. Explaining her wishes for the service to be half Jewish tradition, the other being a personal and romantic send-off, she books him for the service.

Lori orders a dozen red roses to be laid on top of the coffin. Then she visits a printer carefully selecting photographs and planning the order of service. Finally, she decides on the music. She decides to book a pianist to play one of her and Francois's favourite pieces of music by French composer Yann Tiersen. She also arranges for a chapel assistant to ensure two love songs by Jack Savoretti are played on CD.

Having to put her sorrow on hold, busy with all the arrangements, Lori returns home and sits on the sofa in silence. As the sunshine from the window opposite creeps across her face, she thinks of Francois. Playing some of his old voicemails from her cell phone, she can hardly believe he is gone. As a tear runs down her face, she receives a call from Rabbi David.

"How are you and Milo?" he asks.

"Milo is trying to make sense of it. He's very sad, of course. I'm trying to organise things as quickly as possible, but with no help from France, it's difficult. I won't be able to bury Francois quickly, but I'm in contact with the charity now and will have a date very soon. We're going to the cemetery to meet."

"Okay, Lori. I wanted to let you know I will be organising the Tahara."

"Sorry, the what?"

"Tahara. It's Jewish tradition that we cleanse the body before burial."

"Who does it?"

"It will be men, of course. Then he will be dressed in white linen."

Lori feels very emotional thinking about Francois lying dead and being cleansed, but then a sense of comfort fills her heart, knowing that Francois will be surrounded by Jewish people and respected. Despite having never met these people in life, they will be offering him kindness in death. She contemplates this sad thought for a moment, knowing these traditional Jewish rituals are what he would have wanted.

After several fraught phone calls between Lori and Delmare about the funeral, Lori can't help but become impatient with Delmare's insistence on wanting everything to happen quickly. Trying to organise it all, having to learn fast what must be done at a Jewish funeral, Lori tries to be as diplomatic as possible, conscious that Delmare has just lost her son.

"Delmare, you have to understand that I'm alone, and he can't be buried quickly. I have to organise the funeral and lots of other things. We'll have to wait until everything is in place. I'm doing my best!"

"Lori, listen. I'm coming, but I will stay at a hotel. It's better."

"Okay, as you wish, Delmare."

For a moment Lori considers asking Delmare to stay with her again, but she hesitates, feeling devastated and angry at all the people who let him down in childhood. Instead, she finds herself going along with Delmare's suggestion about the hotel, unable and unwilling to comfort her at the moment. She's up to her neck in her own grief, with no desire to prop up anyone from his family at the moment.

On the day of the funeral, Francois's coffin is carried into the chapel by eight Jewish men. Lori is touched by their kindness as she observes them carry him with dignity and pride, like he's one of their own.

Delmare sits with Christophe and Elijah on one side of the chapel, and Lori sits with her close friends and her sister on the other. Periodically, she looks over at Delmare, still hurt and angry and wishing that if only his childhood had been different, he may have been less fragile, possibly even still alive. Soon her thoughts turn to the anti-Semitic attacks, how he must have suffered, wishing that if only she could have known him then, she could have offered him shelter.

The traditional first half of the service comes to an end, and the rabbi sits.

Lori walks to the lectern and explains the second half of the service before reading her eulogy.

"Francois was much more than someone with a mental illness," she begins. She explains how they met online and how he was strong, brave and misunderstood at times, always wanting to battle his way through whatever life threw at him. She explains his own frustrations at his mental ill health making him fragile at times and her admiration for his intelligence and romantic nature, telling the story of him rushing to buy her red roses at a French market as an example. She admits he was not perfect, but who is?

She also describes his wonderful talent for poetry along with his strong belief in God and how proud he was to be Jewish, having made that choice in childhood.

She also describes her poignant memory of when they sat by the crystal-clear aquamarine river in Italy, not knowing then that the next time she would talk about that day again would be at his funeral. Her heart aches as she recalls the joyous moment, locked into the depths of her memory.

"Francois took me for a surprise vacation one day to the wonderful hills of southern Italy. We walked through a village, arriving by chance at a beautiful river, where a few people were dangling their feet in the water to cool off.

"I said to Francois, 'Take off your shoes. Let's do the same.' The water was not deep, but the current was fast. For a moment he hesitated, looking worried, but I said to him, 'It's okay, Francois,' and I took his hand. I sensed at that moment a fragility in him that I hadn't seen before. Then we sat on a rock together, enjoying the water gushing over our feet, cooling them."

Lori's eulogy comes to an end, and the pianist begins to play. As each sweet emotionally entwined note sings out, "Comptine d'un Antre Ete" by Yann Tiersen fills the height and depth of the chapel. This sad but glorious tune is a familiar friend to Lori, as she played it many times before whilst yearning for Francois to be freed from the hospital in France. As she sits and listens, her thoughts are filled with a thousand memories.

She can hardly believe this final door is closing after ten years of them being together in England. She recalls how she waited endlessly for him to be free from that awful hospital, only for him to be cruelly taken away from her again, this time for good. Tears roll down her face at the thought.

A few months pass, and Lori and Delmare still haven't spoken. After a few unanswered calls to Delmare, Lori finally gives up.

Then one day Delmare calls her.

"I tried to call you a few times," Lori says. "Why didn't you answer?"

"Listen, I want to tell you something. Lawrence is dead. He died in August," Delmare replies, referring to her Dutch partner.

"Oh, I see. Well, I can't tell you I'm sorry. He prevented us from speaking to you."

"Lori, why were you so cold to me at the funeral?"

"You have to understand, I was alone, coping with it all, and I was alone when he died. I was so sad he died after all he went through, and I was upset about how you and your family hurt him right from when he was young, apart from your parents."

"Francois was very difficult and aggressive when he was a teenager."

"He was confused, Delmare. He didn't know who to trust. You and your brothers hurt him and confused him, and his father didn't want to know him. He was emotionally damaged, not ill. When you put him in that hospital when he was a teenager, he was angry, not ill."

"I don't want to argue, Lori."

"I don't either. I loved him so deeply, I'm hurting."

"So am I. I was so masked by the medication in England. I could not feel. If I could have felt I would not have coped. I went into a deep depression when I got back to France. That's why I couldn't speak to you, not just because of Lawrence interfering. Francois was my son."

"I know that, Delmare."

"Please forgive me, Lori."

They both begin to cry.

"I do forgive you. I just want you to be honest. Don't blame Francois all the time."

"Okay. You know I love you like a daughter, Lori. My son chose well. He called you his wife, his jewellery. You have a pure heart. You're an angel."

"No, I'm not perfect. I just did my best. I loved him, I still do, and I will forever more. I wanted us to be a family. He wanted that so badly too."

"Ring me any time, Lori."

"I will. You're all I have left of him, of France. I'm so sad. I'll contact you soon."

Two years on, Milo has turned eight. Sitting alone on her bed, Lori begins looking through Francois's belongings, having found it too painful to touch them until then. She takes a clear plastic case from the bottom of her wardrobe and unzips it. Taking out each item in turn, she places them one by one on her bed. These items are among the most precious things that belonged to Francois.

She flicks through his white leather Torah, studying the Hebrew words and wondering what they mean. Then she wraps his tefillin around her arm and places the white embroidered tallit over her shoulders. Sitting in silence, she thinks of him. Filled with a sense of pride and sadness, she tries to imagine how he would have felt when he wore them before her. Then she returns each item to the plastic case.

Taking out one of his jackets hanging in the wardrobe, she buries her face deep into the collar, wanting to smell him, managing to capture the trace of his cologne. Reaching into one of the pockets, she feels something deep inside and pulls out what looks like a business card. On the card are words of French and Hebrew and an address in Paris. Opening her laptop, she looks up the French words on the Internet and discovers their meaning. Then she says them out loud. "May the lord bless you with Zion and see the happiness of Jerusalem."

She places the card in front of Francois's photograph on her dressing table, right next to the small teddy bear he gave her when they first met.

"Yes, my darling," she says, her eyes filled with tears. "I will love you forever, Francois."

CHAPTER 33

Three Hearts

The year is now 2021, and October has arrived. With their relationship now healed, Lori and Delmare speak regularly. As she gazes out of the window of the aeroplane on her way to Nice with Milo, Lori looks forward to reuniting with Delmare, having arranged to stay for ten days.

As they start to descend, the familiar sight of dancing yachts and splendid white ships no longer brings a feeling of excitement but instead a memory of the first time she travelled to France to meet Francois. Her heart is blue that he will not be there to greet her at the other side of their journey.

"Are we nearly there yet, Mum?" Milo asks.

"Almost, my darling." Lori smiles, trying to hide her sadness so as not to dampen his excitement.

After arriving at Delmare's house by taxi, Lori opens the white wooden gate, passing the olive tree in the garden. She peeks through the large sliding window and sees Delmare resting on the sofa. Pushing open the front door, Lori smiles at Delmare as she scrambles to her feet. Their embrace is warm, genuine and welcome. Both of them have tears in their eyes, happy to be together. They understand each other's sadness now that Francois is gone.

"Milo, you're taller, my darling."

"Say hello, Milo," Lori says.

"Hello, Grand-mamie."

Casting her eyes around the living room, Lori sees a menorah inside an arched lit shelf and then a Hamsa in another of the arches. These symbols mean so much more to her now, knowing how important they were to Francois.

After lunch, Lori and Delmare engage in a heart-to-heart discussion whilst Milo plays in the sunshine on the terrace. Their exchange is honest and insightful as they reminisce whilst shedding the occasional tear.

Later that evening, Milo falls asleep on the sofa. Lori gently wakes him. Then, after tucking him into bed, she returns to the living room to chat with Delmare.

"I'm so happy you came, Lori."

"Me too. It's what Francois would have wanted. I miss him so much."

"I understand, my darling. Me too. So strongly. I love you like a daughter; you know. Really, I do."

"I love you too."

They spend their time over the next few days visiting the beach in Villeneuve-Loubet and taking trips to the town of Antibes. Time passes quickly. Then one evening Lori asks Delmare a question.

"I want to visit Francois's old apartment in Victor Hugo in Nice. I can't explain why, but I feel an overwhelming need to visit it, almost like I need to say goodbye to him there. I have dreamt about it many times. Will you come with me?"

Delmare pauses for a moment before replying. Then she nods. "Okay, we go. Tomorrow?"

"Yes, tomorrow good."

Morning arrives. Whilst Delmare takes a bath, Lori prepares breakfast. While waiting for the toast to pop, she takes her coffee out to the terrace. The view of the hill opposite, dotted with white houses and apartments belonging to the residents of the gated community, the beauty of the palm and fir trees and the blooming flowers from the neighbouring gardens is a wonderful site to be had. To the left the blue horizon of the ocean meets the sky whilst the chirping of crickets basking in the sunshine remind her of the times she spent with Francois. Sighing, she can't enjoy her surroundings fully. No paradise feels the same without him.

Going into the garden, Lori finds Milo kneeling on the stone floor playing with sticks, trying to encourage bugs to climb them.

"Mum, is my toast ready?"

"Yes, mind you don't get bitten. Come sit at the table, love."

"Where's Grand-mamie?"

"She's taking a bath. She'll be out soon."

Returning to the living room, Lori stops for a moment, looking at the five small, framed photographs of Delmare's family placed on the marble top bureau. Her mother, father, other brother, one of Delmare herself, and of course, Francois. Then something moves her deep inside. At that moment she has a new perspective on Delmare, understanding her fragility and loneliness. They have all left her, one by one, even her own son, perceived as the weakest of the pack, and yet she had outlived them all, soon maybe even Uncle Gustave.

"Maman, are you okay?" Lori calls.

"Yes, I'll be there soon."

They take a taxi to the train station in Villeneuve-Loubet, then catch a train to Nice. Upon arrival they head for the main shopping district. After taking in several stores, they search for somewhere to eat, settling on an Italian restaurant.

After lunch they make their way to the apartment, eventually arriving at the beginning of Boulevard Victor Hugo. As the three of them walk up the street, Lori imagines Francois walking beside her, the familiarity of the buildings unlocking her memories of him.

"We are near. I recognise these buildings. I wish I had bought a red rose. I didn't see any flower sellers on the way, but I wanted to lay a rose outside the building for him."

"Me too. That would have been nice," Delmare replies.

Just before arriving at the apartment building, they pass a large shrub full of delicate pale pink flowers. Lori picks two, one for her and the other for Delmare.

"Here, we can lay these."

"Yes, we will," Delmare replies.

A few minutes later they arrive. While standing outside the building, Lori is filled with emotion. She looks down at the same large red mat leading to the building's entrance on which she once slept. Then she looks up at the fourth floor, picturing Francois standing at the balcony, smiling down at her.

"It's here. This is the building."

"Yes, darling, we're here," Delmare replies.

"Is this where my daddy lived?"

"Yes, Milo, it was."

Then, just by chance, the glass doors slide open as a man exits the building.

"Quick, let's go inside."

Lori takes one of Milo's hands, and Delmare takes the other.

Once inside the foyer, Lori looks down at the marble floor, then up at the chandeliers all of it just like before, like time had stood still for ten years. She remembers all the times she passed through there with Francois. Taking out her cell phone, Lori films the floor, walls, chandeliers and chairs then the view outside through glass doors.

With tears in her eyes, she turns to Delmare. "I'm ready to go now."

Standing outside the building, Lori kneels down, placing her flower at the foot of the grey-and-white marble pillar next to the entrance, Delmare doing the same.

Taking a deep breath, Lori looks up at the fourth floor one last time.

"Goodbye, Francois," she says. "I love you."

Chapter 34

Moments and Memories and Time

Wiping away a light scattering of rain from a small metal placard, Lori reads the name: "Francois Ronen aged fifty-five years." Kneeling beside Francois's grave in the Jewish cemetery, she has come to visit him, the official gravestone yet to be made.

Now February 2020, it's been almost a year since Francois passed away. It's the twenty-seventh of the month, the very day he died, so she wants to be near him.

"I love you, Francois. I love you so much. I miss you, my darling. I'm so sorry I could not save you."

Tears rolling down her face, she looks down at the placard, still not quite believing he is gone.

Soon it begins to rain again, but she doesn't care. As she looks at some of the other gravestones, she notices the others have small stones placed on their black granite surface. She finds some more inside a stone box. Taking four, she places them one by one on each side of the rectangular placard.

As the rain starts to lighten, she looks up at the sky, thinking about the possibility of heaven and where Francois now resides. At that moment the sun breaks through a gap in the pale grey clouds. She closes her eyes as her tears begin to dry, welcoming the sun's warmth.

Later that evening, Lori and Milo light a candle and place it by Francois's photograph to remember his passing.

Some months later, Lori is shopping in her favourite area of Bristol, Gloucester Road, where she and Francois often enjoyed the delightful area's vast choice of cosmopolitan cafes, shops and restaurants. After a few hours she decides to find a coffee shop, where she can rest her feet.

Just then she remembers one in particular, with little white candles on pale wooden tables. She walks up the street a little farther, and eventually, she finds it.

Stepping into a past moment in time, she orders a coffee and pastry.

Pleased to see the café is quiet, she heads towards the rear, remembering the very table where she once sat with Francois.

The same sound of light jazz surrounds her as she sits. After eating her pastry and sipping her coffee, she closes her eyes. She sees Francois reaching out his hand to take hers then kissing it, just like he did at that very table, neither of them saying a word. She remembers his smile as she looked at his pale blue eyes and into the depths of his soul. She thinks about how, after a difficult time at that moment, it awakened their romance, washing all their sadness away. She remembers how handsome he looked and how her deep love filled her heart once more.

Time moves on, and another year passes. On her way home with Milo, Lori drives by a certain street corner and is gripped by sadness as she recalls how Francois would stand eagerly waiting for her when they had decided to temporarily live apart.

"Are you okay, Mum?"

"Yes, I'm okay, sweetie."

"Why are you sad?"

"I'm not."

"You are, Mum. I can hear you sniffing."

"Sorry, love. I just remembered how your dad used to stand there. Do you remember?"

"I think so, Mum."

"I love you, Milo."

"I love you too, Mum."

It's summer 2022, and Milo has turned ten years old. He has joined a martial arts club. As Lori sits watching him practice with the group, she imagines Francois alongside him showing off his ninjutsu moves as he used to when they first met. She smiles, remembering how talented he was, his skill precise and his knowledge vast. How she wishes he could see Francois now.

Later that evening as Milo plays games on his computer, Lori takes a bath. After getting out and wrapping a towel around herself, she notices one of Francois's old colognes she kept in amongst other toiletries on the window sill. She opens the square glass lid and smells it. As the scent fills the room, her mind fill with a cascade of memories of each time he wore the cologne in England and France, looking smart and handsome.

In her bedroom, she takes out a small plastic packet from her dressing room drawer and holds it up to the light. Inside are two pieces of Francois's glorious large curls. While sitting on her bed, she remembers the hospital and how she cut it after he died, and her heart saddens.

It's now autumn, and Lori and Milo are out walking at a favourite spot of theirs down by a river looking across at Wales. The vast colours of the sky with its greys, pinks and oranges make for a dramatic scene, filling Lori with romantic memories of Francois. As Milo runs ahead, his curly hair bouncing in the wind, just like his father's, Lori listens to Jack Savoretti on her mobile phone, including two of the same songs she chose for the funeral, the lyrics feeling so poignant.

Winter arrives, and one day Lori is on a break from work when she stops by a supermarket to buy some lunch. After eating it in her car, her thoughts turn to Francois. She pulls out her mobile phone and plays some of his old voicemails over and over.

"I know, Francois, my darling, I still love you so much, baby," she whispers.

December arrives, and 2022 is almost at an end. Lori is on her computer looking at gold chains with the star of David, remembering Francois's chain. As she looks at more and more chains, she decides to order one, remembering how Francois flushed his away in an anguished state of mind. After placing an order, a confirmation email pops up saying that the chain will come from a business in New York in three weeks' time.

In New York, inside a jewellery packing room, a middle-aged man places a gold chain in a small brown box. Placing the lid on top, which displays the name of the business in black stylised letters, he pops it into a postal bag along with all the other international packages. The box makes its way to a flight bound for the United Kingdom and eventually to a Bristol sorting office.

One morning Lori receives a knock at the door. It's the postman with a package for her.

She sits on the sofa to open it. Inside is a small object in bubble wrap. She unravels it, revealing a small brown box.

She opens the box and then smiles, looking at a small gold chain as she thinks of Francois.

"Look, Milo, the chain has come."

"Let me see, Mum."

They look at it together.

"Where are you going to put this chain you bought for Dad, Mum?"

"I'll show you."

Milo follows as Lori goes upstairs to her bedroom. She hangs the chain over a corner of a large photograph of Francois on her dressing table.

"There you are my, darling; this is for you," she says, looking at the photo of Francois. After hugging then kissing Milo on top of his head, they both stand there looking at it for a moment longer before making their way back downstairs.

www.ingramcontent.com/pod-product-compliance
Lightning Source LLC
Chambersburg PA
CBHW031256120726
47906CB00003B/765